DANGEROUS DESIRE

"I'm so cold," she whispered against the soft linen of his shirt. "No matter how I try, I can't seem to get warm. Hold me tight, Burke. Help me feel something . . . anything but this."

He took her face gently between his hands. Some long lost emotion stirred inside him, a need to comfort and protect, to take away her sadness, pain, and fear. He bent his head and brushed his lips lightly against hers.

Control slowly unraveled like tightly woven threads that gradually gave way, unwinding, pulling loose all restraint, uncoiling all the rules he'd lived with the last fifteen years.

He pressed his mouth to hers again. Her lips quivered with that vulnerability no amount of angry words or stubbornness could disguise.

He deepened the kiss by long moments, taking away the coldness until he felt her mouth go warm beneath his. Cool, then hot. Ice and fire. She was both and more. . . .

THE TIMELESS PASSION OF HISTORICAL ROMANCES

FOREVER AND BEYOND   (3115, $4.95)
by Penelope Neri

Newly divorced and badly in need of a change, Kelly Michaels traveled to Arizona to forget her troubles and put her life in order again. But instead of letting go of her past, Kelly was haunted by visions of a raven-haired Indian warrior who drove her troubles away with long, lingering kisses and powerful embraces. Kelly knew this was no phantom, and he was calling her back to another time, to a place where they would find a chance to love again.

To the proud Commanche warrior White Wolf, it seemed that a hundred years had passed since the spirit of his wife had taken flight to another world. But now, the spirits had granted him the power to reclaim her from the world of tomorrow, and White Wolf vowed to hold her in his arms again, to bring her back to the place where their love would last forever.

TIGER ROSE   (3116, $4.95)
by Sonya T. Pelton

Promised in wedlock to a British aristocrat, sheltered Daniella Rose Wingate accompanied the elegant stranger down the aisle, determined to forget the swashbuckling adventurer who had kissed her in the woodland grove and awakened her maidenly passions. The South Carolina beauty never imagined that underneath her bridegroom's wig and elegant clothing, Lord Steven Landaker was none other than her own piratical Sebastian—known as The Tiger! She vowed never to forgive the deception—until she found herself his captive on the high seas, lost in the passionate embrace of the golden-eyed captor and lover.

MONTANA MOONFIRE   (3263, $4.95)
by Carol Finch

Chicago debutante had no choice: she had to marry the stuffy Hubert Carrington Frazier II, the mate her socially ambitious mother had chosen for her. Yet when the ceremony was about to begin, the suntanned, towering preacher swung her over his shoulder, dumped her in his wagon and headed West! She felt degraded by this ordeal, until the "preacher" silenced her protests with a scorching kiss.

Dru Sullivan owed his wealth and very life to his mining partner Caleb Flemming, so he could hardly refuse when the oldtimer asked him to rescue his citified daughter and bring her home to Montana. Dru dreaded having to cater to some prissy city miss—until he found himself completely alone with the violet-eyed beauty—One kiss convinced the rugged rancher not to deny Tori the wedding-night bliss that he was sure she would never forget!

Available wherever paperbacks are sold, or order direct from the Publisher. Send cover price plus 50¢ per copy for mailing and handling to Zebra Books, Dept. 3767, 475 Park Avenue South, New York, N.Y. 10016. Residents of New York and Tennessee must include sales tax. DO NOT SEND CASH. For a free Zebra/Pinnacle catalog please write to the above address.

CARLA SIMPSON

SEDUCTIVE CARESS

ZEBRA BOOKS
KENSINGTON PUBLISHING CORP.

ZEBRA BOOKS

are published by

Kensington Publishing Corp.
475 Park Avenue South
New York, NY 10016

First printing: June, 1992

Printed in the United States of America

Prologue

September 8, 1888

The fog wrapped clinging fingers around street lamps and stalked the streets. It draped buildings in a gray cloak, and muted the drunken cackle of laughter from a dance hall, the slurred curses of an abrupt argument, and hurried footsteps on the sidewalks of London's infamous Whitechapel District.

A young woman hurried down the street, hands burrowed deep inside a moth-eaten fur muff. The muff, along with the black threadbare coat worn over the patched brown linsey skirt, with shirtwaist and drooping hat, were all she had against the aching cold of the night.

She increased her pace, anxious to be home within the safe walls of the small flat she shared with another young woman. Since the murders began, it wasn't safe to be out on the streets at night.

She thought of her flatmate, and hoped she was home. The coal stove would be lit, and it would be warm. She didn't like going home to a cold, empty flat.

She cut across the street. A rat stared brazenly back at her from among the flotsam of garbage that littered the gutter. The fog trapped the heavy stench of the sewer, refuse, and horse dung in the cold night air.

At the next corner, she turned and then darted down a nearby alley. It was lined with indiscriminate, rundown flats that looked like old used women all squatted in a row, curtainless windows sagging like heavy exposed bosoms, and crumbling brickwork that resembled worn, faded skirts draped along the sidewalk.

She reached the flat—number 9 at the end—and slipped the key into the lock. There was a soft, warm glow about the room from the coal stove.

The muff was discarded on the small table beside the bed, her fingers brushing against the pale envelope with its elegant handwriting. She had meant to mail it, but had forgotten to take it with her. Tomorrow would be soon enough.

She sat on the edge of the bed and lit the oil lamp on the table. Then she unlaced her shoes. Her feet were wet and cold. She was always cold, and alone. Except here. She glanced at the door to the adjacent room. Her flatmate must have already gone to bed.

She decided to fix a cup of tea. Perhaps her flatmate would join her. There was a knock at the door. She jumped, almost dropping the teapot.

"Who could that be, this time of night?" She wasn't expecting anyone. Perhaps her flatmate had a visitor.

She thought of asking if anyone was expected, but it was dark beneath the door to the adjacent room. She approached the door, bolted from the inside.

"Who is it?" she called out.

"I've got a message."

She frowned, wondering who would send a message this time of night. Still, it might be important. She unbolted the lock.

The door crashed back on its hinges. A blast of cold air whipped into the room, a gust of wind snuffed out the oil lamp by the bedside.

Dangerous shadows plunged into the room. A steel blade slashed through the black night, and the woman's terrified scream died in the swirling mist.

Chapter One

The room smelled of death.

It spilled out of the shadows and wrapped around the hushed whispers of the curiosity seekers who peered in at the window and door. It smothered the air and choked into the throat.

The first thought was always the same—Please don't let it be a child!

A child's death was the worst. So much loss. Lost innocence, lost hopes and dreams, a lost smile. Once a child reached adulthood on the hard streets of London's East End—if they lived that long—hopes, dreams, and smiles were left far behind with the innocence that died in the face of the daily struggle to survive amid poverty and disease.

But this was not a child's room.

It was the room of one of the countless prostitutes who plied their trade in the saloons and taverns of Whitechapel, bartering themselves for a few coins, some drink, a meager meal—selling away their lives.

No matter how many times he experienced it, it always affected Inspector Devlin Burke the same—that sudden shudder, as if he'd been doused with a bucket of icy water, the flash of anguish, the sharp feeling of regret that was hidden behind the hard line of his mouth and the sudden set of his jaw.

His intense gaze scanned the room as he took a mental inventory of first impressions. The uniformed constable in charge, a stocky man with coal black hair and wide-set eyes by the name of Hobbs cleared his throat. "She's over here, sir."

Burke finally looked up, his mouth pulled into a tight frown. "Yes, of course. Let's get on with it." He stepped over to the narrow bed against the far wall. A man pushed his way through the uniformed officers who guarded the doorway. Mr. Sinjin Devoe.

Burke always relied on first impressions. They were instinctive and rarely wrong. His first impression of Sinjin Devoe had been that the man resembled a sleek ferret.

His suits and the overcoat he invariably wore against the bone-chilling London weather were of the finest worsted wool. He was tall and walked with an economy of movement. He was fair with even features that women invariably considered handsome. But there was something in those gray eyes beneath brows perpetually arched with disapproval that Burke didn't quite trust.

Those eyes were cool, remote, thorough. Burke was certain that little escaped their perusal. But there was something else behind those eyes — a void, an emptiness, a complete lack of any emotion. Even rage was better than nothing at all. A man could trust the honest danger of rage. But Sinjin Devoe's eyes were void of all expression, like narrow slits of ice. Burke had learned long ago not to trust a man who showed no emotion.

Burke didn't bother to disguise his irritation at the special assistant who'd been pushed off on him by Chief Inspector Abberline.

Abberline had given him no choice: "He was sent over from the commissioner's office. They have asked us to give him our full cooperation. This is not a request, Burke. It's a direct order."

He'd gone on to explain in an uncompromising tone, "Take him round with you on a couple of your other cases, but keep him away from the Ripper case."

"I've enough trouble on my hands with the press, the home office and Buckingham Palace putting on pressure to end this Jack the Ripper madness. I don't need some ambitious, bureaucratic fool who's never set foot in Whitechapel trying to tell me how go about my work. Between you and me, the man is an idiot, but one we must put up with just long enough to satisfy the commissioner that we're doing our job. Then we can be rid of him."

Burke wished he shared Abberline's confidence at easily getting rid of Devoe. The man wasn't an idiot. He was inquisitive, ambitious, and tenacious, and he was determined to involve himself in the Ripper case in spite of Burke's efforts against it.

After word was sent over that morning that another girl had been found dead, Burke had changed his usual routine. He hadn't gone round to the station first. Instead he left straight away from his flat hoping to avoid Devoe.

Now, as Devoe shouldered his way through the uniformed constables with that unmistakable air of authority, Burke realized the man had an uncanny ability for always knowing precisely where he could be found—either that or someone at the police station was giving him information about the case against Abberline's direct orders.

Burke was inclined to believe the latter. With the meager wages that were paid London's finest, loyalty was easily bought.

"I had a devil of a time finding this place," Devoe cut in, inserting himself between Burke and Constable Hobbs. "What a wretched, stinking little hovel this is."

"It ain't Buckingham Palace, sir," Hobbs replied. "But then if it was it wouldn't suit most of the whores in Whitechapel. The Royal Palace is a bit gawdy and drafty fer their customers," he added in a conversational tone that masked the subtle nuance of contempt behind the words.

Devoe's gaze narrowed, reminding Burke of another assessment—that it might be dangerous to cross him. "The commissioner has been gravely concerned about the gross amount of ineptitude with which this case has been handled. Since this case is not yet solved, I suggest you be about your duties."

Burke saw the instantaneous flash of anger and interceded, placing himself between Devoe and Hobbs. He laid a restraining hand on Hobbs's shoulder. "I need the information from the constable who found the body. If you could get that for me." Then he added with quiet authority, "Now, if you will, Hobbs."

Slowly, the big man backed down. The fists clenched at his sides slowly relaxed. He bobbed his head and muttered, "Right away, sir."

After he left, Devoe brushed at an invisible speck of lint on his coat sleeve. "I went round to your place first thing, but you'd already left." He sniffed with disapproval, "Without telling anyone of your destination. We are supposed to be working together."

Burke ignored the last remark. "You seemed to have discovered my whereabouts without too much effort." He didn't bother to disguise his contempt as he went over to the bed. There was no way to keep Devoe out of this without causing more problems. He grabbed

9

the threadbare coverlet and experienced an almost overwhelming urge to feel the man's throat beneath his fingers.

Beneath the coverlet was a much-mended, satin quilt that had probably once adorned the bed of some member of society before it was donated to the charity house. Both the coverlet and the quilt had been carefully drawn across the bed. Someone, perhaps the murderer, had taken great care to give the bed a neat appearance.

A silk shawl in a garish purple color puddled onto the floor, as if the lady who wore it had just returned and laid it across the end of the bed. But she hadn't just returned. She'd been there for several hours, beneath the quilt, the coverlet, and the satin shawl. Her pale, bloodless hand dangled out from under the edge of the quilt.

"I suppose the wretch was a prostitute like the others," Devoe speculated in a disdainful tone as he joined Burke beside the bed.

Burke smothered back the urge to shove Devoe's teeth down his throat. "Sometimes it's the only way a girl has of makin' her way in the world. It's not as if they choose it because they've nothin' better to do."

"You act as if you sympathize with the poor creatures," Devoe remarked disdainfully.

"I understand how they end this way." Irritation gave way to fury. Burke yanked the covers back, exposing the woman's body and the intricate slashes across the pale torso, the flesh methodically carved, internal organs removed.

For all his cool disdain and air of superiority, Devoe gasped. He tried to swallow but his throat constricted. He gagged as he tried to draw a deep breath.

"Good God!" he exclaimed in a muffled voice behind the handkerchief he abruptly pulled from his breast pocket and smothered over his mouth and nose against the stench of death. He turned away.

Hobbs returned and handed Burke the notes taken by the constable who had found the murdered girl. "Them marks was made the same way as the other two," he said in a quiet voice, then added with sincere sympathy, "Poor thing."

"Was a weapon found?" Burke asked, pushing past the first shock at the sight of the mutilated body. They talked around Devoe as if he weren't there.

"Not that any of my men found, sir. But then the place was already full of people when we got here." He glanced over at the crowd of spectators that gawked at the door and windows.

Burke frowned. "Get them out of here. I don't want anything disturbed more than it has been already."

"Yes, sir."

"Who found her?"

"An old woman across the way. The door to the flat was standing open. She thought it was unusual and came over. That's when she found the body."

"How long ago was that?"

"Just after ten o'clock this mornin', sir. My men arrived here just a few minutes before you did."

Burke cursed softly. "And by the looks of things at least a dozen people have been through here. God knows what might have been disturbed. Get the damn room closed off. No one comes in without my authorization."

"Yes, sir!"

Amid loud protests and disgruntled objections the crowd reluctantly dispersed. They would be back. Burke understood their anger. It came from the fear that gripped Whitechapel District with the Ripper still stalking the streets, and now it appeared he'd claimed another victim.

He turned his attention back to the room. It was Spartan but neatly kept, a small private cocoon with carefully concealed secrets. A young woman had died here. Her meager possessions were laid out on the bedside table, across the back of a wobbly chair, and in the drawers of the narrow chest that contained a few plain but clean garments. The room had its secrets, threads of the fabric of her pitiful existence. It was his responsibility to find those secrets.

Who was she? How had she come to the streets of Whitechapel? Had she been born here or abandoned to the streets as a child? Was there anyone to grieve for her?

Like photographs, Burke stored the myriad details of the room in his memory — the neatly arranged bedcovers that at first concealed the victim like a shroud, everything carefully straightened and tidy, except for the small table beside the bed that tilted at an angle. One of the legs had come off, as if there had perhaps been a struggle and someone had fallen back against it. Although nothing else in the room suggested violence, except for the woman's body.

These details were now part of an intricate puzzle that began

11

weeks earlier when two other women were murdered in precisely the same manner.

Hobbs had returned from dispatching his instructions. Burke didn't look up as he continued his inspection of the room. "What was the girl's name?"

"No one seems to know much about her. She moved in a few weeks ago. Had a hard time comin' up with the rent the first few weeks. Then more recently, she paid on time. Probably hidin' out from someone. Didn't want nobody knowin' her name," Hobbs speculated. "It's common enough in Whitechapel."

Yes," Burke concluded thoughtfully, "she'd come into some money somehow."

"Money?" Devoe appeared at the side of the bed, carefully averting his gaze from the girl's body. His tone was condescending. "The girl was obviously quite penniless. Look at the way she lived." He waved his hand through the air in an encompassing gesture. "A common street girl, a prostitute."

Without the slightest doubt of his conclusion. He added in a superior tone, "It isn't likely that such a girl had any money. Take a look about you, Inspector. This was not a robbery."

Burke's gaze narrowed. He had seen far more than Devoe. It wasn't a robbery that had taken place here. A girl had been brutally murdered for no apparent reason, and Devoe seemed to know far more about the Ripper case than he'd been able to learn in the few days he'd been in the district. Somehow he'd acquired information about the other murders even though Abberline kept the files carefully locked away.

Burke disagreed with Devoe's conclusions. "She wasn't like the others," he said thoughtfully, more to himself, than for anyone else present. There were clues all about them to the sort of life she'd lived the past few weeks if one took the time to look for them.

The small coal stove was hot to the touch. It had been burning for several hours. No ordinary prostitute in Whitechapel could afford the quantity of coal to keep a stove going all night.

Then he noticed the coal bin. It was almost full, an expensive luxury for a penniless street whore. And then there were the curtains at the windows.

They were of good quality, without a tear or mend, and spotlessly clean. In fact, other than obvious signs of a struggle near the bed, the room was immaculate as if someone regularly took a great deal of care to see that it stayed that way. Not the usual habits or amenities of one of Whitechapel's working ladies.

He made no mention of his observations to Devoe as he stepped back to the bed. This time there was no emotion, only cold, impartial observation. The girl's stays were carefully unlaced not cut by the slashes, as if she might have been in the process of undressing for bed when she went to the door. It wasn't something she would have done if the man were a stranger. It meant that she knew her attacker. Then there was the bolt at the door.

It was new, recently installed. The wood was freshly exposed where the bolt was mounted. This young woman had been careful. Yet, Hobbs said the old woman found the door standing open, and there was no evidence that it had been forced open.

Burke gently lifted the woman's hand. She was no more than twenty-five or twenty-six years old at the most. She had once been quite attractive. Now, her skin was achingly cold, the joints of her fingers stiff with rigor mortis.

He discovered something that had obviously been overlooked. With a small pocket knife he carefully removed several black woolen threads from beneath one fingernail.

Devoe moved about the room, searching for other clues. Without a word about his discovery, Burke carefully deposited the pieces of wool thread into a small envelope and handed it over to Hobbs.

The room was silent except for the murmur of conversation from the constables posted at the door. They had seen this sort of brutality twice before, but the shock was still there. Burke looked down at the pathetic, mutilated body of the woman and tried to imagine the events that had taken place in that room.

He was taken back to another time and place, another loss so profound that it had marked his life forever. He had wanted to cheat death then. He found he wanted to cheat it now, for this poor nameless woman.

"Sir? I've found something."

Roused from his painful memories, Burke gently laid the woman's hand back down on the bedcover, and drew the coverlet over her as if he could somehow give her some small portion of the dignity in death that had eluded her in life. Then he followed Hobbs.

It was another room, that had at first gone unnoticed. It was spartanly furnished with a narrow cot, scarred wood dresser, and a single chair. There was a small window at the back. It might have been a closet, it was so small.

A small square of lace covered the scarred dresser top. A threadbare cushion in a pale shade of rose had been placed on the chairseat to ease the hardness of it. On closer inspection, a cheap vase turned out to be a gin bottle. It was filled with flowers. This, too, was a woman's room.

As in the first room, there was no sign of violence, nothing had been disturbed. It was neat, tidy, everything in perfect order. And yet someone had been here recently. Water stood in the washbowl on the small nightstand, as if the woman who occupied this room might have been in the process of washing when she was disturbed. Perhaps by an unexpected visitor.

Two rooms, two beds. Two women?

It was more than a possibility. Even in the poor East End of Whitechapel, it was impossible for a woman on her own to afford the rent on even the most run-down flat, let alone one with two rooms.

It made sense that two women had shared the flat and the rent. But if so, where was the second woman? Who was she?

Had she been there the night before? What had she seen? Had she witnessed the murder and then fled in terror for her life? Or was she simply out for the evening, like so many other prostitutes who had to earn their living off the streets?

Was this her room, or the victim's room?

There were dozens of questions, for which there were no answers. Not yet, but he would find them.

He gave his instructions to have this room carefully examined as well. Then he returned to the first room where two of his constables were involved in a heated discussion with a member of the newspaper.

"Burke!" the reporter exclaimed. "What's happened? We received word there had been another murder?" He craned his head over the constable's shoulder, his gaze fastening on the bed. "Where's the body? Was it done in the same manner? Was she cut up like the other two? Was she a prostitute? Who was she?"

Burke pushed back his irritation as he repeated his instructions that the room was to be completely sealed off from everyone, except himself and his men. The reporter was gently but forcefully re-

14

moved, shouting questions all the way down the street to the edge of the alley where the police barricade had been set up.

He loathed the man. "Parasite!" he muttered under his breath as he scrutinized the room one last time before turning it over to his people to carefully search for any possible clues. But he was forced to admit he had the same questions.

The fog was beginning to burn off. Pale sunlight streamed through the spotlessly polished glass windows. It made the room deceptively cozy and inviting, and glittered off a tiny object on the worn, braided rug.

The pin was intricately designed and felt very heavy in the palm of his hand. It was made of real gold and the perfectly matched stones that formed the petals of a flower were also real. It was very expensive and very old, an heirloom perhaps, the sort of pin a well-heeled lady might own.

Did it belong to the victim? Had it been torn loose as she struggled against her assailant? How had she come by such a costly thing?

"All finished, then?" Devoe entered the room behind him.

"It's obvious no one can tell us anything about what happened here. We should get back and make our report to the chief inspector."

Burke dropped the pin into his pocket. He said nothing of his discovery as he followed Devoe from the room. He stopped at the door and glanced back at the two rooms.

Another woman had been there the night before. He was certain of it. What had happened to her?

Chapter Two

The fronds of a tree fern spread fanlike across the cool marble floor of the solarium. The pale green lace of a Boston fern slowly unfurled. Like multicolored woodsprites, the delicate blossoms of rare orchids, violets, and fuchsia peeked from under the outstretched leaves of coleus and maidenhair.

Light filtered down through hundreds of opaque panes in the glass dome overhead, illuminating everything in perfect, brilliant light.

The temperature was mild, the air was moist. A fine sheen of moisture clung to glass, leaves, and petals, until it collected, and ran in tiny rivulets to the tips and formed quivering, suspended droplets. Overall was the pervading sound of water.

Like soft voices, it played over the senses. It gurgled and ran in complete abandon from the center of the marble fountain, then laughed and tumbled over the rim of the top basin.

It slowed and sighed, swirling gently before it slipped lazily over the rim of the second basin, where it caught for a moment, then whispered farewell. It disappeared in a swirling vortex, to spring forth again moments later from the fountainhead, rippling and giggling, mischievous as a child.

The only other sound was the stroke of a brush across canvas, in steady, rhythmic movements. Then it stopped, only to begin again. Without interruption, the sounds of the water and the brush blended in a subtle symphony.

She didn't hear it at first; the rhythmic click of serviceable shoes, the snap of fabric in the crisply starched maid's uniform.

"Miss?" And then louder, over the sound of gurgling, tumbling water. "Miss Jessamyn?"

Her concentration was broken. Jessamyn Forsythe stood back from the canvas. She frowned as she tried to hold onto the mental images she'd been struggling with all morning.

"Miss?"

Finally, with growing frustration, she said, "What is it, Rose?"

The maid found her, hidden among the clusters of giant potted ferns and tropical trees with her easel, brushes, and paints.

"Mrs. Pierce asked me to bring you this letter. It arrived day before yesterday." By way of explanation, she added, "It was on Mr. Forsythe's desk in the library, underneath some other letters."

Jessamyn made an impatient gesture in the direction of the table covered with glass jars of powdered pigments, a tin of linseed oil, and myriad brushes.

She tried to conjure up the images she'd been working on before she had been interrupted, attempting to refocus her concentration, but they were lost for now. She threw down her brush in frustration and reached for a cloth to wipe her hands.

"It looks real nice, miss," the maid said hesitantly in a heavy Irish accent. "It's one of yer best yet. 'Course, I'm no expert on paintin'. But I know what I like, and I like this one."

Wiping her hands, Jessamyn glanced at the maid with a bemused expression. She'd been working for hours and finally felt that she'd gotten the background right.

It had been difficult to concentrate the past few weeks. She was too preoccupied. Perhaps it would have been better to set the painting aside and go back to it later. But difficult and frustrating as it was, it was also cathartic.

Painting was freedom of expression and emotion, completely unstructured in its form. And yet the discipline it required brought structure to the chaos she'd lived with the past weeks.

She could change color, form, and texture, alter images, add new ones, or abandon them altogether, and begin again. Painting focused and balanced her life, gave back some measure of control, when everything else seemed to be spinning crazily out of control.

She'd only just begun to stroke in the lines of images she'd been contemplating that afternoon. There was no texture, no definitive

17

form. To say it was only a beginning was an understatement, and yet, Rose liked it.

"It's Kensington Park," she explained. "In the fall when all the trees start to change colors."

The girl stepped closer and inspected the canvas, her mouth puckering in concentration. "Ooooh. I can see it plain as day, miss. There's all sorts o' trees everywhere. Oh, I do like it, miss."

Jessamyn smiled. "Those are supposed to be people, Rose. At least they will be when I've finished with them."

"Oh," the maid responded in a small voice. Then she brightened. "There will be trees, won't there, miss?"

"Yes, a great many of them."

"That's nice, miss. A park just wouldn't be a park without trees." She hesitated, rocking impatiently from one spotlessly polished shoe to the other. "Ain't ya goin' to open it, miss?"

Jess set her brushes in the apothecary jar filled with turpentine for cleaning. She looked up with a frown.

"The letter, miss," Rose reminded her. "It has been here, unopened, for two days. 'Course, you'd a had it sooner if Mrs. Pierce had seen it first. It just laid there in the library till Mr. Jarvis found it." The maid fastened lids to the jars of mixed paints and twisted them down tightly.

"It might be important," she rattled on, chattering like a magpie. "Maybe a special invitation now that the season has begun. Miss Lenore always wanted to see every invitation the moment it arrived, even if she did take her time respondin' to them. She always said, a lady shouldn't seem too eager."

At the mention of her sister Jess felt a flash of pain. It had become familiar over the past three weeks. "Yes," she said, a poignant smile gently curving her mouth at the memory. "Linnie always insisted on seeing every invitation the moment it arrived."

"And you wouldn't want to be impolite to Miss Kelly, who sent it. Mrs. Forsythe wouldn't approve of ya neglectin' yer social duties."

Yes, she mustn't disappoint her stepmother, Jess thought, with an equally familiar feeling of resentment. Her head came up suddenly at something else the girl said. "Rose, what did you just say?"

18

"Mrs. Forsythe wouldn't approve . . ."

"No! Before that!"

There was a perplexed expression on the maid's face. "I said that you wouldn't want to be impolite . . ."

"What was the name you mentioned?"

"Oh! that. Miss Kelly, it was. Wot sent you that letter. Mary Kelly. It's right there on the outside of the envelope." Her eyes grew very large. "I didn't mean ta go readin' nothin' personal, miss."

The brushes were thrown down on the table, momentarily forgotten, as Jess snatched up the envelope that only moments before she'd casually waved aside, not wanting to be bothered with some social invitation. The name, Mary Kelly, was written in bold, unmistakable letters. This wasn't an invitation.

Mary Kelly was the name of an imaginary friend she and Lenore had invented as children. Mary shared their escapades and adventures. She was trustworthy and loyal, someone they could tell all their secrets to and never fear betrayal from. It had been years since Jess thought of Mary Kelly.

It must be a coincidence, or a cruel joke. Yet, somehow she sensed it was neither.

Jess started to open the envelope. Her frown deepened at the postmark stamped across the back—Whitechapel. It was one of the poorest, most wretched sections of London, in the East End where those horrible murders had taken place recently. She took a deep breath and then slipped her finger under the seal. She pulled the letter out and began to read.

Dearest Jess,

Forgive me for not writing sooner. I know how worried you must be. There was no time to tell you of my plans, it would have been too dangerous. Even now, I fear sending you this letter. Therefore, I used the name of our dear friend.

I am safe and well. I've been staying with a young woman by the name of Annie Chapman. She's been very kind to me.

Please don't worry about me, and do not try to find me.

You must tell no one about this letter. It is better this way.

I will write again, when I can. You are in my thoughts constantly.

Your loving sister, Lenore.

Jessamyn read the cryptic words scrawled in familiar loops and flourishes across the plain, poor quality paper several more times.

Fear seemed to leap off the paper at her; in the heavy, dark stain where the tip of the pen had hesitated on the paper and the ink bled into puddles, in the lines that skidded hastily and then disappeared, only to begin again in a chaotic rush across the page.

That same fear filled the safe, remote world inside the solarium, and slipped around Jess's heart like a cold, steel band.

"Is anything wrong, miss? Are ya feelin' all right? Yer tremblin'! Should I go fetch Mrs. Pierce?" There was alarm in the girl's voice.

Jess stopped her with a hand at her arm. "No! Please, I'm quite all right." Her face was very pale, and she felt unbearably cold, even though it was mild inside the solarium. So that Rose wouldn't think anything amiss, she added, "It's from a friend . . . Someone I haven't heard from in a very long time."

Her sister's warning—*tell no one about this letter*—made her careful with her words. She managed a smile then, and a lie. "A friend from school . . . in Paris."

"Then it *was* important," Rose smiled with self-importance.

"Yes, very important." Jessamyn carefully slipped the letter back inside the envelope, safe from curious eyes, and put it into the pocket of her work apron.

"In all the excitement over the letter, I almost forgot!" Rose exclaimed. "Mrs. Forsythe said you was to dress for supper. His Lordship is expected this evenin'."

Jess looked up. "Lord Rushmore is dining here this evening?"

"That's right, miss. And Mrs. Forsythe said you wasn't to be late this time. He's due to arrive promptly at eight o'clock." The maid smiled, satisfied with herself that she'd delivered good news with the letter and the instructions that her mistress had been so adamant about.

Jason Deverell, Lord Rushmore, was Jess's brother-in-law. He and Lenore had been married the year before. The wedding was the social event of the season. They lived an idyllic life, in a lavish home, Deverell Hall, with scores of servants. The Deverells were cousins to the Royal Family. Linnie had made a very successful marriage. She was ecstatically happy.

Then, three weeks ago, her sister disappeared. Jason was devastated.

In the weeks since, he'd maintained a careful facade because of his social position. He informed all their friends that Linnie was simply away, visiting friends. Privately, he had several discreetly chosen people looking for her. And in almost three weeks there was still no word, no information, no one who'd seen her, and no clue as to what might have happened. Lenore Deverell, Lady Rushmore, had vanished without a trace.

At first Jess refused to believe that her sister had disappeared, but as days became one week and then two, she was forced to accept the grim reality.

Jason called on them at least twice weekly or sent his footman round with messages for her father to inform them of any news about Lenore. They'd had a brief message from him the previous afternoon. Once again, as before, there was no news of her sister. Each time was more difficult than the last.

Now Jess wondered if he had also received a letter.

"It's a pity Miss Lenore ain't in London," Rose said, as she picked up the brushes Jess had thrown down on the table in her haste to read the letter. "Is she acquainted with Miss Kelly?

The servants in both households had also been told that Lady Rushmore was away visiting friends, outside London.

"Yes," Jess hastily replied. "We were all very good friends." She thought wistfully of their childhood, and longed for that time of innocence. Mary Kelly was their pretend friend. But Linnie had been her real, best friend.

It was Linnie who had encouraged her to take art instruction when they went away to school in Paris, and then persuaded her to take her first finished pieces to Monsieur Gilot, the renowned gallery owner.

Four years ago he established a second gallery in London, and

Linnie once again encouraged her to take her best pieces to him.

Her father and her stepmother, Vivian, assumed that her paintings languished in his gallery, hidden away in some closet to protect her from embarrassment, when other paintings, especially each new one by the renowned and reclusive artist J.B. Dumont, was eagerly awaited and purchased at an exorbitant price, often sight unseen.

J.B. Dumont had taken London by storm three years earlier with the Provence series—visually sensual paintings that brought the earthy pastoral beauty of the French countryside vividly to life.

The first two paintings in the series established a feverish demand for the artist's work. Each new painting was eagerly awaited and art patrons outbid one another to add the latest J.B. Dumont painting to their collection.

Monsieur Gilot recently sold the last painting in the series to a member of the Royal Household. Vivian Forsythe was devastated. She had hoped to own one, even though Palmer Forsythe declared it was far beyond their means.

"If only you could paint like that," she had once remarked to Jess.

Jess glanced at the unfinished canvas that she'd struggled with for days. If only, she thought.

She pulled impatiently at the strings of the apron she wore to protect her clothes when she painted.

"You must help me dress for supper," she promptly informed Rose, pulling off the apron as she crossed the solarium. The heels of her shoes made brisk clicking sounds across the marble floor.

"I'll wear the emerald satin." Her voice echoed in the fading light.

"Mrs. Forsythe said you was to wear the gray silk," Rose trotted frantically to keep up with her.

"And my hair . . . you'll have to do something with my hair."

"I'll put it up for you, like Mrs. Forsythe prefers," Rose suggested, a bit out of breath.

"I'll wear it down," Jess declared firmly.

* * *

She sat impatiently before the dressing table, clad only in petti-coats and a corset while Rose fussed and fidgeted with her hair.

Jess's glossy dark brows, a few shades darker than her thick, naturally wavy hair, drew together over vivid green eyes. Pale, delicate skin created the illusion of fragility that disappeared the moment she looked at someone with that direct, unsettling gaze. Her nose was small and finely boned, at odds with the prominent angle of high cheekbones, slightly stubborn jaw, and determined chin. Her mouth was too full to be considered delicate but suggested instead a subtle sensuality.

She was a study of contrasts—darkness and light, fragile strength, cool fire.

Her expression was troubled. Her hand, usually so calm with a paintbrush, trembled slightly as she reached to brush back a stray tendril of hair that curled rebelliously at her cheek.

The letter from Linnie had arrived two days earlier and lain unnoticed on the desk in her father's library. Her frown deepened as she thought of the cryptic message in that letter—There was no time to tell you . . . It would have been too dangerous . . .

What danger? What had forced her sister to disappear without a trace leaving behind her privileged, perfect life?

Was it something scandalous? Had Linnie somehow com-promised herself as Lady Rushmore?

Jess wondered if her sister might have had an affair, then quickly dismissed the idea. She would never risk her marriage or her position with a casual affair.

Had it something to do with money? Her sister was extrava-gant, even more so now that she was Lady Rushmore. The Deverell wealth was well-known, with vast land holdings, country estates, and several London properties, including the magnificent Deverell estate at Kensington Woods. In addition, Linnie received a substantial inheritance from their grandfather's estate on her twenty-first birthday.

No, Jess decided, money wasn't the problem.

Had Linnie discovered some old skeleton locked away at Deverell Hall, the ancestral family home?

Somehow Jess doubted that would have been enough to scare her sister off. There were enough eccentric and scandalous skeletons in the Forsythe family, beginning with Great-Aunt Eugenie who rode through the English countryside wearing only a ribbon tied about one ankle.

It had to be something else.

Whatever it was, it had frightened her sister badly. Badly enough that she hadn't confided in her.

Dear God, Linnie, where are you? Jess asked herself the question that had haunted her for the past three weeks.

What's happened?

She stared at her reflection in the mirror. Linnie had always been the pretty one with pale golden blond hair, delicate features that suggested an innate fragility, and luminous gray-green eyes. She was intelligent, poised, and articulate. She was also witty and charming. She always knew precisely the right thing to say. Everyone adored her.

Since her marriage to Jason Deverell, Lord Rushmore, her sister had seemed truly happy. Her husband was rich and powerful, heir to one of the oldest and most influential families in England. He was also young, handsome, and wealthy.

After their wedding, they took an extended tour of the continent. Upon their return to London several months later, Linnie threw herself into redecorating Deverell Hall, particularly the nursery. She was eager to have a child very soon.

Jess was convinced her sister would make the perfect mother. After their mother's death, Linnie always looked after everyone else.

Dolls, stuffed animals, even the cook's cat—no one escaped her mothering instinct, not even Jess. As a child she had often found herself trussed up in lacy doll's dresses, frilly pantaloons, and bonnets, and pushed about in a miniature-sized pram.

She tolerated it until the day she discovered the power of rebellion, shortly after her fourth birthday. She stubbornly refused to be dressed like a baby any longer, and fled the nursery through an open window. She'd been in rebellion ever since, and took particular delight tweaking her stepmother's nose—figuratively speaking of course.

She and her stepmother were constantly at odds with one another. Vivian measured success by the title that preceded a name,

24

the number of social invitations one received, and the number of servants in one's household. The only thing that mattered was that both her stepdaughters make advantageous marriages. One title in the family was enough, as far as Jess was concerned.

She was easily bored with endless rounds of parties, balls, dinners, and evenings at the opera. Most young men were shallow, self-centered, and boring. She was aware they considered her to be too outspoken and too opinionated, and she had far too much curiosity for and interest in matters considered unimportant for ladies. Such as social reform, a woman in Parliament, and the right to vote for all women. Quite naturally, it was men who considered it unimportant. And she didn't like to be coddled or patronized, or taken care of. She most certainly didn't care to be told which gown was proper to wear.

Vivian had ordered several new gowns that she considered appropriate from the seamstress without consulting Jess, all in shades of gray, muted browns, and midnight blue that was so dark and dreary she would have to be in mourning to wear them.

As soon as the gowns were delivered, Jess buried them at the far end of the wardrobe behind the heavy wool gowns, coats, and riding habits that were neatly draped in cotton sheeting and stored until winter. She'd been trying to find a way to get rid of them ever since.

"Isn't Mrs. Pierce collecting clothes to be sent over to the charity house for the poor?" She recalled the housekeeper had mentioned it several days earlier.

"That's right, miss. She's got several boxes waitin' to be picked up when the wagon comes round. I put in a few old things meself," she announced. "After all, we have to think of those less fortunate than ourselves." Then she added, "Mrs. Forsythe said she didn't want none of the staff wearin' shabby clothes when we wasn't wearin' our uniforms. Said it would look bad to the neighbors."

"I agree with her completely," Jess announced. Rose watched skeptically as she tore the dresses off the padded hangers. The gowns made a soft, whispering sound as heavy satin brushed against watered silk and taffeta.

25

"By all means, we must keep up appearances. You may have these," she told the girl. "Whichever ones you don't want, put in the charity box."

Rose's eyes widened. "Saints be merciful!" she whispered in awe. "I ain't never had nothin' so fine, miss." She smoothed the heavy silk skirt of one gown with reverence. Then she looked up with solemn eyes and said in a small voice filled with regret, "I can't accept these, miss."

"You can, and you will. Or you may put them all in the charity box and someone else will be wearing them." Jess saw the alarm that immediately sprang in the girl's eyes at the thought of someone else wearing the gowns—perhaps some charwoman or a flower girl down at Covent Gardens.

"Oooooh. I couldn't bear the thought of it," Rose lamented, clutching one gown tightly against her breast. She quickly made her decision. "Thank you, miss! I'll be as fancy as a real lady." Then she added, " 'Course, the other girls at the market won't even speak to me when they see me dressed so fine. They'll think I'm some lady, wot lost my way. You know how it is, miss."

Jess knew precisely how it was—that clearly defined but invisible line between the gentry and the common working classes. They might live in the same house, eat the same food, breathe the same air, but there was a distinction of wealth that separated them as surely as any wall.

A lady must never be seen speaking with a servant, except in the clearly defined terms of their respective positions, and never with a person from the lower classes that she might encounter on the streets. The barriers were clearly defined. Neither expected that they, or the other, would cross it.

Rose was still hesitant. "What will Mrs. Forsythe say about yer givin' them to me?"

"We won't tell her," Jess declared firmly. "It will be our secret. Now, we must hurry. I don't want to be late." When she saw the doubt that still wavered on the girl's face, she repeated firmly, "I'll wear the emerald satin gown tonight."

A half hour later Rose raced around her like a frantic little chicken, fastening the clasp of an emerald bracelet Jess's father had given her, adjusting the cap sleeves of the gown at her shoulders, smoothing stray wisps of hair into the tight coil on top of her head.

Jess raced down the wide staircase, the letter tucked inside the handkerchief pocket concealed in her voluminous skirt. Jason Deverell had already arrived. She heard his masculine voice from the formal drawing room; the elegant, fluid drawl so different from her father's brusque, clipped responses.

It was one of those subtle differences of class between merely well-bred gentlemen and members of the aristocracy who, because of their wealth, titles, and generations of privilege, had acquired a certain effete laziness in their manner and speech.

In spite of the title, the wealth, and the fact that Jason didn't actually *do* anything, Jessamyn liked him very much. He had a keen sense of humor and he tolerated her outspokenness with exceedingly good grace. He once declared that she was his favorite sister-in-law, in spite of her view on politics — particularly as it concerned women *in* politics.

She didn't bother to point out to him that she was his only sister-in-law.

The previous afternoon he had sent word that there was still no information about Linnie's whereabouts. Ever since her disappearance Jess had struggled with her nagging doubts that they weren't doing enough to find her. Now she'd received the letter, and she was certain Jason must have received one also.

She ran across the hallway into the drawing room with its dark, lustrous wood, satin upholstered chairs, rich textured Moroccan carpet, and glistening crystal light fixtures.

"Jessamyn!" She was immediately aware of the censure in Vivian's voice.

"How good of you to join us at last."

She smiled briefly at her stepmother, not trusting what she might say. She refused to allow Vivian to make her angry. Nothing could upset her this evening so certain was she that at last, they might soon find her sister. She greeted her father with a polite kiss on the cheek, and then turned to Jason Deverell.

He was strikingly handsome with dark golden hair, blue eyes and lean, aquiline features. He was tall and moved with a fluid grace that was found only among the aristocracy, and suggested an innate confidence that came from great wealth and a natural strength that came from long hours in the saddle riding to the hunt or horse-racing with his friends.

He was charming and disarming with a quick wit and a distinctive manner that made every woman feel as if she were the only woman in the world. Jess learned long ago that it wasn't flirtation. It was simply Jason's way and explained why so many women of all ages were attracted to him.

It was also part of Jason's charm that he seemed completely unaware of his attractiveness to other women. There had never been even a whisper of involvement with another woman since he married her sister.

He seized both her hands. "Dearest Jessamyn, you look absolutely radiant this evening."

"I heard part of your conversation from the hallway. Everyone seemed to be enjoying themselves."

"Jason was telling me that outrageous story about Lady Anson-Hill and that young man we've seen her with. It's absolutely appalling. She's old enough to be his mother," Vivian explained.

Jess glanced at her father and saw a brief flash of something that could only be described as discomfort. He'd been dreadfully lonely after their mother died. Then he'd married Vivian who was only a few years older than Lenore, hoping perhaps for a companion for his daughters and also for himself. He acquired a young wife that he neither understood nor had anything in common with. There were moments, such as this, when Jess wondered if he regretted it.

Jason continued to hold her hands in his. She anxiously asked, "Has there been word? Have you heard from Linnie?" She was certain that he would tell her now about the letter he'd received.

His shoulders sagged beneath the flawless fit of the exquisitely tailored coat. "Regrettably, no." His voice was grave. "There's been no word at all. Not a trace of her."

"Nothing? Nothing at all?" Surely she must have misunderstood. "Perhaps word of someone who might have seen her? A letter?" She stared at him, her skin suddenly very cold.

She'd been so very certain that he must have received a letter as

28

well. She searched his gaze for something else; a glance, a shift of a brow, that might suggest otherwise, that perhaps he chose to keep it a secret as Linnie had asked in her letter.

But as she stared at him and saw the faint circles beneath his eyes that spoke of sleepless nights, the small lines of frustration at either corner of his mouth, she realized the truth — whatever her reasons may have been, Linnie chose to contact only her.

She was stunned and heard only part of what Jason said, as he went on to explain.

"I spoke with the gentleman I've contacted again this afternoon. He assured me he has the very best people making inquiries. Discreetly of course." His fingers had tightened over hers as if he were clinging to a lifeline. His voice caught with emotion. "I feel so helpless. I can't understand how she could simply disappear without a trace, or why for that matter."

"I'm certain there'll be word soon," Vivian interjected, the oft-repeated sentiment sounding somehow worn and less hopeful as each day had passed.

"It's probably as you first suggested. She's probably taken herself off over some trifle matter without telling anyone. Lenore has always been a little . . . high-strung."

She made it sound as if Lenore were unbalanced or feather-brained, someone who needed looking after.

"Linnie is not high-strung," Jess said. "She's the calmest, most sensible person I know. She had no reason to go off by herself without telling anyone."

"Well then, perhaps she was abducted," Vivian suggested. "The Deverell name is very well-known, and there are all sorts of dreadful people out there."

"Naturally, I considered that possibility," Jason was saying. "If Lenore had been abducted, there would already be a demand for ransom. There's been none. Which is all the more reason why this entire matter must be handled with the utmost discretion. We can't have outsiders knowing about this, or interfering. The scandal could be devastating." He turned to Jess. "It could be very dangerous for Lenore. I know how close you and Lenore are." His voice was gentle, yet filled with his own personal pain. "I deeply appreciate your concern, but I'm afraid I've had to dismiss that

29

fellow you retained."

Vivian frowned. "What fellow? What are you talking about?"

"Sherlock Holmes," Jason explained. "Jessamyn asked him to make inquiries about Lenore."

"You didn't!" Vivian's hand flew to her throat, as if she were about to choke. "The man is notorious. Such a dreadful reputation, always involving himself in some horrible crime or another," she sniffed, as if the thought were unbearable, "often among the lower classes. Whatever possessed you to do such a thing?"

"He has an excellent reputation and a brilliant mind." Jess defended her decision. "He's resolved a great many situations for people whom we are acquainted with. Always as discreetly as possible. He was very highly recommended by Lady Warfield."

"Good heavens! Lady Warfield? The woman can't keep anything to herself." Vivian was almost beside herself. "You didn't say anything about Lenore did you?"

"Of course not!" Jess snapped. "I was very discreet." She restrained her mounting irritation.

"I was under the impression the most important thing is to find Linnie."

"Of course it is, my dear," her father assured her. "It's what we are all most concerned with. But we must be very careful," he went on to explain.

"Lenore is Lady Rushmore now. Everything must be handled with great discretion. It takes very little to start a rumor, or harmful gossip. Both could be devastating for Jason and Lenore."

Discretion? Rumors? Gossip? She couldn't believe what she was hearing.

"In a few months everything will be forgotten when everyone has something else to whisper and snigger about," she pointed out. "What does a little gossip matter compared to Linnie's well-being?"

Vivian cut her off. "Your father is quite right. We must have no more of this nonsense about Mr. Holmes. He brings a certain notoriety to these situations he involves himself in. It's almost as bad as bringing in the police—such dreadful people."

"We must leave the matter to Jason," she continued. "After all he is Lenore's husband. She is his responsibility. I'm certain he will do everything to see that she returns to us safely."

Jess turned to him, pleadingly. "We must do everything we can to find her. Mr. Holmes has an excellent reputation. He'll be very discreet. No one need ever know."

But Jason was adamant. "I'm afraid it's out of the question. I told him quite firmly that I didn't want him involved in this any further. I insist that you let me take care of this." Then his expression softened, and a bit of the old Jason returned in a brief, faint smile.

"I appreciate your concern, my dear. But this is a very delicate matter, and I assure you the very best people are looking for her."

It was then that the butler announced supper. Vivian Forsythe seized the opportunity to change the conversation as she moved between Jason and Jess, and asked him to escort her in to the dining room.

Jess was left no choice but to abandon the conversation with the hope of bringing the matter up later. She allowed her father to escort her in to supper, an uneasy feeling settling low in the pit of her stomach.

Any hope she had of discussing Mr. Holmes further with Jason disappeared over dinner, as Vivian deftly maneuvered the conversation from one topic to another.

She had no appetite and pushed her food around her plate. She was only partially aware of the conversation that flowed around her, and so, looked up in surprise when her name was repeated. Jason asked about her attending opening night at the opera which was only two days away.

"I haven't made any plans."

Vivian frowned. "But, my dear, it's only two days away."

"I haven't made any plans, because I won't be attending," she informed everyone at the table.

Vivian lowered her fork to her plate. "Opening night is one of the most important evenings of the season," she reminded her. There was an even more subtle reminder that it was the most important social event of the season, where dozens of young women met eligible men.

Jess met her gaze across the table. "A dear friend has recently returned from France. She's staying with friends in Hampshire.

31

They've invited me for a visit." She thought of Charlotte Eddelson, an old friend from their French Academy days who lived in Hampshire. She'd visited her often, and Charlotte could be relied upon.

Vivian was stunned. "You're not thinking of going?"

"Actually, I've already accepted."

"Isn't this rather sudden, my dear?" her father asked.

"Not really. I simply forgot to mention it. The past few weeks have been very difficult."

"Perhaps it will be good for you to get away," Jason suggested. "I know how upset you've been. Hopefully this will all be over by the time you return. Naturally, we shall all miss you." Then he asked, "How soon are you leaving?"

"Actually, quite soon. I was thinking about tomorrow."

"I see," Vivian said woodenly, with a hint of the disapproval she dared not voice further in front of Jason Deverell.

"I suppose there's nothing we can say to change your mind."

"No," Jess said firmly. "You can't. It would be exceedingly poor manners to change my plans at this late date." It was the one excuse that Vivian, who always prided herself in being the standard bearer of social propriety, could not and would not argue against.

"We'll send word, of course, the moment we hear anything from Lenore," her father assured her.

"Thank you. I would appreciate that." The moment she informed them of her plans, she realized that her father and Vivian would want to know who she was staying with. Yes, she would tell them that she was staying with Charlotte. Charlotte could be relied upon to help Jess carry off her own disappearance.

"It would be more comfortable for you to take the train," Vivian suggested, and Jess realized it would leave the elegant new coach her father had just purchased for Vivian's use.

"Yes, of course. Whatever you think."

"And you must take Rose, of course."

Jess was confident she could persuade Rose to take a small vacation, say perhaps to Brighton where her sister lived, with those new gowns in her case and several gold crowns in her pocket.

"I'll have Rose pack the new gowns to take with you. They

would be appropriate for the country," Vivian chatted on, completely unsuspecting of the true direction of Jess's plans.

"We shall miss you, of course," her father spoke up for the first time, repeating what Jason had already said.

He seemed to be struggling with something more as he pushed a piece of roast lamb about his plate. But he fell silent as if the thought suddenly eluded him, or perhaps it was too difficult to express.

Jess thought of all the lost moments between them. She wanted him to say something more, but, as always, there was Vivian between them.

"Of course, we shall miss her," her stepmother interjected, making the sentiment seem somehow shallow and meaningless. "It will be good to get her mind off this dreadful situation."

Jess realized that was all Linnie's disappearance meant to them — a *dreadful situation* — to be resolved as quickly as possible before anyone else found out and there was a scandal.

Any remaining doubts Jess might have had about her hastily made plans quickly disappeared.

The following morning she would leave the train at the first stop and hire a hansom cab.

Her sister's letter had been posted from Whitechapel. Her search must start there.

It was the only clue she had. That, and a woman by the name of Annie Chapman.

Chapter Three

The hansom lurched away, churning up a mixture of garbage, mud, and horse dung that clogged the street, geysers spurting from beneath each wheel. Jessamyn jumped back, but not before the disgusting ooze spattered her boots and the hem of her skirt.

The skirt was a plain brown linsey wool. She'd found it, along with the shoes, shirtwaist, and shawl in the charity box at home. At the time she thought the clothes couldn't look more pathetic. She was wrong.

She pulled out a handkerchief and tried to remove some of the stain. Her head jerked up at a warning shout.

A horse-drawn wagon followed by several lumbering cattle bore down on her. The cattle snorted and bawled, pushing and shoving through the street, their stumps of nubby horns frightening to someone who'd never seen a barnyard animal before in her life.

Ignoring feminine delicacy along with the hem of her skirt, and the piles of garbage and horse dung, Jess ran for the doorway of a nearby shop.

She clutched her valise against herself like a protective shield as she flattened herself into the doorway. Shoving and drooling, the cattle pushed past her down the street. A second man ran after them with a long switch in his hand which he applied when they slowed their pace.

Her black felt hat, which she had borrowed from her maid, was askew on her head and hair streamed down about her shoulders as Jess peered out from the doorway. Of all the things she had prepared herself for, a herd of cattle roaming the streets of London was not one of them.

She hastily repinned her hair and straightened the hat. When she was certain there were no more cattle coming her way, she stepped from the doorway of the shop.

Gone were the wide, familiar avenues that bordered stately Belgravia and Grosvenor Square. Gone, too, were the carriages and private coaches, and the elegant town houses with their pale Georgian facades.

They were replaced by narrow streets crowded with carts, wagons, and drays, and gutters that ran thick with every imaginable sort of filth and waste.

The smokestacks of nearby factories loomed overhead through the thinning mist and belched their own waste into the leaden sky, draping everything with a film of gray soot. It heightened the pervasive gloom and despair that hung in the air like a smothering weight.

Dingy laundry hung from ropes strung across alleys. Doors to shops gaped open, displaying dead poultry, slaughtered livestock, and staring dead fish strung up along sagging overhangs.

Jess swallowed back the hollow feeling that had clawed at her stomach ever since she took the cab from Victoria Station, after sending Rose off to visit her sister in Brighton.

While other passengers had boarded the train, Jess slipped into her private compartment and changed into the cast-off clothes she'd brought along as a disguise. She left the train just before it pulled out of the station, and hired a driver to take her to Whitechapel.

Now all the doubts and uncertainties she hadn't allowed herself earlier that morning threatened to smother her.

How could she possibly hope to find her sister with nothing more than a letter postmarked from Whitechapel? She hadn't even an address, and as she stared at the buildings that surrounded her a familiar feeling of helplessness, that she'd lived with ever since Linnie disappeared, returned.

She had no idea where she was — at least not precisely where she was. This *was* London, but a part of London she'd never seen before. She felt abandoned, like a stranger in a foreign country.

A small cart rumbled up the street. The driver was hunched over as if trying to coax every shred of warmth from his thin clothes that resembled innumerable holes held together by a few thin threads.

He was a shrunken little creature with a high forehead that disappeared into a thatch of matted gray hair, jammed into a knit cap. His eyes drooped over sagging cheeks shot through with tiny veins that spread like the silken strands of a spider's web, growing thicker as they converged on his large nose, where they stood out in sharp relief against his sallow skin.

He pulled hard on the reins and the cart creaked to a stop. His hands were scarred and gnarled, the joints swollen with arthritis, like deep burls in an ancient old oak. But there was no outward sign of pain as he grabbed hold of the side of the cart and swung down with amazing agility.

The cart was mountained with piles of garments, rags, and bits of yarn. He was one of thousands of ragpickers who roamed the streets, scavenging or trading for odd bits of cloth or old clothes.

"Good day ter yer, miss." He touched the brim of his cap. "An' a right cropper of a day it is, too. Spivey's th' name, an' I got a rare bargain t'day—some quality wool an' a good bit of linen. Are yer buyin' er sellin'?"

"I beg your pardon?"

He looked at her through the narrow slits of wrinkled eyes. His mouth twisted in a smile that revealed one badly yellowed tooth, in barren, rotted gums.

"Beg me pardon, do ye?" He looked her over from head to foot. "A right topper young lady like yerself don't need to go beggin' fer nothing. Yer sound like a bleedin' swell."

"A swell?"

"A nob, gentry, quality folk . . ." he explained, making gestures as if he were holding a cup of tea, small finger extended outward, "like yer was some grand lady."

She was tired and hungry, her clothes were badly stained, and she suspected she was probably lost. She remembered something her maid had said, about clothes not making a real lady, and she laughed softly. The clothes might disguise what she looked like, but there was no disguising how she talked.

He squinted at her. "Somethin' wrong, miss?"

"No, Mr. Spivey there's nothing wrong, but I was wondering if you could tell me where I am?"

His eyebrows shot up, smoothing out the mapwork of wrinkles on his face. He looked as if he thought she might be daft.

"What I mean is, could you tell me if this is Whitechapel?"

"Yer mean yer don't know?"

"Well, not exactly. You see, I just arrived in London," she explained, reciting the story she'd decided to tell if anyone asked. "I'm trying to find my sister. I received a letter from her. It was mailed from Whitechapel."

"Don't s'pose I could int'rest yer in a bit of linen?" he repeated.

She started to say that she didn't need any linen. What she did need was information. But something stopped her. This was London, the same city where she had been born and raised. But it was a far different London from the one she was familiar with.

The rules of society, where she might pay a few coins to obtain information, didn't apply here. She had to learn a new set of rules, and the first was that business was conducted before any information was offered.

"I could use a good piece of wool for a coat."

Mr. Spivey's eyes lit up. "Got jus' the piece, I do." He circled around to the back of the cart. With the precision of a shopkeeper who knew precisely where each item in his store was kept, he burrowed down through the mountain of rags and garments, and immediately came up with a green wool coat.

"It's a mite big," he commented, eyeing her sharply. "Yer a wee, little thing. But there's the more ter keep yer warm of a cold evenin'." He held the coat aloft for her inspection.

It was a man's coat, wide in the shoulders with large pockets.

The fabric was stained but in good condition. She made a pretense of inspecting it very carefully, at the same time wondering what she should offer for the coat.

She made a great pretense of frowning as she examined the frayed cuffs, remembering how the cook at Carrington Square criticized each piece of fresh fish and produce that was brought round to the kitchen in an attempt to drive down the price.

"The cuffs are threadbare," she remarked thoughtfully. "And I don't know if I can get those stains out." The truth was she hadn't the faintest notion how to remove the stains, but Mr. Spivey didn't know that.

"What do you want for it?" she finally asked, having completed her inspection.

"I do 'ave a substantial investment in that piece. I intended it fer me poor widowed sister . who lives in Houndsditch." He rubbed his gnarled hand over his chin. "She's got six kids an' 'er 'usband up an' disappeared on 'er. She could make good use o' that coat."

"With six children I don't suppose she could pay you much for it," Jess replied.

"No, that be true. Still I couldn't part w'it fer anythin' less than a 'arf crown." He fixed her with a solemn stare, as if even that price were a great sacrifice.

"A half crown? It's not worth more than three shillings," she informed him bluntly, an expression of faint disgust on her face that she'd seen the cook use countless times when trying to drive down the price of an item she wanted to purchase.

Mr. Spivey clasped his hand over his heart. "Three shillings?" he squawked. "Yer wound me ter me very soul, miss. I've a livin' ter make, an' a sister with eight youngins to feed." His eyes rolled back in his head.

"I thought you said she had six children."

One eye fixed on her steadily. "Well, there's the two orphinks that sorta adopted Gert—she's me sister." He shook his head sadly. "She's a kind soul. Jus' naturally took 'em in, she did."

"Of course. And it must be difficult to provide for eight children."

38

"That it is." He shook his head. "That it is."

Jess said reluctantly. "I can't afford a half crown, although it is a fine coat. But I'm certain you'll be able to get your price for it." She handed it back to him.

"True enough." Mr. Spivey eyed her carefully, undoubtedly watching for any change of expression to indicate that he might still get the full price for the coat. She turned and picked up her valise and started to walk away from him.

"Then again," he said thoughtfully, "one in the 'and is worth two in the bush, ol' Spivey always says. S'pose I could let yer 'ave it fer say . . . eight shillins?"

Jess stopped and said without turning around, "I'll give you four."

"Seven!"

She finally turned around. "Five!"

He groaned. "Six shillins, an' that's me final offer. Givin' it away, I am, at that price."

"Done!"

Mr. Spivey reluctantly handed over the wool coat. "Yer drive a 'ard bargain, miss. Me nieces' and nephews' stomachs will be scrapin' their backbones because o' it."

She took the coat and put it inside the valise, hoping that any former occupants, of the crawling variety, had already vacated the coat. Mr. Spivey pocketed her money and looked up at her sharply.

"If'n yer needs ter find someone in Whitechap'l, the place to go is the bloody peelers."

"I beg your pardon?"

"The peelers! Police, much as I 'ate to say it. Spend most of me time avoidin' 'em," he said under his breath with a hint of disgust. "They know everyone 'ere about on both sides."

"Both sides?"

He snorted impatiently. "Both sides!" he repeated, as if by shouting, he could make her understand.

"Yer 'ave the peelers on one side o' th' law, and then yer 'ave the fences, informers and thieves on th' other. The closest police station is on Commercial Street. Two ov'r and one up."

She assumed by that description that two over and one up meant two streets over and one up. She could walk it in just a few minutes.

Mr. Spivey climbed aboard the cart and sat on the hard bench seat, staring straight ahead. He wore a contemplative expression.

"It's on me way. Could take yer there," he suggested, and then added, "Fer a price o' course." He turned a narrow eye on her. "Say, fer three shillins?"

She smiled at his shrewdness. It was on his way, and he was offering to give her a ride, for three shillings of course, which would recover the full price he'd originally wanted for the coat.

"I paid two shillings to come all the way across London," she informed him. "I'll pay you one shilling."

His face set with a stubborn expression. "Two."

She could be just as stubborn. "One shilling, or I shall walk."

"Yer drive a 'ard bargain, miss. Get yerself up 'ere. One shillin' it is, and poor ol' Delilah will be droppin' in her tracks from th' extra weight."

Delilah, no doubt, was his horse. She already appeared to be about to drop in her tracks. Jess climbed atop the cart while Mr. Spivey continued lamenting all the reasons this latest transaction would be the ruin of him.

He whistled to the horse. "Get on, Delilah! Move yer ol' bones! Only one shillin', darlin'. There'll be no extr' 'ay t'night."

It was an interesting journey through Whitechapel. Occasionally he stopped to pick a rag out of the gutter, or paw through a pile of trash for some hidden treasure that might be found.

She could have walked the distance in half the time, but she would have been deprived of Mr. Spivey's colorful conversation about the people they encountered along the way. He only knew a few of their names, yet he *knew* all of them.

He smiled and waved at them, asking about their family, their latest ailment, and any trouble with the peelers. Then as they drove past, he whispered their various illegal talents and encounters with the police. They finally pulled to a stop on Commercial Street.

"That be the place." He gestured across the street. Jess stepped down from the cart and paid him the shilling they'd agreed upon.

His hand brushed hers. Then he pulled back. He rubbed his fingers across his chin, and his voice was suddenly gruff.

"I 'ope yer find yer sister. Young girl like yerself shouldn't be alone. It's not safe, in a place like Whitechapel." Then he cleared his throat.

"Yer be careful, miss."

"Thank you, Mr. Spivey."

He chuckled, exposing shriveled gums. "Mr. Spivey. Ain't no one ever called me that before. Kinda' like th' way it sounds."

He slapped the reins over Delilah's rump. The cart rumbled away and he shouted back over his shoulder, "I'd 'a given yer the coat fer four shillins."

"I would have paid eight shillings."

He didn't look back and he didn't turn around. For a moment she thought he might not have heard. Then she saw his shoulders shake with laughter, and he called out to his horse, "Ho, Delilah. We been robbed, darlin', and by a right topper little thief at that."

The Commercial Street police station was a two-story brick building that filled the entire corner of the street. It had a slate roof and double windows on either side of the entrance. A row of tall, narrow windows faced the street on one side. The other side of the building was a solid brick wall at the alley. Narrow brick steps led up to the front entrance.

At the top of the steps a constable escorted a man inside the station. He weaved unsteadily on his feet and mumbled something unintelligible.

"C'mon, Gilly," the constable ordered gruffly. "Give me any more of yer trouble and it'll be Newgate fer accosting a constable."

The man stumbled and cursed, struggling against the metal cuffs at his wrists. His head came up briefly, and his gaze wob-

41

bled past the constable. He grinned foolishly at Jess. She stepped out of their way.

"Get on with yer, Gilly," the constable ordered. "Th' inspector has a few questions ter ask yer. Come along easy now, or I'll 'ave to lock yer up."

"I already told yer," Gilly grumbled. "I don't know nothin'."

"Inspector Burke still wants a word wi' ya. Come along agreeable now, or I'll use this." The constable placed a hand on the short club secured at his belt. Gilly grinned again.

"Yer be careful with that now, guv. Yer jus' might hurt yerself with that thing."

"No more trouble from yer now!" The constable pushed him into the police station.

Jess followed them at a safe distance. Inside the station, she stopped and stared. Nothing she encountered out on the street had prepared her for this.

There were approximately a dozen people in the station, but the noise made it seem as if it were ten times that many—all arguing, shouting, and protesting loudly.

Each was trying to tell their version of some story to a uniformed constable over the noise and confusion as everyone talked at once. A police sergeant, his face puckered like a belligerent bulldog, attempted to bring some order to the confusion from where he sat behind a long, raised counter.

The sergeant peered down at her from over the edge of the counter. "What do yer want?"

She jumped as if she'd been poked through with a hatpin.

"I need to speak to someone . . ."

"Wot about?"

"I'm trying to find someone . . ."

"Has there been a crime?"

"No, I don't think so . . . I don't know."

"Missin' person yer say?" The sergeant frowned. "Mr. Ludlow be in charge of that," he informed her.

"Could I see Mr. Ludlow?"

"He's not 'ere right now." A faintly bemused expression crossed his pugnacious face. "Might say he's missin'." His face split in a wide grin. When she didn't laugh with him, he coughed and cleared his throat.

"Wot's yer name?"

She hesitated, and then thinking of the disguise Linnie had been forced to assume, "My name is Jess . . . Kelly. Perhaps I could see someone else."

"Yer'll 'ave ter wait. Yer can sit over there." He wrote her name down on a piece of paper and pushed it aside, pushing her aside just as easily.

"It's very important," she persisted. "I would like to see someone now."

"Oh yer would, would yer?" he cocked his head as he glared at her over the edge of the counter. "And would yer also like us to serve yer tea and crumpets while yer wait?"

She'd never mastered the fine art of verbally putting one in one's place as Linnie had, so that the person was only vaguely aware that it had been done and spent the next several minutes trying to decipher the exact meaning of all the things that had been said to him. She'd never had the patience for cool, slicing wit, which she was absolutely convinced would be wasted on the sergeant.

Instead, her reaction in such situations had always been much more direct, with several well-chosen and colorful comments that instantly leaped to the tip of her tongue. Comments that had been overheard in the servants' quarters when she was a small child, and which she discovered — much to her stepmother's mortification — usually brought immediate results.

She suspected, however, that the sergeant would be far less than cooperative if she told him what she really thought. And Jess had never been considered foolish. Impulsive perhaps. Headstrong certainly. But not foolish.

The problem was everything she'd learned brought up with every advantage and privilege at Carrington Square was of no use here. As she'd quickly discovered, this part of London was very different.

"You'll 'ave ter see Mr. Ludlow," Sergeant Sweeney repeated, and dismissed her as he focused his attention on a thick stack of papers before him. It was obvious that all further discussion was pointless. She turned and collided with a small boy.

"Watch where yer goin'!" he hissed.

He was dressed in ragged, oversized men's clothes and scrambled past her to the front of the counter. Undaunted by the height of it, he launched himself up the front of the counter and grabbed hold of the edge.

" 'ey! Sweeney!" he shouted. "I gotta see Mr. Burke. It's important."

"Eh, Mickey!" the sergeant greeted him. "Wot's it about this time?"

Tiny Mickey clung to the edge of the counter with tenacious fingers, nose perched over the edge like a sharp-eyed ferret, his oversized shoes scrabbling against the front of the counter to gain a precarious foothold. His legs were skinny and dangled at least eighteen inches off the floor.

"It's about that case wot 'e's workin' on," Mickey explained. "Got some information he wanted 'bout that woman wot got herself all cut up."

"All right," the sergeant waved in the direction of a wood gate that led to offices at the back of the station. "Endicott, 'ere, will let yer through. And if ya kick the front of me desk one more time I'll deliver yer over to the workhouse meself."

Mickey brought his knees up to his chest and then kicked away from the counter, landing in the center of the room at Jess's feet.

"Rotten peeler!" he muttered under his breath as he spun past her and through the gate where a uniformed constable, obviously Mr. Endicott, sat officiously guarding the back of the station house. Without knocking, Mickey let himself into the first office.

Whatever information Mickey had for Inspector Burke, it was obviously important—more important than trying to find someone who was missing. Jess frowned and sat down to wait.

A young girl slouched into another chair nearby. She was crying, making loud snuffling noises, occasionally drawing her sleeved arm under her nose.

The pervasive smell of the streets clung to her. She fought back her tears, her chin thrust out stubbornly, as if she were ready to take on the world.

At a nearby desk an old man was describing someone he'd seen to the young constable. The old man's hand was heavily bandaged and trembled as he drew it across his wrinkled forehead, recalling the man who'd beaten and robbed him.

She longed to draw these people, to capture their expressions and that inner strength each stubbornly clung too. She saw it in wary glances and defensive gestures. It filled their conversations—like an angry fist they shook defiantly in the face of adversity. She took out her tablet and pencil.

She sketched the young girl first, her hand moving across the paper in quick, practiced movements, capturing character and emotion. She sketched the police station in the background, including Sweeney behind the high counter.

She resisted giving him short floppy ears, a pugnacious flattened nose, and drooling jowls. Instead she emphasized the contrast between the immaculate uniforms the constables wore and the disheveled rags worn by Mickey, the girl, and the old man.

When she had finished sketching the old man, she began another sketch of the man he had described to the young constable. He was observant and gave specific details—the way the man wore his hair, the high forehead, the shadow of cold eyes, a small scar, the meager growth of beard that covered the man's face. She was almost finished when a woman's loud screech echoed across the station.

"You bloody rotter! Yer can't keep me 'ere!" she screamed at the top of her lungs. "I'm a respec'able business woman! I earn my keep! Yer got no right to roust me like that!"

The woman was dressed in a gown in a startling shade of purple. It had once been quite stunning with cap sleeves, low bodice and a high black lace fichu. Only remnants of the black lace remained, cut away or perhaps torn away to reveal the plunging neckline of the bodice. It was several sizes too small for the current occupant, and her ample breasts bobbled and

45

threatened to escape as she struggled to free herself from the two constables who tried to restrain her.

The hem of the skirt was pinned high up over one leg, secured at the waist with a frightening chartreuse bow. It revealed a length of leg that could only be described as porcine, encased in a black stocking secured by a red garter that cut into the ample flesh of her thigh like the band about a length of summer sausage.

Her hair was several different shades of brown and trailed down her back in a disheveled tangle. It was difficult to tell the color of her eyes for the vivid make-up she wore that gave her a rather owlish appearance.

Her cheeks were smudged with bright crimson spots and her mouth was a wide slash above a set of double chins. Her skin was pale and mottled, slipping in crepy folds about her neck. Jess felt a stab of pity for her as she sketched every detail. It quickly disappeared.

"You touch me agin and I'll kick yer bloody arse!" the woman screamed. "I ain't done nothin' wrong!"

"The charge is stealin', Maude," the sergeant informed her, from the safety of his chair behind the counter.

"One of yer customers made a formal charge — said yer pinched 'is wallet las' night."

Maude lunged at the counter and tried to claw her way over the top. She looked surprisingly strong.

Two uniformed constables were immediately on her, ducking and lunging to avoid her nails and teeth.

"It's a bloody lie! Wot reason would I 'ave to pinch the blighter's wallet? He gave me that money 'cause I showed 'im such a good time." She lashed out with her feet, then collapsed, resembling a crumpled hothouse flower.

"Yer got no right to keep me 'ere!" she wailed pathetically. "It ain't me fault 'e couldn't get it up! I don't give refunds!"

"Sit down!" the sergeant shouted at her, and then warned, "One more word, and I'll have yer locked up!"

She was shoved into a chair, but was undaunted. "I got business appointments ter keep with important clients. I can't stay."

46

"It's one o'clock in the afternoon, Maude. None of yer *clients* is out and about this time o' day," the sergeant pointed out, apparently with some knowledge on the matter.

"I got one waitin' fer me!" Maude informed him. "A good payin' one, too, all set to do me when these blighters busted in. If he's gone when I get back—" she threatened, only to be cut off.

"Get outta' that chair one more time, an' I'll have yer put in chains!"

Maude glared back at him, but remained sitting in the chair. "I wanna see Burke!" she demanded.

Jess listened with growing interest. It was the third time she'd heard that name mentioned. Whoever he was, Inspector Burke seemed to know a great many people.

A telephone—a fairly new invention that was gaining popularity in London because of the ability to speak with someone across the city by simply speaking through the instrument—sat atop the desk within the sergeant's reach. It was also within Maude's reach as she suddenly squirmed free, flung herself over the edge of the counter, and grabbed it.

Unfamiliar with the workings of the instrument, she began shouting into the earpiece, screaming the inspector's name over and over, while the sergeant tried to grab it away from her.

Maude twisted out of his grasp, lost her precarious perch on the counter, and tumbled over backward taking the telephone with her.

Several uniformed constables converged on her at once. Gilly, the man Jess had encountered as she came in, leaned forward in his chair and cheered her on.

"Sweeney! What the devil is goin' on out here?"

The door to the private office Mickey had gone into opened so abruptly that the opaque glass windowpanes rattled. A triumphant smile curved Maude's red mouth.

"Burke!" she shouted happily from where she lay on the floor. "Come to me rescue, luv. Look wot this lout done ter me!" she made a face at the sergeant, who had lunged across the counter in an attempt to retrieve the telephone, and found himself sprawled across Maude on the floor.

"Laid me low, 'e did. I coulda broke me neck. As it is, I got a 'orrible pain in me arse. I may never work again!"

"For God's sake, Sweeney!" he remarked as he crossed the station. "Get off the floor, man!"

Sergeant Sweeney tried to untangle himself only to become more hopelessly snarled in Maude's skirts and hamlike legs.

"Beg pardon, sir," he muttered, attempting to leverage himself away from Maude's gaping bosom. She smiled up at him, obviously enjoying the situation and her triumph in gaining an audience with Inspector Burke.

Maude winked at Sweeney. "I don't give nothin' away fer free, luv. If'n yer plannin' on stayin' there yer gonna 'ave ter pay up jus' like all me customers."

He tried to free himself once more, but found himself firmly planted between Maude's legs.

Several uniformed constables tried to offer assistance, smothering back wide grins. There were several loud coughs and one or two choking sounds from other inspectors who had come into the station to see what all the commotion was about.

Inspector Burke stepped into the melee to help extricate the sergeant. Maude laughed and rolled her eyes with great enthusiasm. When Sweeney was on his feet, she held out her hand to Inspector Burke.

"Give us a 'and, luv," she said with a flirtatious smile. "Ya wouldn't leave a lady lyin' on her back, now would ya?"

The inspector shook his head. "In your case, m'dear, we might all be safer for it." He took hold of her hand and pulled her to her feet. She leaned into him and pressed her gaping bosom against his arm.

"It's over now," he informed the crowd of assorted onlookers that had gathered. "Get on with yer business."

He spoke with a hint of an Irish accent, which Jess recognized immediately. It was barely perceptible, but the soft rolling cadence betrayed him. It intrigued her.

"What is it you've done now?" he asked Maude as he slipped her arm through his. He escorted her across the station to a

48

desk in the corner as if she were a grand lady setting out with a beau to the ball. He pulled out a chair for her and then sat down. Their heads bent in conversation. He nodded occasionally, his mouth pulled into a frown—a very appealing and intriguing frown, Jess thought.

His face was dark and strong, the chin square cut, the nose was aquiline except for a slight bump as if it might have once been broken. His chin was square cut, adding to the impression of strength, or . . . stubbornness.

His mouth was wide with a faint crease at one corner as he sat, chin resting against long, straight fingers, a thoughtful expression creating an identical crease between straight dark brows.

It was a powerful, handsome face, but not a forgiving one. There was humor, but she sensed it had been honed by a sharp, perhaps even biting, wit, instead of easy laughter.

With an artist's scrutiny, she caught subtle nuances—the contrasts of character in the lift of one black brow as he listened intently, the unexpected quirk at the corner of his mouth as his lips curved into a smile revealing a startling sensuality.

His gaze was downcast as he listened to Maude, crescents of thick black lashes curved against dark skin that conjured up visions of a Gypsy ancestor. It was impossible to see the color of his eyes. They would be dark, Jess decided, like the rest of him.

His hair was thick and framed his head in impatient black waves as if he were in the habit of driving his hand back through it. There was an intensity in every movement that suggested restlessness, as if this part of his work was tedious for him. He rose abruptly and patted Maude's shoulder reassuringly.

"If the man has brought a formal complaint, it will have to be investigated," he explained to Maude. "But there's no need for you to remain here if I have yer word that you won't leave until the matter is settled."

"Where would I go, luv?"

Burke wasn't charmed by that seductive smile. "Any one of a dozen different places if you thought you could get away with it."

"I won't let the bloody bastards send me to Newgate!" she threatened. All sensuality was gone, replaced by a wariness that emphasized the lines in her face.

"It won't come to that," he assured her. "You'll have to trust me on this."

Maude's face pulled into a frown. "Yer give me yer word they won't send me over? I couldn't survive in that place."

"It will be all right, Maude." And then he added, "As long as you continue to help me. But you'll have to be a good girl. If this happens again, I won't be able to help you."

"All right," she muttered. Then she angled a look up at him and a slow smile spread across her face.

"Yer a right decent man, Burke. Not like them other bastards." She gestured toward Sweeney. Then she snaked out a hand and stroked the front of his coat.

"I could be real grateful fer all yer've done fer me, Burke."

Jess suddenly stopped sketching. A faint smile quirked at the corner of the inspector's mouth.

"Didn't you mention a gentleman friend was waiting for you?" he reminded Maude.

Maude sighed and slowly stood up to leave when it was obvious he wasn't going to accept her offer. "It's only Archie, an' 'e'll keep. Fancies 'imself in love with me, 'e does. Proposed marriage the last time 'e was in town."

"Perhaps you should accept his offer," Inspector Burke suggested.

"Thought about it, I did. But then I got to thinkin', if I got meself married, me 'usband might want me ter quit me work."

"That is a possibility."

Maude snorted. "Couldn't live with that. Can't see meself livin' in Blackpool or Soho, raising up a passel of brats. Besides," she winked at him, "wouldn't get to see the likes of you no more." She went on with a sweeping gesture that encompassed the police station. "I couldn't bear to give up all this." She turned to leave.

"Take care of yourself, Maude."

She blew him a kiss. "Yer jus' come 'round whenever yer feel like it, luv. I always got time fer yer."

Jess watched as Maude sauntered out of the police station. She stopped briefly in front of the counter and gave Sweeney a big, broad smile.

"See yer around, Sweeney."

When Jess looked back around, Inspector Burke had returned to his office. The door was closed only a few minutes before Mickey burst out of it. He grinned from ear to ear, and clutched a shiny coin in his fist. He scampered past Jess, the money undoubtedly already spent several times over. Whatever he'd told Inspector Burke, he'd been handsomely rewarded.

The sergeant had resumed his position behind the high counter. More than ever, he resembled a stubby bulldog.

Jess closed the sketchpad and put it away. It was late, and she had no idea when Mr. Ludlow would return, if at all. She had no alternative plan. She had to see someone today about finding her sister.

Sweeney was bent over his paperwork as relative calm returned to the station. She was certain the response she would receive if she spoke with him again. She glanced at the closed office and quickly made her decision. Little Mickey had made it seem so simple.

She hesitated only a moment, then when Sweeney turned away she slipped past the front counter to the wood gate where the young constable, Mr. Endicott, sat at his post.

He looked up and smiled. "Wot can I 'elp yer with?"

"I need to see Inspector Burke," she told him firmly as if she had every right to make that request.

"Wot about?"

Jess took a deep breath and repeated exactly what Mickey had said, keeping her voice low. "It's about the case he's been working on." Of course, she had no idea what that might be. "I have some information." Then she added, "Sergeant Sweeney said it was all right."

The constable looked past her to the front desk as if looking for confirmation. Sweeney didn't look up. He was concentrating on the papers before him. The young constable looked back at

Jess, and she gave him what she hoped was a dazzling smile. For one heart-stopping moment she was certain that he was going to call out to Sweeney.

Then he finally said, "All right, then," and opened the gate for her. Without a backward glance, Jess swept through the gate. Any second she expected Sweeney to call out. But there was nothing. She didn't knock at the door, but opened it and quickly stepped inside.

The office was small and overcrowded with a spartan desk, file cabinet, and two chairs. Inspector Burke sat in one of those chairs behind the desk, his head bent forward.

He didn't look up, but continued writing notes in the file that was open in front of him. She was certain he hadn't heard her come in. She was wrong.

"Has Hobbs gotten back yet?" the inspector asked, obviously thinking that she was someone else. "I want to know what he found over on Hanbury Street. And for God's sake don't let Devoe get word of this. The man's incompetent. Probably needs assistance to relieve himself." All this, of course, was said without looking up.

She shifted uneasily from one foot to the other, wishing at that moment that a hole might open up in the floor.

Her sister would know precisely the right thing to say at a difficult moment like this. But Jess had never possessed Linnie's skills for the articulate.

She should have thought of something bright or witty. Better yet, she should have made her presence known the moment she walked in, as any proper, poised lady would have done.

But she'd gotten little sleep the night before and had nothing to eat that morning. Her nerves were raw with worry for her sister, not to mention the frustration of wasting precious time cooling her heels outside for almost two hours. She wasn't at her best, and her usual bluntness got the better of her.

"That must be rather awkward. My sympathies to Mr. Devoe."

Chapter Four

The scratching of pen on paper stopped abruptly. Inspector Burke slowly looked up.

The hole that Jess' had wished for only moments before couldn't be big enough, she decided.

Then she made a discovery—Inspector Burke's eyes were blue—a deep, piercing, completely disconcerting . . . and disapproving blue. They should have been black or in the very least dark brown. But they were an incongruous, striking color that had the effect of completely unnerving her.

"Mr. Devoe will be grateful for your sympathy," he commented without changing expression. He didn't lay down the pen, but held it poised over the paper, a reminder that she had interrupted him and was in the very least unwelcome.

Under normal circumstances she would have been polite, matter-of-fact, and gone directly to the point, as she had with Mr. Holmes. But these were anything but normal circumstances. At any moment she expected Sergeant Sweeney or Constable Endicott to come through that door and remove her.

She was in a strange part of London where she knew absolutely no one, except of course, for Mr. Spivey, who could not be considered any sort of acquaintance. Even if he could be, she had no idea where to find him. She knew of absolutely no other place to go.

She also knew absolutely nothing about Inspector Burke, but from what she'd overheard outside his office, he seemed to be a man of some responsibility and competence. She didn't have time to wait for Mr. Ludlow, and if today passed without some result she would either be forced to stay here and start over in the morning, or return home, which she would not do.

Having had that hasty discussion with herself, she replied, "I'm trying to find my sister. She came here several weeks ago."

Actually, she had no idea how long Linnie might have been in Whitechapel, or if she was still there. All she had was the letter, postmarked four days earlier. She rushed on before he had the opportunity to summon someone.

"There's been no word from her." Another lie in the growing list. The web expanded and became more complicated, as she carefully worked her way through what she could tell him, and what she dare not say in order to protect Linnie.

"She should have written. It's not like her to go off without sending word." Jess dared not tell him about the letter or its contents. It would raise questions she was not prepared to answer.

"I have to find her. I'm very worried. I'm afraid something may have happened."

"She's a very responsible person, always looking out for everyone else. Please, Inspector. You must help me." She clasped her hands together and buried them in her lap.

He sat back in his chair, fingers curled around the pen. "We have a man who usually handles situations with missing persons," he explained.

"Yes, yes, I know. Mr. Ludlow. But he's not here, and I don't know when he shall return. It's imperative that I see someone today." She met that disconcerting blue gaze and was reminded of something she'd discovered earlier—his weren't easy eyes. They were contemplative, scrutinizing, and revealed absolutely nothing about the character of the man.

She could usually discern a great deal about people simply by watching them. He was a contradiction. She caught several glimpses of different expressions that played across those strong features, but none remained long enough to put a label to what he was thinking.

Mr. Spivey was simple to understand, as were Maude, Gilly, and even Sergeant Sweeney. But Inspector Burke was an enigma.

He gave away absolutely nothing about himself either by word or gesture. It was unsettling.

Then he shifted in his chair as if he were suddenly restless, possibly a signal that their conversation was at an end. She fully expected him to call out for Endicott to remove her to the outside office, there to wait for Mr. Ludlow's return.

She'd already woven enough lies for a spider of legendary proportions. She quickly decided to add still another.

"I was told that I should ask for you, that you would be able to help me."

One straight, dark brow arched. "Who told you that?"

Jess swallowed uneasily. What name could she possibly give him that he couldn't check, and discover the lie?

Maude, whose conversation with the inspector, she'd heard in the reception area?

Somehow she thought not. Maude was shrewd. She'd convinced Burke to let go with a promise of good behavior. She was also a survivor. Jess had seen the statistics on the women who lived in the East End.

Their life expectancy was painstakingly short due to poverty and disease. Somehow Maude had managed to live to a substantially mature age. Jess suspected she looked out only for herself.

What about little Mickey?

He was a born entrepreneur, who bartered information for money. She had no doubt he'd expose her for the liar she was for far less than he'd received earlier for the information he'd brought the inspector.

And then there was Gilly, whom she'd quite literally bumped into when she came in.

He had obviously been quite intoxicated, and she remembered that on the few occasions that her father had taken a few too many brandies, he had absolutely no recollection of it afterward. It was a dismal possibility at best, but the only one with any real potential.

"Gilly said I should speak with you. He said you could help me find my sister."

55

"Gilly?"

"Yes, that's right. Please, you must help me. I don't know anyone else in Whitechapel." That much was true enough. She waited, hoping desperately that the drawn-out silence indicated that he was considering her request.

Had she noticed skepticism in his tone? Perhaps he realized that she was lying? She felt as if there were a sign hung around her neck with the word *liar* spelled out in large letters. She wasn't any good at this, but for Linnie she'd lie to the Archbishop of Canterbury himself.

"He is a liar, a cheat, and a thief," he remarked thoughtfully, leaving far more unsaid—that he perhaps considered her to be the same. Once again she noticed the soft roll of words, the hint of Ireland that slipped around the hard edges of the direct question, and she wondered about Inspector Burke.

This was the nineteenth century after all, and the empire prided itself in being very progressive. Still, there were issues that plagued society—the homeless, the deplorable conditions in the workhouses where small children were forced to work, illiteracy, lack of any rights for women, and the age-old appalling treatment of the empire's own subjects from Scotland and Ireland like bastard children that it wished to ignore but couldn't.

It was practically impossible for a Scot or Irishman to rise above the most menial of positions without the benefit of sponsor or connection. Inspector Burke made no attempt to disguise that he was at least part Irish. The hint of accent that remained came from the passage of time. It was a long time since he'd left his native Ireland. And in that time he had acquired the elevated rank of inspector. Although her stepmother Vivian would have pointed out that he was still a policeman, with the predictable shudder of revulsion she reserved for someone she considered to be of a lesser station in life.

Inspector Burke went on to say, "Gilly would sell his dear sainted mother for a pint of ale and never think twice about it or feel even the least bit regret except that he'd try to find a way to do it again in the future. And you say that yer a friend of his?"

"We met just after I arrived in London."

"I see. And where is it that yer from, Miss . . . ?"

"My name is Jess Kelly." She told him precisely the same thing that she'd told Sergeant Sweeney.

"I'm from . . . Brighton." Then she hastily added, "My sister is also from Brighton."

Also from Brighton. How very precisely she spoke, Burke thought. He made a few notations and looked up, a slightly bemused expression.

"Of course. And what is your sister's name?"

"Then you will help me find her?"

"How could I possibly refuse someone who's a friend of Gilly's?"

She slowly let out the breath she'd been holding. Her hands relaxed. She wondered if it was considered another lie every time it was repeated or if it counted as just one lie. It was a dilemma for someone who'd always been so bluntly honest.

"My sister's name is . . . Mary Kelly."

"When was the last time you heard from her?"

"Almost a month ago, when she left home."

"What does she look like?"

"She's tall, and she has blond hair and dark eyes. She's very pretty." He looked up at her then with that speculative expression that she'd noticed before. It had that same unsettling effect on her, as if he were looking for more than she was willing to tell.

"We don't look very much alike," she hastily added. "Mary favors our father's side of the family. I favor our mother's."

He frowned again. "What about your parents? They allowed you to come to London alone?"

Another part of the web. She said simply, "There is no one else."

"What sort of . . . work does your sister do?"

She sensed a hesitation in the question. There was even more when it came to an answer. She had no idea what to tell him, even if it was a lie. Linnie had never worked a day in her life. They were raised with servants, and Linnie's marriage had

57

placed her in a position where the word didn't even exist.

She looked at him uncertainly. She had to be very careful. She needed a plausible answer. She thought of what she knew of Whitechapel—the poverty, disease, the horrible conditions in the workhouses. She remembered what she'd seen that morning—the taverns and dance halls, shops with rotting produce, the fetid smell of butchered animals; Mr. Spivey, Maude, Gilly, and Mickey. And she knew the reason he'd looked at her the way he had.

No one chose to come here if there was any other place they might go. The working conditions were deplorable, the living conditions much worse. Yet Linnie had come here and disguised herself as Mary Kelly. Why? What was she afraid of?

Inspector Burke was waiting for an answer.

"We heard there was work in the factories. She was going to find a position first, and then send for me."

"The factories?"

"Yes, that's right."

Burke glanced down at her hands clasped in her lap, and noticed the skin drawn white across taut knuckles. Her fingers were slender, finely tapered, and made him wonder about the work she sought.

Her clothes were plain and serviceable, mended in a few places, the shoes too large. Her features were fine-boned, almost elegant. Her brows were sleek, dark wings over expressive eyes the color of soft jade. Her mouth was full above a strong chin, and her wide jaw reminded him of something that had once been said about him.

"Yer too stubborn fer yer own good, lad. Stubborn pride will bring yer not but grief, a sore head, and more bruises than yer know wot to do with."

Jess Kelly was proud, he thought. And stubborn. Whatever the circumstances of her life had been, it hadn't robbed her of that.

Her clothes weren't uncommon for a young woman of modest means. Yet, they were uncommonly clean, right down to the oversized button-top boots. And her hair was clean. It gleamed, a healthy, dark rich color beneath the ridiculous hat she wore.

She had mentioned Gilly. He frowned. The only women Gilly knew, or cared to know were the whores who frequented the taverns and earned a bed for the night by spending an hour on their backs.

Burke knew most of them, or at least recognized them— women like Maude who arrived with or without husbands, usually with a half dozen children to feed, from the same number of fathers whose names were forgotten as quickly as their faces.

How did a woman on her own, with children to feed, earn a living? In one of the many factories, as this young woman wanted, or needed him to believe? In one of the countless sweatshops, or worse yet in a doss house like Maude?

If disease didn't kill these women, then poverty did. And they left behind children, like Mickey, to carry on their wretched legacy.

All those women had the same look about them—the weariness, the false-bright hope that was quickly smothered beneath the oppressive weight of too much drink, too little coin, the unchanging despair. And then there was the physical side of it—the sallow skin robbed of health and vitality that clung too tightly to bones without muscle to support it; eyes that should have known some light of meager joy but were filled instead with a sort of glazed acceptance; the brittle smiles that hid the edge of desperation.

Jess Kelly wasn't like those women. She was different.

Perhaps it was the way she folded those elegant hands in her lap, or the way she straightened her slender back, or carefully averted her gaze, allowing only the briefest eye contact before she looked discreetly away. Or perhaps it was the slight, almost imperceptible hesitation of careful answers to his questions.

She was lying. He was certain of it, and she wasn't very comfortable with it. Perhaps that was the reason he'd begun to write down the bits and pieces of information she relinquished almost grudgingly. He wanted to know more.

"Is there anything else you can tell me about your sister? Something that might perhaps help us locate her."

Jess hesitated and then decided there wasn't any reason not to tell him the name in the letter. It might be helpful. "She mentioned a young woman by the name of Annie Chapman."

Burke wrote the name down. It meant nothing to him, but it was better than nothing at all.

"Do you have a likeness of your sister? A photograph perhaps that might help us?"

"No." Jess's heart sank. She should have thought to bring a photograph, but that, too, might have created problems. All the photographs of Linnie would have shown her in elegant, fashionable gowns, far too expensive for a young woman of modest means to own.

She looked up then, a hopeful expression on her face. "I could draw a picture of her."

Burke looked up from the notations he'd been making, with the intention of turning them over to Ludlow when he came in.

"You fancy yerself an artist, Miss Kelly?" he asked, with some bemusement.

"I like to draw," she said simply, offering nothing more.

His expression was thoughtful. What young woman of her situation had the time to draw?

"By all means, Miss Kelly."

He expected a simple, unskilled effort at best that would be of little benefit to him, and watched as she opened the shabby valise at her feet and pulled out a tablet of paper and a charcoal pencil. She folded back several pages and he couldn't help but notice that she'd drawn other pictures, although it was difficult to discern her competence. She finally turned to a blank page and began to draw.

The pencil made faint, scratching noises across the paper. She hesitated, momentarily distracted by a knock at the door, and then quickly went on as if she were intent on finishing as rapidly as possible.

He'd been expecting young Endicott with some word of

Hobbs. It was Hobbs himself who poked his ruddy face around the edge of the door. Burke motioned him into the office and indicated for him to close the door behind him to prevent anyone outside the office overhearing their conversation.

"Beg pardon, sir." Hobbs ducked his head in apology as he saw Jess seated before the desk.

"I jes' got back, sir. An' I foun' somethin' I thought you should know 'bout straight away." He hesitated and glanced uncertainly at the young woman.

"It's all right," Burke assured him, unconcerned about her overhearing a conversation that couldn't possibly have any meaning for her.

He came around the desk and sat on the edge very near Miss Kelly, where he might also get a look at the picture she was drawing.

"What did you find?"

"Took a couple of men, jus' like you told me, an' we went back to 'anbury Street to have a more careful look inside th' flat. Without Mr. Devoe," he added in a quick aside.

Jess looked up. Evidently Mr. Devoe was not well thought of.

"Well?" Burke asked.

"We moved th' furniture about, jus' like you suggested, sir, and one o' th' men found this." He pulled a piece of folded paper from the breast pocket of his coat.

"What is it?"

"It's a letter wot fell behind th' bed," Hobbs went on to explain. "Must o' happened durin' a struggle o' some kind."

"What does it say?"

Hobbs's expression was a mixture of reluctance and grim satisfaction at having found something of importance that had previously gone undiscovered.

"We know who the young woman was wot got murdered. Her name was Mary Kelly."

Chapter Five

With a strangled gasp, Jess stared at the uniformed constable. Her face was ashen. The tablet of paper slipped from her numbed fingers and fell to the floor with a dull thud. She tried to draw a deep breath but couldn't breathe past the tightness in her throat.

"No," she whispered in disbelief. But even though her lips formed the word, no sound came out. Then she was on her feet, and screaming it, desperate to hear it and believe it, denial hard and painful in her chest.

"No! She's not dead! I won't believe it. It's not true. I would know if something had happened to her. I would know it!" she insisted.

She was pale and trembling. The soft jade of her eyes had gone to a stark black color as the irises expanded, thinning the green to thin bands that all but disappeared. Burke was certain she was going to faint, but she didn't.

For the first time he noticed how small she was, rigid with angry denial as she stood with slender fists clenched at her sides. She would hardly reach to his shoulder, yet she stood there as if she'd take on the world, or in the very least, anyone who tried to make her believe that it was her sister they'd found murdered.

He saw the hard glitter of tears, but she fought them back as well as the hysteria that edged her voice. She clung to the fragile thread of control with a fierceness he'd seen only a few times in his life. He knew almost nothing about her, but he admired her strength.

"My sister is not dead," she said vehemently. "Do you understand? She is not dead!"

Hobbs had been stunned at her reaction. Now, he looked at Burke in bewilderment.

"Sister?"

The sketchpad was momentarily forgotten. Burke gently but firmly pushed her back into the chair, before the fierce energy abandoned her and she collapsed completely.

"I'll explain," Burke said in a quiet voice as he motioned Hobbs aside. When he'd finished with what little he knew, Hobbs whistled softly through his teeth.

"Wot yer gonna do now, sir?"

Burke took the letter that Hobbs and his men had found during their second search of the flat at Hanbury Street. His expression was tight.

"She'll have to identify the body before we can be certain."

Hobbs looked past him to the woman. "Not the usual sort we see. She's a pretty little thing." Then he added, "Doesn't look much like her sister."

"No, she doesn't. I'll put the letter with the other items found during our initial search." He turned with Hobbs toward the door. "Say nothing of this to anyone until we know for certain who the dead woman is. Especially not Devoe."

"Right yer are, sir. Chief Inspector Abberline said we was to follow yer orders. Mr. Devoe would likely have a fit and fall in the middle o' it if he knew we found more evidence that he missed when he searched th' flat 'imself."

"That he would. I'll take care of the necessary report to the chief inspector."

Hobbs hesitated at the door. "What about the young woman? I feel badly fer frightenin' 'er like that."

Hobbs was a big brute of a man, far more intimidating than any weapon he could have carried. Burke had seen him subdue three men at the same time with little effort, yet he was completely undone by a slip of a girl.

"You had no way of knowin', man," he offered consolingly, then added, "She has far worse ahead of her."

"Aye," Hobbs nodded grimly, remembering the grisly scene they'd encountered when the body had been found. Burke closed the door and then turned around.

Routines. His work was filled with them. The routines of petty thefts, questioning witnesses or possible suspects, the countless files, reports, and seemingly endless paperwork that cluttered and slowed down the critical elements of an investigation. It was all routine, and he loathed it.

There were times when the emotions that went along with it became routine as well. A victim's anger, bitterness, even fear. He encountered so much of it on the streets, had lived with it his entire life, that he seemed to absorb it until a numbness set in that made him more or less immune to any feelings.

Once in a while, though, something or someone got to him. They got beyond the numbness and slipped inside to a place where a shred of the person he once was or might have been, existed. He supposed that was where hope survived, although it had been so long since he felt it that he doubted it existed.

Still there were moments when the cynicism and the cool, calculating logic was set aside and he existed on pure emotion.

It existed for Mickey, and the others like him, because he had once been like Mickey. It gave him an understanding and an empathy that could only come from shared pain. But his feelings for Jess Kelly, and the pain he knew she experienced, were unexpected, like something lost a long time ago and thought lost forever.

There was something about her, small and fragile as she was and clinging to that chair, that went deep inside him. It was the pride and stubbornness that he sensed earlier. It gave her the strength that she needed now.

Without realizing that he'd touched her, he looked down and found his hand resting on her shoulder. The need to comfort and protect her surprised him.

"We'll need to know for certain," he said quietly, wondering if she understood at all, or if the strength even remained.

She nodded. Her eyes were wide and stark, yet hauntingly beautiful. She was deathly pale and held herself stiffly erect in the chair, as if she would collapse if she allowed herself to relax for a moment.

He stooped down and picked up the tablet that had fallen to the floor. The picture of her sister was only partially finished. It was impossible to discern any of the features. He fanned through the other pictures, allowing her a few more minutes to compose herself.

He was stunned. She had told him that she liked to draw, as if it were a hobby or simple pastime. It was more than that. She was gifted, truly talented, with an ability that was almost frightening in its intensity and perfection for detail.

Maude, Mickey, Sergeant Sweeney. He recognized them all. But she'd done more than merely draw pictures of them. She had somehow managed to capture the inner person as well — Maude's shrewdness tinged with an air of sadness, Mickey's impish excitement matched by an almost feral survival instinct that made him seem less a child, and Sergeant Sweeney represented by the comic caricature of a bulldog in a constable's uniform.

His gaze came back to her. Where had she acquired such skill? Had she been born with it? Or had it been finely honed somehow? The likenesses were absolutely perfect, including the one of himself.

It was the same face he saw every morning in the oval mirror above the washbowl when he shaved. He recognized every hardened line and angle. But he saw something more that he wasn't prepared to acknowledge, and quickly flipped past that particular page until he returned to the one she'd begun of her sister. He frowned slightly at a sudden thought.

"If you were to finish this picture, it wouldn't be necessary for you to make an identification." He struggled with the need to somehow make this easier for her. She stunned him once more with the vehemence of her answer.

"No!"

Without touching her, he felt as well as saw the shiver that trembled through her, and hated himself for feeling anything at all that made him less than cynical and hard.

"No," she said again, much softer this time, almost a whisper. "Please understand. I have to see . . . I have to know for certain . . ."

He did touch her then, overpowered by the need to somehow lessen some of her uncertainty and anguish through the simple contact of taking her hand in his. She didn't pull back, she didn't respond at all, except that her gaze came up to his, pleading in its intensity.

Her eyes were completely dry, the dark irises all but disappeared,

65

exposing the soft green and the turmoil of emotions behind them.

"All right. I'll take you over." He thought of telling her what she might expect, and then realized that he had no idea how to prepare her for it.

If she were a man, one of his fellow inspectors, or even one of the other women of his usual acquaintance, he would find something to tell her, something within his experience and common to hers that would somehow make it less unpleasant.

He caught himself up, surprised that he thought of her as different from other women he knew, and completely at a loss as to why, except that she *was* different.

"If you need a few more minutes . . ."

"No," she said, with more determination than strength. "I don't want to wait any longer." It has to be now, she thought, before I lose my courage, before I run away wishing that none of this had ever happened. "I have to know."

"It's nearby. If you'd like a moment to prepare . . ." he suggested. She nodded, and he showed her to a small water closet at the back of the station.

Alone, she splashed water on her face and then mechanically tried to bring some order to her disheveled appearance. She caught a glimpse of her reflection in the mirror above the washbasin and touched her hair, an automatic gesture that seemed somehow ridiculous under the circumstances.

Still, she felt compelled because of all the ways she and Linnie had always been so different. Linnie was always so beautiful, so proper, her clothes and hair always perfect.

It seemed to Jess that she always floundered happily around in her sister's wake if never her shadow, with rumpled skirts and awkward crinolines, hair aflight, and hats askew.

She removed the sad little hat and smoothed her hair. Then she looked down at the shabby skirt and threadbare shirtwaist that she'd donned as a disguise, and almost laughed out loud. She'd always gone her own way and done precisely as she pleased, and how she pleased.

Dear God, she prayed. Please, don't let it be her! It can't be. I need to tell you something, Linnie, she wanted to scream out loud.

I need you to be the perfect one, she thought, even it if drives me crazy, then *I* don't have to be perfect. I need you to be beautiful and poised, so that it's not important whether *I* am or not. I need you to be confident and witty, so that *I* don't have to be. I need you, Linnie, she thought, if for no other reason than to be able to say it.

For several moments she wondered if she could simply stay there and never go outside, never have to face what waited. But it wasn't possible. She let herself out of the small room. Inspector Burke was waiting for her.

She thought she felt his hand, steadying and comforting under her elbow as they walked down the hallway at the back of the police station, but she wasn't certain.

Her legs were unsteady, and she was afraid they wouldn't support her, yet she remained upright and walked. It was a hollow, unreal feeling, as if every sensation, each emotion, even the sights and sounds about her, like a dream ceased to exist.

Through another door and down another short hallway. It was dimly lit, gas fixtures puddling pale light on brick walls. It wasn't cold, yet she shivered. It seemed they walked forever, yet it couldn't have been more than fifty feet. The entire time, he kept a firm hold on her, as if he understood.

At the end of the hallway he spoke briefly with a man dressed in a white cotton overcoat, and Jess was struck by the odd notion that he must be a physician.

Her numbed thoughts refused to think any further, or she would have perhaps understood.

"Miss Kelly?" And then a little louder. "Miss Kelly."

How many times had he repeated the name?

She had no idea and glanced up for some indication of what was expected of her. She felt the gentle pressure of Inspector Burke's warm fingers through the thin fabric of her sleeve.

"Are you certain you want to go through with this?"

His voice was inexplicably gentle, offering her escape if she chose it. She mentally clung to the warmth she heard there, needing both his voice and his touch in ways she couldn't possibly have explained. She nodded adamantly, incapable of anything more. The man in the white coat led the way through another doorway into a small room.

Her immediate impression was that everything was white, almost blindingly so. White chairs, white counters, white walls and ceiling. And a white table in the center of the room, draped with a white sheet.

There wasn't any way to spare her what she had to see. Burke knew that, and still felt the urgency to turn her away, to shield her eyes, to somehow take away the shock and horror that were second nature to him, so that she would never have to experience it. But she saw everything when the medical examiner pulled back the sheet.

She saw the pale lifeless torso, slashed with maddening precision, the pallid greenish tinge to the skin, the purplish black shadows at the eyes, mouth, and fingers.

It was necessary for her to see it all, so disfigured was the slashed face, that it was impossible to be certain of the woman's features. She stood there, silent, and impossibly cold, as if she were no more alive than the pitiful woman who lay on that table.

Jess forced herself past the numbness, forced herself to look and see, and somehow think.

She couldn't tell! She didn't know if it was Linnie! Then panic engulfed her, that she might never know. She looked down at the pale hand, with that purplish skin. With unsteady fingers, she gently lifted that lifeless hand, so cold and rigid.

She felt no horror or revulsion at touching someone who was dead. A greater need to know forced her past the horror. It might be Linnie, who'd always soothed and comforted her, who bandaged her childhood wounds and eased the deeper wounds when they lost their mother. How could she possibly be afraid to touch her?

She slowly turned that cold, lifeless hand over, and realized that as she did so she repeated a silent prayer.

Chapter Six

The fingers were stiff, cold, and lifeless. Jess looked for the familiar half-moon scar at the tip of the small finger arcing down from the fingernail, acquired when she accidentally slammed Linnie's finger in the door when they were children.

It wasn't there! She checked again to be certain that her eyes and her imagination weren't playing tricks on her. There was no scar. It wasn't Linnie!

She looked up at Inspector Burke. The words wouldn't come out. All she could do was shake her head.

The walls seemed to close in on her then. The rigid self-control that she'd clung to ebbed away. Everything about her was reduced down to a single gray pin dot before her eyes, and she felt as if her arms and legs suddenly weighed several hundred pounds. She was falling and was powerless to prevent it.

The last thing she remembered was that Inspector Burke's eyes should have been dark. They were *very, very* blue.

Burke saw the emphatic shake of her head. Then her hand came up, in a fluttering gesture as if she were trying to brush something away, or perhaps grab hold of something for support. There was nothing, and she slowly slumped against him as if she were a cloth doll.

He picked her up and carried her back to the police station next door. Chief Inspector Abberline's office was closest. He knocked and heard Abberline's acknowledgment. At his second more urgent knock Abberline opened the door himself.

"What is it?" the chief inspector demanded, his irritation at the interruption evaporating when he saw the young woman in Burke's arms.

"Good heavens! What happened?"

"My apologies, sir. There is no other place where I can take her." The other offices were small and uncomfortable. In addition to two wingback chairs, a small leather-covered settee sat against the opposite wall, a few of the comforts afforded the chief inspector.

Because of his position Abberline often met with members of the home office, Scotland Yard, and various members of society in their efforts to assist in the campaign against poverty and crime within his district.

It all took precious time away from the equally important task of solving crimes and apprehending criminals. He was a simple but educated man, who'd worked his way up from constable to chief inspector, and he wasn't at all certain that he liked it. He much preferred being in the thick of things as he was constantly telling Burke.

He'd been especially pleased when he had been given instructions from his immediate superiors to personally assist in solving the recent series of ghastly murders that had occurred in Whitechapel.

He requested that Devlin Burke also be assigned to the case. They were a great deal alike, although their backgrounds were very dissimilar. They both believed in the need for a system of law and order, although for equally dissimilar reasons, and both were smart enough to know that occasionally one had to step outside that system in order to solve the crimes that one encountered.

Abberline was several years older than Burke. He'd worked on several cases with him, and liked him very much. He was direct, uncompromising, occasionally ruthless. He knew the streets better than any man he'd ever encountered on either side of the law, and had a similar disdain for the interference of society nobs who thought they could make the world better, or in the very least improve conditions in the East End, with their charitable donations of food, clothes, and money.

Occasionally they discovered that the problem lay deeper than food, clothes, or a few coins in a man's pocket. That it had to do with a man's integrity, his ability to better his lot in life and make something of himself. When that happened, it was possible to make changes, however slowly they occurred.

Burke was an example of that, though there were few who knew it, or knew of his orphaned life on the streets of Dublin and the crimes he had committed in order to survive, and his struggle out of the poverty that could have easily killed him.

Burke hadn't volunteered that knowledge. It came out in bits and pieces over the years when he confronted and struggled with something out of his own past on the streets. Somehow he held onto his pride and his honor, and he was trustworthy.

There were times in the past when Abberline had to rely on that trust. Burke had never let him down.

There was a bond between them that went beyond their work, more that of brothers. At least as close as Burke would allow. It was necessary. Oftentimes a man in this profession couldn't be certain who he could trust. Abberline knew he could trust Burke. The converse was true as well, which did nothing to explain why at that moment Inspector Burke was standing in the doorway of his office holding a woman in his arms.

"What have you done now?" Abberline asked with a bemused expression as Burke swung through the doorway.

"She fainted."

"You do have a way with the women, lad," Abberline exclaimed as he stepped to the side of the doorway. "I thought perhaps ol' Maude might have given you a bit of trouble. I heard her screamin' even though the door was closed."

Abberline peered over his shoulder. "Who is this young lady?"

"Her name's Jess Kelly. She arrived in London this mornin', or so she says."

Abberline gave him a quizzical look. "You suspect otherwise?"

"I don't know what to believe. She said that she received a letter from her sister several days ago, mailed from Whitechapel. She came looking for her."

"What is the sister's name?"

"Mary Kelly." Burke also explained about the letter that Hobbs and his men had found in the flat over on Hanbury Street that morning, written by Mary Kelly.

"I thought there was a strong possibility the murdered woman might be her sister."

"You took her over to the morgue." Abberline's expression was grave. "Was it her sister?"

"No. But apparently her sister lived at the flat at one time. The letter that Hobbs found proves it."

"What about the murdered woman?"

"In her first letter, Mary Kelly mentioned that she was staying with a woman by the name of Annie Chapman."

"Then the murdered woman may be Annie Chapman," Abberline surmised.

"It would seem so. At least we have a name now, which is more than we had before. I'll ask around. Someone on the street may have known her."

Abberline was thoughtful. These recent murders—three of them now, all in the same manner—had proven especially difficult to solve.

"It would help if we had a likeness of the dead woman. Someone might recognize her and be able to give us information."

Burke's expression was grim. "Her face was badly cut. The physician stitched up her as best he could, but there's only so much he can do."

Abberline looked down at the young woman who lay still as death on the settee. "She's a strong one to see something like that. I've seen stout men pass dead away at the sight of what a knife can do."

Burke nodded. "She'll need something strong when she comes round. Perhaps some tea." He stood and started for the door.

"Stay, lad," Abberline told him. "It will only upset her further to see an unfamiliar face when she comes round."

"I'll have Endicott find some of that tea you keep for Maude."

When he had gone, Burke laid his fingers against her throat.

Her breathing was shallow as to be almost nonexistent. Her pulse was so faint he couldn't feel it at all.

He turned her over onto her side, and unfastened the buttons of the shirtwaist. Her skin was cool and soft as satin at the hollow of her spine, where his fingers brushed as he pushed back the two halves of the garment. He found the strings of the corset.

Damnable contraptions, he thought, frowning at the pale satin strings that laced down the length of her back to her waist, restricting her breathing. The satin ties had knotted, and he cursed them as well, struck by how incongruous the elegant, satin garment was with the shabby clothes she wore.

Probably a cast-off garment that she had acquired from an employer or from a charity box, he thought as he took a small knife from his pocket, and cut the laces. The closure immediately opened and almost at once he saw her slender back relax and expand as she took a full, deep breath.

A healthier color immediately spread across her skin, and she didn't seem quite so cold when he gently took her by the shoulders and turned her over, and then again when he felt for the pulse at her throat.

It was rapid and thready, but her natural pink coloring fully returned, driving away the shadows beneath her eyes, and the whiteness around her mouth. Her eyelids quivered like the frantic, uncertain beat of a butterfly's wings when it first emerges from the cocoon. Then her lashes fluttered upward, revealing the clear, bright jade of her eyes. There was an unexpected innocence there, bright in its intensity, and then that magnificent jade color darkened with confusion and the shadows of remembered things.

Her lips were softly parted as if she would ask a question when she remembered precisely what it was she wanted to ask. It made the innocence all the more poignant, and again Burke felt that unbearable need to protect her. From what she had seen and what she would remember in the next few minutes when memory returned completely.

He recalled that he had once thought she wasn't beautiful. He

73

was wrong. She was extraordinarily pretty, with those haunting green eyes that had a way of looking at him, as though she saw past all the barriers he kept carefully in place. It was a disconcerting realization for someone who'd always managed to keep all but one person at a distance.

But it was more than that. Her beauty lay in the emotions fully exposed on her delicate features. She would never be able to hide anything. In the short time since she'd walked into his office, he'd learned a great deal about her just from those emotions.

She was stubborn and proud, and cared deeply about her sister. There were things in this world that were unknown to her, but she confronted them with a strength he could only wonder at. There was absolutely no fear in her.

She had an incredible talent for looking through the most dismal, wretched aspects of life to the heart within. He saw that in her pictures.

Whatever the circumstances of her life, she'd never been a victim. He suspected that Jess Kelly would never be a victim. Beneath the secrets she carefully guarded for whatever the reasons, she had a rare strength and courage.

It was there in her eyes now as she looked back at him, the memory of what she'd seen in the morgue once more clear and sharp. He also saw the unasked questions.

"This is Chief Inspector Abberline's office. I brought you here after you fainted."

She had no clear memory of it. The last thing she remembered was . . . those incredible blue eyes of his.

She looked away, suddenly uncomfortable as if he could read her thoughts. He sat beside her at the edge of a settee in a large, comfortable office. Inspector Abberline, whoever he might be, was not present. The door was closed.

She still felt light-headed and pressed her fingers against her forehead, breathing in slowly and deeply until the world seemed to right itself again.

"How long have I been here?"

Again there was that curious, very proper way of saying things that he'd noticed earlier.

"Only a few minutes."

"And Inspector Abberline?"

"He thought you needed something to drink when you came round. You were very pale." He watched as she brushed back the tangle of glossy dark hair that had spilled over her forehead. It was an elegant gesture, and he frowned as it recalled an unwanted memory from the past.

"I'm feeling much better now." She struggled to sit up, but feeling the coolness across her bare back flattened herself against the back of the settee.

"What happened to my clothes?" she demanded.

The old memory from the distant past was gone, and he regarded her with a smile at the obvious irony of defending her virtue.

"Your clothes, such as they are, made it impossible for you to breathe properly." He held the small knife aloft. "I loosened them for you."

Whatever color she had regained, drained from her face, only to return in a shade of deep crimson. She was incredulous. "You cut my clothes?"

It was difficult to tell precisely what it was that bothered her—the damage to her corset strings or perhaps feminine modesty, which considering the common way she was dressed, appeared unlikely. By her clothes, she was no more than a common street girl, if somewhat talented artistically. He'd never known a street girl to bemoan a little loss of dignity, especially where a man was concerned.

"Is it the clothes yer worried about or that I might have seen yer backside? I assure you, you've nothing I've not seen already on a great number of previous occasions." He saw those eyes go from soft jade to deep emerald.

"It's not that," she snapped. "I just don't like to be . . . touched. It's not . . ." She caught herself just as she was about to say that it wasn't proper, or worse, that she'd never been touched by a man before. Not that she wasn't aware of what went on between a man and woman. Linnie had filled her in on those particular points. And, of course, in France where she went to school the word *modesty* didn't even exist.

"You were saying?"

"That it's not . . . *necessary!*" she blurted out, for lack of anything more appropriate at the moment. Admittedly, it sounded completely absurd.

"It seemed *necessary* at the time. You were turning blue."

She glared at him, not at all certain where the anger came from.

"I would have recovered sufficiently without you ruining my clothes."

"They're not ruined."

"They most certainly are," she informed him and reached behind her.

"These strings are worthless. I can't tie them. They're not long enough."

With her usual talent for bluntness she waved them as if they were ties on a package. The color of his eyes deepened, and she could have sworn they crinkled at the corners. She scooted back on the settee and struggled to lace the impossibly short corset ribbons.

"You don't need to wear a corset," he informed her with equal bluntness. "I could encircle your waist with my two hands."

Her head snapped up. The discussion of corset strings with a man, and a stranger at that, was almost more than she could tolerate.

"It is none of your concern whether or not I need to wear it. The point is, if I can't retie it, I'll be wearing it about my ankles."

"My point precisely. You don't need it."

She opened her mouth to tell him that what she did need was some privacy so that she could finish putting herself back together, but she decided that would only undoubtedly get her in more trouble.

76

"Here," he took her by the shoulders and turned her around as if she were a child.

"What do you think you're doing . . . ?"

"Be quiet, or you'll have the entire constabulary in here."

Jess snapped her mouth shut and silently endured while he quickly—and with suspicious efficiency—laced her corset. Before she could protest, he also fastened the row of buttons at the back of the shirtwaist.

"I'm sorry you had to go through that," he said as he finished. "I know how difficult it was for you to see that."

She realized he was talking about identifying the body of that poor woman. This gentle, caring side to him that bordered on tenderness, completely unnerved her. She didn't know how to respond. She preferred him angry, antagonistic, even silent.

She finally said with a small shiver, "I had to know for certain, if it was . . . *Mary.*" She wrapped her arms tightly about herself as if the cold had returned. "Thank God it wasn't," she whispered, closing her eyes as she tried to block out the images of that white room.

"I understand what it is to lose somethin' that you love fiercely," he said in a quiet voice as his hands rested on her shoulders. "I'll do what I can to find yer sister. Obviously, she *was* living with the woman we found."

"Then that woman must be Annie Chapman, the woman my sister mentioned in the letter I received."

He nodded. "It would seem that way. If you could finish the picture of your sister, perhaps someone will recognize it and may be able to tell us something about where she might have gone." He didn't add that he wanted very badly to find Mary Kelly, if she was still alive, to discover what she might have seen the night Annie Chapman died. There had been blood in the second room of that flat, raising the possibility that the murderer, who was fast gaining a notorious reputation, might have claimed more than one victim. But there had been only one body.

Did that then mean that he had gone after the second woman, whom they now believed to be Mary Kelly, and was

77

unsuccessful in his attempt to kill her?

Or had he succeeded and they had yet to find the body? It would be a distinct change in the pattern the murderer had already established in the previous three murders, and he thought it unlikely. Still, it was a possibility that couldn't be ignored, even though he chose not to mention it to Jess Kelly.

"Yes, of course I'll finish the picture," she eagerly assured him. "Then we can begin looking for Mary. The sooner the better."

Burke's gaze narrowed. "My men will find yer sister," he informed her bluntly.

She started to protest, "I want to help . . ."

"That's entirely out of the question."

"I came here to find my sister." Her voice rose as she got out of the chair. "She doesn't know anyone here. She's probably badly frightened by what happened."

"That is a possibility," he acknowledged grimly.

A thought occurred to her then that she hadn't yet considered. "If she was there when it happened, she may have seen something." The cold feeling returned to the pit of her stomach and became a knot of fear.

Burke nodded. There was no point in denying what she knew to be true. But perhaps he could convince her of the foolishness of her plan to stay by being brutally honest with her.

"It appears that the murders were not random occurrences. They've been very carefully thought out, planned, and executed." He chose his words carefully, between what he needed to tell her in order to make her understand the danger they were dealing with, and what he could not say because there was no proof of anything yet. They were still looking for needles in haystacks as far as clues and witnesses were concerned.

"The two other victims were prostitutes. Now that we know the third victim's name, we must find out if she was also a prostitute. Until now we've had only vague descriptions of at least a dozen possible suspects, but nothing that has been of any use to us.

"There is a possibility that your sister might be able to identify the murderer," he went on to say. "We'll do everything we can to

78

find her, but you must stay out of it. Three women have already died. It may not end there."

She knew precisely what he'd left unsaid and it confirmed her own fears. "You said that you understood what it was to lose something that you loved fiercely. Then you must understand that I can't leave until I find my sister."

He was caught by his own words. And the reality was that he couldn't force her to leave. She'd done nothing wrong, she wasn't a criminal. She was free to come and go. And he'd already discovered that she would do precisely as she pleased.

Once again he felt that inexplicable need to protect her, while at the same time experiencing a growing frustration.

At a sudden knock at the door, he snapped, "What is it?"

The door opened fractionally as if the person behind it were reluctant to enter the room. Endicott poked his head around the edge of the door and smiled hesitantly.

"Chief Abberline asked me to bring this fer the young lady." He opened the door a few inches more and held out a cup as if offering proof that the interruption was not his idea.

Greeted by uncomfortable silence, he looked from one to the other and swallowed uncertainly.

"I'll just leave it on the desk then, sir." He glanced at Burke.

"By all means do so and be done with it," Burke said irritably.

"Yes, sir." The tea was carefully deposited on top of the desk. Endicott gave Jess a brief look, then wisely left the office. When the door had closed behind him, Burke turned on her and took up his argument once more.

"This is no place for a young woman, especially a . . ." He stopped then, suddenly at a loss for what to say, or perhaps deciding against what he had intended to say.

"Yes, Inspector?"

The problem was, he didn't know precisely what it was he was about to say. He knew virtually nothing about her. Her clothes were quite ordinary and of poor quality. By her own words, she had no money, and no other family. Her sister had come here to find work. In this part of London, work for women was limited to the workhouses, factories, and prostitution. And yet . . . what? The problem was, he didn't know, and so he retreated to the safety of a different argument.

"You're not familiar with London, especially Whitechapel. It would be too easy . . . A young woman can easily find herself taken in with the wrong people, or worse yet, she might end up . . ."

"Murdered?" she calmly asked when he seemed to have trouble saying the word.

"Yes!"

"That is a risk I shall have to take," she said in a determined voice. Then her hand came up and she pressed her fingers against her forehead. Much more quietly, but with equal determination, she added, "I haven't the means to go elsewhere. So you see, I really have no other choice, even if I would consider it."

He paced across the office, trying to find some means to make her understand. He turned and paced back.

"You can't simply live off the streets. This isn't the country." He stood toe-to-toe, towering over her and yet shouting as if she were having some difficulty hearing him and he could somehow make her understand if he only spoke louder. They were both unaware that the door had opened. Chief Inspector Abberline stood in the doorway of the office.

"Perhaps a little louder would do the trick, Inspector," He suggested, making them both look around abruptly.

"Heard you shouting from the outer office. Is there some difficulty?"

"I was explainin' that it would be best if Miss Kelly returned home." His accent had thickened appreciably. "I assured her we'll do everything to find her sister."

"Of course," Abberline concurred, a thoughtful frown on his face. Burke visibly relaxed, taking that as at least tacit agreement.

Jess hadn't the strength to argue with him further. She hadn't eaten all day. That, on top of the earlier shock over her sister, and the dreadful experience of seeing that other poor woman, made her suddenly weak again.

Abberline's gaze narrowed. "Are you quite all right?"

"I'm just a bit light-headed."

"Confrontations with mules can to that to you," he agreed with a trace of a smile that he only vaguely attempted to hide as he gave Burke a brief look.

"Sit down then, Miss Kelly, and have some of this 'tea.' " He pushed the cup across the top of the desk toward her. For the first time, she noticed that he'd brought her valise and sketchpad with him.

She accepted the cup and took a sip. Her eyes widened, as she swallowed and discovered the tea wasn't tea at all, but exceedingly strong whiskey. It burned all the way down, causing her to gasp for air which immediately made her cough uncontrollably.

"That'll brace you up," Abberline remarked as he laid the sketchpad out on top of his desk. "Was anything of her sister's found at the flat on Hanbury Street?" This was directed at Burke.

He hesitated and then said, "There was no money, only a few rags and other garments."

"Then it seems, Miss Kelly, that you are without means."

When she was finally able to find her voice again, she repeated what she had already explained to Inspector Burke. "I was to join my sister here. We hoped to find work."

"I see. That does create a problem, and things being what they are here in Whitechapel . . ."

She assumed that he, too, was looking for reasons that she should leave, and she quickly added, "I have no home. There is no other place for me to go."

"Hmmmm," he replied again, opening the sketchpad on top of his desk. "I quite understand. In other words, you must remain here."

She nodded, grateful that at least he was capable of understanding.

"Endicott has informed me that these are your drawings."

Without waiting for her reply, he added, "They are quite remarkable. You've caught that young imp Mickey, and of course Maude. But by far my favorite is Sergeant Sweeney."

Lest he disapprove, she hastily explained, "I didn't mean for anyone to see that one." He surprised her then.

"Might I keep it?"

"Yes, of course."

He smiled. "I'm no art patron, but anyone can see that you have a remarkable talent, Miss Kelly." He turned to the sketch she'd made from the old man's description.

"Endicott informs me that you made this sketch from a description given by a man who was robbed."

"I wasn't eavesdropping . . ."

He held up his hand. "There's no harm done, Miss Kelly. In fact you've given me an idea." He sat back in his chair, chin propped on his steepled fingers, lost in thought. Finally he asked, "Is it possible for you to draw anyone from a description?"

"Yes, I suppose so," she answered hesitantly, not at all certain what it was he was getting at. "It depends on how observant a person is. I can only draw what they describe to me."

"I quite understand. What if several people described different aspects of a person? Say, perhaps mannerisms, characteristics, color of eyes, height, weight, style of dress, a way of walking?"

"It would be possible to make a composite sketch, although I have no idea what it might look like when it was finished."

Abberline was soft-spoken with pleasant, even features. He looked more like a banker or solicitor than an inspector of police. He gave her a contemplative look across the desk.

"That is the mystery. One, which I would like very much to solve. Wouldn't you agree, Inspector?"

Burke had paced across the office, and was standing with his back to them. She caught the movement from the corner of her eye, as he abruptly turned. He said nothing but stood, leaning against the far wall, arms crossed, disapproval obvious in his expression.

Abberline stood then and smiled evenly, unaware or unaffected by Burke's lack of response. He came around the desk and leaned back against it, one arm folded before him, the other hand propped against his chin, much like a lawyer presenting a case before the magistrate.

"You are in need of employment. We need to solve these dreadful murders. We have been unable to do so because we have yet to acquire an accurate description of the murderer."

"One witness gave us the color of eyes, another gave us a description of the way the man walked. Still another described the way he was dressed. We have dozens of witnesses who have given us dozens of descriptions, some of which match, others that don't, and more that simply confuse the issue."

"The information is in countless files, written down by a half-dozen inspectors and an equal number of constables. I have endless descriptions of the man who may be the murderer and absolutely no idea what he looks like. I believe, Miss Kelly, that you may be able to help us by using your artistic talent.

"Therefore, I am offering you employment. We don't usually employ citizens in our work. But occasionally we can arrange for special compensation to individuals who are in a position to assist us with information. I can't offer you a great deal of money, but it would be enough to live on. It would solve the immediate problem so that you won't be forced to live on the streets."

Burke pushed away from the wall, objection written in every line of his face.

"Sir, there have already been three murders. Is it wise to involve her in this?"

"She won't be directly involved. She can work here at the station from the information we have in the files. If necessary, we can bring in witnesses again and have her speak with them. Perhaps one of them has remembered something they neglected to tell us."

"But, sir . . ."

"I understand your concern, Mr. Burke. But this is *my* decision. I believe Miss Kelly may be of assistance to us." He gave Burke a long look as if waiting for him to make further comment. Inspector Burke snapped his mouth shut. Clearly, he understood that further objection or argument was unwanted and perhaps unwise.

"Good." Abberline circled back round his desk and returned to his chair. He smiled at Jess. "When can you begin?"

"I suppose I could begin now."

"When was the last time you had something to eat?"

"Last evening," she replied hesitantly, still a little dazed by the swiftness with which everything had been decided.

Abberline always thought everything through very carefully and thoroughly. But when he finally made a decision he acted upon it quickly.

"Tomorrow morning will be soon enough for you to begin," he announced. He reached into his vest pocket and pulled out several coins.

He gave them to her. "Consider this an advance against your wages." Then he looked up at Burke.

"I believe something to eat might be in order, and she'll need a place to stay. Endicott might know of a place," he suggested.

"Endicott lives with his sister and her family." Burke clearly was not pleased with the turn of events. "He wouldn't know a respectable boardinghouse from a doss house."

Abberline smiled at him. "I'm certain you'll come up with something. I'm making you responsible for Miss Kelly's well-being."

"Sir, . . ."

"That is an order, Mr. Burke."

Chapter Seven

The expression on his face went absolutely still.

Only moments before he'd been close to anger. Now his eyes were cool and unemotional. It was impossible to guess what he was thinking. She found that far more disconcerting than the anger.

With that same cool detachment he walked over to her valise and picked it up. Without a word he turned and strode out of the office.

"Are you tenacious, Miss Kelly?" the chief inspector asked with a slightly bemused expression.

She watched Burke as he threaded his way across the crowded station. Her gaze snapped back to the chief inspector.

"I've been accused of being very stubborn."

"Excellent. You'll need it. And a strong pair of legs."

It was a dismissal and a hint of what was to come. She hastily grabbed the sketchpad.

"Thank you, Mr. Abberline."

She discovered precisely what he meant by a strong pair of legs. It took three strides to equal one of Inspector Burke's. He was already out the door and halfway down the front steps to the street before she passed Sweeney's desk.

A rather large, foul-smelling woman stood in the middle of the station, like a soldier ready for combat. She was dressed in a discarded man's coat with all the buttons missing except one fastened over the rolling sea of her large bosom. A scarf was knotted under her equally ample chin. She wore stout boots, and waved a dead fish through the air at Constable Endicott like some medieval weapon.

The fish, along with several conspicuous stains of dubious origin smeared across the skirt, accounted for the stench.

Jess dodged around the unhappy fishmonger, nimbly wove her way through a cluster of smudge-faced children who all resembled little Mickey in their manner of dress and colorful language, and darted out the front entrance. She spotted Inspector Burke standing at the curb. With her hand clamped down on her wayward hat, she quickly ran down the steps and joined him.

Though nothing in his expression indicated it, she knew he disapproved of the orders he'd been given. It was in his stance, the solid wall of his back turned toward her, his refusal to even acknowledge her presence.

Her upbringing and background had prepared her for dealing with all manner of social encounters. Nothing, however, prepared her for Devlin Burke.

Without a word he held out the valise and let it fall with a thump to the sidewalk. Then he stepped off the curb and crossed the street without a backward glance. She stared after him.

"Of all the . . ." she muttered under her breath, anger battling with indignation. She seriously considered kicking the valise into the gutter. Then she gave even more serious consideration to kicking Inspector Burke in the shins. How dare he treat her as if she were no more than a . . . a common street girl!

Then it struck her, that was exactly what he thought she was—precisely what she had wanted him and everyone else to think. It was a little disconcerting to realize that she'd been so convincing in her disguise.

She grabbed the valise and plunged across the street, side-stepping a cart drawn by a sagging horse, several piles of horse manure, and a dead rat in the gutter. Several blocks later she finally caught up with him outside the Swansea public house.

He didn't bother to hold the door open for her. Instead he simply walked in, leaving her to struggle with the bulky valise, the door that snapped shut behind him, and a bewhiskered patron who reeked of sour ale and several other unidentifiable odors, and who leered at her with a drunken smile.

She was becoming rather skilled at dodging both immovable and movable objects, especially those that swayed on their feet. She found Inspector Burke, a tankard of ale on the table before him.

She was disheveled, her hair tangled about her shoulders, and the hat was hopelessly askew. Her arm ached from the weight of the valise, and she suspected there was a blister rubbed on her heel from the oversized boots as she clumped down the street after him.

Burke looked at her with thinly disguised amusement. She was quite a sight. Rumpled, her clothes too large, that ridiculous hat slipping sideways off her head, her hair in wild disarray, as if she might have been rolled under a carriage, yet with color staining her cheeks, and fury sparkling in those vivid eyes — rumpled and disturbingly beautiful.

"Sit down before you fall down," he suggested irritably. "Or before you choke to death on whatever it is yer tryin' to say."

She sat down in the opposite chair with unladylike exhaustion. The tavern keeper appeared at the table.

"Afternoon, Inspector. I see Lollie already fixed yer up with a bit o' ale."

"Hello, Tripp. Have you seen the Mudger about today?" Burke inquired.

"Not lately. The Mudger only comes in when 'e's got a bit of business ter conduct, or a hole in 'is gut wot needs filled." Then he added, "A bit late fer lunch, ain't it, Inspector?"

"Not for me. Bring another tankard of ale and one of Lollie's kidney pies for the girl."

"A wee mite she is," Tripp observed as he flicked crumbs from the table with a towel. "I'll bring two pies. Lollie has just that many left in back."

The way they were talking around her made Jess feel as if she were some sort of recalcitrant child waiting for punishment to be meted out over some misdeed. She glared at Burke.

87

"Mr. Burke . . ." They were interrupted once more as Mr. Tripp delivered the tankard of ale to the table and set it before her. She pushed it across the table.

Burke promptly pushed it back at her and said sharply, "Drink it."

She seized the tankard and took a swallow. The ale was dark and strong, with a frothy foam at the rim, and left a thick aftertaste that clogged her throat. When she finally quit coughing and looked up through watery eyes, she found Burke watching her with a bemused expression.

"Drink a lot, do you?" he asked. He reached across the table and wiped the foamy mustache from her upper lip. The hard scrape of his callused thumb against her lip was unsettling. She sat back in the chair, carefully wiping the rest of the froth from her mouth, wondering what it was in the ale that made her lip seem to burn.

Mr. Tripp returned with the meat pies then. She concentrated on the bowl before her. It was a combination of stewed vegetables and savory meat with thick gravy, served in a deep bowl and covered with a thick dough crust. Her stomach rumbled loudly at the enticing aroma. Mr. Tripp grinned broadly revealing a gaping row of crooked teeth.

"Hey, Lollie!" he shouted back over his shoulder. "Warm up th' other pie. She may be jus' a small bit but she's got a right topper appetite. It's growlin' fierce, an' Mr. Burke is payin'."

Jess was still trying to make him understand that one pie was more than enough when he cleared away the empty bowl and delivered the second pie.

She scooped at the edge of the flaky crust.

When she looked up again, Mr. Tripp was grinning broadly from ear to ear, shouting at Lollie to come out and have a look at the little miss with the big appetite, and the second bowl in front of her was empty.

The tankard was also empty and there was a warm, deliciously contented sensation seeping into her fingers and toes.

Burke tossed several coins down on the table, and rose

abruptly. He thanked the tavern keeper, and then without a word, left the tavern.

It took a few moments for her to realize through the contented haze of the ale and delicious food, that he'd left her once again. She grabbed the valise and sketchpad, thanked Mr. Tripp and Lollie for the delicious meal, and ran out of the tavern after him. He stood at the curb, beside a vacant hansom.

"Thank heaven," Jess muttered under her breath, grateful that she wasn't going to have to run across the whole of London after him.

"Twenty-four Abbington Road," Burke called out to the driver as he climbed inside without even a backward glance to see if she followed.

She quickly scrambled after him, certain he would have liked nothing better than to leave her behind. The narrow skirt hobbled her, and she would have gone down in the gutter had he not clamped strong fingers around her wrist and pulled her into the cab.

She fell against him, her hat tumbling into her lap, hair sweeping loosely over one eye.

"It's a wonder you survived the journey to London," he muttered, setting her as far away from him as the small quarters of the hansom would allow. The double doors snapped shut and the hansom lurched away from the curb.

It's a wonder someone hasn't punched you in the nose! she wanted to shout back at him as she shoved her heavy hair back into place and dragged the valise onto her lap.

He ignored her, staring silently out the opposite window. It was obvious that he didn't care to carry on a conversation with her. She settled back into the hansom, wedging her small shoulder behind his on the narrow seat. They swayed through late afternoon traffic in uncompanionable silence.

Streets and squares flickered past as they wove through the congestion of drays, carts, and more hansoms. Peddlers and vendors, a man selling fresh eels, meat pies, and plum duff, filled the sidewalks.

A boy darted out into traffic as it slowed and then stopped altogether. A thick wad of newspapers was jammed under his arm. He poked his head in one hansom after another, or waved a folded paper aloft to a tradesman who sat atop a wagon.

A cripple, with his legs gone below the knees, was strapped to a square piece of board mounted on four small wheels. His hands were thickly wrapped in layers of ragged cloth. He propelled himself with amazing speed, stroking along the cobbled sidewalks with those padded hands, weaving in and out with amazing agility that belied his handicap. A large cup of matches was clamped between the stumps of his knees as he rollered along, calling out to people on the street, "Matches fer sale."

At one corner a young girl sold beribboned bouquets of flowers. She was dressed in a plain skirt, scuffed boots, a ragged shirtwaist, and indiscriminate hat.

She called out, "Flowers fer the pretty ladies," reminding Jess of all the times she'd passed by others like her without a thought to where they lived or how they survived by peddling flowers. It emphasized the stark contrast between this part of London and the world she knew at Carrington Square. A short while later they pulled to a stop at 24 Abbington Road.

It was a modest brick house, tall and straight, in a row of other identical tall and straight buildings, except for the difference of display windows and professional signs hung over doorways, or from ironwork cross-arms that declared the crafts of milliner, bootmaker, or apothecary.

Twenty-four Abbington Road was on the fringe of Whitechapel, in a working-class neighborhood where rooms were let for rent. Burke let himself in the front door. Jess wedged through the narrow opening, valise and sketchpad tucked under her arm, just before the door snapped shut.

There were footsteps at the back of the house. A woman, several years older than Jess, with rich, auburn hair, and dark luminous eyes, came toward them down the hallway.

She was attractive with a mature beauty of soft, rounded features, elegant hands, and a smile that conveyed a certain experience of those years, which made Jess suddenly feel awkward.

"Burke, me luv," the woman exclaimed. "Where yer been hidin' yerself?" She reached for him, wrapping her arms about his neck. "It's been a mite lonely round 'ere, luv," she cooed up at him.

"I've been working long hours," he explained. "I need a favor."

She smiled up at him, an intimate expression that darkened her eyes. "All yer 'ave ter do is ask, luv. Yer know that. When 'ave I ever refused when yer needed somethin'."

"I've brought someone along." He angled his head over his left shoulder. The woman followed his glance, craning her neck around that wide shoulder. Her eyes widened speculatively at sight of Jess.

"Well, wot 'ave we 'ere?" she exclaimed, an auburn brow arching with an expression that could have been anything from surprise to amusement.

More than a little put off at being inspected as if she were a curiosity, Jess let the valise thump to the floor.

"My name is Jess Kelly."

"Cor! She's a bold one ain't she." Then the woman added, "Me name's Belle Rossi. I own this place."

"She needs a room," Burke explained. "She's working down at the station for a while."

Speculation cooled those dark eyes. "Wot sort o' work?"

"Drawing pictures from descriptions of suspects," Jess interjected as she leaned around his shoulder.

"She's working for Chief Abberline," Burke clarified, giving her a nasty look.

"Sorry, luv. Both yer and Abberline are outta luck. All me rooms are let. I rented the last one yesterday morning to a young couple from Derby."

"You'd a known that if yer ever came home at night," she added with an intimate smile.

"It will only be for a short while. You could put her in with one of your other tenants," Burke insisted.

"They'd like that!" Belle smirked. "Especially since the other single tenants are all men."

"What about yer flat? You've only that mangy cat. You could put her up for a few days."

"Don't yer be talkin' badly 'bout Melrose. He likes yer. Besides, me nephew is here for a visit. He's got the extra room."

Jess was tired of being treated like excess baggage that Burke was forced to drag along behind.

"I shall find a place on my own," she announced. "You needn't feel any responsibility toward me whatsoever, Mr. Burke. And I don't care to be discussed as if I were a fixture on the wall."

"Not a timid one, is she?" the woman remarked as she struggled with a smile.

"No, she's not," Burke muttered.

Jess shouldered her way around Inspector Burke.

"Perhaps you know of another house where I might find a room," she inquired, ignoring Devlin Burke.

"There ain't no other place," Belle informed her. "Not 'round 'ere leastways. That room o' mine was the last one on th' block. Unless yer want ter stay in Whitechapel District."

"She can't stay there," Burke stated flatly. "It's too dangerous. She'll stay in my flat."

A tiny little alarm went off in Jess's head. "Oh, no. I couldn't do that. It just wouldn't be . . ."

"Wot?" Belle demanded. "Not proper?" The expression on her face clearly indicated she thought such an idea ridiculous.

Jess was caught in a trap she'd cleverly woven for herself. A common street girl in dire circumstances wouldn't concern herself about the propriety of staying in a man's flat. She'd undoubtedly welcome the opportunity.

"It wouldn't be right," she insisted. "Putting you out of your room. I can sleep downstairs. Perhaps in the parlor," she suggested.

"You can't sleep in the parlor," he informed her bluntly.

"She could always find a place in one of the doss houses," Belle suggested, receiving a dark look from Burke. She merely shrugged her shoulders. Jess had no idea what a doss house was and suspected she didn't want to know.

"She'll stay in my place." He seized the valise and carried it up the stairs. Jess had no choice but to follow.

His rooms were on the second floor. They were cool and dark, the windows hung with worn dark green drapes. The globes of the ornate gas wall lanterns were freshly polished. There wasn't a speck of dusk anywhere, and the wood floors gleamed dully. Evidently Belle Rossi was an immaculate housekeeper.

Two upholstered chairs sat before the hearth. The worn fabric on both had been creatively patched so that contrasting pieces of fabric appeared to be part of the original design. The carpet had long since faded to muted shades of hunter green, wine, and dark blue.

A desk sat against the wall beside the hearth. An oil lamp for reading, several photographs of children, and a black-and-white cat who obviously considered the desk his personal domain, sat atop the desk. The overall appearance was worn and a bit shabby, yet comfortable, and not at all what she might have expected of a man who lived alone.

"Melrose!" Belle exclaimed. "There yer are, luv." She scooped up the cat in her arms and nuzzled her cheek into his fur.

"He musta sneaked in when I was cleanin' this morning. It's his favorite room. Burke claims he don't like cats, but don't yer believe it. Animals knows about people. Melrose wouldn't spend a minute up here if he thought he wasn't wanted."

"Probably has fleas," Burke muttered as he turned up the gas lantern at the wall.

"Melrose?" Jess asked with amusement as she reached for the cat. He went to her willingly, snuggling into the curl of her arm.

"He wandered in a couple years back," Belle explained. "Like other strays and men wot come in off the street. Finds themselves a roof, good food, and a warm bed, and move right in. Then one day they're gone. They're all like that." In spite of her harsh words, it was obvious that she was fond of the cat.

Melrose stared up at Jess with contemplative, yellow eyes. His fur was soft as satin with contrasting black patterns on white. His ears were covered by twin black patches that extended down

93

around both eyes, giving him the look of a masked bandit. There were vivid black patches across his back, and his tail was also black.

He lay on his back, cradled in her arms like a baby, his eyes closed to half slits, and rumbling with contentment.

"He likes yer," Belle admitted grudgingly. "He don't take ter everyone." She reached for him then.

"Meals is included in the rent," Belle informed her. "Since Burke is never 'ere I s'pose yer can 'ave his portion. Breakfast is at eight o'clock, supper is at seven. An' I don't bring trays up."

It was clear that Belle Rossi didn't like her, but for the time being Jess was determined to get along with her.

"Thank you. I'll try not to be any trouble."

"Oooooeeee! She's a right proper little bit, ain't she. Acts like a reg'lar little lady the way she talks. Better be careful, Burke, yer ain't used ter nothin' so fancy." She left then, Melrose tucked under her arm.

"Remember, supper is at seven," she called over her shoulder. "If yer not 'ere, yer miss out."

"She's a good sort," Burke said in a quiet voice, that made her wonder about his relationship with the woman. "She comes off a bit harsh at times. It's because she's had a hard life." It was all the explanation he offered. He went into the adjacent room then, taking a heavy coat off the peg beside the wardrobe. He pocketed several other items.

She had followed, wanting to explain that she hadn't meant to impose on him. They collided at the doorway as he was coming out of the room. His hands came up at her shoulders, steadying her. Her breasts were pressed against his chest, her hips wedged against his. She quickly stepped back and crossed to the far side of the sitting room.

"I'll reimburse you for my portion of the rent, until I can make other arrangements." She stood in the shadows near the hearth, where she wasn't likely to get in his way again.

"That won't be necessary." His gaze narrowed as he watched

her. "Abberline won't be able to pay yer much. Save what you earn."

"That's quite all right."

Silence expanded in the room. She felt his cool speculation and kept her gaze averted. Finally he crossed the sitting room. He dug into his pocket and thrust several coins down on the desktop.

"There's enough for the fare of a hansom in the mornin'," he announced.

Her gaze snapped up. "You're leaving?"

He looked at her then and once again she was aware of that lean animal intensity.

"Aye, there's a man I need to speak with, if I can find him."

"The one called the Mudger?"

Those blue eyes narrowed. It wasn't the first time that she surprised him like that. There was very little that slipped past her. He would have to be more careful.

"The Mudger is a fence." At her confused expression he explained, "He's a merchant of sorts. He knows practically everyone in Whitechapel. He may be able to tell us something about Annie Chapman."

She darted across the room. "I'll get my sketchpad."

He grabbed her wrist, stopping her. "That won't be necessary."

He saw the flash of pain in her eyes and immediately released her wrist. It was delicate, the bones fragile like the wing of a trapped bird, slender as a child's in his large hand, reminding him of his first impression—that she was vulnerable, just as Megan had been vulnerable. He slipped on the coat as he turned toward the door. She followed him, coming round at him when he went to the desk.

"If you find the Mudger, he may be able to describe someone to you. I can draw that description."

"You'll not go with me," he said bluntly.

Her chin angled stubbornly. "And why not?"

The way she said it made him think of a proper society lady, who had just been informed that there wouldn't be any Yorkshire pudding for supper.

"Because the only women who go there are prostitutes and whores. Unless, of course, you've a mind to change yer accommodations for the night. In which case you might be able to earn a bit more than the few pennies you'll earn from Abberline. Then again you might not."

She jerked back as if she'd been struck. Her face was pale. For a moment he thought she might faint. There were shadows of pain and wariness behind her eyes. For the first time in a long time, he regretted treating her the way he had. But he wouldn't change his mind about taking her with him. He muttered an oath as he turned back to the desk. He opened the center drawer and retrieved a small paper packet, which he jammed into his coat pocket.

"We'll begin work on the sketches in the morning," he repeated firmly as he turned to leave.

Something stopped him at the door—something that slipped in at the edge of his brain. Perhaps it was the harshness of his words, perhaps it was the silence in the room that echoed after. With another oath he swung back around.

She had followed him, perhaps to argue, or follow. She stood very near, pale and small, angry and defiant. A memory pulled at him—Megan. Jess reminded him of her, in more ways than he cared to admit, or wanted to admit. There was that same fragility, the vulnerability that reached deep inside him and made him feel things he'd rather not feel, that same wistful expression, hoping for things that might not be possible.

The difference was in the stubborn angle of the chin, the defiance in those jade eyes. Megan had never possessed that strength or determination.

Several pins had come loose in her hair. Thick waves tumbled at her neck and shoulders. He caught several strands between his fingers. It was like rich, dark satin.

She stared at the ribbon of hair wrapped about his hand. A disquieting urgency built along her nerve endings. His hands

96

were large, with long, blunt-tipped fingers which were lightly dusted with fine black hair. Those fingers slowly twining through her hair, dark blending with dark, was like an intimate joining.

Her lips parted but no words came out. There was only the quiver of her lip, the breath suddenly caught in her throat, the urgent heat that explosively charged the air about them.

She pulled back, freeing the long tendril from his grasp, leaving the pin behind. His fingers closed over it.

He stared down at it for a moment. Then he looked up. With surprising gentleness he returned the pin, securing it in the soft coil of hair above her ear, his fingers grazing the pale skin at her cheek.

Her skin burned where he touched. She wanted to pull away, at the same time she wanted to turn into his touch, and brush her lips against his callused palm.

What would it feel like? she wondered. What would he taste like?

Her thoughts stunned her. No man had ever roused these feelings in her before. They were new, confusing, and more than a little frightening. Her gaze angled away from his at the same time she physically pulled away from him, to a safe distance where he couldn't reach out and touch her.

"In the mornin'," he repeated, his voice oddly different, deeper, thickened around the words. Then he was gone, the door slamming after him.

She watched him leave from the window of the small sitting room that looked out over the street below. He turned and walked to the corner where he hailed a hansom. She let the worn curtain fall back into place.

She quickly repinned her hair. Then she scooped up the coins from the top of the desk and dropped them in the small leather pouch at the bottom of her valise. When the time presented itself, she would return every last coin to the chief inspector.

It was late. There was only perhaps another hour of daylight left. She put on the worn coat she'd bought from Mr. Spivey and let herself out of the room, locking it with Burke's key.

On the street she turned and walked to the corner as he had. Within a few minutes a vacant hansom approached from the adjacent street. As she climbed inside, she paused and looked back over her shoulder. She was certain she saw the curtain at the downstairs window fall back into place. She closed the doors and gave the driver the name she'd overheard at the Commercial Street police station.

Hanbury Street was only a few blocks from the Commercial Street police station. It took only a few inquiries for her to find the exact location of Annie Chapman's flat. The murder had given the place a sort of notoriety.

It was a small, pathetic hovel across an alley. Number 9 was painted in whitewash beside the door, which was stoutly locked. She learned from a young boy playing stick ball in the street that the police had completed their search of the flat the previous day.

She gathered the coat more tightly about her, holding herself against the aching coldness that had settled in the pit of her stomach. She had to know more. She had to get inside that flat.

She peeked in at the windows, but they were covered by curtains that made it impossible to see anything. She stepped back, struck by an odd notion that she couldn't quite put her finger on. Then it came to her as her gaze swept over the line of identical flats that clustered the alley.

This one was the only flat with curtains at the windows. And from the looks of them through the smudged windows, they were of good quality. It was so like Linnie, that even in this dreadful place she had insisted on curtains at the windows.

Try as she might to hold them back, tears choked into her throat. What had happened? Why had her sister run away to a place like this?

"Hey! Wot yer doin' hanging about?"

She jerked around and came face-to-face with a shriveled woman dressed in a man's coat, boots, and a wide-swinging skirt that hovered over her girth like a suspended tent. A hat was squashed down over her straggly white hair, and worn knitted gloves were wrapped about her gnarled hands, the fingers cut out. One eye squinted up at her—the woman was very short—the other eye was glazed over with a milky white haze.

"Get away from that door! I don't allow no one ter come pokin' about," the old woman squawked, producing a crude wood cane which she aimed at Jess's head.

"There ain't nothin' ter see. Damned police! Damned newspaper people! Won't never be able to rent it out wot with them crawlin' all over the place."

It was then that Jess realized this woman must be the landlord.

"I'm looking for a flat to rent," she quickly spoke up before the old woman launched the cane at her again.

"Go on with yer!" She gave Jess a deprecating look with her one good eye. "Where would you come by the means to rent a flat?"

"I have money, and I need a place to stay," she lied, willing to pay the price of a month's rent merely to look inside.

"How much yer got?"

"How much is the rent?"

"Half crown per month. Includes all the furnishins, coal is extra. There's two rooms. Yer could let the other one out yerself, like the last tenant." There was, of course, no mention that the previous tenant had been murdered. "Ain't seen yer about. Must be new to this part o' London."

"I just arrived yesterday."

"Figured as much. Yer don't talk like yer from hereabouts." Her gaze narrowed once more, wrinkling her face like an old squashed prune. "How'd yer hear bout this place?"

"A young boy told me about it."

"Must be that little beggar always playin' sticks. Well it ain't no never mind ter me. That's the price, take it o' leave it. Got another bloke interested in rentin' it out."

Jess doubted anyone else was interested in renting the flat so soon after the murder. The police had finished their work only the day before. And there weren't any prospective tenants standing about.

"I'd like to see it first."

"I'll get me keys."

The old woman waddled across the alley to another identical flat. She returned with several keys attached to a large ring.

"I rents all these out fer the owner. He lives over in Tottenham," she said as she slipped a key into the lock and pushed the door open.

"Rents is due on the first. Yer don't pay, yer out on the streets. I don't pay no mind to anybody yer have come visitin'. Jus' make certain they ain't the quarrelsome type. An' I'll have me boy, Jocko, put the fear in that fella wot keeps comin' round, so's he won't be botherin' yer. That is unless yer lookin' ter pick yerself up a few *gentleman friends*." She gave Jess a knowing wink.

"What sort of fellow came around here?"

"Oh, yer know the sort. Looks like he ain't got more 'an th' price of ale in his pocket. He come around right reg'lar till a few days ago. The girls wot rented this place always let 'im in. Must be a real strong lad." She winked at Jess. "If'n yer get my meanin'."

"Yes, of course," Jess answered. "What did this fellow look like?"

"Oh, a right reg'lar sort, light hair, a bit thin in the face, but with a ready smile. A real charmer with the women."

Jess made a mental note of the description. It might be useful later. The old woman showed her the room then.

It had been cleaned. Any signs of struggle or death that had remained after Annie Chapman's murder were now gone.

She had brought her sketchpad along, but she was certain that if she tried to draw the inside of the rooms she would be asked to leave.

Instead, she added to the mental list of details that now included a vague description of the man that had been seen at the flat.

More than that, she tried to imagine what her sister's life had been like here during those brief weeks.

She had told Burke and Inspector Abberline that she would know if her sister were dead. As she walked about the room, she sensed

100

only a sort of pathetic loneliness, but none of the fear or aching loss that she'd experienced at the loss of her mother.

She was confident her sister was still alive. She needed to believe it. But where was she? She pushed open the door to the adjacent room. The room was tiny, hardly bigger than a large wardrobe, yet it contained a narrow bed, small dresser, table, and chair.

"Yer could charge 'alf the rent fer that extra room," the old woman suggested as she followed her about.

Jess walked about the room. Her sense of her sister was stronger here. She was certain this had been Linnie's room, cramped and barren as it was, and such a startling contrast to even the most utilitarian storage rooms at Deverell Hall.

"Well? Wot'll it be dearie? I got ter know," the old woman called to her from the first room. "Won't find another like it in all o' Whitechapel."

It was then Jess saw it, that splatter of crimson color on the threadbare carpet that no amount of scrubbing could wash away—blood.

The boy on the street had told her that Annie Chapman had died in the first room. He'd been one of the first people to see her and had described it in great detail. But something had happened in this room as well. This blood was fresh, dried only in the past few days.

The room wobbled uncertainly, the walls seemed to close in on her. She felt that cold hollow ache of fear in the pit of her stomach. It expanded and spread, until she was unbearably cold and shaking.

Linnie had been here. This had been her room. Was it her blood staining the threadbare carpet?

She forced her legs to move, one halting step, then another. She was afraid she would collapse, then she couldn't have stopped if she'd tried.

She ran past the startled landlady, plunging out into the street, and directly into the arms of a man who stepped from the dark shadows at the door.

Chapter Eight

"What the devil are you doin' here?"

She screamed as she collided with Devlin Burke.

He grabbed her, his fingers closing around her arms. He was equally stunned, and he was angry. His fingers tightened, bruising her beneath the fabric of her coat.

"What *are* you doin' here?" he demanded again, shaking her.

Her hands were clenched into tight fists, fingernails cutting into the palms of her hands. Surprise gave way to anger.

"Why didn't you tell me?" she demanded furiously. "You knew about the blood in that other room!" she accused, very near tears. "That was my sister's room, and you didn't tell me! What else have you found that you haven't told me about? What are you hiding? Why won't you tell me?"

She was hysterical, vivid green eyes bright with tears. Her face was ashen, void of color, like it had been in the morgue when she saw Annie Chapman's mutilated body. Once again Burke was struck by the startling contrast of strength and vulnerability.

She'd fainted at the morgue, but there was no danger of that now. She was angry, furious to the point of doing herself, or someone else, physical harm as she tried to free herself from his grasp.

She was like a wild animal, cornered, defending herself against something that was terrifying in its power to destroy — fear.

He saw it behind her eyes, raw and painful, like some primitive creature hiding in the shadows. She refused to give in to it, refused to believe that her sister might be dead, instead turning on him, oblivious to the pain as he tried to restrain her.

He loosened his hold for a moment and then pulled her into

his arms so that she was caught, unable to run away. Her fists were pinioned against his chest. She struggled, wearing herself out, until exhaustion and tears overwhelmed her, and she collapsed against him.

He stood in the middle of the alley, ignoring the curious stares of the tenants who had poked their heads out of windows and doors at the commotion, trying to somehow comfort her.

The landlady stared at them. A sharp look quelled her curiosity and she scurried off across the alley to her own flat, grumbling about "damned peelers who was too busy calmin' hysterical ladyfriends when they shoulda' been protectin' law-abidin' citizens from crazed murderers."

The fight had gone out of Jess. Once again she was fragile and vulnerable, stirring unwanted memories out of his past, recalling another time and another young girl who had been too fragile to survive.

He'd lived with death and violence as a child. As a grown man he saw death on the streets every day. Through the years he had convinced himself that nothing could hurt him again. Even the mindless brutality of these recent murders hadn't penetrated the hard protective shell he kept firmly in place . . . until today.

He realized that Megan's death had affected him profoundly. He thought he'd escaped it along with the past. But he saw too much of Megan all over again in Jess Kelly. Perhaps it was because she seemed so fragile and lost, perhaps it was because she was so small, barely reaching his shoulder, or perhaps it was that disquieting innocence he sensed beneath the brave facade.

Whatever it was, it reached inside him. Before he realized it, he brought his hand up and stroked her back, quieting her with gentle words that slipped out of the shadows of his own childhood, when someone whose face he couldn't recall had quieted his own worst fears, and the silent rage that burned in his young heart.

"Don't hold it in, lass," he whispered against the softness of her hair. "Cry it all out, until yer can't cry anymore.

"I know what it is to fear somethin' and ache fer it until it seems yer insides will burst. Get it all out, so that it doesn't eat at yer no more, and when yer done, we'll talk."

She burrowed against his chest, the sobs muffled against the front of his coat as the fight went out of her. Gradually he felt the tension ease until her slender shoulders sagged and her fists unclenched, and she stood clinging to the front of his coat.

"Come along, then," he finally said, wrapping his arm about her shoulders and pulling her away from that flat on Hanbury Street.

"It's gettin' dark, not a good time to be about."

When they arrived back at Abbington Road he asked Belle to bring hot tea up to his flat.

He lit a fire at the hearth. The warmth gradually drove back the shadows in the room. Melrose had slipped into the room and lay on the hearth rug, his paws curled under his chest. His eyes were closed to narrow slits, the tip of his black tail lifting and falling slowly with contented grace.

"You knew about the blood, didn't you?" Her hands were tightly wrapped about a cup of tea. The heat that seeped through as she cradled it in both hands somehow helped her focus the pain of that discovery. Even with tear-stained cheeks and red nose she was beautiful.

"Aye, I knew."

She'd recovered sufficiently during the ride back. Now only the anger remained, carefully held in check. He'd always admired that ability in a man, but thought it impossible in a woman. They were usually far too emotional.

"Why didn't you tell me?"

"It didn't seem necessary at the time," he answered bluntly. When she started to protest, he held up a hand and continued. "It proves nothin', except that there was blood in the second room."

Her throat was tight. "My sister's blood."

He was brutally honest. "Perhaps. Then again, perhaps not."

He knew what he would see in her eyes then, a sort of desperate hope, a need to believe that what he was saying was true. It was there when she looked up at him, along with something else — determination. She would insist on the truth, whatever it was.

"Your letter and the one we found at the flat make it fairly certain that yer sister lived with Annie Chapman. But we can't be certain she was there the night Annie died."

"And you can't be certain that she wasn't."

"There's been no other body found in the three days since Annie died. I believe yer sister is alive."

Her voice broke and went to a soft whisper. "Unless you just haven't found her . . . yet."

"It's not his way," Burke said. When she looked up at him again, the expression in her eyes cut at his heart. She wanted so much to believe in any other possibility.

"What do you mean, *not his way?* That sounds as if he has a particular style. That would mean . . ." Her eyes widened then. "You believe these murders are connected? Perhaps committed by the same person?"

"Aye," he acknowledged solemnly. "They're connected. The last three murders have been committed by the same man. It's all very methodical. The victims have all been approximately the same age, all women, and all prostitutes." He couldn't look at her then, so he paced the room, stopping before the blazing fire at the hearth.

"The manner of death is always the same as well, a knife, used by someone who has a great deal of skill, and in a manner that is very methodical. The marks are practically identical, made from the right to the left side of the body." He turned then and found her watching him, her eyes fixed and stark.

"He takes great pleasure leavin' his victims so that they're certain to be found, almost as if he were flaunting it."

"Or sending a message to others?" she whispered softly.

"Aye."

105

"Then it's not ended."

He shook his head, his mouth a thin, hard line. "No, it's not ended. He'll kill again. And yer sister is somehow involved. In the very least, she may be able to identify him. My guess is that she's gone into hiding. We have to find her."

Gone into hiding. It was the reason Linnie had disappeared over three weeks ago. But why? And now she was forced to hide again, somehow caught up in something horrible and frightening.

"Is that where you went tonight?"

He stood at the hearth, one arm resting against the mantel, a cup of tea in his other hand. She wouldn't have thought him the sort to drink tea, but ale or something stronger instead. He looked down at the cup, frowning slightly as if weighing what he would tell her.

"One of my people on the street heard that the Mudger knew of a fella who was keepin' company with Annie Chapman. I haven't had any luck findin' the Mudger yet. He's a wily old fox, knows of places in this city that no man has ever seen. He hasn't been about in several days. Probably knows that I'm lookin' for him. If I can find this fellow that the Mudger knows, he may know somethin' about yer sister."

Jess understood what he left unsaid. "And if she's still alive, she's in danger because of what she may have seen."

"Aye. And if you stay, that danger could come to you as well." She looked up then.

"That old woman at Hanbury Street mentioned a man who came around to Annie Chapman's flat. She said *both* women knew him."

He looked up at her then, the frown deepening, but a different light in his eyes. "Did she say anything about him?"

"She gave a vague description — height and his hair color. She said he always had a smile. She said he charmed all the ladies."

"That might describe half the able-bodied men in Whitechapel. It would help if we had a better description of the man."

"Could he be the one?"

His expression was thoughtful. "Possible. Whoever killed Annie and the others has to be someone who could get near, someone they felt they could trust, perhaps even someone they knew.

"Now you understand my meanin' that it's not a safe place. Goin' out about late in the day is especially dangerous. You'll not go out again like that."

"But there's nothing for me to be afraid of. You said all the women were prostitutes."

"Aye, all wearin' skirts, shirts, and coats."

She knew precisely what he was getting at — those clothes could be found on hundreds of women in Whitechapel. It was also what she wore.

"Perhaps it was someone all the women knew," she suggested.

"A customer?" he said bluntly.

She felt her face go warm. "Yes, I suppose that is what I mean. But in that case I'm perfectly safe."

Then she realized what it was that she'd revealed to him, her face went crimson. "What I mean is . . ."

There was a faintly amused expression on his face, at the trap she'd so neatly laid for herself. "What is it that yer meanin', Jessie?"

The easy familiarity with which he said her name unnerved her even further. No one had ever called her Jessie.

"I came here to find honest work," she insisted. "Just like my sister. I'm not in any danger."

His eyes narrowed as his expression changed again. "Perhaps yer more in danger, because of what you know."

She blinked and stared up at him. "I don't know anything."

He watched her steadily. "Perhaps not, but perhaps yer sister mentioned somethin' before she came here. Perhaps there was another reason that might have something to do with Annie Chapman."

What did he know, or what had he guessed? Her gaze slipped away from his.

"I already told you. My sister came here three weeks ago to find work. I was to join her. I received only that one letter posted four days ago from Whitechapel. And I came to look for her."

"Aye, that's what you told the chief inspector."

"It's the truth. I've told you everything that I know."

Her gaze wavered downward, focusing on the cup of tea—her third—that she held in both hands. Fatigue pulled at her. She had no idea what time it was. The fire hissed at the hearth as expectant silence expanded between them.

He'd discovered a long time ago that when a person insisted they were telling the truth, it was usually a lie. He let the silence draw out, using it to watch and think. Finally, he said, "You've a long day ahead of you. Mr. Abberline will have a lot of work for you. You'd better get yer rest."

She didn't want to rest, not yet. "You don't think I can be of help, do you?" She wanted an answer for something that had bothered her all afternoon. She couldn't rid herself of the feeling that he resented her involvement.

"That remains to be seen. You've a passable talent, and God knows we've not been able to come up with anything more substantial in the way of a description. I've no argument with yer helpin' out whatever way you can."

"Then it's me you don't like."

His eyes were cool, completely void of any emotion. "I've no feelin' about yer one way or t'other. I've been given orders and I'll carry them out."

"And you always do precisely as you're told, don't you, Inspector!" His expression never changed, didn't alter by so much as a glance, or shift of his mouth.

"The only thing that matters is findin' the murderer. And I'll find him. You have my word on that."

His word, when she had told him more lies than she could count. Could she believe him? Could she trust him?

Her cup rattled as she set it down abruptly and stood. "I'm very tired. I'd like to go to bed now."

His gaze narrowed. "All right. Take the bedroom fer yerself. I'll sleep out here."

"I couldn't do that. If you have extra blankets, I'll sleep out here."

"You'll have the use of the bedroom," he repeated in a tone of voice that suggested there would be no more discussion of the matter. "Mr. Abberline won't like it if yer fuzzy-headed in the mornin' on account of a poor night's sleep."

"What about you?"

He put more wood on the fire. "I'm used ter sleepin' in the streets. One night on the chairs won't bother me. As I said, I'm rarely here."

It made her wonder where he passed other nights, and she thought of Belle Rossi. She noticed the looks that had passed between them and guessed their relationship was more than that of landlord and tenant.

She hadn't the strength to argue with him over the bedroom. She suspected it would be pointless. Devlin Burke struck her as the sort of person who rarely lost an argument.

She undressed by the light of the lantern on the bedside table, leaving her clothes where they lay. She'd forgotten to pack a gown, and slipped beneath the mended covers clad only in the thin chemise she wore under her corset.

The door opened abruptly, and Burke filled the doorway. He obviously felt no need for polite formalities such as knocking before entering, even though it was his bedroom. The rules of society that she'd lived by her entire life, with rigidly defined rules of propriety between unmarried men and women didn't apply here. Those rules didn't exist in Whitechapel, or for Devlin Burke, for that matter. He was obviously quite accustomed to sharing a room with a woman.

"Is everything all right, then?"

She pulled the mended quilt up about her shoulders, even though the room suddenly seemed very warm.

"Everything is fine. Thank you."

109

She refused to look at him. He suppressed a smile at her apparent embarrassment at having a man in her room—or more accurately *his* room.

Only a short while earlier they had been arguing with one another. Now there was an unspoken truce.

"This old house is drafty. It gets cold at night," he explained as he opened the trunk at the foot of the bed and took out several blankets.

She glanced through the opened doorway to the two chairs before the hearth. "Those chairs don't look very comfortable."

He looked at her then with a speculative expression. "Is that an invitation?"

Her mouth went dry. She could have sworn he grinned at her before she looked away, her cheeks red with embarrassment.

"What I meant was . . ."

"I'll be fine," he assured her, saving her further embarrassment. "But don't think I'll be givin' you all the blankets." He spread one over the top of the quilt.

When she looked at him again, only a hint of a smile remained at his mouth. Then, unexpectedly, he bent over her, smoothing the quilt and blanket, tucking them in about the edges as if she were a child. His fingers brushed her bare shoulder, sending tremors across her skin, as he tucked the edges about her neck.

"I'll not have you freezin' to death. I'd be hard-pressed explainin' to the chief inspector."

Her gaze met his. His face was only inches from hers. Those dark blue eyes had gone to black. She could smell the faintly woodsy smell about him that was part woodsmoke, part spice, and part secrets, completely incongruous with who and what he was. She could feel the heat of his skin, near yet not touching.

Not an easy face, she'd thought when they first met, but a strong face, with sharp planes and angles, a strong chin, and that strong mouth.

She felt an almost overwhelming desire to touch his mouth, to trace the fullness with her fingertips, to feel the texture and warmth of his skin, to smooth the faint crease at the corner, to learn all the subtle moods found in each expression.

Surely her interest was only artistic. But there was a tiny, unrelenting voice deep inside her that whispered liar, and made her wonder if her concern earlier had been only that, or an invitation.

An odd expression flashed across his face, then it was gone, and he stepped back from the bed. On his way out, he stopped at the doorway.

"We'll find yer sister." He turned then and left the room, pulling the door closed behind him.

"Please, leave it open."

He looked back in surprise. "Afraid of the dark, lass?"

"Not at all," she responded tartly. She glanced down at his feet. "Melrose won't be able to get in if the door is closed."

Burke glanced down at the cat with its distinctive black-and-white markings. Melrose rubbed against the doorjamb. They exchanged glances, one confident yellow, the other suspicious blue.

Then with a dismissive flick of his tail the cat trotted across the room and leaped onto the bed. He immediately located the softest place just under the edge of the quilt where he could hide and observe everything that went on in the room. He curled into a tight ball.

"Probably does have fleas," Burke snorted with disgust.

"He wouldn't allow it," she assured him, stroking the satin-soft fur. "He's very fastidious."

"Do as yer please, but it won't be my fault if yer scratchin' in th' mornin'."

As he went out the door, he added, "I leave early each mornin'. I have lotsa' work to do, an' I can't be waitin' round fer you to get ready. If yer not ready I'll leave without you."

She watched as he moved around the sitting room adding more wood to the fire, pushing the two chairs together, then settling himself with a few muttered words.

Melrose snuggled against the curve of her body. He purred with satisfaction, his eyes closed to lazy slits of smug superiority.

She wasn't afraid of the dark. She'd never been afraid. It was Linnie who had been afraid as a child, while Jess had challenged whatever mythical monsters that might lurk there to come out and do battle. Leaving the door open with that reassuring glow of light wasn't for herself, it was for her sister, like a candle left in the window.

Some time later Burke turned, the blankets twisting about his legs. Melrose appeared at the doorway of the sitting room and regarded him with what he suspected was an expression of high amusement. He hurled a pillow at him.

The cat nimbly side-stepped the feathered missile, sat down a few feet away, and proceeded unconcerned to clean himself.

"Better not have fleas," Burke threatened as he shifted his position for the dozenth time and finally dozed off.

He awoke the next morning with cramped muscles, a stiff neck, and Melrose perched in the middle of his chest. They exchanged glares. When he tired of their mutual disgruntled staring, Melrose hopped down onto the floor, drawing Burke's attention to the fact that the flat was unusually quiet, cold, and except for himself and the damned cat, completely empty.

He lunged out of his makeshift bed, very nearly tripping in the tangle of blankets that wound around his legs on his way to the bedroom. It was empty.

The curtains were pulled back at the window, revealing that it was well into the morning. The bed was made, and she was gone.

He stormed out of the room. The cat scuttled out of his path to a place of safety on top of the mantel where he regarded him with an expression of faint disgust as if to say "You overslept. What did you expect?"

Burke jerked the door open and went out into the hallway to look for her there. Instead he found Belle Rossi, on the landing at the first floor, staring up at him.

"Mornin' luv," she cooed delightedly.

"Where is she?" Burke demanded.

"Has yer little guest flown the coop?" she asked with mock surprise and a twitch of a satisfied smile as she hitched up her skirts and climbed the stairs. She reached the landing and gave him an appraising look from his tangled dark hair down to his rumpled pants. "Yer wouldn't have had such a bad night down at my place, Burke," she sighed softly.

With an oath, he stalked back into his flat. She followed with the good sense to keep several feet behind him.

"I 'eard someone go out early enough. Thought it was one of me other tenants. Left yer in the lurch did she? Must be losin' yer touch, luv."

"What time was that?" He ignored the rest of the unwanted comments as he scooped the blankets off the floor and tossed them across the chair. He glared at Melrose, who escaped to the opposite end of the mantel and exited to the floor.

"There yer are, darlin'!" Belle exclaimed. She scooped Melrose up in her arms. "Yer 'ave to stay outta 'is way when he's in a foul temper," she warned the cat with a meaningful glance at Burke, as if the cat understood every word.

"He's not use ter the ladies takin' a cropper on 'im."

Burke growled as he went into the bedroom, splashed water into the bowl, and lathered his face with shaving soap.

"Are you going to tell me what time she left?"

Musta' been 'bout seven thirty when I 'eard the front door close. What 'appened up 'ere last night anyway? Not that it's any of my business."

She let Melrose out for his morning rounds, then carefully inspected the room, taking in every detail of the two chairs shoved together to make an uncomfortable bed, the tangled blankets, and the neatly made bed in the bedroom through the door that stood ajar. Then she found the envelope on the desk with Burke's name on it.

"Looks like she left yer a note, luv." She didn't bother to disguise the satisfaction in her voice. Burke emerged from the bedroom, soap scraped away from half his face. He snatched the envelope from her hands and tore it open.

Inspector Burke,
I'm accustomed to leaving early each morning. I have a great deal of work to do. You weren't ready on time, so I left without you.
Jess Kelly

The message was blunt and irritatingly familiar. If he wasn't mistaken, those were almost the exact words he'd said to her the night before.

Cheeky, he thought with more than a little aggravation and a small smile. He thrust the letter down on the desk and returned to the washbowl to finish shaving, an odd thought struggling at the back of his brain.

"Do you know how to read and write, Belle?"

She glanced up abruptly from the letter, certain she'd been caught at eavesdropping, then realized he couldn't see anything from where he stood. She let out a small sigh of relief.

"I know how to scribe me name, an' I know me numbers. Need that fer market and the rents so's me tenants don' cheat me. Never 'ad the time or inclination fer more 'an 'at.

"Yer know how it is, Burke. Only the bleedin' swells gots the time fer readin' books. As fer writin', who 'as time to practice makin' letters over and over with fancy little loops and curves. It's all I can manage to scribble out some numbers."

She watched as he scraped the soap from his other cheek, and felt a sharp pang of loneliness. It had been a while since he'd shared her mornings or her bed.

Burke paused, staring at Belle's reflection in the small oval mirror above the washbowl as she stood at the doorway. *Letters with fancy loops and curves.*

It described the writing in that note. Belle was right. Who had

114

time for anything more than the crudest scratches and scrawls? Certainly not most of the people found in Whitechapel or any other part of London, or Dublin for that matter. He had acquired those skills by sheer tenacity, painstakingly self-taught, driven by the certainty that if he was ever to raise himself above the circumstances of his birth that he had to have them.

Those skills, and a cunning education on human nature learned from the streets, were the means of escaping the poverty he'd been raised in. His hatred for the woman who'd given birth to him and then abandoned him infused him with a burning hunger to achieve more and have more than the life she had sold him to.

He'd scraped and fought his way out of the gutters. He mimicked every fine gentleman he ever encountered, acquiring the skills of manners and speech.

Occasionally the years spent on the hard streets of Dublin betrayed him, the accent of his youth slipping through in a moment of anger. Just as Jess Kelly had betrayed herself. Hers wasn't the speech or meager writing skills of a common street girl. Somehow she had acquired an education, but her clothes were rags, and she obviously hadn't eaten a decent meal any time recently before she came to Whitechapel.

It appeared the circumstances of her life weren't much different from his own. Yet he couldn't set aside the feeling that she was lying.

He glanced at his reflection in the mirror above the washbowl as he wiped the last smudges of soap from his face. There were times he didn't like what he saw—someone who had become too hard, too cynical, even brutal at times.

His life was littered with enough lies and deceptions to hang ten men. It gave him a certain edge for uncovering lies that other people told, while protecting his own secrets.

If she had lied to him, it was only a matter of time until he caught her. And whatever secrets she was keeping, he would expose them as well.

Chapter Nine

She was to be paid a half crown for each full day she worked, six days a week, with Sundays off to attend church. Chief Inspector Abberline apologized that he couldn't pay her more. She assured him that it was more than enough, estimating that it made her sketches worth approximately one shilling apiece, a rare bargain she realized with a secret smile, if she were of any noteworthy talent.

Mr. Abberline put her to work immediately. It was painstaking, reading through countless written statements from witnesses, passersby on the street, anyone who might have seen something at the time of the three murders. Although the files were neat and orderly, the descriptions were a hodgepodge, making the work time-consuming and difficult.

She began with descriptions taken after the first murder of Polly Nichols. There were dozens of them; known acquaintances, people she had been seen with the night she died, a man she had boasted was a new customer.

Some descriptions were thorough, others were hardly more than a few vague details. A sketch was made for each one.

Constable Endicott's assistance was invaluable. He read each description for her, repeating details, translating some of the unfamiliar slang words taken down in the reports. Within a few days sketches covered every available surface of the office where they worked.

Late one afternoon, Endicott had taken several sketches to Chief Abberline's office. She continued working, bent over the desk, attempting to make a composite sketch from several similar descriptions. She gradually became aware that someone was watching her. She looked up. Burke was standing in the doorway.

"Didn't mean to interrupt you."

She laid down the pencil and rubbed her hand. She frowned as she studied the drawing she was working on.

"That's all right. This isn't going very well. It's like trying to fit together pieces of a jigsaw puzzle." She looked up then. He had a thoughtful expression on his face and she realized she'd made another slip. She doubted that most people in Whitechapel had the time for jigsaw puzzles.

"It's just that it's very confusing," she rushed on to explain. "It's as if there's a man out there with a thousand faces."

He said nothing as he approached the desk, filling that small, cramped office with restless energy. He wasn't usually at a loss for words. She seemed to sense his uneasiness and immediately became alarmed.

"Have you learned something about my sister?"

"No," he reassured her, standing before the desk. He didn't sit but remained standing instead.

Her voice broke softly. "I'm never certain whether that's reassuring or not." And then as if she felt the need to reassure him, or perhaps herself, "I want to find her. But until I do, at least I can still hope that she's still alive." She looked up at him then, her eyes wide and searching. "I don't suppose that makes much sense."

It made perfect sense.

She was so small, she seemed no more than a child bent over her school texts, studying intently to earn a passing mark. She stirred something within him, a protective instinct that left him feeling vulnerable and uncertain. It was a long time since he'd felt that way.

"Aye," he said, his voice low and intense. "Uncertainty keeps hope alive. It's the certainty of somethin' that takes away all hope. I understand, Jessie."

It was the second time he'd used her name that way, like an endearment, almost intimate in the way he said it. It was unset-

117

tling, reminding her that he was far easier to understand when he was angry. At least then there was no misunderstanding.

"Then you haven't found the Mudger yet."

"Not yet, but we'll find him," he assured her. "There's a certain aspect of character he can't hide."

"What is that?"

"Greed. The Mudger likes his money. I've got men watchin' the people he does business with. Eventually he'll show his face and when he does, we'll have him."

"Is that what you came to tell me?"

"No."

He stood there, looking down at her, his eyes dark and contemplative, as if he couldn't quite decide how to begin.

He'd come into the office to apologize, something he rarely admitted or felt the need for. He'd been wrong about her sketches, although for the life of him he didn't understand why he felt she should know about it. Except that he'd watched her for days, sitting there in that office, bent over her drawings.

"Yer work is remarkable, Jess," he finally said, as he picked up one of the drawings she was working on. He frowned as he studied it, a street scene with several people drawn into the sketch. There was a life to the sketches, an intensity of emotion that went beyond surface images.

"You've already helped us locate several other people who may have seen something at one of the murders."

"But we're still no closer to the identity of the murderer," she reminded him, expressing some of the frustration she'd experienced over the past several days. "I want to help."

"You have, a great deal. We've accomplished far more than we could ever have hoped for. Chief Abberline is very pleased."

She sensed that still wasn't what he wanted to say. Whatever it was, he was having great difficulty over it.

"I was wrong objecting to Abberline's idea," he said finally. "I'm rarely wrong."

"And even more rarely admit it?" she suggested with a faint smile, careful not to gloat over the small victory of his apology.

He smiled then, too, a heart-stopping smile that transformed his face. The hard line of his mouth dissolved into a wry grin. The crease at the corner of his lips softened into a dimple. And his eyes . . . God help her, his eyes held a rare joy and laughter that took her breath away.

She'd thought him handsome before, but in a hardened, almost cynical way that hinted at the danger he was capable of. This was someone different, someone who rarely escaped from behind the cold facade . . . someone she suddenly longed to know more about.

"Aye, yer have the truth of it there, lass," he admitted with thickened accent.

It seemed some of the barriers had come down between them. She suspected it was unwise to take advantage of the moment, but she had no choice.

"I'd like to do more than this." She made a sweeping gesture over the top of the desk.

"In what way?"

She took a careful breath. "I could ask questions about Annie Chapman, and Mary."

"No." It hissed out, a low, emphatic sound edged with a sharp warning.

"But I was able to find out about that young man who visited Annie. Your men knew nothing about that. The people you speak with might hold something back. They might be willing to talk to me if they thought I was just a friend."

"No!" He threw the sketch down on the desk. It wasn't a simple warning any longer. "I know what yer speakin' of, but I told you before, yer not to get involved. It's too dangerous. Three women have already been killed. Do you want to be the fourth? What good will yer be to yer sister if yer throat is cut?" They were hard, angry words.

"What good am I to her sitting here, drawing pictures?"

"It's the only way you'll be allowed to help!" he told her bluntly as they stood across the desk from one another.

"I want to do more."

"No!"

She was dangerously close to losing her temper. She leaned across the desk at him.

"I may come and go as I please. I haven't broken any laws. You can't tell me what to do."

"Aye, Jess, I can. If yer interfere again you'll be sent away."

Sent away? Where? To one of the workhouses, to get her out of the way? Surely they couldn't make her leave. It was a frightening thought. But far more disquieting was the fact that she had a great deal to hide from them. She'd already learned that Burke had a reputation for being thorough.

How much would it take for him to learn the truth about her? What had he already learned either on his own or that she had mistakenly revealed about herself? She couldn't allow him to find out. She had to protect her sister. They mustn't know anything.

"Don't interfere, Jess." His voice softened, but the warning hadn't. Was it possible he knew what she was thinking?

She scooped up several more sketches, and rounded the desk. He grabbed her arm as she tried to push past him.

"It could be dangerous."

She allowed herself to look at him then.

"It appears I don't have a choice."

"No, you don't."

She jerked her arm free of his grasp and fled the office.

With a sort of childish glee she drew horns, a hooked nose, and several disgusting warts on the picture she'd been sketching.

Across from her, Endicott closed the file they'd been working on with a snap and reminded her that it was late and time to go home. He seemed to be waiting for her.

"Please, go ahead without me," she insisted, shoving the sketch to the bottom of the stack and beginning another. "I want to finish this last sketch today."

Endicott dug the sketch from the bottom of the stack.

"Except for the nose, horns, and warts, it looks exactly like

Mr. Burke." He looked across at her with humor glinting in his eyes.

"Yer don't like him much, do you."

"No, I don't. He's rude, overbearing, and very . . . Irish!"

"That's jus' the way yer see him, Jess. He's not always that way."

"I suppose he's like that only when he's dealing with women and children," she suggested, although she knew she was wrong.

He'd been kind to Mickey that first day they met, and gentle and considerate toward Maude. He obviously had a great deal of affection for Belle. He got along with drunks, thieves, and beggars. She seemed to be the only one he disliked intensely.

"He usually gets along with most everyone, unless they cross him. He's a fair man."

"That's my point precisely." She stabbed at the sketch with her pencil.

"Yer jus' outta sorts, 'cause yer tired. That's enough fer t'day, Jess. Yer should be on yer way before dark. Would yer like me to escort yer home?"

It was then she realized that she hadn't seen Burke all day. It was just as well. After their last encounter she'd decided it was best to avoid him as much as possible. He'd been adamant that she wasn't to interfere in the investigation. He wouldn't be at all pleased if he discovered she had no intention of keeping her promise.

"It's not far, I'll be quite safe," she assured Endicott. She didn't want him accompanying her when she left the police station. Before he could press the matter, she hastily packed the tablet and pencils away in the small valise, along with the sketch of Devlin Burke.

He protested. "Mr. Burke said I was to see that yer got 'ome safe."

"It's not necessary, and I'm certain you have somewhere else you should be. Your sister will be expecting you for supper. Or perhaps some young lady?" she suggested, knowing precisely the effect the comment would have.

He blushed, color spreading across his lightly fuzzed cheeks. He didn't quite meet her gaze.

"It ain't no bother, Jess. And it was Mr. Burke's orders."

She could see that she would have to outmaneuver him if she was to get away from the station unescorted.

"I'll need a few minutes of privacy then," she said as she slipped on the patched coat she'd purchased from the ragpicker and tucked the valise under her arm. "I need to use the convenience." He went absolutely crimson to the roots of his hair.

"I'll jus' wait fer yer here then," he stammered.

"I won't be long." Jess smiled, and then left the office for the back of the station, where the water closet was located. She hesitated, hand on the latch, and glanced back over her shoulder.

Endicott closed the file they'd been working on and put it on the stack to be returned to Chief Abberline for safekeeping. His back was momentarily turned toward the doorway. She quickly slipped down the hallway, out of sight.

It was the same hallway that led to the medical examiner's rooms. Visions of Annie Chapman's poor mutilated body swam before her. She pushed past and found another door that opened onto an alley. She let herself out.

It was late afternoon. The sun, a fiery crimson ball in the haze of smoke and soot from nearby smokestacks, had slipped down behind the sagging roofs of factories and the twin spires of a nearby church. The crisp bite of fall was in the air. Fog crept up from the river on cat's feet, muting the late afternoon to gray dusk.

She crossed at the corner, glancing down each street, searching for a creaking cart piled high with rags and discarded garments, with an old man hunched on the driver's seat against the growing night chill, and an equally creaky horse named Delilah. It was almost dark when she finally found them.

She called out. There was no mistaking that dappled gray horse. But the driver didn't seem to hear. She called out again. He turned at the next corner. She hitched up her skirts and ran after him, finally catching him halfway down the next block. He jerked around in surprise, his wrinkled eyes widening as he recognized her.

"Whoa, Delilah! Well, if it ain't the miss wot bought that fine coat th' other day." The old eyes narrowed. "I see yer wearin' it."

"Yes, it's a fine coat. It was a good bargain."

He nodded, lips caved in around gums that were almost toothless. "Yer laid me low with that deal, lass. That piece was worth twice the price."

"That's what I came to discuss with you. I need something else, and I was certain you could help me." He stared at her with narrowed eyes as if he were about to refuse. The reins were tight in his hands. His expression was skeptical.

"I found employment. I can pay you," she assured him.

"How much?" he grumbled. It was late and he wanted to be on his way home before dark.

"A half crown?" She thought it a fair offer merely for information.

"Wot is it yer be needin'?"

"I need information about a man."

He clamped his mouth shut, and she was certain he was going to refuse without hearing anything further.

"I can pay you well for the information, more than you'll earn in a month with that cart."

He seemed to make up his mind then. "It'll cost yer a gold sovereign," he informed her.

"That's more than the price of a dozen coats," she exclaimed.

"Take it or leave it. Information is more costly than rags."

It was highway robbery, and they both knew it. Could she trust him not to simply take her money and disappear.

Probably not, unless she made it worth his while not to.

"Very well," she agreed. "One sovereign now. And three more when you find the man I'm looking for."

Spivey slapped his leg with glee, lips pulling back in a lopsided grin.

"Done! Who's th' bloke yer lookin' for."

"He's called the Mudger. I was told he buys and sells things."

123

Spivey gave her a long look. "Aye, that he does, an' a more dang'rous feller yer'd never want to meet. Sell his dear mother's soul, 'e would, if th' price were ter 'is likin'."

"Won't be easy ter find, an' 'e ain't th' sort wot takes kindly ter people askin' fer him."

"It's important," she insisted.

"Awright," Spivey grumbled. "It'd take me a year to earn that kind o' money with ol' Delilah." He sucked in his lips.

She handed over the single gold sovereign. "Where shall we meet? How will I find you?"

He pocketed the coin and then gathered the reins. He slapped the reins over Delilah's rump and the cart rumbled off.

"Right 'ere, four days from now, at midday. I'll have somethin' fer yer. Ho! there. Get along, wit' yer, Delilah."

She watched as he disappeared into the gathering gloom. The lamplighter was lighting the street lamp at the corner. She quickly walked toward that glowing beacon. It was almost dark now. She hailed a hansom at the corner and gave him the address on Abbington Road.

Lights shone at the ground floor windows as she stepped from the hansom and paid the driver.

"Yer missed supper," Belle snapped, as she cleared plates from the table in the dining room. She disappeared through the door to the kitchen, arms piled high with plates. She didn't return.

Jess climbed the stairs. There was no light glowing beneath the door of Burke's flat. It was locked and silent. As she inserted the key in the lock a small shadow darted from the shadows on the landing and rubbed against her skirt.

When she opened the door Melrose scuttled into the room ahead of her with a twitch of his tail.

"Good evening, to you, too. Please, come in."

Her supper that night was one of the apples she'd purchased from a street vendor. Melrose clearly did not consider apples to be acceptable fare. He turned down her offer, settling himself on the corner of the desk nearest the hearth while she spread out the sketches she'd brought to work on.

She worked through the evening, making composite sketches of the ones she'd made earlier that day, adding a new sketch of the man the landlady had described on her visit to Hanbury Street. She was unable to match it to any of the others.

It was almost midnight when she finally turned down the gaslights. She let Melrose out. He slipped down the stairs, disappearing in the direction of the flat at the back of the house. She left blankets neatly folded on the chairs by the hearth.

They were still folded in the chair the following morning.

The small office where she worked with Endicott was next to Burke's office. When each sketch was finished it was taken to his office and added to the growing stack. He went through the files, providing them with new descriptions, bringing in some of the people so that she could work with them directly.

When he was gone, wherever it was he went off to, she worked with Endicott and Chief Abberline. She overheard comments and conversations, learning a great deal simply by listening.

She discovered that Sergeant Sweeney was more bluff than bluster, and resembled a great overstuffed toy bear.

Endicott was young, eager, and completely loyal to Burke. He worked twice as hard as anyone else. He was conscientious to a fault, and she soon realized, completely infatuated with her. It made him gullible. He believed anything she told him, which made it easier to elude him each day when she left the station.

Sergeant Hobbs was a hard man. He'd been constable for twenty years. He'd been married but his wife had died. Now his work was his life and his fellow constables were his family.

And then there was Mr. Devoe. She'd been warned by Chief Abberline the first day, that she was not to discuss her work with Devoe.

She was working late one morning. Several constables had taken out their kits containing their meals. Others had departed for the local public house. Endicott cleared his throat for the third time. She finally looked up.

"Enough, Jess!" he protested. "I'm wastin' away from hunger, an' yer better have something ter eat as well, or we'll be pickin' yer up off the floor again."

"I'm sorry. I didn't realize it was so late." She studied the sketch she'd been working on.

"Don't wait for me. I'll eat something later."

"You'll waste away if yer don' eat, Jess. There's not much ter yer as it is." Then he brightened with a sudden idea.

"Would yer have supper with me, Jess? Me sister's a right topper cook. She'd like ter meet ya."

She was flattered by the invitation, and a home-cooked meal was tempting. In the past two weeks she'd returned to the house at Abbington Road only once in time for dinner, and then just as everyone sat down to eat. Belle made it clear she was not pleased.

However, she suspected there was more to the invitation than mere concern for her appetite. Endicott's intentions were plastered all over his eager young face.

"That's very kind, but I have something to do tonight."

"Yer always got somethin' ter do, Jess," he complained with more than a little disappointment. "Where is yer goin' all the time?"

"I've made some friends," she answered vaguely, as she made a final change to the sketch she was working on.

"I though yer didn't know nobody in Whitechapel."

"I've met a few people."

"Be careful, Jess," he warned gently. "Don't be out late. I wouldn't want ter see nothin' 'appen ter yer."

She touched his hand with genuine affection and reassured him. "I'll be careful."

He blushed then. If he suspected she wasn't telling him all of it, he said nothing more. He broke open his kit and offered her part of his lunch.

"Sis always packs more 'an I need. I'd be right pleased if yer'd let me share it with yer."

She accepted one of the large slices of fresh bread, with sliced

126

cheese and a fresh apple. They were sharing a companionable picnic spread across the top of the desk when they were interrupted by Inspector Devoe.

He was tall and lean, wearing a suit of clothes far more expensive than a mere inspector's pay allowed. His hair was pale, not a strand out of place. The curved mustache at his upper lip was thick and equally pale, almost disappearing into his upper lip. His eyes were ice blue, an unsettling, opaque color, that made it seem there was nothing behind them.

"Endicott!" he snapped. "Where are the files on the Ripper murders. And where the devil is Burke? I was to accompany him this morning."

The *London Times* had received several letters, supposedly sent from the murderer, ridiculing the efforts of the police, and signed with the name Jack the Ripper, as the sender was calling himself.

There was no way of knowing if there was a connection to the murders, or if the letters were simply the nonsensical ravings of a lunatic mind, or some poor soul craving notoriety.

Endicott gulped down a large chunk of bread. It was dry and lodged in his throat, adding to his obvious discomfort. He finally swallowed, his face flushing with embarrassment.

"Beg pardon, sir. But Mr. Abberline has everythin' locked up in 'is office."

"Where is Chief Abberline?"

"He's out, sir. Had a meetin' 'cross the city."

"And Inspector Burke?" Devoe asked, his elegant mouth thinning tightly.

"Mr. Burke left early, sir." Then Endicott added, "Before you came in."

"A regular occurrence," Devoe bit off with thinly disguised fury. "Everyone is always out and about. With such diligence this case should have been solved weeks ago." His fingers drummed along the desktop, thumping on the stack of sketches. He seized the sketch on top of the stack and examined it, his patrician features edged with mild disdain.

She'd known men like him all her life. They were pompous

and overbearing, impressed with themselves and their effect on others they considered to be their social inferiors. They paid more attention to the fabric of their suit than a woman did to the fabric of a gown. And they gossiped and connived worse than any woman. Men like Devoe were so busy admiring what they considered their own superior wit they were easily outwitted.

"What the devil is this?" he asked.

Endicott glanced at her helplessly, clearly caught in a dilemma. He had his orders from Abberline, but Devoe was also a superior. No matter how he responded, he would be in trouble.

"Well, uh, you'll have ter see Mr. Abberline 'bout that sir."

"I'm not talking with Mr. Abberline at the moment. I'm asking you. If you value your position at all, you will answer me." His hands closed over the sketches that had been so painstakingly drawn.

"They're sketches," Jess informed him bluntly.

"For what purpose?"

When she first met him she thought him handsome, with a certain sophistication and self-assuredness that reminded her of Jason Deverell. She imagined most women found him attractive. But she sensed something cold, almost ruthless about him.

"Who requested this?" he asked.

Endicott's discomfort grew. "Chief Abberline."

"Has this to do with the recent murders of those prostitutes?"

Endicott glanced uneasily over at Jess. "Yes, sir. And other cases," he was deliberately vague, trying to reveal as little as possible about the importance of the sketches.

"Who drew them?"

"Well, uh . . ." Endicott's voice trailed off. He was uncertain how to respond. If he told what he knew he could well face reprimand from Abberline. If he refused, he could well face reprimand, or worse, from Devoe.

"The sketches are mine," she announced, bringing those cold eyes around to her.

"Who the devil are you?"

"Mr. Abberline hired me to make these sketches from

128

descriptions."

He carelessly flipped through the drawings, the paper crackling.

"A meager talent," he sniffed. "What can he possibly hope to learn from this?" He made a dismissive gesture through the air.

"The drawings have already helped locate several witnesses wot was seen at the different murders," Endicott argued. "Chief Abberline an' Mr. Burke are followin' them up now." He realized then that he had perhaps said too much and snapped his mouth shut.

"I fail to see how these will be of any use."

Jess saw the fury in Endicott's eyes. She stepped between them. She reached behind her and grabbed Endicott's arm. She squeezed hard, warning him to say no more.

"The things that people remember about someone often have more to do with emotions and expressions rather than physical features," she explained. "Expressions reveal far more about a person than a scar or the color of eyes, or some other distinctive mark, although those are always helpful."

"Do you believe that you can actually sketch these expressions and produce something useful?" There was a note of derision, along with doubt, in his voice.

"Yes."

"What are you working on now?"

She'd begun a new sketch when he first stepped into the office. She turned it for him to see. The features were as yet indistinct, except for the shape of the face and the eyes.

"What does this reveal?" he demanded.

"Perhaps you can tell me."

He studied the drawing. "A high forehead, possibly above average intelligence," he surmised. "The fellow is a cold person, I think, perhaps dangerous. Not a fellow to be trusted. Definitely the criminal sort."

She kept a straight face. "What makes you say that?" She immediately saw the hint of superiority in the lift of a tawny brow.

"It's in the eyes, of course. One can always tell a person by his eyes." He warmed to his superiority. "I don't like the eyes. I definitely would not trust this man. Probably a thief." Then he looked at her.

"Well? Are you going to finish it."

"I suppose I should," she agreed and quickly sketched, leaving absolutely no doubt as to the identity of the subject.

"There, I believe that does it," she announced, turning the tablet around for Endicott and Devoe to see.

"Cor!" Endicott exclaimed. "It's you, Mr. Devoe. Like lookin' in a mirror, it is!" He beamed and then obviously remembered Devoe's earlier assessment of the preliminary sketch.

"Er . . . wot I mean is, it sorta' looks like yer, sir," he hastily added. Then, "Beg pardon, sir, Sergeant Sweeney needs my help with a bloke." He quickly left the office.

"As I said, a passable talent," Devoe remarked stiffly at the trap she'd cleverly set for him. "And an utter waste of time." Then he turned on his heel and stalked out of the office, calling out to Endicott as he passed him that he wanted to see Burke the moment he returned.

"Yes, sir." Endicott nodded, then muttered to himself, "Acts as if he's chief inspector, the way he's always orderin' everyone about." He looked up at Jess as he came into the office.

"Were yer goin?"

"I'm going home," Jess slipped on the coat she'd purchased from Mr. Spivey. Odd choice of word—home. Stranger still that she thought of it as that.

"I'll go along with yer," he reached for his uniform jacket. "Mr. Burke said I was ter escort yer to 'is place."

She already had her coat buttoned, the valise tucked under her arm. She grabbed her hat and slipped out the door.

"I'll see you tomorrow," she called back over her shoulder, cutting across the station, leaving him to fumble with his coat buttons.

"Jess! Hold on!" But she was already out the front entrance and down the steps.

She darted across the street and ran to the corner, where she

130

hailed a hansom. She gave the driver instructions, and the hansom jerked away from the curb.

Burke stepped from the shadows at a nearby doorway. His dark blue gaze narrowed as he watched that slender figure emerge from the police station and dart across the street.

Where the devil was Endicott? he thought furiously, as he watched her cut across to the opposite corner, and wave down a hansom.

It lurched down the street, the opposite direction from Abbington Road. Endicott was nowhere in sight.

Burke reached the other side of the street in long-legged strides, the hansom still in sight. A second hansom approached. It was occupied. Burke motioned the driver over.

"Already got me fare," the driver informed him and started to guide the horse away from the curb.

"Police," he snapped. "I need this hansom," he informed the driver bluntly. "I'll pay three times the usual fare."

The driver considered it, then shook his head. "Wouldn't be right, guv'ner. 'Sides, 'ow do I know yer are who yer says yer are?"

"You'll know right enough when I have yer certificate to drive this hansom pulled. What's it to be, man?" Burke demanded.

"Right yer are, guv'ner!" the driver exclaimed, thumping on the top of the hansom, and yelling to his passengers, "Out yer go, gents. Police business."

They alighted, grumbling and complaining. Burke reimbursed them for their fare and climbed in after them. "There's another hansom a half block down. Catch it an' there's a full crown for yer trouble."

The driver tipped his hat. "Right yer are, guv'ner." He snapped the reins and the hansom lurched away from the curb. "Fer a crown, I'll race this thing in the Derby. Hold on ter yer 'at and don' stand up."

Chapter Ten

It was late afternoon, no longer light yet not quite dark. A thin ribbon of pale light lingered at the rooftops. The streets were filled with shadows that ran together, plunging the sidewalks and buildings into early darkness.

Carts and wagons rumbled past; drivers making their last deliveries, vendors pulling empty carts home from market, all eager to be home and warming themselves before a fire. She waited for Mr. Spivey in front of a tavern on Middlesex Street.

The traffic thinned, the streets emptied. Twice she heard the sounds of a horse-drawn vehicle approaching, steel-rimmed wheels grinding on the cobbled streets. A produce cart—leaves of limp cabbage falling into the street—slowly rolled past. A hansom, approached from the same direction, but turned before reaching the corner.

The owner of a tanner's shop appeared in his doorway, trailing the acrid stench of animal hides from inside the shop. He shut the door, pulled the shades at the windows, and turned the sign at the door so that it read CLOSED FOR THE DAY.

There was a sudden burst of laughter from the tavern. A man and woman emerged, supporting each other. They crossed the street, somewhat unsteadily, then disappeared inside a lodging house.

She was cold, or perhaps it was the sudden sense of loneliness that engulfed her. She was far from home, dressed like a pauper, completely cut off from anything or anyone familiar. There was no one to rely upon but herself. But there was also a newfound sense of freedom. She could come and go as she pleased and answer to no one if she chose not to. Her artistic talent was appreciated and accepted as it never had been by her family.

But even as she marveled at the irony of her newfound freedom on a darkened corner in a part of London where no proper lady of society would dare venture, she realized there was no such freedom for her sister. Linnie was in some kind of dreadful trouble. Until she found her there was no freedom for either of them.

She pulled the frayed lapels higher about her neck, trying to coax more warmth from the coat, and silently prayed that Mr. Spivey hadn't forgotten their meeting. It was a long way from Abbington Road, too far to walk if he failed to arrive, and she couldn't be certain she would find another hansom that time of day.

The night air went to a soft mist. A shadow separated from the others and lengthened toward her. A man, thickly dressed against the night chill, made his way precariously down the sidewalk in her direction. She stepped out of his way, but he stumbled, grabbing at her to steady himself.

He smelled of stale food, perspiration, and sour ale.

"Outta th' way!" he grumbled, wiping the soiled sleeve of his coat across his nose. Then he looked up and stared at her through bloodshot eyes that slowly focused.

"Sorry, luv!" his tone immediately changed and he swayed closer, reaching for the front of her coat. He smiled, a lopsided, gaping expression.

"How 'bout a toss?"

She had no idea what he was talking about and suspected she didn't want to.

"No! Thank you." She politely refused as she tried to pull free of his fingers. For someone who was obviously quite intoxicated he was surprisingly strong. She finally pulled free.

He stood there, swaying about unsteadily yet remaining upright, as if his feet were anchored in cement while the rest of his body kept moving. He stared at her with an odd expression, then hiccupped, belched, and made a dismissive gesture through the air with his hand.

"No matter. Don't s'pose I could raise ol' Harry t'night anyways," he muttered, exhaling a thick cloud of fumes. "Too much gin does it every time." Then he gave her a gaping smile filled with something that might have been regret if he had been sober, and staggered off down the sidewalk, singing off-key, hiccupping loudly, and having great difficulty with his legs.

Toss indeed! she thought as she turned abruptly and headed in the opposite direction. And what had he meant by *old Harry?*

She turned at the sound of an approaching horse cart. Mr. Spivey pulled Delilah to a stop at the curb.

"I thought you might have forgotten," she exclaimed with relief as she ran to the cart.

Mr. Spivey grunted in response. "Thought about it," he admitted bluntly. "Damned cold out this evenin'. Winter's comin'." Then he gave her a sharp look from beneath ragged brows.

"Yer got th' rest of th' money?"

"Yes! I have it here," she replied. "Do you have the information?"

He nodded. "I got it, right enough. Let me see them coins first."

She pulled a small bundle, wrapped in a handkerchief, from her coat pocket. She unwrapped it in the light from a nearby street lamp that had already been lit. Mr. Spivey's eyes glowed the color of the golden coins. He nodded.

"Th' Mudger is stayin' at one o' his places over on Aldgate. Number eighteen. He has a flat there where he stays sometimes. Been there fer the last several days."

"Is he there now?"

Spivey shrugged. "He was there late yesterday. Can't say 'bout t'day."

Frustration returned. What if his information was wrong? How would she find him again?

"Can you take me there?"

He shook his head. "Yer got the information. That was th' deal."

"Yes, I know. But I may not be able to find another hansom this time of night. I'll give you another sovereign if you'll take me to him." She saw the greedy glint in his eyes.

"O' all right," he finally said. "I've already missed me supper. Climb aboard," he snapped. "Ain't got all night."

A hansom sat around the adjacent corner. As the cart rumbled off down the street the driver called down from his perch behind the cab.

"Wot yer want ter do, guv'ner?"

Burke watched the ragpicker's cart until it turned at the next corner. "Follow, but far enough back so as not to draw attention."

Jess stepped down from the cart. Before handing the extra coin to Mr. Spivey, she asked, "Could you possibly wait for a few minutes?"

"Can't be stayin'," he snapped. " 'Tis late. Got ter be gettin' 'ome. This be outta me way, as it is." He pocketed the additional sovereign with the others and gathered the reins. In a softer tone he added, "Yer can get a lift at the corner. 'Tis right busy at night." Then he whistled to Delilah.

She stood for several minutes, watching until the darkness absorbed Delilah and the cart, and the distant creaking of wheels was smothered by the gathering mist.

The street was deserted. Lights appeared in some of the windows of the surrounding buildings, like eyes that glowed and watched. There was a loud crash, and a cat squalled from an adjacent alley. It was a frightening sound, like a woman's terrified scream. It set her already taut nerves on edge. She hurriedly looked for number 18.

The numbers were carved over the doors. She tried the latch. The door opened and she let herself into the building. There was a door down the hallway to the right, a stairway to the left. Taking a deep breath, she knocked at the door. There was no answer, and she knocked a second time. The door was finally jerked open, and a face appeared in the narrow space.

"Wot yer want?"

In the shadow of the doorway, concealed from the light, it was difficult to determine anything about the face. The hair was scraggly and long and the skin smooth, which suggested it might be a woman and not the person she was looking for.

"I'm looking for someone called the Mudger," she inquired hesitantly.

Beady eyes stared back at her with undisguised suspicion. "Ain't nobody 'ere by that name." The door started to close. Jess stopped it with her hand.

"I was told he's staying here. I have to see him," she insisted firmly, and then added, "He's expecting me." The door opened fractionally.

"Oh, he is, is he?" A pinched face poked out through the narrow crack. Jaundiced eyes scrutinized her. The old woman sniffed. "Might be at that. There's women traipsin' through 'ere all times of the day and night, but that ain't no concern o' mine. Top o' th' stairs, dearie, second door ter the left." And then the door slammed shut in her face.

"Thank you very much," Jess muttered.

The foyer was dimly lit, with only a single gas lantern at the far end of the hall. She turned toward the stairway. A hand clamped over her mouth. An arm grabbed her about the waist, cutting high under her ribs, and pulling her off her feet. She was dragged out of the building, down the steps, and then hauled into the dark recessed doorway of an adjacent building.

Terror sliced through her brain, recalling images of Annie Chapman's mutilated body. Then it churned into her throat, but there was no scream. She was suffocating.

She struggled, clawing at the arm about her waist, kicking with both feet, at the same time she tried to jerk her head free of that smothering hand.

"Jess! Be still!" A voice hissed.

The sound of her name finally penetrated the fear, logic taking over, forcing its way into her paralyzed brain. It was someone she knew.

Burke!

She quit struggling then, and he removed his hand from her mouth, setting her to the ground.

"You!" she whispered furiously as she whirled around. "What are you doing here?"

"I might ask the same of you."

"You followed me!" she accused.

"It seemed the thing to do since you decided to disobey my orders."

"Your orders . . . !" she gasped. "You forget, Inspector, I am not one of your officers or constables to be ordered about."

"That's right yer not. Which means yer have even less reason to be here. Now, what *are* you doin' here?"

She smothered back the fury that tightened in her throat. "I found the Mudger," she announced. "I came to ask him questions about my sister."

"I know all about the Mudger. Two of my men found him yesterday."

"Yesterday?" she stared at him. "Why didn't you tell me? Have you spoken with him? What did he say about the man who was seen at Annie Chapman's flat? Did he know the man's name?"

Burke clamped a hand over her mouth to silence her. "He hasn't told me anythin' yet. He wasn't here yesterday. Imagine my surprise when I followed you here."

He was not amused. She dragged his hand away. "Why didn't you tell me?" she demanded.

"I'm not obliged to tell you anythin'. Yer not involved in this case. Yer simply workin' for the chief inspector," he pointed out in a tight voice. "What the devil were you thinkin' comin' here like this, alone, this time o' night? When I specifically told you to stay out of it."

"And I told you that I'll do whatever's necessary to find my sister. If I'd known you had already found the Mudger, it wouldn't have been necessary for me to come here," she pointed out the obvious.

"Well, it's not necessary now." He grabbed her by the arm and whirled her around, propelling her down the sidewalk, away from the building at number 18 Aldgate Street.

He recalled the exchange he'd seen between her and the ragpicker, the coins glinting dully in the light of the street lamp. It was more than she could possibly have earned working for Chief Abberline. Where had she come by that amount of money?

An ugly thought nagged at the back of his mind—there was only one way a woman in Whitechapel acquired that kind of money. His fingers tightened about her arm.

From the moment he first met her, he'd felt an almost overwhelming need to protect her. She had a way of looking at him with her heart in her eyes, all the emotion exposed and naked in those green depths. He realized that it was all a lie.

She was a terrific little actress. She put Lily Langtry to disgrace. He'd been taken in by that soft look behind her eyes—a young woman newly arrived in London, without a penny to her name, desperately searching for her sister.

He'd been had—a person who shilled, connived, and lied with the best of them—and he didn't much like it.

He dragged her down the sidewalk and around the corner. A hansom waited at the curb. He jerked open the door, picked her up and tossed her inside. When she sprang forward to protest, he slammed the door in her face.

"Take her to the Commercial Street police station," he ordered the driver. "Ask for Sergeant Hobbs. He's to escort her to number Twenty-four Abbington Road."

She shoved the doors open. "You can't do this! I won't be sent off. I have to find out what he knows about Annie!" Burke ignored her as he continued his instructions to the driver.

"Don't stop till you arrive at the station, an' don't let her out of yer sight until you hand her over to Sergeant Hobbs." Then to insure that his orders would be carried out, "She's a dangerous sort, wanted by the police for several crimes. Do as I say and you'll have a handsome fare fer yer trouble."

Then he added as an afterthought. "If she gives you any trouble, yer have my permission to take that buggy whip to her backside."

Buggy whip indeed!

Her hands shook as she paced the floor, recalling Burke's parting words. Each time she turned and paced back across the small sitting room of the flat, she came face-to-face with Sergeant Hobbs.

He was like a great, large mastiff with a thick, wide forehead, broad, flat nose, and a powerful, square jaw. His skin was craggy and hung in thick pockets at his cheeks. He was thickset with powerful arms and wide hands. Not the sort of man one argued with or tried to charm.

He'd been silent during the ride over from the station. Before that, he hadn't said more than two words to her. When the driver gave him Burke's instructions, he simply nodded, grabbed his hat, and climbed aboard.

Hobbs had lit the fire at the hearth. It appeared he assumed he would be there for several hours. Belle brought supper up to them, without her usual complaints about the lateness of the hour. Hobbs ate heartily, mopping sauce from the rich stew with a fat, puffy dumpling, while she continued to pace the room.

"Yer should eat," he said, around the mouthful of dumpling. It was the first he'd spoken since they left the Commercial Street station. "There's hardly no flesh on yer bones as 'tis."

She smiled, moved by his unexpected concern for her. She reminded herself that he had once been married, and according to Endicott he continued to grieve over that loss. Appearances could be deceiving. God knows her appearance was more than a little deceiving.

Still, it was difficult to imagine a man of Hobbs's size and gruff manner capable of tender feelings. Just as it was difficult to imagine Inspector Burke capable of any concern for anyone, much less a benevolent attitude when it came to meting out punishments.

When she thought of his parting threats, her appetite waned to a faintly nauseated sensation in the pit of her stomach.

"I'm not hungry," she said and silently worried just how angry Burke might be when he returned. He didn't seem the type to sit and calmly discuss some point of disagreement.

Would he have her dismissed for interfering? He'd been angry enough, and heaven knows he'd told her in no uncertain terms that she wasn't to involve herself.

She decided he wouldn't go that far. They had made tremendous progress with the sketches she'd provided them so far. But she was certain he wouldn't simply let the matter go. He was too angry with her — angry to the point of violence.

She saw it in those cold, hard eyes, heard it in the furious quiver of his voice and the thickened accent that wrapped around each angry word, felt it in the bruises his fingers left on her arms.

He'd been furious enough to strike her. If she wasn't quite so angry herself, she would have been more cautious. Once again her rebellious temper had gotten the better of her.

Endicott had said that Burke was a fair man. She wondered.

What would he say when he returned? More important, what would he do?

Would *he* follow his own recommendation to the driver? The possibility made her uneasy. But unless he carried a buggywhip around with him, she considered it unlikely. She argued with herself that physical punishment was archaic, something that belonged in medieval times. Although she was aware that it happened on rare occasions even within polite society—a swollen cheek, or a faintly discolored eye that necessitated careful application of powder, a certain stiffness when one walked, and the too-hastily offered excuse that one had been clumsy and stumbled, or collided with an opened door.

She didn't understand women who tolerated such treatment. No one had ever laid a hand on her—not her father, or any man within her circle of friends. But this wasn't Carrington Square, and the man she was dealing with wasn't her father, or one of the gentlemen of her acquaintance.

"Yer goin' ter wear a hole in that carpet," Hobbs pointed out, as he poured two cups of tea. He held out one of the cups to her.

She took it, not because she wanted the tea, but simply because she needed something to do with her hands. It had been over three hours since Burke threw her bodily into the hansom with those specific instructions.

"Do you think he found the Mudger?"

"Mr. Burke usually gets wot he's after. An' he knew fer a fact that the Mudger was stayin' over on Aldgate. He was waitin' ter catch him there unawares. That is until you decided to go callin'."

She preferred not to discuss that particular point. "What sort of person is the Mudger?"

"Oh, he's a right miserable sort, an' 'e can be difficult to deal with. He's as hard as they come, streetwise, and twice as mean. He'll give the inspector a bit of a go. But in the end, Mr. Burke will get the information 'e wants, or 'ave the Mudger takin' up new accommodations at Newgate."

"You respect him," she said with more than a little surprise. She'd learned from the beginning that very little respect existed between the uniformed constables and the plain-clothed inspectors. There was an invisible barrier that separated them, as if the inspectors considered themselves above the men who walked the streets and alleys of London.

One notable exception was Mr. Abberline. The men he commanded seemed to respect him enormously. He was soft-spoken, amiable, and fair. He didn't hold himself above others.

On the other hand, there was widespread resentment for Mr. Devoe. He had come from another department with the home office. He didn't live in Whitechapel. He belittled everyone with the exception of Chief Abberline, for obvious reasons. He was considered an outsider, an intruder, who had no real understanding or empathy for the people on the streets, or the men he worked with.

Burke didn't seem to fit into either mold.

Hobbs set his cup down with surprising care for a man of his size. His black eyes fixed on her, heavy pouches of his face settling into a thoughtful expression.

"Aye, I respect him. He's a good man. Don't hold 'imself above others jus' because he made 'nspector. He don' 'esitate to get 'is 'ands dirty. Like them murders—nasty business. And goin' after the Mudger. Others might send someone else round ter question 'im. Not Mr. Burke. Takes care o' things himself, no matter th' risk. Not afraid of any man. An' he 'as a feelin' fer the common folk, the ones that go hungry, an' sufferin'."

She remembered the look on his face, when he'd taken her to identify the woman who turned out to be Annie Chapman. There had been a fleeting compassion in his eyes that was almost painful. She had seen it before that, with the little boy Mickey. And she'd seen it when he looked at her.

"Comes from the streets 'imself," Hobbs went on to explain, "He understands wot it's like fer the poor wretches, havin' ter steal an' whore themselves jus' ter survive." His eyes narrowed thoughtfully. "He's a fair man, too, tho' yer might not think it at first. Comes off a bit 'ard sometimes, but that's because o' where he come from. No 'ome as a child, and a bit of a tangle with the law himself."

"A fair man," she repeated thoughtfully. Endicott had said the same thing of him. She wondered how one remained fair growing up as he had.

"I hope you're right about that."

"A bit concerned, are yer now?" he asked. Something that very much resembled the beginning of a smile twitched at the edge of his mouth.

"He was quite angry," she admitted.

Hobbs nodded. "That's the Irish in him. Makes fer a right nasty temper. But there's no one else ol' Hobbs would rather 'ave with 'im on th' streets. He's a good man with 'is fists, quicker with a knife."

"I suppose I should consider myself fortunate that all he mentioned was a buggywhipping."

"There's some truth to that," he agreed, then surprised her by saying, "My Sara was a headstrong woman. Ev'ry now and then we use' ter go round and round, arguin', shoutin' at one t'other. On occasion 'twas necessary ter let her know who the boss was."

She shivered at the thought of the damage a man the size of Hobbs might be capable of.

"Don't look so distressed. I never did her no real harm. An' whenever we went at it, she threatened me with a teapot."

She looked at the chipped teapot that sat on top of the small table. She could have sworn he chuckled.

"We went through a sizable number of teapots. She had right deadly aim. But afterwards . . ." his voice was low and stunned her with its sudden softness. "Th' makin' up is half the fun o' it." He looked down at the teapot then. "I'd buy a cartful of teapots ter have it all back again."

It was a surprisingly tender moment. She didn't know what to say she was so taken aback. Then he looked back up at her again, his face set with those heavy pockets, his beady eyes fastened on her.

"A good argument never hurt no one. Clears the air, gets things out in the open."

"I hope you're right," she said. Then she heard the downstairs door opening and closing.

"That'll be Mr. Burke," Hobbs announced and stood.

"Wouldn't you like another cup of tea?" she offered, hoping to delay him at least until she had a chance to determine Burke's mood.

He stood and buttoned his uniform jacket. He shook his head. " 'Tis late. Best be on me way." Then he winked at her.

"The pot's empty. Sara always said they was easier ter get her aim right when they was empty."

She smiled weakly. "I'll try to remember that."

A few moments later, Burke came through the door. His overcoat was covered with a sheen of moisture, his dark hair was damp, and there were deep lines at the corners of his mouth.

"That will be all, Hobbs." Not a word of greeting, just dismissal, and it seemed that none was expected. All her cool, collected composure slipped by several degrees.

"Good night, sir." Hobbs glanced at her briefly, then added, "See yer and the miss in the mornin', sir." Then he let himself out.

Burke took off the heavy overcoat and hung it on a hook at the door. He unwound the woolen scarf about his neck and emptied his pockets. Then he crossed to the hearth and warmed his hands at the fire. Silence drew out interminably, and her nerves grew taut. It was impossible to guess what sort of mood he was in.

Finally she could stand it no longer. At the risk of making him angry all over again she had to know if he'd learned anything.

"Did you find the Mudger?"

Without turning around, without so much as looking up, he nodded, "Aye." One word.

She went to the hearth. "Did you ask him about the man at Annie's flat?"

"Aye."

Frustration mounted. "Did he know him? Did he give you a name? What did he tell you?"

"Why did you go there tonight?"

She blinked at him. "I explained that already. I went to find out what he knew about Annie."

"Without telling me," he said bluntly.

So, this was the way it was to be. She'd hoped he would be in an amiable mood. The anger was still there. She heard it in his voice.

"It seems you already knew where to find him," she pointed out, avoiding a direct answer.

"Why didn't you tell me of it *first?*" he persisted with bulldog tenacity.

"Because you wouldn't have allowed me to accompany you."

"Precisely!" his hand came down on the top of the small table, sending teapot and cups rattling.

"I explained that you weren't to be involved in this. You were only to do the sketches Abberline hired you for. Yer can't be goin' off on yer own. It's too damned dangerous."

"You've been looking for him for days, and weren't able to find him," she pointed out. "I wasn't certain he would be there. I didn't see the risk in finding out if he was there."

"Didn't you?" he shouted, not giving her the opportunity to answer. "And I suppose when you found him, yer intended to politely say 'excuse me, but Mr. Burke want's ter speak with you about three murdered women. If you'd be so kind as ter stay here 'til I can bring him round.' "

"Well, no . . . not that precisely."

Not that precisely! What *precisely* did yer think you would do when you got there? Do you have any notion the sort o' man the Mudger is? Do you know wot it is he does? The nature of his work?"

He was more than angry, he was furious. She heard the subtle change in his voice, the dangerous edge that went suddenly low and warned that it might not be wise to argue further.

"Do you?" he demanded, not about to let it go.

"I was told that he buys and sells things," she answered hesitantly. "I suppose he's a merchant of some kind." And then with a small defiant tilt of her chin she added, "Not unlike Mr. Spivey, who was very kind and helpful." She thought she made her point very well. After all, Mr. Spivey had been no threat to her at all.

"Good God, Jess! Have yer no sense at all? The Mudger is a dangerous man, the lowest sort of filth that crawls in the gutters."

How dare he say that to her, as if she were a helpless child who needed protection from herself. At that moment the teapot looked very inviting. Her fingers itched to feel that smooth porcelain surface just long enough to hurl it at his head.

"I have sense, Inspector!" Her fingers curled tightly into the palm of her hand. "Enough sense to find the Mudger without your help! Enough to realize that without him I may never find my sister!"

"Enough to know that he buys and sells women jus' like you? And for a helluva lot less than yer paid the ragpicker," he informed her bluntly. He saw the shock and momentary confusion in her eyes and took advantage of it as he turned on her.

"Aye, Jess, he's a procurer. He provides women to other men for a price. That's the sort of merchant he is." He jerked her chin up with his fingers, forcing her to look at him.

"Do you have any notion what might have happened?" he demanded, his fingers tightening, as if he could physically make her understand.

His face was very near hers, his eyes dark and angry. There was something in his voice that seemed to ache out of him from some deep, dark place that held all his secrets.

"Why should it matter to you?" she cried out, glaring up at him. Then she pushed at his hand and jerked away from him. She was angrier than she'd ever been in her life. She didn't owe him any explanations, and he wasn't about to receive any.

She strode furiously to the bedroom, determined to end the conversation. She heard his softly muttered curse. Too late, she realized that the anger had changed.

He caught her just inside the bedroom door and spun her around. His eyes had gone to black: dark, emotionless, cold as if something lay dead behind them. His fingers tightened around her wrist until she thought the bones would crumble.

"It shouldn't matter at all," he repeated, his voice dangerously calm. "But God help me, it does. And somehow I have to make you understand."

She stepped back, twisting her wrist, hoping to dislodge his fingers, hearing only part of what he said. She was too furious to hear the subtle warning. He jerked her toward the bed and flung her down on top of it.

"If you won't listen to reason, then by heaven, I'll find another way to make you understand!"

Chapter Eleven

She choked with fury as she came up off the mattress, struggling against the downy thickness that tried to swallow her. He grabbed her, hauling her upright with no more effort than if she were a rag doll.

She kicked at him, trying to crawl to the other side. His fingers clamped around both her wrists. In less effort that it would take to draw the quilt, he dragged her back across the bed.

Her hair had come down about her shoulders, her shirtwaist was dislodged from the band at her skirt. The hem rode up around her knees.

"I hate you!" she screamed at him, taking aim at his head, wishing for all the world that she had that teapot.

"Be that as it may, Jess. You have to learn to obey yer betters."

Unable to push her disheveled hair back from her eyes, she blew furiously at it. "I suppose you think you qualify for that?"

"Aye, at the moment. And since you refuse to listen to reason, you'll have to learn the hard way. Like a misbehaved child." The fingers of one hand clamped over both wrists.

"How dare you treat me this way! Let me go!" she screamed with all the ladylike effrontery that twenty-four years of indoctrination into polite society had provided.

"Don't be givin' yourself airs, Jess. I told you that I'd do whatever was necessary to make you understand." He sat at the edge of the bed and dragged her across his bent legs with a jerk of her arms, driving the air from her lungs as she collapsed, his knees driving into the soft apex below her ribs.

When she was finally able to draw a breath again, she demanded furiously, "What do you think you're doing?"

"Lesson number one!" His large hand came down across her bottom with a loud, resounding whack.

Her entire body convulsed, her wrists jerking against his grasp. She was so stunned she couldn't speak for several moments. When she did, she was more than furious.

"How dare you!" she spat out, twisting and thrashing across his bent legs.

"Two!"

She went rigid as his hand fell a second time. Her teeth were tightly clenched as she gathered her strength. She tried to jerk her wrists free again.

"I hate you!"

"Yer entitled to that," he told her. "Three!"

"Let go of me! You, you . . . bloody peeler!"

His hand hesitated momentarily in midair, then he concentrated once more on his task. She had to be taught a lesson, and short of locking her up . . .

"Four!"

She shrieked and struggled all the harder, trying to leverage her elbows into his lap. It was no use. In growing frustration and pain, she sputtered, "Damn you! You, you . . ."

"Five!"

"Damned arrogant. . . . Irishman!" she screamed.

"You can do better than that," he encouraged her. His hand came down again.

"Six!"

She stiffened and jerked as his flattened hand connected with her bottom. There was no curse, no scream this time only a stunned gasp that was immediately choked off.

Seven, eight, nine . . .

Her body tensed for each blow, but she remained silent. The only thing she allowed him was an occasional painful gasp when his hand fell and she could no longer control the pain that radiated from her bottom. In between, she gathered herself, bracing for the next one, stubbornly refusing to give in to the screams she wanted to hurl at him. She would rather die than allow him that satisfaction.

He mercilessly counted each stroke. She forced herself not to think of the pain that jarred through her body, but instead concentrated on the reason she'd come to this part of London in the first place.

Then she was aware that he was no longer counting.

He had let go of her wrists, and took hold of her arms, gently lifting her off his knees and shifting her across his lap.

She sat stiff and unbending, her face turned away, refusing to look at him. It took all her strength to bring her ragged breathing back under control along with her turbulent emotions. No one had ever struck her before.

She would hate him later. At the moment it was all she could do not to break down crying hysterically.

Her shoulders trembled from the effort it took just to remain where she was and not allow him to see how very close she was to losing that last shred of control. She wouldn't allow him that further humiliation.

He cursed under his breath. He'd never known anyone to be so willful, so mule-headed, so . . . He could have sworn that she was Irish. She had that same stubborn streak that he knew only too well. She sat absolutely still and so rigid that her body trembled from the force of it. Her eyes were clamped shut and she had bitten down on her bottom lip, cutting tiny white half-moons cut into the tender flesh.

A single tear squeezed from between her closed lids and trickled down her cheek. One tear that completely dissolved all his anger. It slowly slipped down the curve of her flushed cheek, leaving a pale, wet streak. Then it caught at the edge of her tightly clenched jaw.

That single tear unleashed a flood of emotion. He lifted his hand to her cheek, touching the wetness. He lifted her chin with his fingers and tried to turn her face toward him. She jerked her chin away, refusing to look at him. He persisted.

"You gave me no choice, lass," he gently explained. Though she tried to hold herself from him, he finally pulled her against him and put his arms around her. He rubbed her back as he held her, stroking small circles in the taut, rigid muscles.

She shuddered as a sigh caught in her throat, much like a child who'd disobeyed and then worn herself out with tears. Eventually there was less resistance in her taut body. He tucked her head beneath his chin. She seemed small and fragile, as if she might break.

Her breath caught in a small, dry sob and she hated herself for it. Inside, she held herself very tightly, the pain wrapped around other emotions. But the soothing motions of his hand on her back slowly wrapped around the pain and eased it.

She wanted to curl into him, to lay her hand against his chest and feel the warmth of his body. Doubt, uncertainty, and fear ached cold and hollow inside her. She'd been so cold for so long. She wanted it to go away. She wanted to feel safe and secure again. At that moment, in spite of the fact that he'd spanked her soundly—a fact that she wasn't at all certain she would ever forgive him for—she felt safe and protected, as if everything really would be all right as long as his arms were about her.

His lips moved against her hair. Her skin was warm and flushed, the tears dried to pale streaks.

"I never meant to hurt you, little one," he said almost apologetically, his cheek pressed against her hair.

It was soft, like dark satin beneath his beard-roughened skin. He rarely felt regret. He felt it now. But as much as he disliked the manner of punishment, he wouldn't apologize for the need of it.

Her breath came out in jerky whispers of tiny sobs all strung together. She didn't fight or pull away. He sensed the emotions she struggled with; the anger, pain, and humiliation. She was like a small wounded animal that needed to be kept safe.

"It won't happen again. I promise you that." He meant every word. For reasons he couldn't begin to understand, he knew he'd rather die than ever hurt her again. "There'll be no more need of any punishment as long as I have your word that you'll not interfere again."

She stiffened and jerked away from him. Her slender shoulders trembled at the effort it took. She looked at him then, her eyes wide, dark as moss in forest shadows.

She thought that he had finally understood, that in spite of her mistake in judgment in going to the Mudger's flat, she wouldn't—couldn't—refrain from doing whatever was necessary to find her sister.

She realized that once again, she was wrong. It took a great deal of effort to keep her voice under control.

"I have to find my sister," she said. Let him assume whatever he chose from that. She immediately felt the muscles in his legs go rigid. His warning was gentle but firm.

"You'll not interfere in any way," he warned. She stood then, a bit shakily, and stepped away from him, deciding that it was safer to put distance between them.

"I won't go near the Mudger again," she agreed, giving him that small concession.

He came up off the bed, too smart to be trapped with that carefully worded promise. "You'll do nothing," he said flatly.

She heard the anger that slowly came unraveled in his voice. She braced herself, gathering her own strength.

"I'll do whatever is necessary to find her."

"Damn!" he shouted. "Have you learned nothin' at all! I explained the danger to you. I won't allow you to be involved."

"Have *you* learned nothing at all?" she demanded. "My sister's life is in danger. You once said you knew what it was to lose something that you loved. If you understand that, then you must understand how I feel."

"Understandin' is one thing. Common sense is another. And you've proved you have none." He stood over her, his face taut. His fingers curled into tight fists. For a moment she thought he was going to grab her and spank her again. She saw the conflict in every rigid muscle, felt it in the angry words. She sensed that it took every last ounce of control he had not to drag her over to that bed again. But he didn't.

Instead, he swore vividly and then suddenly turned and walked to the door, as if he could no longer trust himself to stand that close and not strike her. He stopped at the door, and turned to glare back at her.

"I'll keep my promise not to do you physical harm, Jess. But by God, I'll find another way to keep you out of this!" he vowed.

"Get out!" she shouted furiously at him, disregarding for the moment that the room she was ordering him out of was in fact his bedroom.

The expression on his face was hard, equally stubborn. "Aye, Jess, I'll get out. You can have it all to yourself. But don't even think about sneakin' out and goin' callin' on the Mudger tonight, or any other time for that matter. I won't be far away, jus' downstairs."

Downstairs, with Belle Rossi? For some inexplicable reason that, more than his threat to stop her, completely infuriated her.

"It makes no difference to me where you sleep!" she shouted, that fragile thread on control finally snapping. "You may sleep, downstairs, upstairs, or in the street for all I care. After tonight, I won't impose on you any further, Mr. Burke." If she wasn't so tired and sore, she would have left then.

"Do you really think that makes any difference, Jess?" he asked.

His voice had gone suddenly soft, low, and dangerous. She realized that it *didn't* matter where she stayed. As long as she worked for Chief Abberline, he would be able to find her. And he knew as well as she did, that she wasn't about to walk away from the strongest link to finding her sister.

She saw the look of satisfaction that glinted in those blue eyes and she hated him all over again for his smugness.

"Good night then, Jess. Pleasant dreams," he said with complete self-assurance and closed the door behind him.

She was so furious that her hands shook. The tears she wouldn't allow herself to cry earlier welled in her eyes.

Damn Irishman! she thought. At that moment, she wished she could get her hands on that teapot.

Then her watery gaze fell on the washbowl and pitcher on top of the washstand beside the bed. She grabbed the pitcher and threw it.

It hit the door at the precise location of his head only moments before with a loud crash, and shattered into hundreds of pieces.

Chapter Twelve

"This is Jimmy Cassidy of the *London Times*," Mr. Abberline made the introductions in his office. Jess had just arrived. Burke sat beside the desk while Sinjin Devoe took up a position of authority beside Abberline. Jimmy Cassidy nodded a greeting, coming partway out of his chair in front of the desk.

"Mr. Cassidy has been writing articles about the murders for the newspaper," he went on to explain. He seemed to choose his words carefully, his hands folded before him on the desk, his expression somber, his tone edged with an almost imperceptible disapproval that she had learned to pick up on over the past few weeks working with him.

The relationship between the police and the writers for the newspapers was uneasy at best. The Ripper case, as it was now called, had proven to be very difficult to solve. Lurid stories with sensationalized details of the three murders had appeared in all the newspapers. Undoubtedly Jimmy Cassidy was responsible for some of those articles, which fueled the fear over the unsolved murders and perpetuated the panic that had spread across the whole of London.

Jimmy was young. He looked hardly older than Jess, long-legged and wiry, with a thatch of red hair, millions of freckles, and inquisitive blue eyes. He nodded.

"Please ter make yer acquaintance. Mr. Abberline tells me that you've made some sketches of possible suspects."

She avoided looking at Burke, as she had ever since their last argument. She'd decided that the best way to avoid a certain situation was to ignore it. He'd been out on the streets most of the past few days and there had been no opportunity for conversation, not that she had any intention of discussing her intentions regarding her sister. Instead, she glanced expectantly at Mr. Abberline, wondering how she should respond.

It seemed an evasive answer was perhaps best. After all, she didn't care for any undue attention or probing questions from a member of the newspaper staff.

"I've been assisting Chief Abberline at his request. I simply wanted to help any way that I could. It was his suggestion to make sketches from descriptions given by witnesses."

"I've told him of your talents," Abberline went on to explain. "The home office has decided that we should publicize the sketches. Mr. Cassidy and the *Times* have generously extended their cooperation in the matter. We will be working with them on the progress of the investigation."

She looked at the chief inspector with surprise. His gaze met hers briefly and held her in some silent communication. He had previously forbidden everyone involved with the case from speaking to anyone about the details of the investigation, in the hope of preventing widespread panic over the murders. The fewer details that were made public, the greater the possibility they could maintain calm in the city.

He'd been battling interference from the home office for weeks. They wanted results and had sent Sinjin Devoe to accomplish those results, or in the very least keep them apprised of the progress in the case. It hadn't taken long for her to discover that everyone involved in the investigation right down to Sergeant Sweeney, who sat at the front desk, resented Devoe's presence, and maintained a closed brotherhood of silence where the investigation was concerned.

All information had to be cleared through Chief Abberline or Mr. Burke before it was released to anyone. Even her sketches had been kept under lock and key in Abberline's office, except for the composites she worked on in the evenings.

On more than one occasion, Devoe had cornered her about the sketches. Each time, she had lied her way out of a demand to see them, by explaining that she didn't have them. His latest demand had come the day before. She could only assume that he'd met with the same resistance from Chief Abberline. She wondered if Devoe had his hand in the involvement by the newspapers. He seemed quite satisfied with the fact that Abberline was now in a position where he was being forced to cooperate and produce the sketches, as well as all available information.

Chief Abberline was clearly caught on the horns of a dilemma: reveal too much about the murders and he might be aiding the murderer about whom they still knew almost nothing; reveal too little, and rumor and speculation abounded with stories worse than the truth, bringing the home office down on his head.

At any time they could remove the case from his authority. He walked a tightrope that was being drawn tighter with each day that passed and no suspect was arrested. Still, though his face was drawn and tight, his voice was even, perfectly controlled. Not so Burke. He was furious with this latest mandate that had come down from the home office.

It was there in the hard lines at his mouth, the irritated shift of his long-legged body, the cold glare he fastened on Devoe who was in conversation with Jimmy. Abberline laid a restraining hand on his arm and gave him a hard look. Burke restrained that dark Irish temper.

"Mr. Cassidy has received letters from the man claiming to be the murderer," Abberline explained. "The most recent just yesterday. He's agreed to share the contents with us, along with information that he's learned, as a fair trade for our cooperation."

"That's right," Jimmy spoke up enthusiastically. "Signed himself, Jack the Ripper, just like the first time. This letter will run in tomorrow's edition."

"Then you believe that it's authentic?" Jess asked, knowing there had been doubts about the first letter, whether or not it had actually been sent by the person responsible for the murders, or merely some pathetic unbalanced person who simply claimed to be the murderer.

"We can't ignore the possibility that this man may indeed be the murderer," Devoe interjected with authority. "He seems to know a great many details about all the murders. Now he's made the suggestion that the police are involved in an attempt to hide some of the facts." His gaze leveled on Devlin Burke. Burke started out of his chair, but Abberline stopped him with a restraining hand.

"We've all been under a great deal of strain, trying to find the murderer. I won't tolerate any criticism of this district or any of my men. If you have accusations to make, Mr. Devoe, then I suggest that you make them directly to me and I will deal with them in an appropriate manner."

Jess was uneasy. From the moment she'd first met him she hadn't liked Devoe. He was too cold and calculating, that gray shaded expression behind his eyes, so that one could never be certain what he was thinking.

Abberline was precise, methodical, painstakingly honest and forthright. In the short time she'd worked with him, she'd learned that he was genuinely kind.

Devlin Burke was volatile. Behind the facade of that cool, blue gaze was a restless energy and a temper barely held in check. He was a complex man, who gave very little of himself away, as if he had to hold it all in very carefully. There was more hidden away inside about himself, than he revealed to anyone. In his own way, he was honest, forthright, and completely loyal to those he trusted. Those he didn't, she suspected didn't want to meet up with him. She suspected that he believed in revenge against those who betrayed him.

Hard edges or smooth ones, Devoe was a person not to be trusted. Everything he revealed about himself had a contrasting side, an opposite, so that one never knew him, or what to expect of him. He was the sort who held himself from everyone else about him and trusted no one. The cool reserve that others mistook for disdain, she suspected was a carefully concealed ruthlessness.

She didn't like Sinjin Devoe at all, and for reasons that had no substance. It was simply a feeling she had, an artist's observation of the subtle nuances of character.

Tension in the office drew out. If not for Abberline's not too-subtle reminder she suspected that Burke would have thrown Sinjin Devoe out of the police station bodily. Abberline understood just how dangerous that could be. Devoe was not a person to cross unless one's back was always guarded.

Devoe backed down. He smiled at her then; it was not the first time she'd been exposed to that cold, calculating charm.

"We felt, in the interest of cooperation, that now might be the time to publicize some of your sketches, my dear. In the hope that someone might recognize one of them."

She glanced briefly at Abberline, saw the subtle warning expression in his eyes, then his gaze focused on a point across the office. The message had been clear: *tell him nothing of importance.*

She answered discreetly, knowing full well that her only chance to find her sister lay with Abberline.

"It's been a very slow and difficult process. I've made several sketches, but there have been dozens of descriptions, all greatly varied. It would be premature to focus on any one sketch at this time. There simply haven't been any two descriptions alike." She thought of mentioning the composite sketches she'd been experimenting with and immediately decided against it.

"I've assured Mr. Cassidy that he has our full cooperation, as long as it doesn't jeopardize any aspect of the investigation." Abberline went on to explain. "He's asked to see something today. I'm certain there must be *something* you can show him."

"Yes," she answered hesitantly. "I believe that I have a half dozen which are ready." She understood what he hadn't said—show Jimmy Cassidy sketches, any sketches, as long as they weren't of anyone identifiable. She could only guess that it was a ploy to keep Jimmy occupied and the home office temporarily pacified.

"I would like to see the sketches as well," Devoe interjected. "The home office is most interested in any progress. The sketches should run in the newspaper tomorrow if possible, along with the letter. That is, if they are of any substance."

"Very well, that will be all then," Abberline cut in, dismissing everyone. Then, as if it were an afterthought, "Jess, may I speak with you a moment?"

She waited by the door as everyone left. When they were gone, Abberline indicated that she was to take a chair. He closed the door.

"I've been very pleased with your work, my dear. Inspector Burke explained the progress that you've made with the composites. Fascinating process."

"Thank you."

"Needless to say, it is important that we cooperate with the home office on some level, and they have been adamant about printing the sketches in the newspapers. But it isn't necessary to print all of the sketches. I appreciate your not mentioning anything about the composites. With the great discrepancies we've received in descriptions, I believe the composites may hold the key to identifying our man."

"They're not ready yet. There's still a great deal of work to do. And I can't even be certain that it means anything. I keep adding to them each time we receive a new description."

"Yes, I know how painstaking it must be. That is why I want you to hold back the composites. There is no need giving the *Times,* or the home office information that may be . . . shall we say inaccurate."

She knew precisely what he was suggesting. "I have three or four sketches which I think will pacify the home office and the *Times.* I doubt that anyone who sees them will be able to identify an actual person."

"Very good, my dear," he was obviously greatly relieved. "I am grateful for your discretion in this matter. I need time, my men need time, not hand-holding with the home office, or mollycoddling the press.

"I will say, that we've stumbled upon a startling possibility that I cannot go into. I'm certain that you understand the need for discretion. Suffice it to say that it might greatly hamper our efforts if either the home office or the press were to know of it." Then he smiled at her with genuine warmth. The fatigue and strain was heavy about his eyes and mouth.

"I have great faith in your talents, Jess. I believe you will come up with something substantial. I'm also aware of the reason you're here in Whitechapel. We will make every effort to find your sister. You have my word on that."

"Thank you, Mr. Abberline." He held up a hand as he stood and came around the desk. His expression had become stern, almost formidable, reminding her that no matter how kind and forthright he was, he had also risen to the rank of chief inspector because he was tenacious and had exemplified himself.

His voice was firm, his tone uncompromising. "I must insist that you refrain from any direct involvement in this investigation, other than your responsibilities to me with these sketches. It's much too dangerous for you to go about on your own."

Her gaze immediately went to the door, where Burke had stood only moments before. He said he'd stop her from pursuing information. He'd used the one weapon against her that she dare not challenge—Mr. Abberline's support. Without it, she would be put out on the streets, her position and her access to any information about her sister immediately ended.

Abberline read her thoughts. "Mr. Burke said nothing to me about this. I wouldn't lie for him if he had."

She carefully controlled the cold edge of fury. "I find that difficult to believe."

"Be that as it may, I assure you it is the truth, my dear. Although I am aware there has been some difficulty between you and Inspector Burke, it was Sergeant Hobbs who spoke to me of the matter."

She had seen Hobbs the very next day after her confrontation with Burke. He'd been concerned for her after he left that night. She remembered his look of surprise when she told him about the pitcher, and his asking "Did it break?"

She assured him that it had, with very satisfying results, which she had cleaned up the following morning.

"My Sara said the same thing," he'd told her with an amused glint in his eye. "Said it was the most satisfying experience she could find short of cracking me up side the head with it."

Jess had heartily agreed, wondering how much more satisfying it would have been had she cracked Burke up side the head.

"It seems Sergeant Hobbs was concerned for your welfare," Abberline was saying. "He mentioned that you reminded him a great deal of his wife, and something else about a teapot." He looked at her inquiringly.

She smothered back a smile. "It was a water pitcher," she clarified. She looked up briefly and could have sworn there was laughter behind the solemn expression on his face.

"Nevertheless," Abberline said, bringing them back to the discussion at hand, "I must insist that you not pursue any aspect of this investigation." His meaning was more than clear. He shook his head sadly.

"These murders are a nasty business, and now we have the newspapers to deal with as well as the home office. I have no idea where this will all end. The only thing we know for certain is that this fellow, who calls himself Jack the Ripper, is still out there. He's killed three times. I'm dreadfully afraid that he will kill again, unless we can stop him." He gave her a nod. "Cooperate with Mr. Cassidy as far as we've discussed. Anything else must be approved by me or Inspector Burke."

"I understand."

"Very well, my dear. Be pleasant to Mr. Cassidy, but don't let him charm you. Remember, these newspaper fellows have no souls, let

158

alone discretion or scruples. They've sent him here to pry and snoop and dig up information that they believe we're hiding from them."

"I'll be careful." She smiled. She might not have cared for society gossip and rumor, but there wasn't a female alive who'd been reared on it who couldn't best a newspaper writer any time she chose to.

Jimmy Cassidy and Sinjin Devoe were badgering Endicott to show them the sketches when she walked in. Over Endicott's polite but careful refusal, she heard Jimmy say, "Mr. Abberline gave his approval. Said I was to have whatever I needed."

"There are several sketches which would be appropriate," Jess intervened. She saw the obvious relief on Endicott's face. "Mr. Abberline emphasized that you should see all of these."

For the next hour she provided several sketches that she'd made from the earliest descriptions and long since abandoned as too incomplete of detail to be of any use. If Endicott was aware of the game she played, he said nothing of it. He'd never liked Devoe, and he regarded Jimmy Cassidy with that same guarded resentment of all constables.

Jimmy was good-natured and congenial with a razor-sharp wit and a keen intelligence. He asked dozens of questions, most of which she answered vaguely. She told him he would have to see Chief Abberline. He was constantly looking about, watching everything that went on around them, while carrying on a steady conversation.

Nothing escaped his scrutiny, and she found herself wondering if he was making notes on some invisible tablet in his brain that would later appear in the newspaper. She was careful of everything she said. When in doubt, she said nothing at all.

She saw Burke only once that afternoon as he came out of his office. Hobbs stopped him and handed him a piece of paper. Burke said something in response, and then quickly left the police station. She stared after him, wondering where he was going in such a hurry.

"What about this sketch? Jess?" She looked up. Suddenly she was aware that it wasn't the first time Jimmy had asked the question.

"Yes," she answered. "That is one of the most important sketches." Another lie. They seemed to come so easily. Her gaze fastened on the front door of the station. She wished she could follow Burke, wished she knew what it was that had caused him to leave with such urgency.

* * *

Burke crossed the street at the corner. It was late afternoon, almost dark, and bone-chilling cold as the wind came up off the river, cutting down the streets, and blasting its icy breath at street corners. He pulled the ragged lapels of the cast-off coat tight about his neck, and affected a shuffling, crippled gait, familiar from his youth on the streets.

His face was buried beneath the knit cap, a moth-eaten muffler wrapped high about his cheeks. The bawdy sounds of a nearby tavern cut through the brittle air. Raucous laughter mingled with the smells of stale garbage, warm ale, and coal smoke.

A body heaved through the opened doorway and tumbled out onto the sidewalk. A second man burst out the door, fists raised in sparring position as he stood over the man who lay in the street.

"C'mon now. Show me wot yer got," he roared drunkenly, moving round the prostrate man in a sideways crab walk. "Nobody says words against me, Nellie." He sparred at the air as he weaved about, hardly more steady on his feet than his companion, who lay in the gutter at his feet.

Burke slipped past them and the small crowd that had gathered, mugs hoisted in exuberant support of one contestant or the other. The warmth inside the tavern was as welcome as it had been when he was a lad, stealing on the streets, sneaking into taverns for a warm pint, eluding the constabulary for a bit of food taken from a merchant, or a purse taken from some well-heeled swell.

Like any tavern in Whitechapel or Dublin, the Rose and Thistle had a peculiar brand of welcome that was loud, off-color, and offered simple pleasures for simple people who could hope for little more in life. It was times like these when he realized he hadn't come all that far. It was in his blood; the ease that allowed him to move among them, and not be noticed.

Except for one particular set of watchful, young eyes. Mickey spotted him and quickly worked his way through the crowded tavern.

"Is he here, Mickey?"

"Comes round late in th' evenin'. Lean sort, fair hair, an' a nasty rattle in 'is lungs."

He patted Mickey on the shoulder. "You've done well, lad. There'll be an extra coin in it for you." He reached into his pocket and gave the boy three coins instead of the two agreed upon.

160

"Want me ter hang 'round an' point 'im out ter you?" Mickey asked enthusiastically in hopes of another coin.

"Get yerself home, Mick. Yer mother'll be worried about you."

The boy's expression fell and he looked away. "Got no one waitin' fer me, Burke. Me mother died a fortnight ago. Th' landlord, ol' Mr. Luty, says as how he could let the room fer twice the price, an' put me out on the street."

Burke squeezed the boy's shoulder with heartfelt sympathy. "You can't stay on the street, Mick. It's too dangerous."

"I'll be all right," young Mickey brazened it out. "I got friends."

"No sort of friends who'll take care of you, lad. You come round to the station in the mornin'. I'll have somethin' for you, if you'd care to consider it."

"Work?" Mickey looked at him incredulously. "Yer know 'ow I been gettin' by on the streets, Burke." He was aghast. "You did the same, an' you come out of it all right. Told me yerself."

"Aye, I know well enough. And many times I've looked the other way over yer thievin'. But the day will come, lad, when I won't be able to look the other way no more. And it'll be Newgate fer yer new home."

"Maw always said as wot I'd end up there."

"She wanted better for you, Mick. The offer stands. You come round, I'll see that you have a place to live, food in yer belly, and somethin' fer yer future the way yer maw wanted."

Mick shrugged uncomfortably. "Best be on me way." On his way out the door he turned back for a moment.

"I'll think about it." And then he was gone, disappearing into the shadows and the gathering mist.

"Hello, luv. Buy a girl a drink?"

Burke looked up with some amusement at the whiskey-thickened voice that purred seductively at his elbow.

"Hello, Maude."

She stared at him, trying to see through the layers of hat and muffler. "Burke?" she asked incredulously.

He shook his head. "Not tonight, luv. Just a bloke off th' streets lookin' fer a drink to warm 'imself, and a little information," he told her, and she immediately understood.

"Who yer lookin' for?"

"Fella by the name of Toby Gill. Mick said he comes round the Rose some evenins. He's slender built, fair in th' face, with bad lungs."

She nodded. "I seen 'im around." She was careful to keep her voice low, her smile inviting, and her hands inquisitive. It wouldn't do to have anyone guess that she was talking to a peeler. She owed Burke a lot. He'd gotten her out of more than one bad scrape with the constabulary.

"Wot yer want 'im for?" she asked, slipping her hand through his arm, hugging it against her breast. She'd always fancied how it would be to have him warming her bed at night.

He deliberately avoided a direct answer, instead saying the words he knew were of far more interest to her. "For a half-crown."

She smiled, slipping her hand inside the front of his coat. "I'll send round word if he comes in. Fer another 'alf crown, I'll do you over at me place after closing time."

"Yer worth more than a half crown, luv, but on an inspector's pay . . ." he shrugged.

"That's always yer excuse," she grumbled with a girlish pout, that produced deep lines at the corners of her mouth and revealed the years spent on the street. "Truth is, Burke, I'd do yer fer nothin' on accounta . . ."

"On account of what, Maude?"

"On accounta past favors. I could make yer feel real good on a cold night." Her hand lowered, stroking him.

His hand closed over hers, bringing it back to the top of the counter, where he held it in his.

"Yer too much woman fer me, Maude. I might not recover. Then who would keep the streets safe?" he gently refused, easing her past the rejection, knowing only too well the desperation behind the casual offer.

"Yer a 'ard case, Burke," she grumbled. "If yer don' want nothin' to ease wot's between yer legs, wot can I get yer, luv?"

"A draft of good Irish whiskey and Toby Gill when he comes in. And there's a full crown in it for you."

"Always did say yer was all right, Burke. I'll get yer whiskey, and Toby Gill when I see 'im."

Burke sat at a table in the corner. Two small tumblers of stout Irish whiskey burned through the night chill. He nursed a third, and waited. It was worth the wait.

Long after midnight the whiskey was liberally doused in thick black coffee, and Toby sat across a desk from Devlin Burke at the Commercial Street police station.

"I swear on me mother's grave, Inspector. Annie was alive when I last saw her."

Burke doubted he even knew his mother, much less where she was buried. "When was that, Toby?"

"Two, no three days before . . . before that awful thing happened to her."

"Why did you try to run away when I asked about her?"

"I know the peelers is lookin' fer the bloke wot did them murders. Me and Annie got together real reg'lar. I was afraid someone might think I 'ad somethin' ter do wi' it."

"Did you?" Burke immediately shot back at him.

"No! I swear it, guv'ner. I was over at the 'orspital that night, real bad with th' fevers I get sometimes. They let me out late."

Toby Gill's hands shook badly and he coughed incessantly, occasionally bringing up dark spittle on a stained cloth he wiped across his mouth.

He wasn't an old man in years, but in time spent in the workhouses, factories, and on the streets. Like so many others, the meager money he occasionally stole or hustled could have gone for medicine to ease the lung disease that was slowly killing him, instead of whiskey and pints of ale.

"You were seen comin' out of Annie's place the night she was murdered. I have a witness who'll swear to it," Burke informed him.

Toby's shoulders slumped with resignation. "Oh all right! I went round ter her place that night. But I swears she was already dead. I had nothin' ter do wi' it. I'd never hurt Annie."

"If you had nothin' to do with it, then why didn't you come forward with this information?"

Toby laughed then. It brought on another fit of coughing. When it was once more under control, he looked at Burke. "Who's gonna believe me guv'ner? Annie's dead, and I says I was there. Everyone's gonna naturally think wot I did it."

"But I swear to you I didn't do it. I wouldn't 'urt Annie fer nothin'. We was friends." He slumped wearily, his shoulders thin and spare beneath the coat that hung on him.

It was easy enough to check with the local hospital about the night Annie Chapman died. It was possible that Toby could have killed her after he left the hospital, but looking at him Burke had his doubts about that. The man was wasted by the disease that filled his lungs. Annie Chapman had been a good-sized woman. Toby probably didn't weigh much more than she had.

It just didn't make sense that Toby was the murderer. According to the physician who'd examined all three victims, the killer had to have tremendous strength and weight to overpower his victims so completely and then inflict the brutal wounds. It was for those reasons that it was assumed the murderer had to be a man.

It was also for those reasons that Burke was convinced Toby Gill was telling the truth. He wasn't physically capable of overpowering a woman of Annie Chapman's height and weight, much less creating that much damage.

His fist came down on the desktop, emphasizing the frustration of the entire case. It was always the same. Possible leads that went nowhere. Descriptions that were meager at best, while the fear and panic grew. Then he remembered a promise he'd made, and another possibility of someone who might know something about the night Annie Chapman died if he could find her.

"What do you know about a young woman by the name of Mary Kelly?"

"Ah, c'mon, Jess. Yer've told me nothin' 'bout yerself," Jimmy Cassidy looked at her from under twin thatches of red brows. "By now, I've usually persuaded the ladies ter have supper with me."

"I'm certain there must be a great many of them," she responded.

"One fer every night o' the week," he boasted with a wide smile. "C'mon, Jess, have supper with me tonight."

"I wouldn't want to impose. *Thursday* might not approve."

"Thursday?" Then it occurred to him precisely what she meant, and he grinned. "Oh, I don't have any special arrangement fer tonight. Besides, I'd like to find out where you come by that fancy way of talkin'. I'd say the West End, maybe yer was a lady's maid fer some fancy swell. Am I right?"

"I arrived in London only a few weeks ago," she answered evasively.

"There yer go again. No country girl would say 'I arrived only a few

164

weeks ago'. Yer know I'm right," he pried with good-natured tenacity.

"Unless she learned it from the lady she worked for," Jess suggested.

"And which lady might that be?"

"Do you think the person who wrote those letters is actually the murderer?" she asked.

"You've done that four times in the past half hour," he complained.

"I beg your pardon?"

"You don't have to go beggin' nothing from me, Jess. You know perfectly well wot I'm sayin'. You've changed the conversation round four times in th' past thirty minutes. And that's sayin' somethin' since I'm usually the one tryin' to wheedle information out o' people." He laughed. "Jus' like one of them fancy society ladies gossipin', at some fancy dress ball, always talkin' round somethin' then slippin' somethin' in sly and sneakylike. That's wot yer remind me of."

"Or perhaps a newspaper writer?" she suggested and he hooted with laughter.

"I like yer, Jess Kelly. An' I'm not givin' up on you. You'll have supper with me, sooner or later."

It was sooner than later, when she discovered that Jimmy was indeed very good at uncovering information. He'd been at the Commercial Street police station less than half a day and he'd already learned the name of the man who'd been with Annie Chapman the night she died—Toby Gill.

According to Jimmy, Toby Gill frequented a tavern called the Rose and Thistle.

That afternoon she eluded her usual escort by leaving earlier than usual. Everyone was either busy or hadn't returned yet off their shift. No one saw her leave. She went in search of the Rose and Thistle.

It was located on a street like so many others in Whitechapel with refuse swirling in the gutter, an odd assortment of vendors and merchants closing up business for the day.

A man pushed past her on his way inside. He nodded, smiled appreciatively, and offered to buy her a pint. She politely refused and remained outside, looking for someone who fit the description of Toby Gill.

It soon grew dark, the light from the tavern and the gay tinkling of a piano spilling out of the doors of the Rose and Thistle each time a customer went in.

She'd never been in a tavern before. It was loud and smoke-filled with sawdust on the floor. She was dressed much the same as several other women she'd seen go in, but still she felt the stares that fell her way. The man who'd spoken to her outside looked up. His face broke into a huge grin.

"Well 'ello, luv. Did yer decide to give ol' Lem a try?"

"No, thank you. I'm looking for someone."

"Now, that's no way ter be, luv," he coaxed as he dropped an arm about her shoulders and pulled her against him. "I got me a few quid, a powerful thirst, and a bit o' an appetite. If yer know wot I mean." He winked leeringly at her. His hand, draped over her shoulder, lowered slightly so that his fingers clasped over the swell of her breast through her shirtwaist and coat.

Having spent the last three weeks in Whitechapel, exposed to' all sorts of unexpected encounters, she did understand precisely what he meant.

She looked him straight in the eye and exposed the handle of the small club from inside the fold of her coat. Endicott had given it to her for protection.

"I understand perfectly, darlin'," she said with mock sweetness. "And if you touch me again, you'll be wearing this, right between your teeth."

He jumped back, withdrawing his hand. "I didn't mean no harm." He continued to back away.

"I *do* mean harm," Jess informed him bluntly. His hands spread wide as he held them up.

"Take 'er easy, luv. Jus' tryin' ter be friendly. Yer better go easy or the night is likely ter be long and lonely."

"What's the problem, Lemmie?" a deep-throated, feminine voice asked from behind Jess. She turned and immediately recognized Maude, the woman she'd seen that first day at the police station.

Her bright red hair was piled high on her head, and she wore a plain shirtwaist and nubby linsey skirt. She held a pint of ale in one hand and a cigarette in the other.

"Hey, don't I know you?" she exclaimed.

"Yes, I was at the Commercial Street police station three weeks ago. You were speaking with Inspector Burke."

"That's right. Now I remember. Yer was sittin' there, pretty as yer please, drawin' pictures. Wot can I do yer for, luv? A pint o' ale, or perhaps a young man?" she winked.

"Well . . . no . . . Thank you," Jess replied with some bemusement. "That is, not exactly the way that you're suggesting. But I am looking for someone. A man by the name of Toby Gill."

"Is that right? He's right pop'lar round here lately. Several folks been askin' after him, includin' Inspector Burke."

That didn't surprise Jess. "Do you know where I can find Mr. Gill?"

"Well not right off, I don't. He comes through once in a while for a bit o' ale. But I could maybe get a message ter him fer you."

"I would appreciate that. I'd be willing to pay you for your trouble."

"No trouble at all luv, especially if there's a few coins in it."

Jess took paper and pencil from her sketch case and wrote down her name and the address of the flat on Abbington Road. Better that than to have Toby Gill show up at the police station asking for her. Burke would be furious, she might well be dismissed, and she didn't think her backside could withstand another spanking.

"Tell Mr. Gill that I am also willing to pay him for the information I want." She pressed the note into Maude's hand.

"It's very important."

"All right, dearie. I'll tell him."

Jess handed her several shillings and then turned to leave.

"If it's that important it's worth more 'an that!" Maude exclaimed.

"You're quite right, and you'll have more, *after* I hear from Toby Gill," Jess assured her.

Maude snorted as she stuffed the note into the pocket of her skirt with an expression of grudging admiration. She'd thought the girl no more than a pretty little mouse the day she saw her in the station, all composed and quiet. Not someone to stick in one's memory. In fact she'd completely forgotten about her until she walked into the Thistle.

Maude was usually able to connive, cajole, or shill coins from just about anyone. But she had to admit, the girl was no mouse.

The following day, the *London Times* ran a lengthy article on several pages of the newspaper about the latest developments in the Ripper murders. It included the contents of the latest letter supposedly sent from the murderer, along with sketches of possible

167

suspects by Jess Kelly who was working with the London Police.

And Toby Gill sent a message to the flat at 24 Abbington Road. Times were hard. If someone was willing to pay him for information, he was willing to sell it.

Chapter Thirteen

The Magpie and Stump was a pub on St. Giles Road. It was made of stone and mortar, with heavy wood beams, and sat squat on the sidewalk like a well-fed cat contemplating its next meal. Small paned bow windows on either side of the entrance glowed with light from inside, like twin cat eyes staring out into the gathering gloom.

There was a stone overhang from the second floor establishment, denoted by a worn, faded sign swinging in the winds that read simply, SILAS FORTNEY, leaving Mr. Fortney's particular occupation to speculation. Discretion of this sort was common in Whitechapel, where many businesses operated discreetly, their locations known only by word of mouth and reputation—whether legal or illegal. The Mudger called himself a merchant.

As she stood on the sidewalk across the street from the Magpie and Stump, Jess wondered if Mr. Fortney was also the same sort of merchant whose reputation needed no advertisement.

It was dark and cold, uncertain weather whipping up a gusty wind that billowed her slender skirt one moment, then wrapped it about her legs the next.

She knew it was unwise to venture out after dark. A madman stalked the streets of Whitechapel. With grim certainty Burke and Chief Abberline were convinced he would strike again.

After the most recent article along with her sketches appeared in the *Times,* they redoubled their efforts to find him before that happened. Every constable and inspector worked double shifts, scouring the streets, questioning countless people, following every lead of information no matter how insignificant it seemed.

She'd seen Burke only once in the past three days. He was haggard, as was everyone, his features taut, emphasizing the hard lines and planes of his face. He had spoken to her briefly to tell her that he'd learned nothing new about her sister.

In spite of the argument they'd had over her previous interference, and the coolness between them since, she had been profoundly touched by the fact that he had taken the time to inquire and then tell her of it. An awkward moment had followed. Nothing was mentioned of the shattered pitcher. Then, after several moments of uncomfortable silence, during which neither of them could think of what to say, he had asked if she was all right.

She had assured him that she was, amazed at his concern. She hadn't been able to sit down comfortably for almost two days after their last encounter when he'd been *concerned* about her. She decided she was better off without so much of his bloody concern.

Because of that last encounter his insistence that she not pursue her search for her sister on her own, and Abberline's explicit instructions to the same, made her hesitate and look about her. She was risking a great deal by coming here—she was risking more if she didn't. She gathered her coat tightly about her, as if gathering her resolve, and crossed the street.

The heavy oaken door to the Magpie and Stump swung open as a man and woman entered ahead of her. There was the momentary burst of conversations, laughter, the clink of glass mugs, suffused with the inviting warmth from a stone hearth, and the aroma of hearty food. The small pub was crowded, overflowing with wood tables and chairs, a long, high counter from behind which ale was dispensed at a frantic pace, and customers engaged in food, drink, and a heated game of darts against the back wall.

She slipped in unobtrusively, blending in with her worn clothes and moth-eaten coat, the crumpled hat squashed down over her hair. She quickly looked about, looking for a face that resembled the sketch she'd made from the description Jimmy Cassidy had given her.

She searched the faces that crowded at the bar, bent in conversation, or gathered at the back wall. None fit the description of Toby Gill, and a slow panic began to build. After all these weeks he was the only one she'd been able to find who might know something about her sister. What if he didn't come? How long would it take to get another message to him? If he didn't show this time, would he even agree to meet with her?

She knew that Burke had questioned him, but he hadn't been arrested. He wasn't the man they were looking for. But what if he became frightened and went into hiding? She'd never find him.

"Jess Kelly?"

She jerked around and came face-to-face with a gaunt, haggard young man, whose flesh seemed to hang on his bones. He was young, with fair hair, and watchful gray eyes. Toby Gill.

"Yes."

"There's a table in the corner." He pushed past her, moving along the side wall to the far corner not far from where the heated game of darts was in progress. He took the chair in the corner, sitting in the shadows.

"I was afraid you'd decided not to come," Jess said as she took the chair opposite. With an artist's eye for details she tried to assess Toby Gill.

Like so many others in Whitechapel, where steady work was hard to come by, he was dressed in meager clothes that had been mended several times. He sat hunched over as if he held himself against the cold, although it was pleasantly warm inside the pub. His coat hung off his shoulders, emphasizing his thinness rather than concealing it. There was several days' growth of golden stubble on his chin, his skin was pale and sunken at his eyes and in the hollows of his cheeks. He probably wasn't more than thirty years old, but there was an agedness behind his eyes that made him seem much older.

He made a response and might have said more but he was seized by a harsh, racking cough that seemed to drain his strength. When it finally subsided he gave her a faint smile.

"Thought about not comin', but th' message said there was coin in it fer me. An' truth is, I could use a bit o' change in me pocket. It gets colder at night, and rooms at the lodgin' house cost a bit. That is, if the offer still stands."

"Yes, of course." As she had so many times over the past few weeks, she felt an overwhelming anguish. Her privileged life had

171

sheltered her from people like Mr. Spivey who bought and sold rags for less money than she purchased her paints or paper; Maude who made her meager living from her laughter and her body; little Mickey who stole to survive; and Toby Gill, whose only hope for a next meal perhaps now lay in the information he could sell her.

It would have been so easy and far more comfortable to remain sheltered from people like that. But she wasn't any longer, and she suspected that it was impossible to go back to that safe, sheltered world where everything was perfect—where she always had enough to eat, warm clothes to wear, a roof over her head, and a fire at the hearth—and not be haunted by what she had found in White-chapel.

"Would you like something to eat?" she asked with a vehemence that seemed close to anger, because he was so pitifully thin, and because she had been shielded and protected from people like Toby and Maude, and because she resented it. He declined with a shadow of a smile.

"Perhaps something to drink?"

The smile deepened. "A bit o' ale would help ease th' chill. Ain't got much appetite." The owner of the pub eventually brought two pints of the dark frothy ale.

She pushed her mug aside, not particularly fond of the bitter drink, while Toby drained his. When he glanced at the one before her, she pushed it toward him. It, too, was quickly emptied. He set the mug down with a small, sheepish smile.

"Helps ease the cold inside. Don't never seem to be able to get warm no more." It was a hesitant, careful smile, that revealed several bad teeth. But behind it, she saw a genuine charm.

"You wanted information," he reminded her, a careful, expectant expression on his face. "That's wot Maude said yer was payin' for." It was a subtle reminder that he expected to be paid for his time and trouble. "She also said you was acquainted wi' Mr. Burke."

"Yes," she answered carefully, not wanting to frighten him or make him suspicious. "I'm trying to find my sister. He's been helping me."

"Yer sister?"

"Yes, it's the reason I came here. I received one letter from her

172

several weeks ago. She was staying with Annie Chapman at the time." She watched his face for any change of expression, either recognition or that sudden furtive glancing away that she'd come to recognize when a person didn't care to speak of a particular matter. She saw only mild curiosity mixed with guarded speculation.

"Her name is Mary Kelly," she maintained the disguise, because she knew her sister would never have used her real name. "Do you remember her?"

He shrugged. "Annie always had a new flatmate. They was always comin' an' goin'. Stay a few weeks or a month, long as they could pay their part o' the rent, and then they'd be gone and there'd be a new one. Otherwise Annie couldn't afford th' rent wot with wot's charged fer rat-infested rooms in Whitechapel." There was a note of disgust in his voice. He accepted another mug of ale when it was brought round.

Jess took out a sketch she'd made of her sister and showed it to him. "This is what my sister looks like. She's very pretty, with fair hair and blue eyes. She's slender and a little taller than I am." He studied the sketch intently.

She went on to explain, "The letter was dated only the week before when I received it. She would have been staying with Annie at the time of . . ." she hesitated then, visions of Annie's body on that table in the morgue all too vivid.

"When poor Annie got herself kilt," Toby said quietly, downing a long swallow of ale.

"Yes. I know you were friends with Annie. I'm very sorry."

"I didn't do it, you know," he defended. "Mr. Burke thought it at first. But I couldn't never harm Annie." He looked up at her then, his eyes bright with moisture.

"Annie was more than jus' me friend. We was real close. She took care of me—ever since I got this misery in me chest. I wouldn't never hurt her." He wiped at his eyes then, glancing about to see if any of the other men had noticed. Jess laid her hand on his, wanting to comfort him.

He went on. "I was there that night." His shoulders moved beneath the coat. She realized he was trembling. "I went round late, 'cause I didn't want to bother her none when she was wi' a customer.

After all, she had to earn a livin'." His mouth worked as he struggled with his emotions.

"But poor Annie was already dead. Jus' layin there. I pulled the covers up over her, 'cause I couldn't stand seein' her that way. Then I jus' ran." He looked back up at her then.

"There weren't nobody else there. I looked because I was afraid that other woman—Mary Kelly—mighta been hurt, too. But she weren't there. Nobody was there. I jus' ran, 'cause I figured as how everybody would think maybe I did that to Annie."

Toby picked up the sketch and stared at it for a long time. "I remember her," he said with a nod. "Only saw her once though. Annie told me as how she was her new flatmate." His expression changed, his mouth twisting with a sad frown.

He wiped at his eyes again with his coat sleeve, and Jess looked away for a moment, deeply affected by his sadness.

"I remember Annie sayin' as how she could likely keep the flat since she 'ad someone to share the rent wot could pay her half on time, plus extra fer coal wot wi' winter comin' on an' all. Things was startin' to look up for her."

"Can you remember anything else?" Jess asked, desperate for anything he could tell her.

"There ain't no more to tell. Only saw yer sister once er twice. I remember as how she was real private, always keepin' to 'erself in that back room when she was about. Most times she jus' let 'erself out so as not ter bother Annie and me when I come round, or when Annie was entertainin' other gentl'men."

Again, she felt that overwhelming fear inside. Her sister was always so refined, elegant, and proper. She'd often reprimanded Jess for her outspoken, blunt ways of expressing herself. Whitechapel and the people who lived there were as remote to her sister as the far ends of the earth.

Whitechapel and its overwhelming poverty were something her sister read about in the newspapers, discreetly lest her husband, Lord Deverell, learn of it. It wouldn't do for a peeress of the realm to expose herself to such indelicacies when there were other more acceptable means of occupying her time, such as weekends spent in the country entertaining the Prince of Wales, whom Jess had never met but whom she understood was a boring, somewhat common-looking young man.

But something had happened—something dreadful enough that her sister had fled her privileged life and disappeared on those same streets of Whitechapel, hiding out, living in secret among thieves, beggars, and prostitutes.

"How did she seem?" She was desperate for anything he might be able to tell her. "Did she look well?"

"As I recall, she looked fit enough. A bit pale maybe, but not sickly. Annie said as 'ow they was eatin' real good, 'cause Mary could afford ter pay fer vegetables and meat."

"Do you have any idea where she might have gone afterward?"

There was no need to explain what she meant by afterward. Toby shrugged his shoulders, and shook his head slowly.

"Yer sister weren't there that night. Like I told the inspector, it was late and bitter cold. I went round ter Annie's place thinkin' as 'ow she could maybe put me up fer the night, if she didn't 'av a payin' customer. She did that sometimes. We 'ad an understandin' that way. Helped each other out, we did.

"But like I told him, there weren't nobody there. I didn't see nothin', 'cept poor Annie, an' she was already dead. That's why I ran like I did. Figured the police would think as how maybe I did it if I stayed there."

"Please," she implored him as frustration set in. "This is very important. Do you remember anything that was mentioned—the name of a place, perhaps some plans she was making, anything at all about where she might have gone?"

He shook his head. "Like I said, she kept ter herself. Never said more 'an two words all the times I was there. Real standoffish an' unfriendly like, as if she didn't care to say 'ello."

Or perhaps because she was terrified, Jess thought. Her frustration grew, at being so close and yet unable to learn anything that might tell her where Linnie had gone.

"She might be stayin' wi' someone else," he suggested. "Scared tho' on accounta Annie bein' murdered an' all. Everybody in Whitechapel heard about it."

Jess shook her head. "She doesn't know anyone."

"Maybe one of Annie's chums," Toby suggested. "They looked out fer each other on the street, 'specially after the murders started. Lotta good it did Annie," he said, his voice suddenly gone low and thick.

She understood why Burke hadn't arrested Toby. He couldn't have killed Annie. He was too sick and weak, and he'd obviously cared a great deal for her. He was genuinely grieving for her.

He wiped his nose. "She looked out fer others, like she looked out fer me. Annie was a good ol' girl, always had a smile and a kind word fer everybody. If she had a few coins, she shared 'em. Never let nobody go cold er hungry if she could help it." He looked up at Jess then.

"Why would anyone want to hurt Annie?"

"I don't know. If the police can find an answer for that, perhaps they'll find the person who did it." She reached across the table and touched his hand, trying to offer some small comfort.

"What about Annie's friends? Do you know any of their names?"

He nodded. "Lizzie Stride 'ad a place over on Caber Street, but she got throwed out on accounta' she couldn't pay the rent. Annie said as how she moved in with Cathy Eddowes. But I don't know where?" He looked up at her then. "I could ask around and find out fer you. 'Course, it would cost you."

"I would appreciate that, and naturally I'll pay you for your trouble."

He grinned at her then, a charming and at the same time pathetically wan smile. "A few pints is all I need ter 'elp me through th' night."

She stood to leave then. She laid several coins on the table, more than enough to pay for the ale, several good meals, and perhaps a few nights lodging. Toby kept the smaller ones and pushed the others back across the table.

"Yer sister was a friend o' Annie's. That makes her a friend o' mine, too, and you th' same. Jus' th' cost o' a few pints will be enuf."

"No," she insisted, leaving the rest of the coins where they lay, and leaving him no room for argument. Her eyes misted. In this impoverished part of London, remote from the artifices of polite society, where friendship was acquired according to family name and fortune, she had the influence of neither and had still found a friend. Was her sister as fortunate to have found another friend she could trust?

"It's the least I can do, to help find my sister," she said, then added with heartfelt gratitude. "Thank you, Toby."

"I ain't given yer nothin' yet," he responded.

"You've given me a great deal by your kindness. More than you know."

He concentrated on the mug set before him. He ran a thin hand across his mouth. "I'll send word round fer you when I find out where Liz and Cathy is stayin'. Maybe they'll know somethin' 'bout yer sister." Then he added in a quiet voice. "I hope so, Jess. The streets is no place ter be fer a young woman nowadays. Yer shouldn't be out an' about. Best get on home, if yer gotta place ter stay."

Then he grinned at her, a charming, lopsided smile that for a moment banished the sickness from his eyes. "Otherwise, yer welcome to stay wi' me and we'll find a doss house when the Magpie closes fer th' night."

His offer was forthright and uncomplicated, for two people to share some comfort and human warmth, possibly more as far as Toby was concerned. Oddly enough she wasn't embarrassed or outraged by his suggestion.

"I have a place." Then she thanked him, because in spite of all the social propriety that she'd been raised with she understood the sincerity behind the offer.

He tipped his full mug to her. "Good evenin', Jess Kelly."

The next two days passed interminably. As each hour disappeared and no word came from Toby, she began to lose hope. Perhaps he had forgotten about their agreement, perhaps he'd been taken ill and been unable to make any inquiries, possibly he hadn't yet been able to find either Liz or Cathy, or possibly he'd taken advantage of her situation and her generosity.

No, she refused to believe that, even though everything she'd been raised with told her she'd been a complete fool to trust a homeless, penniless street person who sold information for a pint of ale and several coins.

Her finances had dwindled substantially. Still, she insisted on paying Belle for the use of Burke's flat, especially since he was never there. Belle accepted the money with a shrewd glint in her eye, which made Jess suspect that she probably still charged Burke the full amount, but that was not her problem.

However, before too much time passed, she would be forced to obtain more money, especially if she was able to locate Annie Chapman's friends. If she wasn't able to find them through Toby's efforts, she would still need money to continue her search. She wasn't leaving Whitechapel until she'd found her sister.

She returned to the flat on Abbington Road early in the evening, the third day. She'd worked until after seven o'clock on changes to some sketches with Mr. Abberline in his private office, since Devoe never stayed past five o'clock, and Jimmy Cassidy had to get back to the *Times* to file his latest story.

Like everyone else, Abberline was tired, frustrated, and anxious about not being able to obtain any hopeful leads to the murderer's identity. The article with the letter and her sketches had brought hundreds of responses from people who were certain they'd seen at least one of the men in the sketches. It created an exorbitant amount of work to follow up each response for men who were already overworked beyond the limits of human endurance.

Abberline and Burke worked as many hours as anyone else. Their rank afforded them no special privileges. In fact, each inspector was expected to make increased efforts. They worked round-the-clock each day.

She'd heard from Endicott that Abberline hadn't been home in days. Burke slept on a cot in the constables' room at the back of the police station. Extra clothes had long since been removed from his flat at Abbington Road. At least she wasn't given to wonder where he slept at night.

They had struck an unspoken truce of sorts. Burke inquired how she was or what she was doing whenever he saw her. She was certain he checked up on her whereabouts from the other constables, but she gave him no reason whatsoever to think she was doing anything other than following his strict orders about not involving herself.

She let herself into the flat with the key that Burke had provided.

Melrose rubbed against her leg on his way into the small drawing room. Evidently Belle had put him out for the evening, or was out herself. She hadn't appeared in the front parlor as she usually did, full of criticism and remonstrations about Jess's tardiness, something she seemed to take great pleasure in.

Jess fumbled for the matchbox on the table. Her fingers finally brushed against it, and she lit the gaslight on the wall. With a soft hiss, light glowed into the room, creating shadows at the fireplace and in the corners, pooling softly on the tops of worn, scarred furniture. She took off her coat and laid it across a chair.

It was odd how familiar and comforting those meager furnishings had become over the past few weeks — it felt more and more as if she were coming home each time she opened the door. It was then she saw it — the small piece of folded paper that had been slipped under the door.

At first she thought Belle might have started leaving her notes about her tardiness for meals. Then she remembered that the best Belle could manage was her name and a few numbers.

She read the note.

Jess,
Liz Stride and Cathy Eddowes are stayin' at #3 Mitre Square.

Your friend, Toby

His name was signed with awkward, broken letters, like a child's handwriting. The note itself had obviously been written by someone else who could read and write.

"Thank you, dear Toby," she whispered, pulling her coat back on, and gathering her small reticule that contained her money.

It was past eight o'clock in the evening. Not exactly the proper hour to go calling, but she had to find Liz Stride and Cathy Eddowes as soon as possible. She prayed she could find a driver this time of night.

She had to walk three blocks to Sheffield Street, then cross over to Harcourt. She finally found a hansom. The driver cautioned her about being out that time of night. She thanked him and then insisted he take her to Mitre Square. Fortunately he knew the location.

It was some distance away. It must have been well after nine o'clock when the hansom turned and then slowly came to a stop. She pushed open the doors.

"Is this Mitre Square?"

"Up a ways, miss. The street's blocked off."

She looked up the street. She saw several people walking about in the light from the street lamps. Closer still were several carts and drivers, and other people gathered at what appeared to be two wagons drawn crosswise across the street only a short distance ahead.

"Best stay inside, miss," the driver informed her as she stepped down. She paid him his fare.

"Thank you. I'll walk from here."

Several people had gathered about just ahead, blocked from going any further by those two wagons and uniformed constables. Everyone talked at once, speculation running through the gathering crowd. Jess heard someone say, "They've found another one."

She grabbed one woman's arm. "What's happened?"

"Don't know, dearie. Jus' got 'ere meself. Heard someone say there's been another murder." Jess pushed past her to the edge of the crowd. She looked down the street and saw more uniformed constables moving about, heard the echo of orders being given and somewhere further, the shrill urgency of a police whistle.

She flattened herself against a storefront and ran at the edge of the crowd, keeping her head down, ignoring comments as she pushed past people. Then the crowd thinned. She ducked across the entrance to an alley, where several other people had gathered.

A man ran past her in the opposite direction. His shoulder brushed against hers. The force of the blow staggered her, sending her momentarily off balance. She would have stumbled and fallen, except for the wall of the boardinghouse at her back.

She heard a mumbled, "Sorry, my dear," sensed his momentary hesitation as if he might stop to inquire if she was all right, then he disappeared into the crowd behind her.

Undoubtedly one of the police inspectors she'd seen gathered at the far end of the street. Police wagons were blocked across it. She made her way along the sidewalk, keeping to the shadows. Occasionally there was the sudden arc of light from a hand-held lantern as one of the constables crossed the street, or appeared at a doorway. Then they swung away, disappearing down an adjacent side street, only to reappear further down several seconds later. The police were looking for someone.

A familiar, uneasy sensation tightened in the pit of her stomach. Slowly, she shouldered her way through the crowd. She deliberately moved away from a uniformed constable who stood guard to prevent anyone from passing by, waited until he'd turned in the opposite direction, and then slipped through the barricade of wagons into the concealing shadows along the sidewalk.

She ran among the shadows, quickly moving down the street toward the small knot of police constables, wagons, and others who had gathered.

As she approached the corner, there were no more shadows to hide in. Here, she was conspicuously the only woman about. As she darted across the street she noticed the street sign — Mitre Square.

She heard bits of conversation:

"Did anyone see anything? . . . What about the witnesses . . . ?"

"Get all their names. . . . Search every street . . ."

"Th' old man over there said 'er name is Liz Stride . . ."

"Poor thing. Her throat's been cut. Jus' like the others . . ."

At the sound of that name, Jess pushed frantically past a uniformed constable.

"Hey, miss. Yer not s'posed ter be round here. Stop 'er, Smitty."

She pushed past the man called Smitty, running along the sidewalk. A face was blurred and vaguely familiar, then she pushed and shoved people aside, desperate to get past them.

It couldn't be! her thoughts screamed in her head. Liz Stride — Annie's friend!

"Jess?" The voice was familiar.

She didn't stop, but kept shouldering her way through, slipping past constables and inspectors, ducking under elbows, side-stepping, and then squeezing past before anyone could notice, or stop her.

"Jess! Wait!"

She plunged through the edge of the crowd into a small space that had opened up and stared down at the body that lay on the cold, cobbled stones.

Chapter Fourteen

It was Liz Stride.

Jess heard the name again as she pushed her way through the crowd that had gathered. Then she saw her.

She stared, horrified, at the young woman whose body lay exposed and mutilated. Blood pooled and ran in tiny rivulets about the cobbled stones, a dark inky color in the wavering light from the lanterns.

Her clothes had been slashed away from the front of her body. Deep wounds had sliced open layers of skin and tissue, exposing the organs underneath. One arm was extended away from the body, her hand starkly pale against the dark night, the dark cobbled stones, and the dark blood.

Jess stood there, unable to move, unable to breathe. It was cold. The cold seeped inside her, until there was only a numbness spreading over every emotion, so that all she could do was stare mutely like those around her.

"Jess!"

From somewhere far away, a voice called out. She heard it several more times before she realized someone was calling her name.

"What yer doin' here?"

Slowly the voice penetrated the numbness around her senses. She looked up and saw Endicott shouldering his way through the crowd toward her.

"Get Mr. Burke!" he shouted back over his shoulder. Then she felt his hands at her shoulders. He tried to pull her back through the crowd, away from Liz Stride.

She felt as if she were moving in slow motion, her feet and legs too numb to walk. She didn't want to leave. She wanted to stay there.

"Do you have a blanket?" She looked up at Endicott.

"It's all right, Jess. Come away. Yer don't want to see that." His arm was around her. She pushed it away and turned on him.

"Get a blanket!" she demanded. "A coat, something . . . anything. Cover her with something." Her voice quavered.

"Don't let them see her like that!"

"What the devil is goin' on here? Endicott?" That voice, edged with anger, was familiar. Then, "Bloody Christ! Jess! What is she doing here?"

"I don't know, Mr. Burke. I looked up an' there she was, standin' there at the edge of the crowd."

Strong hands closed over her arms. When she resisted, she was firmly but gently pulled through the crowd.

"Come away, lass." When she was unable to move, those hands pulled at her insistently. Reality shifted back into place. Some of the numbness left her legs and she began to walk, although she was certain she would have fallen if Burke hadn't kept firm hold of her arm.

Curious faces looked back at them as they moved through the crowd. There were comments of disgust.

"Bloody peelers!" one man spat out. "They let the murderin' bastard kill again."

She closed her eyes for a second. She still saw Liz Stride's body behind her closed lids, every detail frozen in her numbed thoughts. Burke ignored the comments, his hand firm on her arm as he guided her through to the back of the crowd.

"It was Liz Stride, wasn't it?" Her voice ached in her throat. She tried to look back, sickened and stunned by what she had seen, yet unable to pull herself completely away. One horrified thought wouldn't go away—it could have been her sister.

"Come away, Jess. Don't look again. You don't want to see it." It wasn't an order. There was no anger in his voice. She moved like a sleepwalker, unaware of the steps she took, unaware of anything except the sight of that body lying there, cold and dead on the cobbled stones.

He escorted her to a police wagon. It was an enclosed vehicle with padded seats used for transporting several men. A uniformed constable sat atop. Burke helped her inside the wagon, out of the cold night air. He sat across from her.

"It was her, wasn't it?" she demanded, her eyes haunted and stark, filled with the horror of what she had seen.

"Aye," he said slowly, watching her through the shadows inside the wagon. "I'm told that was her name."

She sat across from him, her hands buried in her lap, huddled against a cold from which there was no escape—the cold emptiness of shock.

"What are you doin' here, Jess?" he asked gently. "How did you find out about this?" He reached out and took her clenched hands into his larger ones, wrapping warm strength around the numbing coldness that had completely absorbed her.

"Jess?"

She finally looked up. "I found out that Liz Stride was a friend of Annie Chapman's."

It was as if someone else spoke, her voice seemed to come from some faraway place, but not inside her. She didn't think there was anything left inside, no warm place, safe from what she had seen.

Her shoulders sagged and her head bent forward. She expected him to yell at her about disobeying his orders. Oddly enough he didn't so much as raise his voice. But he wanted answers.

"How did you come by that information?"

"I spoke with Toby Gill. He told me."

"And you thought that if you talked to her she might be able to tell you something about your sister."

She nodded. "Toby said they were all friends, they looked out for each other." She looked up at him then.

"Is that how the others died?"

His voice was low and stark. "Aye, it's the same. Like some damn bloody ritual the bastard is performin'."

She swayed slightly and he immediately shifted across the middle of the wagon to the seat beside her. His arm closed around her and he pulled her against him.

"I wish to heaven you hadn't seen it," he said quietly.

"I needed to see it." Her voice was hoarse. "Until then I didn't understand. She turned into the solid strength of his shoulder, her

185

hand clasped the front of his coat. She shuddered. "He must be mad."

"Aye, lass. That he is. Completely mad, and he's still out there." Then his shoulder moved beneath her head and he straightened.

"I'm sendin' you back to the flat," he said gently. She pulled back.

"No! I can't leave. I won't. Please don't send me away, Burke. I have to speak with Catherine Eddowes. She might know something about what happened to Liz Stride."

His blue eyes narrowed in the thin light from off the street. "Who the devil is Catherine Eddowes?"

Jess struggled to organize her shattered thoughts. Seeing Liz Stride that way had completely unnerved her. She was shaking, the words coming out in jerky half-sentences.

"She lived with Liz Stride, not far from here. Toby gave me the address in Mitre Square."

He suddenly sat back, holding her away from him. "Are you certain about this?"

Her teeth chattered from the cold that began to seep in. She nodded. "Yes. Toby told me they shared a flat after Liz was put out of the room where she was staying before. He sent this round to the flat when he found the address." She showed him the piece of paper with the message and Toby's childishly scrawled name.

Burke leaped past her, out the double doors. Endicott had followed them to the wagon and had waited discreetly outside.

"Stay with her!" Burke ordered the driver. "Don't let her out of your sight even for a moment. Is that clear?"

"Yes, sir!"

Jess had started to follow him out the wagon. He turned back to her. "Yer to stay here, Jess. There's no compromise on this and I won't stand for you disobeyin' me again. It's either that, or I'll have you taken to the station." She nodded her agreement.

"I'll stay here. I promise I won't interfere."

"That's what you said last time."

"Last time you shouted at me." He gave her a slightly bemused look. Then he whirled around to Endicott.

"Come with me. And bring a half-dozen men."

* * *

She had no idea how much time passed. It was dark and cold inside the wagon. The driver had climbed down and provided her with a lap blanket. She wrapped it tightly about her, but it was no use. She couldn't get warm no matter how she tried. And always the nagging question—What was taking Burke so long?

She'd noticed the street sign for Mitre Square when she first arrived. The flat that Catherine Eddowes shared with Liz Stride couldn't be far away.

Still they waited.

She saw uniformed constables and plain-clothed inspectors moving quickly about in a flurry of activity. Orders were given. A nearby wagon was moved forward. It pulled through the barricade and stopped just beyond.

There were shouts and the sporadic flash of hand-carried lanterns arcing through the thickening night air as constables moved down the adjacent streets.

Then she heard the shrill, piping sound of the policeman's whistle splitting through the cold night air. Her head came up, and she reached for the door. It was an eerie, piercing sound that she'd heard all too frequently the past few weeks. It sent a chill through her.

"What is it?" she asked the driver.

"They've found somethin', miss," he answered. "Maybe someone lurking about the streets. Best stay inside, like the inspector ordered. It's turned right nasty out tonight."

"How long have they been gone?"

"Not long, miss." She knew he lied. It had been at least an hour. What was keeping them? What were they doing? Had they found Catherine Eddowes's flat? What had she been able to tell them? Or had they joined the street-by-street search for the killer?

Her nerves were worn thin. She shivered, pulling the blanket about her shoulders.

How much later was it that she heard voices approaching? She jerked upright, muscles complaining. She was stiff, frozen through. The doors opened.

"Did you find her?" she asked Burke anxiously.

"C'mon, Jess. I'm takin' you home. There's no more can be done here."

187

Endicott was with him. She jerked back and looked from one to the other. The street had gone quiet about them. The other wagon was gone. Occasionally the light from a lantern bobbed in the distance as the search continued. It must have been well after midnight.

She sat back, suddenly uneasy and wary. "What is it?" she demanded, looking from one to the other.

"You have yer instructions, Mr. Endicott," Burke said with quiet authority. Silent understanding passed between them.

"Yes, sir. Will you be goin' back to the station tonight, sir?"

"I'll be takin' Miss Kelly home first."

"Right yer are, sir. I'll inform Mr. Abberline." Then he was gone. Burke gave instructions to the driver atop the wagon to take them to the flat on Abbington Road. Then he crawled inside and took a seat across from Jess.

"What is it. What's happened?" she demanded, fear slicing through the coldness, building along her nerve endings. "Did you find Catherine Eddowes? What did she say?"

There was no light inside the darkened interior of the wagon as it moved down the street. Somehow it hadn't occurred to anyone to light the interior. Jess clung to the edge of the bench seat across from Burke. There was a small glass window in each side of the doors at the back. Occasionally the glow of a passing street lamp, flickered through, briefly illuminating the interior.

Burke's voice was low and heavy through the darkness that surrounded them.

"Aye, Jess. We found Catherine Eddowes," he said quietly. "She's dead."

There wasn't a sound inside the wagon. It lurched and swayed around corners and across the uneven surface of one street after another.

"No," she finally said refusing to accept it. "That's impossible. She can't be . . ." the last word wouldn't come past the tightness in her throat. With a ragged whisper she said, "It's not possible." Pushing it away, refusing to believe it.

He was beside her then, gathering her into his arms, pulling her tight against him.

"There's been some mistake," she insisted.

"There's no mistake, lass. We found her at the flat she shared with Liz Stride."

"No!" she said stubbornly. "It's not true." Yet some small part of her knew that it was true. It had been there in Endicott's voice, only she hadn't wanted to hear it.

In spite of all her struggling, he pulled her against his chest, his large hand cupping her head, cradling her against him with his other arm. "Shhhhhh," he gently comforted. "Easy, Jess. Don't think about it now."

But she couldn't stop thinking about it. It must be true. Burke wouldn't lie to her. He had no reason to lie. Her hands were clenched into fists of denial.

"It can't be true."

"I wish it wasn't, lass. I wish it with all my heart." He cradled her against him the remainder of the ride back to Abbington Road.

She had no sense of time. It seemed the entire evening had passed in a blur of seconds, yet she understood that it must have been hours. When the denial eased into silent acceptance, the coldness returned and spread to her hands and feet until every part of her ached with it, and a violent trembling began.

Burke held her tight and she clung to him, needing to feel the coarse wool of his coat, the heat that permeated through his shirt and coat, the hard, solid strength of his body.

"Come along, Jess." His shoulder moved beneath her cheek.

Every time she closed her eyes she saw Liz Stride and Annie Chapman's bodies, cold and lifeless, their skin completely bloodless. She was certain she wouldn't sleep for a very long time. But she'd crawled inside herself like a small wounded animal, trying to find some safe place away from the horror. She finally stirred.

She hadn't dozed, although she was emotionally and physically exhausted. Still she jerked upright, her body rigid and tense, as if bracing herself for another shock.

Burke dismissed the driver and escorted her up the steps into the house. It was early morning, perhaps two or three o'clock. No one was about. Someone, perhaps Belle, had left a single gaslight burning in the hallway. Wordlessly, they climbed the stairs. Each step was mechanical, driven by some unconscious command.

Inside the small flat she immediately went to the hearth and knelt

189

before it, wadding bits of paper and adding small pieces of wood to get a fire started. When the fire caught, she put on several larger pieces of wood, then set the screen before it.

She hadn't realized before how unusual it was that Burke used wood instead of coal. Of course they used wood at Carrington Square. But it wasn't readily available in this part of London. Still, she preferred the faintly spicy smell of wood smoke over coal.

It was odd that she would think of something like that at a time like this, as if she needed to think of such mundane matters to focus her shattered thoughts.

When the fire was lit, she quickly went about the room, turning up every lantern and light, until the room glowed brightly. Belle would complain about the extravagance, but she didn't care. She wanted light instead of shadows, and heat to drive away the aching cold she hadn't been able to get rid of since she came to Whitechapel.

"Jess." His voice was gentle, no angry words, no reprimands, no orders.

"Let me turn up this last lamp," she said, unaware that her voice was brittle, taut, as if it would break at any moment, and her along with it.

"It's always so dark in here. I don't like the dark."

As she passed by him, he took her by the shoulders and gently restrained her.

"I know yer hurtin', lass." He slowly pulled her into his arms. He'd removed his coat and she felt the soft nubby texture of his shirt. How could she be so cold and he not seem to feel it at all.

"I wish you hadn't seen that tonight. I wish I could take it away, and make the world safe."

"I never used to be afraid of the dark. Linnie was the one who was always afraid." She shivered in his arms. "Now I hate it when the sun goes down each day."

He frowned slightly as he held her. Linnie? Undoubtedly she had been speaking of her sister. Perhaps it was a nickname. He knew she was still in shock over what she'd seen that night.

"I dread every new day that comes because I'm afraid I'll find out that she's dead. And I dread the end of each day, because it's dark, and she still hasn't been found."

"I know, lass. I know." He gathered her closer, feeling the shock that trembled through her, trying to give her some of his warmth.

"Please hold me tighter, so that I won't feel the fear," her voice quivered. "You don't fear anything, do you, Burke?"

His arms tightened about her, understanding far more than she could ever know.

"There's things every man fears, lass, no matter who he is. No one is free of it. It's always there in some form to tear away at you. When it does, you have to hold on, hold tight."

He'd been weaned on fear, lived with it his entire life, until he was numb from it. He knew she was feeling that numbness now — the shock and disbelief that the mind at first refuses to accept. When the numbness was gone, the tears would come. She needed to cry, to get past the pain and horror. He'd cried all his tears long ago.

She held him tight, her arms about his lean waist, her hands flattened across his muscular back. She buried her face against his shirt. She couldn't seem to get close enough. She wanted to feel . . . something . . . anything except the emptiness and loneliness and fear, that she'd felt the past few weeks.

"I'm so cold," she whispered against the soft linen of his shirt. "No matter how I try, I can't seem to get warm. Hold me tight, Burke." Her voice broke then as reality began to return. Her head moved beneath his chin as she turned her face into his neck.

"Please make it go away . . . make the cold go away." Her fingers were curled into the front of his shirt. She looked up at him then. Her face was pale and sad, her eyes were wide and stark, filled with deepening shadows until soft green had gone almost black, her lower lip trembled.

More than ever he was aware of how small and slender she was, and of the vulnerability that lay in those haunting shadows at her eyes.

"Help me feel something . . . anything but this."

He took her face gently between his hands, cradling it. Some long-lost emotion stirred inside him, a need to comfort and protect, to take away her sadness, pain, and fear. He bent his head to hers, and brushed his lips lightly against hers.

The contact was brief, like the stroke of a feather, the barest touch of skin against skin, stirring warmth against numbing cold. His

191

breath brushed against her mouth. There was no response, just the cool contact of her lips. His hands slipped over her shoulders and he kissed her again, focusing her shattered emotions on his mouth on hers.

Gradually, he felt the smallest response as her mouth moved hesitantly against his. He started to draw back but her hands stopped him as they came up to his face, holding him as she pressed her mouth more firmly against his.

Her slender fingers trembled against his beard-roughened skin, then spread along the hard bone at his jaw, holding him for her kiss, giving in to the need to feel something more than the pain and fear.

His hands opened and spread across her back as he held her, stroking small circles in the taut, rigid muscles. Her body quivered like a tightly drawn rope that must either ease or snap. His strong fingers stroked the slender cords and tendons. Eventually he felt the tension seep out of her, the muscles and tendons relax. He pulled away. A sigh shuddered through her, then caught in her throat as he changed the angle and kissed her again.

He felt the anger, pain, and fear that she struggled with, his mouth against hers. He'd confronted her anger, he understood her pain, but the fear tore at him unlike anything he'd experienced for longer than he could remember. It trembled through her. It was cold at her lips.

Control slowly unraveled like tightly woven threads that gradually gave way, unwinding, pulling loose all restraint, uncoiling all the rules he'd lived with the last fifteen years. He felt it slip through his fingers like slippery strands that he tried to hold onto. But the more frantically he tried to hold on, the more quickly it slipped away. Like trying to hold on to water, or the wind. It was there, he could feel it, but he couldn't confine it, couldn't bend it to his will.

His fingers trembled against her skin. Weeks ago when she'd fainted, she'd been like warm satin in his hands. Now she was pale, the skin across her cheeks and her lips, cool to the touch. What would it take to make her skin go warm like that again?

There had been women who had given him that understanding. Megan with the sweet innocence of youth so quickly lost on the streets of Dublin in order to survive. He had discovered his first kiss with her. But all too quickly the innocence was destroyed by others and Megan was dead.

There were other women along the way from youth to man-hood—whose faces he couldn't recall, who shared the nights under a meager blanket finding warmth with exploring hands and quickly clasped bodies. And later there were a few he'd stayed with longer than a single night. But there hadn't been anyone after Megan, who made him *feel*.

Not until now.

From the very beginning, Jess Kelly had slipped under his de-fenses and pushed him beyond the edge of control, forcing him to feel things he'd left in the past and never wanted to feel again, because the price was too high. And she asked for nothing in return, except that he help her find her sister.

He pressed his mouth to hers again. Her lips were cool and quivered with that vulnerability no amount of angry words or stubbornness could disguise.

Darkness and light, night and day, as if she were two people, and he'd only caught glimpses of both, yet knew neither one.

He deepened the kiss by long moments, taking away the coldness as his hands had eased the muscles at her back, until he felt her mouth go warm beneath his. Cool then hot. Ice and fire.

She was both and more as her mouth shifted, then angled against his. She was liquid fire, her mouth sweet, her small tongue experi-mentally touching his.

She was hesitant and uncertain and made him burn with a wild reckless urgency. She stripped away every last thread of his control, exposing a raw and aching need that he'd buried deep for fifteen years.

"Burke." His name shuddered out of her in an equally urgent and needy whisper as the kiss ended and another began. Her nails cut through the fabric of his shirt and created tiny half-moons in the dark skin underneath as she clung to him.

The lines that had defined her entire life were no longer clear. She'd stepped out of one world and into another. The longer she lived in this world, the less she understood of the one she'd left behind.

"I can't feel anything except the pain." Her breath caught in a small, dry sob. "Please make it go away. Please, Burke." He pulled her against him, holding her tight, his cheek pressed against her hair. It was soft, like dark satin against his beard-roughened skin. He closed his eyes, breathing in the sweetness of it.

"I wish I could take it all away, lass," his lips moved against her hair. She angled her face up toward his, her mouth brushing against his chin until she found his mouth with small, caressing strokes that slowly undermined every excuse or argument.

He traced the curve of her upper lip with his roughened tongue, making tiny feather strokes. At each corner, he dipped his tongue into the small indentation, then stroked back lingering in the middle.

He pulled her upper lip between his. The breath shivered out of her somewhere between a whisper and a sigh. Her lips parted and he slipped inside. She tasted of sweetness and unshed tears and made him ache.

The intrusion was startling, hot and wet, as she tasted the fullness of him, stroked her tongue tentatively against his, then changed the angle and took him more deeply inside.

He tasted dark, hard, and sweet, creating unexpected sensations as he moved inside her, tiny bursts of pleasure igniting where they were joined, then slowly pulsing into every part of her body with each stroke. It was intimate, wildly sensual, and made her skin hot. Each taste built the pleasure and a restless energy that made her want to touch him — the lean tendons at his arms as he held her, the softness of his mouth, the hard muscles on his chest.

She pulled her bruised mouth from his, aware of the dark sound he made in his throat. Her fingers stroked up his lower arms, her nails scraping the flesh underneath the sleeves. Eyes closed, driven by the fear and anger, she wanted to feel more. She pressed her mouth against the front of his shirt.

He felt the shirt go wet against his skin — wet heat. He groaned, taking her head between his powerful hands, as if he would pull her away from that intense contact. Then his long fingers stroked back through her disheveled hair, and he crushed her to him, his mouth plunging down over hers.

His face blurred and she felt the sudden, hot brush of his breath, then the violence of his kiss that bruised her mouth, crushing her lips against her teeth, bringing the faint taste of blood.

There wasn't a sound in the room, not even the creak of a floorboard, nor the hiss of the fire. It was completely silent as if everything were momentarily suspended in time. There was only that wildly sensual sound deep in his throat and her own startled gasps.

Her fingers skidded over each feature of his face as she clung to him. Not an easy face, but one she'd ached to touch from the moment she first saw him, to feel the texture, every contour, shape, and hard line.

Touch. She was fascinated by the roughened beard that tingled at her fingertips, the indentations of deeply etched lines at the corners of his mouth, the contrasting softness of his mouth.

Taste. His mouth was warm, sweet, and softly violent, stunning her in ways she'd never dreamed. She pulled back, but sensed that it was already too late. His mouth closed over hers again, with a new taste—heat. And her last ounce of control disintegrated.

She closed her eyes, holding his image behind her lids, closing out everything else as her senses took over. Anger and restraint, bruising softness, sweet fire. She wanted more, and slipped her fingers back through the dark waves of his hair, changing the angle, drawing him closer, deepening the kiss by long moments, until her lungs ached, but she no longer cared if she drew another breath.

Then the tip of his tongue brushed along her lips with a new tenderness that almost made her cry out, and discovery began again. Her lips parted. She drew in a deep breath, then shuddered anew as the wet velvet of his tongue slipped inside. Each touch was like the stroke of a feather, infinitely tender, teasing, making her want even more—controlled violence.

His breath shuddered out of his lungs and burned across her cheek, and then he was kissing her again, slipping inside then withdrawing, until she held him between her hands so that it was impossible for him to withdraw completely, holding him inside her so that she could experience the wonder of an even deeper sensual discovery.

Her arms slipped about his neck, as her tongue tangled with his, and she tasted a wild, forbidden heat. His fingers braceleted her wrists. Instead of pulling her away, he deepened the kiss as his hands slowly lowered down the length of each arm, until he held her about the waist. Then he slowly fanned his fingers open, each thumb stroking down over the fullness of each breast, grazing each distended nipple that strained against the taut fabric of her shirt-waist.

Through the thin cloth he felt the sudden tightening of flesh as her nipples grew pebbly and hard. She quivered in his hands, gasping as the kiss broke and then began again. Her hands slipped to his shoulders, clutching at him, fingers biting into the fabric that covered hard muscles.

Her mouth was soft and full, pliant beneath his one moment, demanding the next. Her breath mingled with his as the angle changed, then she cried out softly as he plunged inside once more, meeting him with equal strength, equal demand, and equal hunger.

Taste, touch, sight, sound, smell — as an artist she was intensely aware of all of them. But she'd never been aware before as a woman.

He was a dark shadow standing over her, fascinated by what she couldn't see as well as what she could: the rustling of fabric against fabric the harsh rasp of his breathing; her own startled gasps the pungence of wood smoke mingled with the traces of night air, damp wool, and redolence of man; the nubby fabric of his shirt; the heavily corded muscles across his shoulders.

All of it focused in the taste of him at her mouth — wildness, smoke, and heat.

One large hand spread down her back, cupping her bottom through the fabric of her skirt. The other grazed her cheek, then slipped behind her neck. He arched her away from him, breaking the kiss as his mouth lowered to her throat.

She was suspended, held by those powerful hands as he cradled her. Her hands clasped his shoulders. His mouth moved down her throat to the curve at her shoulder where the collar of the shirtwaist gaped away. Her eyes slowly closed as her fingers clenched over hardened muscles, pulling him to her. Then he pressed his mouth against the front of her shirt, as she had done to him, the fabric wet beneath his hot mouth.

"Burke." His name shivered from her lips. It might have been protest, it might have been something else. Whatever it was, it was too late.

His teeth grazed over the distended nipple that was dark through

196

the wet fabric. She shuddered then, holding him tight against her. He swore softly and picked her up, the curse drowned out by the crash of the bedroom door back against the wall.

He laid her across the bed, his long body pressing her into the thick mattress. There was no time to think, no time to protest. There was a wildness in him that she couldn't have stopped if she'd wanted to.

The heat of his mouth, the memory of it at her breast focused a single thought—she wanted him to go right on touching her, until there was no more coldness, until it was gone, and she could feel again.

His fingers closed over her wrists, drawing them slowly over her head. He held them there, gently pinned with one hand. Then his other hand slowly stroked down over her left breast, the heat of his fingers burning through the fabric. He tore it open.

The night air chilled her bare skin where the shirtwaist was ripped away. She gasped as his mouth closed over her bare breast, wet and hot. She strained in an instinctive effort to free her hands, but he held her fast. She cried out, arching against him.

He stroked the taut nipple with his tongue, then took it between his teeth, biting softly, causing tiny fingers of pleasure to shaft downward through her body. The distended peak was thick, dark, and hard as he pulled it inside his mouth. Her body shuddered beneath him.

Gradually his fingers loosened about her wrists and he released her. Nothing restrained her except the wild heat of his mouth.

Through half-closed lids she watched, stunned and fascinated by the stark contrast of the dark beard on his face against the pale skin of her breast; the soft pink of his tongue stroking her dark nipple, then closing over her so that dark and light became one sensation that centered low inside her.

It was as if a satin ribbon were being pulled tighter and tighter each time his mouth tugged at her breast. Her hands clasped his shoulders. A wild restlessness built along her nerve endings. Then the restlessness became more urgent, almost frightening as it took control. Her fingers bit into the flesh at his shoulders as if she would push him away. But instead, her fingers bit into the dark tanned flesh, and she clasped him against her as the rhythm increased;

biting, tugging, stroking, throbbing deep inside her.

His fingers brushed against her thigh, the skirt drawn up by slow inches, until he found the layers of cotton and silk underneath. Slowly, he peeled away layer upon layer.

A ragged breath shuddered out of her, then caught as she felt his fingers against the bare skin at her hip. Her lungs ached, while her body tensed in some unknown anticipation as his thumb slowly stroked down over the indentation below the curve of her hip. Then his hand fanned down over her stomach.

His fingers caressed the taut flatness of her stomach until he found the soft silk between her legs. His fingers slipped through silken tendrils until he found soft folds of flesh. He parted her, stroking wet heat. She was softer than silk.

She should have been shocked and horrified. No man had ever touched her so intimately. Instead there was a startling new awareness as consciousness splintered into smaller, separate sensations: the soft, worn patches of fabric at her fingertips as she clutched the quilt beneath her; the cool smoothness of wood as her other hand brushed against the headboard; the oily pungence of the gaslight that mingled with the scent of his dampened skin; the wild restlessness that expanded inside her; the strong hand that clasped her hip and held her fast; the rough stroke of his callused fingers over her throbbing, sensitized flesh; the urgency spreading upward through her taut body; then the sudden, invasion as his fingers slipped inside her.

She arched upward, gasping for air. The breath shuddered in her lungs as his mouth closed over her breast.

"Jessie," he breathed against her swollen flesh. It was an intimate, dark sound that seemed to come from somewhere deep inside.

Her breathing was ragged, half gasp, half sob. Her nails bit into the hard muscles at his shoulders. Then she felt the pressure of both his hands at her hips. He slowly rocked her body against his, and she was aware of hard erect flesh through fabric against her stomach.

The wool fabric of his pants grazed her sensitized flesh, creating a wild heat inside her. She gasped. His mouth bruised down over hers and he swallowed the sound. She clung to him, trying to pull him closer.

His hand moved between them. She heard the sound of clothing being tugged away, then felt the startling heat of hard exposed flesh against the cleft of her body. Then the heat was inside, startling and intimate, shattering the fear, destroying the night shadows, until there was only that solid presence moving deep inside her.

It was still dark outside when she awakened. The heavy curtains were drawn at the window. Light from the hearth in the adjacent sitting room pooled through the doorway onto the bare wood floor. There was a soft hiss as the fire burned low.

Jess stirred. Then memories of the night before returned. She sat up in the bed, immediately aware of her nakedness beneath the thick quilt, and a slightly bruised sensation in her body.

Burke was gone. There was a note on the table beside the bed, saying only that he had to return to the police station.

Her hand trembled slightly as she brushed back her disheveled hair and other memories returned: the harshly whispered curse when he first made love to her; then the unexpected tenderness when he made love to her again, more slowly; and afterward, when he held her and whispered, "I'm sorry, lass. I never meant to hurt you. I didn't know."

He'd stayed with her several hours, holding her against him, until she had fallen asleep. And then he left.

The door swayed open a few inches further, and a small shadow slipped into the room with feline grace.

Melrose sat in the middle of the carpet, staring back at her with wide-eyed speculation, as if to ask, "Well, what did you expect?"

"I don't know," Jess answered with a small, shaky smile. "This sort of thing isn't usually discussed at afternoon teas and garden parties." Then she closed her eyes and struggled to control her uncertain emotions, trying to banish the images of Burke's heavily muscled body naked against hers.

At those darkly intimate thoughts and the memory of what had followed, her body was suffused with a sudden heat and a deep ache below her stomach at the memory of his body moving inside hers.

She should have been stunned and shocked. God help her, if she kept her eyes closed she could still feel his hands on her body, and she was profoundly shaken by an undeniable truth—she had wanted that intimacy as she had never wanted anything in her life. Somehow, she had known what would happen. Perhaps she could have—should have—stopped it. But she hadn't, and now he was gone.

She thought of Toby Gill and his casual invitation. It was a harsh reminder of the difference between the rules of society she'd been raised with, and the rules people lived with on the streets of Whitechapel, including Burke, where life was uncertain and precarious, where one didn't know where the next meal might come from much less where one would sleep at night. All artifice was stripped away, and life at times was reduced to the pleasure one could find in a single moment.

She shouldn't have come here, she didn't belong. Not in a place like Whitechapel or with a man like Burke.

"But I had to come," she whispered. The cat stared at her, stoically silent. Then he bowed and stretched and lazily sauntered over to the bed. He stopped abruptly, his attention suddenly fastened on something on the rug.

He batted at it with one paw. The tiny object tumbled and rolled, then caught the light from the hearth and sparkled.

"What is it, Melrose?" she asked, smiling at the cat's playful antics. Then she frowned slightly.

"What have you found?" She slipped from the bed, holding the quilt tightly about her, clinging to the shabby, threadbare comfort it offered. She knelt and picked up the tiny object.

It was a lady's jeweled pin, the tiny stones set in the shape of a flower. She recognized it instantly. It was her sister's pin. But what was it doing here?

Burke. That cold knot of fear returned.

He must have found it at Annie Chapman's flat. But why hadn't he mentioned it, and why wasn't a notation made of it on the list of personal items taken from the flat by the police?

That knot tightened.

What did Burke know? What was he hiding?

Chapter Fifteen

"Never saw nobody wot likes to get herself cleaned up like you do," Belle Rossi grumbled for the dozenth time as she stepped out of the bathing room next to the kitchen.

"It ain't healthy, an' it ain't natural. You'll catch yer death of cold this time o' year." As if dirt and grime were seasonal afflictions. The hem of her skirt twitched back and forth, like Melrose's tail, as she stomped off down the hall, head held high as if the very thought of bathing once a day was loathsome.

"It'll cost yer extra for the hot water," she called back over her shoulder. "I'll add it to wot you already owe me fer the meals I throw out on accounta yer never 'ere on time fer supper."

Jess didn't bother to remind her that she asked her weeks ago not to prepare any meals for her. It all fell on deaf ears. Belle Rossi disliked her for reasons that undoubtedly had nothing to do with cleanliness and everything to do with Devlin Burke.

After she had gone, Jess closed the door and set the latch against any further intrusions.

Water poured into the metal tub in a thin, vaporous stream through a copper pipe connected through the wall to a boiler at the gas stove in the kitchen. She turned on cold water from a second copper faucet. Soon the entire room was shrouded in clouds of warm steam. She quickly undressed and stepped into the tub.

Belle frowned on bathing too often and discouraged her other tenants from it, with the exception of Devlin Burke. She never said a word of criticism about the late hours he kept, or his requests for the use of the bathing room. She fixed him warm meals any time of the day or night, and had on occasion — Jess was certain — provided him alternative sleeping accommodations as well.

Jess chose not to think of it as she unpinned her hair and slipped beneath the water. She quickly scrubbed her entire body and her hair with the soap she'd purchased from the apothecary when she first arrived in Whitechapel.

It was French-milled, with a soft floral fragrance that permeated the steamy room. The wife of the apothecary had talked her husband into buying the soap from a traveling merchant who lost his way about London and found himself in Whitechapel.

The apothecary despaired of ever selling the half-dozen cakes of soap in the satin-lined box. They sat on the shelf for over a year. In all that time he had only been able to sell two pieces to a young woman a few weeks earlier.

When she questioned him further, Jess realized that her sister had been his customer. There was very little he could tell her, except that the young woman was very pretty, although shabbily dressed. However, much to his surprise, she had more than enough to pay for two cakes of soap.

The apothecary had no idea who the young woman was or where she lived. He saw her only once after that. She returned to purchase some laudanum because she was having difficulty sleeping at night.

Just that easily, Jess's path had crossed her sister's.

There was nothing more the apothecary could tell her, but she was so grateful to learn from someone else that Linnie was apparently well and safe at the time that she purchased all the remaining cakes of soap from him. It was an extravagance given the state of her rapidly dwindling finances, but well worth every penny.

She sat in the warm water, the fragrance of the soap clinging to her skin. Only now she allowed herself to think of everything that had happened the night before.

She shivered at the horrible memory of Liz Stride's body on the cold cobbled stones, sinking deeper in the water as if the heat from it could drive away the sudden chill beneath her skin. Then she thought of Devlin Burke.

She wrapped her arms about her as she leaned back against the steel rim of the tub. She looked down at her body through the soap-clouded water that rippled against the skin at her shoulders and across her breasts.

She closed her eyes, trying to block out the memory of what had happened the night before, but it followed her there. It was all the more intense shrouded in the darkness behind her eyes as she recalled the images of two bodies intimately joined, and Burke's hands touching her.

The water moved against her breasts like warm hands surrounding and enclosing her. Satiny waves swelled against her nipples and they suddenly went taut beneath that lapping motion like the heat of his mouth.

She rubbed her hands down over her arms against the sudden goose bumps that tingled across her skin. Then down over her hips and further down the length of her thighs—every place that he had touched, trying to determine if there was any difference in her because of what had happened.

She felt the same—the bend of her knees, then up over her thighs to the bones that protruded softly at her hips. She had washed away traces of blood at the inside of her thighs, but nothing else was changed. There were no outward marks to remind her—almost as if it hadn't happened.

Then beneath the velvet water her fingers brushed the small cluster of tightly coiled curls at the juncture of her thighs, and the distended nub of swollen flesh at the cleft of her body.

She had never touched herself so intimately, and no one had ever touched her until last night. At the time she had been too overwhelmed by other senses to fully comprehend what was happening. When she had finally realized, she was too stunned to respond.

He had touched every part of her with his hands, and then his body had joined with hers in that most intimate way, pushing inside her with a force and intensity that she was certain she would never survive.

She realized now just how limited her knowledge of what happened between a man and a woman had been. Just prior to her sister's wedding, in the privacy of their shared bedroom, Linnie had elaborated what had been explained to her.

The entire process seemed a formidable undertaking, although not frightening. It dispelled some of the unusual stories she'd heard gossiped about by her unmarried friends.

When Jess thought about it, the entire process seemed quite logical, and if one was only required to participate for the purpose of having children then it didn't seem so objectionable at all. That was the point where her knowledge of more intimate marital relations ended.

It left out such details as how one goes about such maneuvers — with clothes on, or removed? It also neglected to elaborate about other possibilities, such as kissing, touching, and the matter of size.

As an artist she knew that people came in varying sizes. It had never occurred to her that *that* particular observation applied to all aspects of the body. Even through her dazed senses when Burke pulled both their clothes away she had been stunned by the size of him pressing hot against her. There was some small part of her that cried out that she was too small, that she would surely break.

There had been that first tautness, a split second of pain as if some barrier had been breached, and then the thick fullness of him pushing inside her. She didn't break. Instead, her taut muscles eased about him with some instinct of their own, the wetness he'd created in her slicked him past the sensitized folds and throbbing nub of flesh, until he was held solid inside her.

Now, experimentally, she traced her fingers over that distended nub of flesh that he had so intimately touched. It was sensitive and tightened even harder under her fingers like a bud coiled so tight that she ached at the touch. The ache spread, radiating up through her stomach, causing her nipples to pucker and harden.

She gasped from the intense, raw pleasure it created along every nerve ending — tiny echoes of the sensations Burke had created in her body. That, too, had been lacking from her sister's explanations.

Once more she curled beneath the water, letting the liquid heat surround and soothe her. She had to think. Everything her sister had explained to her, everything she'd heard gossiped about by her friends, had to do with marriage, betrothals, and committed relationships, and absolutely nothing to do with her relationship with Burke.

They weren't lovers. She didn't even consider them to be friends. Friends could rely upon and trust one another. Burke was a complex, hard man who she suspected neither trusted nor relied upon anyone but himself. He'd lived most of his life on the streets. He was handsome, but dangerous, a loner who looked out for one person — himself.

They would never have met if her sister hadn't disappeared. They had absolutely nothing in common, they lived by different rules. From what she had seen on the streets of Whitechapel, what had happened the night before between them, was commonplace — a little comfort on a cold night, as Toby or Maude would say. She'd been upset and frightened, more than any other time since coming to Whitechapel. Realistically, that was all she had wanted from him as well. She was foolish to think it meant anything more.

It was all resolved in her head. Rationally, logically, she knew that what had happened meant absolutely nothing to Burke. It explained why he had left so easily afterward.

She surged out of the water, sending waves of water crashing angrily over the rim and washing across the floor in her haste to escape the water. She hastily grabbed the cotton bath sheet from the small table nearby and quickly wrapped it about her shivering body. She convinced herself that it was the coolness of the water that made her tremble even though her skin glowed pink.

She quickly dressed in the clean clothes she'd brought with her and twisted her damp hair into a tight coil at the nape of her neck. Then her fingers brushed against the floral jeweled pin that she'd brought along and hidden beneath her clothes on the table.

She suspected Belle was inclined to snoop around in the flat when no one was about, considering all the times she had returned to find things moved about and Melrose locked inside.

The pin — Linnie's pin — was cool to the touch, the brilliant stones glinting back at her with multihued facets.

She forced the night before out of her thoughts. She had to accept that it wasn't important — certainly not important to Burke. She had to get past it, forget it, and focus on the reason she had come to Whitechapel.

Five women were dead. The one person who had known all of them was Toby Gill. She had to find him.

* * *

It was midmorning when she arrived at the Rose and Thistle. They weren't open for business, and of course Maude was gone. But one man who had slept the night under a table and claimed to know Maude well, was able to tell her where Maude lived.

She had a room at a lodging house. It was rundown, the walls of the narrow hallways dripping with moisture, floorboards sagging underfoot, and the distinct scurrying sound of inhabitants other than people filling the shadows. It was a rabbits warren of cubbyholes, alcoves, and one-room niches, all filled with sleeping bodies. For a coin a boy directed her to Maude's room.

"Go away!" A deep-throated voice bellowed as she knocked persistently.

She knocked again. The door finally jerked open, and Maude peered out. She was disheveled, her bright red hair a tangled mass, and heavy, dark makeup had seeped into deeply etched lines about her eyes. She clasped a mended quilt about her body, one bare shoulder exposed. There were obviously several well-chosen comments on the tip of her tongue. Then her eyes widened in surprise and recognition.

"Wot yer doin' 'ere?" she asked.

"I need to talk to you," Jess hastily explained. Maude cast a quick glance over one shoulder and pulled the door more tightly closed so that only her face was showing in the narrow opening.

"Wot the devil is so damned important this time o' day? Can't yer see I'm busy?" she grumbled, keeping a firm hand on the door to prevent it from opening any further.

Although she couldn't see into the darkened room through the narrow opening, it was obvious that Maude had someone with her—undoubtedly a man. Under any other circumstances, Jess would have been completely mortified. She didn't have time for it.

"It's almost noon," she said impatiently. "I must speak with you." Then she added, "There have been two more murders."

Maude stiffened. "Yeah, I heard 'bout that."

"You already know?" Jess was stunned. The police were very careful to keep this sort of thing quiet as long as possible to avoid any more panic. But then as she had learned, in Whitechapel there was very little that happened that everyone wasn't aware of almost immediately. And the recent murders brought a special element of fear that seemed to hasten even the slightest bit of gossip or rumor.

"Then it's even more important that we talk. I have to find Toby Gill."

Maude's mouth twisted with a frown. Her expression was wary. "I ain't seen him since I gave 'im yer message. What's it all about?"

Jess quickly explained that her sister had been living with Annie Chapman, and that the women she'd been looking for earlier were friends of Annie's.

She finished by explaining, "Liz Stride and Catherine Eddowes were murdered last night. I was on my way to talk to them when I found out. Toby knew all of the women who have been killed. He may know something about it. He might have seen Liz Stride or Catherine Eddowes. It's very important that I find him. You're the only one who can help me."

She shrugged. "I ain't heard from Toby since I gave 'im yer message."

"Then perhaps we could find him together. You have to help me." When Maude still hesitated, her mouth twisted into an uncertain frown, she added, "I'd be willing to pay you."

To Jess's surprise Maude still hesitated. Finally, she said, "Give me a minute, luv." She closed the door in her face.

Jess stood there for several minutes, uncertain whether to stay or leave. Finally, the door opened again and Maude stepped out into the hallway, carefully closing the door behind her.

She was dressed in a shirtwaist and skirt with a thick sweater buttoned across the front. A knit cap was pulled down over her hair. Her face was washed revealing a dusting of freckles across the wrinkled skin. She wore fingerless gloves, scuffed shoes, and stockings with gaping holes.

"Yer got money with ya?"

"Yes," she answered hesitantly. "I brought what I have left."

"You'll need it," Maude informed her. "Information don't come cheap. Toby's probably laid up someplace sleepin' it off," she speculated. "He don't have a reg'lar place, like these deluxe accommodations." She made a sweeping gesture with her hand. "Usually just finds 'imself a cot fer the night in one of the doss houses. Last time I just waited till he came round to the Rose again. It might be days before he comes back this time. Especially if he knows the police is lookin' for him."

"But no one else knows about this."

Maude laughed, a harsh sound deep in her lungs. "He's smart enough to figure it out on his own, luv. If he knew all them women, then he knows they'll get around to considerin' him a prime suspect in them killins."

"But he couldn't have had anything to do with them. He's not the sort."

"Yer right enough about that. He don't have the strength to do wot that fiend done to them women, cuttin' them like that. But the police will still be lookin' fer him fer the same reasons yer want to talk to him—to find out wot he knows."

"Then it's all the more important that we find him right away, before he disappears completely."

Maude agreed. "Right yer are, luv."

"Which doss houses might he have gone to?"

Maude laughed, a low, coarse sound in her throat. "There's dozens, luv. An' not fancy like this place. This is the Palace compared to wot you'll find out there. Not exactly the sort for someone like you."

"I have to find him," Jess insisted. "My sister's life depends on it."

They spent the entire afternoon going from one lodging house to the other, searching doss houses and taverns, asking countless people on the street if they had seen Toby. No one had seen him. It was as if he'd vanished just as her sister had.

Several times Jess had the distinct impression that someone was following them. But each time she looked back over her shoulder there was no one there, except the odd assortment of vendors, hawkers, shills, draymen, and people who lived on the streets. No one was lurking about, or scuttling among the shadows.

Still she couldn't rid herself of the feeling. It was late afternoon when she and Maude returned to the Rose and Thistle.

"I'll buy yer a spot o' ale," Maude generously offered, with the money Jess had paid for her time jingling in her pocket. "Toby might show up t'night."

Jess was tired, hungry, and thirsty. Even a mug of thick, dark ale seemed appealing. But it was already past four o'clock, and the last of her money was almost gone except for a few shillings that would barely pay for the fare of a hansom to take her across London.

"Thank you, but I must go. There's something important I must do," she explained. "If you hear from Toby, please have him contact me immediately."

"Dearie, fer this kind o' money I'll have the queen herself contact you."

The sun slanted low over the rooftops of buildings as she left the Rose and Thistle. The sky had gone from blue to cold, pale gray. She quickly found a hansom and gave him the address at Marylebone Lane .

"Do you know it?" she asked when he looked at her incredulously.

"Close enough, miss. I know Marylebone *Road*. Can't be far from there. I can find it, if anyone can." He hesitated, then squinted down at her skeptically from under the rim of his stovepipe hat held on his head by a muffler tied under his chin.

"But that's pretty near across the whole of London. It'll take better part o' an hour to get there."

"It shouldn't take more than a half hour if we get on right away." Still he hesitated.

"It'll be a sizable fare, miss."

"Will a half crown be enough?"

He looked up with a startled expression. "More 'an enough, miss. For a half crown . . ."

"Yes, I know. You'd take me to the Royal Palace for that much money."

He tipped his hat. "That I would, miss. Climb aboard. I'll have yer there in twenty. No one knows the streets o' London like ol' Tarkin."

She climbed inside the hansom and pulled the narrow double doors closed across the compartment, closing out most of the chill wind that had come up. A man stepped from the dark shadows at an adjacent alley. He waved down another hansom and quickly climbed aboard. It plunged down the street at a frantic pace, swaying from side-to-side through thickening late afternoon traffic, always within sight of the first hansom.

* * *

The crowded hub of central London was left behind. The staid edifice of the Exchange, austere Banker's Row, and the ornately frescoed buildings of Parliament gave way to the Georgian facades of small businesses, exclusive clothiers, jeweler's salons, importers of rare artifacts, and the few prestigious art galleries that solicited to an aristocratic clientele.

The driver, Tarkin, reined to a stop at the curb before the establishment of Françoise Gilot, gallery owner and procurer of fine artwork.

The discreetly lettered sign to the right of the brass and wood door declared simply his last name *Gilot*. His reputation as the most knowledgeable and discreet art dealer in London required nothing more.

A small, private gallery occupied the front salon of the building, where Gilot displayed the finest of European artwork—by appointment only—for his wealthy patrons.

In the private sitting rooms the daughters of London's aristocracy received art instruction—an acceptable indulgence for proper young ladies of society—from the small elite staff of artists personally selected by Françoise Gilot.

Jess stepped down from the hansom and paid the driver the agreed amount. "Please wait. I'll only be a few minutes, and there will be another half crown for you."

He tipped the brim of his hat. "Right yer are, miss." Then he straightened his back in spite of the bitter chill that whipped down the street. He was aware that his rig was oddly out of place among the elegant private coaches with high-stepping teams of matched horses that passed by, just as the young woman he'd brought was out of place in this part of London.

To all outward appearances, she was a common street girl, dressed in plain, drab, cast-off clothes, no better than a charwoman or a doxie. But there was a hint of elegance beneath the squashed felt hat, a certain poise as she instinctively held the hem of her skirt away from the water that swirled in the gutter, and an unmistakable air of confidence that no doxie would have had in this part of London, with its gleaming black coaches, ladies in expensive, elegant gowns, and gentlemen in finely-tailored waistcoats, satin vests, and boots undoubtedly polished by a footman.

At this time of day Jess knew most of the staff and their aristo-cratic young students would be gone for the day. She rang the bell, announcing her arrival, and then, instead of waiting for the foot-man to open the door, she quickly let herself in, not wanting to draw attention to herself by waiting at the door.

Instead of the footman, Jacques Bernier, a dapper little French-man, it was Monsieur Gilot who appeared, perhaps thinking that one of his patrons had returned unexpectedly.

Françoise Gilot often worked late into the evening, organizing displays of newly acquired artwork for his patrons, cataloging ac-quisitions for other patrons and writing correspondence to other gallery owners throughout London and Europe in search of a particular painting or lithograph requested by one of his clients.

The formal entry was filled with shadows. He had obviously not been expecting anyone and the gas lamps in the entry had not been lit. The only light was from the adjacent formal salon where he met with all clients in an elegant atmosphere, serving them delicate French pastries with tea or coffee laced with cream, cinnamon, and chocolate.

He frowned in the half-light when he saw her, taking in the shabby skirt, threadbare midlength coat, and squash hat, her fea-tures hidden in the shadows.

He was elegantly dressed as befitted his position as successful gallery owner and art connoisseur in a long coat and pants of the finest black worsted wool, a gray satin vest, and a crisply starched linen shirt. In deference to his artistic eccentricity, his slightly long hair was smoothed back from a rounding face. He had a pencil-thin mustache instead of the muttonchop whiskers that were fashionable among English gentlemen, and wore a single eyeglass at his left eye. It was attached to a fine gold chain about his neck.

"We are closed for the afternoon," he announced with a disdainful tone and a disapproving arch of his right brow.

"Ah, c'mon guv'ner," Jess said sweetly, in her best imitation of an East End accent, "yer wouldn't turn away a girl on a night like this, would ya?"

He stiffened visibly. "As I said, mademoiselle, we are closed for the day. This is an art gallery, not a charity house. I have a regular staff. I have no need of a charwoman, or whatever it is that you do."

"How about a few coins then, luv?" she suggested, enjoying her game, at the same time being aware of the sad reality made by the distinction of her clothes.

"I donate to several charitable organizations, mademoiselle. Now, I must ask you to leave."

"Not even a ha' penny, sir?" she asked as she finally stepped from the shadows and into the light that poured into the hallway from the formal salon.

Monsieur Gilot stared at her. Then his eyeglass popped loose and he gasped. "It is possible? Mademoiselle Forsythe?"

She smiled. "Good afternoon, monsieur."

"But, but . . . Mon Dieu! . . . I do not understand. . . ." he gestured with helpless confusion at the clothes she was wearing.

"It's a very long story. I need your help. And as always, I must insist upon your usual discretion." Then she added emphatically, "No one must know that I have been here, or that you have seen me."

"But of course, mademoiselle," he rushed to take her hand, then tucked her arm through his. As he escorted her to the familiar private studio on the second floor, he assured her, "The last student left some time ago. Everyone else is gone, including Jacques. No one will know that you have been here. You may rely upon absolute secrecy."

The small private studio at the top of the stairs was dark. But during the day natural light from skylight windows in the ceiling flooded it with perfect light.

The air was cool and faintly musty, with the redolent smells of heavy oil-base pigments and linseed oil and the sharp bite of turpentine.

Monsieur Gilot turned up the gaslight at the wall. It filled the room with shadows that outlined spiky sable brushes of various thickness and width, standing on end to dry in tall apothecary jars. Bottles and jars of many different sizes were clustered on shelves at one wall, some filled with clear liquid, others filled with primary colored powders of yellow, red, and blue, and secondary colors of green, purple and orange.

Two paintings sat on easels against one wall, draped with cotton cloth to protect them from dust and exposure to the sunlight that normally filled the studio. A third easel sat apart, also carefully draped, the painting not quite finished.

Solace. It was the one word that came to mind, as Jess walked into the small, familiar haven and let her senses fill with the sights, smells, colors, and textures. Mr. Gilot walked beside her with silent understanding as she lifted the cotton dust cloth from first one painting and then another.

Chambord, Chenenceaux, and the most recent, Azay-le-Rideau — all chateaux of the Loire Valley in France, and the subjects of the latest series of paintings by the renowned artist, J.B. Dumont. The colors were rich and vibrant, capturing the verdant hillsides, lush vineyards, and the imposing chateau of the fabled Loire Valley of France. Each was uniquely evocative of the style established by J.B. Dumont, contrasting the wealth of ancient aristocratic families — symbolized by the imposing chateau — with the timeless pastoral beauty of the French countryside, peasants who worked the fields and vineyards, and simple stone and wood-beam cottages.

Monsieur Gilot had praised the Loire series, declaring that it would be even more successful that the famed Provence series. Over the past several months the three paintings had gradually taken form. Each was now carefully draped, their existence shrouded in secrecy according to the artist's wishes.

No one but Gilot and the artist was allowed inside this small private studio. Jess carefully scrutinized each painting. Finally she made a decision. "Sell the Chenenceaux."

He could barely contain his excitement. "The usual arrangement, mademoiselle?"

"Yes, three hundred pounds sterling on advance against the final sale amount. I shall take one hundred pounds with me this evening, with the balance is to be deposited into my account."

Gilot clasped his hands together excitedly. "These will be even more successful than the Provence series. I already have a buyer for the next J.B. Dumont painting, sight unseen." His dark eyes glistened. "What about Chambord, or Azay-le-Rideau? I could sell them immediately."

"No," she was adamant. "Only Chenenceaux for now." Monsieur Gilot suddenly stiffened. He looked past her to the doorway, a frown on his face.

"The gallery is closed, monsieur," he announced.

Startled by the intrusion, Jess whirled around. She gasped as a man stepped out of the shadows.

Chapter Sixteen

"Monsieur! I must ask you to leave at once! We are not receiving patrons this time of night." Gilot repeated vehemently. He gave the stranger a deprecating look.

It was obvious from the stranger's appearance that he was not the usual client. His clothes fit well enough but were of common cloth, and there was the unmistakable air of the streets about him, something dangerous and vaguely threatening that had Gilot drawing up defensively.

Devlin Burke slowly walked into the small studio. In the soft glow of the single gaslight that had been turned up at the wall, he carefully walked about the room, touching the sable-tipped brushes, picking up a jar and swirling the colorful powdered pigments about inside, uncapping the bottle of turpentine to smell the sharp odor.

His attention to every detail was as meticulous as it had been that day in Annie Chapman's flat, or the night before in the room Catherine Eddowes shared with Liz Stride in Mitre Square. Then his gaze fastened on the Loire Château paintings and the distinctive signature in the lower left corner of each.

He turned then, his face filled with hard lines and angles, anger carefully controlled in every rigid feature. The expression behind his eyes was cold and speculative.

Not an easy face. His voice was low and harsh, edged with that same hard anger.

"What is this place?"

She realized then that there was no way for him to know. The sign beside the front entrance simply said *Gilot*. For those unfamiliar with this part of London there would have been no clue in that name to explain. Nor would there have been anything inside the house where he obviously followed her from the street.

The formal salon was that, a formal area where Gilot met privately with his esteemed clients. The paintings they came to see were kept carefully draped and stored, brought out from the back gallery only upon request for viewing. The private rooms, where lessons were given, were in another part of what had once been a private town house in the fashionable part of London.

"Who are you?"

Monsieur Gilot was not a big man. He was no taller than Jess and portly in stature yet he started across the studio in purposeful strides. Jess stopped him with a hand at his sleeve.

"It's all right, Françoise. Leave us."

"But, mademoiselle . . . !" he protested. "It is not wise."

She shook her head. "It will be all right. This is Inspector Burke of the police," she hastily made the introduction. Gilot looked from her to Burke with uncertainty.

"Please," she insisted, and then reassured him, "I will be quite safe." She wished she could be certain of that. Burke was angry. No, she realized, perhaps furious was a better word. She had never seen him so angry, rigidly controlled, as if he didn't trust what he might do if he relaxed that control for a single moment.

Gilot finally nodded. Reluctantly, he left the studio. But he hesitated a moment at the door.

"You have but to call out, Mademoiselle Forsythe, and I will have every gendarme within several miles here instantly. I don't care if he is an inspector." He deliberately left the door to the studio open. She turned to face Burke.

She'd been caught in a lie of her own making. Now her thoughts raced as she tried to decide what to tell him. Could she trust him? She felt the cool gold of Linnie's pin at the bottom of her pocket.

What had he been doing with the pin? Why hadn't he turned it in at the station with the rest of the articles taken from Annie Chapman's flat? Did he already have his own suspicions about Mary Kelly?

She was determined to protect her sister. Enough rumors, speculation, and notoriety already surrounded the killings. The newspapers would have a field day if they knew the wife of a peer of the realm was involved. Yet she wondered how much he already knew or suspected. Enough, she realized, to have followed her here.

He's got no use for liars, cheats, or thieves. Could the truth possibly save her?

"What is this place?" he repeated in a low voice as he made an expansive gesture about the studio with his hand.

She decided to try for the truth. "This is an art gallery owned by Monsieur Gilot."

"And this particular room?"

"A private studio used for painting."

"J.B. Dumont's studio," he speculated accurately. So, he had noticed the signature on the paintings.

"What is this all about, Jess? Or is it Mademoiselle Forsythe? Or some other name?" he suggested with tight-lipped fury.

Having had some experience with his anger in the past, she braced herself. The night before was forgotten. Then she saw comprehension in the sudden narrowing of those cold blue eyes.

"Or perhaps J.B. Dumont?"

Her back was rigid as if she'd been physically backed against a wall. She answered simply, "Yes."

His gaze fastened once more on the paintings, then back at her, as if he were trying to make the physical connection between the woman he'd gotten to know over the past few weeks and the bits and pieces he'd heard or read about J.B. Dumont.

There was no place in his life for art, still he knew what went on in the whole of London and beyond. Oftentimes solving a case depended upon it. And during his misspent youth on the streets, surviving as best he could, he'd acquired a passable knowledge of what was valuable and what was not. The artist, J.B. Dumont, had established a reputation for being as reclusive as he — or apparently *she* — was talented. He couldn't begin to imagine the amount of money a Dumont painting cost.

Jess Kelly, J.B. Dumont, Miss Forsythe — obviously all the same person. He realized that it all made perfect sense — her artistic talent, her manner of speech, the fine satin undergarments he'd discovered when she fainted that no common street girl could ever hope to own. It was all a lie.

She was no pathetic, impoverished young woman forced to live off the streets. When he thought of what Abberline paid her for the sketches, he almost laughed out loud. It was a pittance compared to a three-hundred-pound advance for one painting. The only question was—Why?

"You have a great deal of explainin' to do, Miss Forsythe, or Dumont, or whatever the hell it is yer callin' yerself today." His voice quivered, his face was void of all expression, somehow more frightening than the rigid expression of anger.

"And you have some explaining to do as well," she informed him bluntly, refusing to be backed down by it. She reached inside her pocket as she walked toward him across the studio. She laid her sister's jeweled pin down on the table that contained the paint pigments and brushes. It glowed in multihued colors of ruby-red, sapphire-blue, and emerald-green. "This belonged to my sister. I want to know how you came by it."

Burke frowned. He always kept the pin with him, afraid someone else might see it and ask where he'd gotten it. He didn't understand how she could have come by it. He looked at her then, forced to remember the night before, and understood. He must have lost it at the flat, and somehow she'd found it.

Frederick Abberline, Chief Inspector of Police, looked up sharply. There were dark circles under his bloodshot eyes, and his face sagged with fatigue.

"What the devil are you talking about, Burke?"

"Her name is not Jess Kelly."

"Well if it's not Kelly, then what the devil is it? And how, precisely, is it of any importance?"

It was the second time in less than a minute that he'd mentioned the devil, causing Jess to wonder if such invocations might conjure up that fork-tailed little demon.

She'd never seen Abberline lose control. He was perilously close to it now, pressured by increased demands to solve the Ripper murders, and now with two more killings that brought the total to five. She saw Jimmy Cassidy in the outer station as they walked through. He smelled a story and wanted information.

Abberline was trying to keep details of the murders secret, but he was hindered by the demands of the home office and the agreement he'd been forced to make with the press.

If they didn't cooperate with Jimmy, he'd obtain details from other sources, most of it inaccurate, fed by rumor and speculation. But correct or not, he would eventually get his story. It was a matter of being tenacious. How long would it take him to find out about the woman who'd been staying with Annie Chapman?

She wished she'd been able to find Toby, but there were no messages when they returned. Her last hope was that he might have sent word to the flat on Abbington Road. But at the moment there was absolutely no hope of going there. She had two furious men glowering at her.

"Will someone please explain what is going on here?" Abberline demanded. Burke looked at her.

"Are you going to explain? Or do you want me to?"

Jess's hands were so tightly clasped that her knuckles had gone white. She still needed their help. Without it, finding her sister was hopeless. A saying from her childhood popped into her brain—one of those long lost thoughts instilled by one in a long line of humorless nannies. "Oh, what a tangled web we weave, when first we practice to deceive."

Unlike the spider that wove those intricate webs, she was the one who'd been caught.

"My name is Jessamyn Forsythe."

"Forsythe?" Abberline repeated, his temper thinning. "Very well, it's not Kelly. I fail to see how that bit of information is of monumental importance."

"Tell him the rest of it," Burke ordered in a tone that suggested it would be unwise to refuse.

"I also go by the name, J.B. Dumont."

The expression on Abberline's face suggested slight confusion, that quickly disappeared.

"Dumont! The artist, J.B. Dumont?" His expression was now one of incredulity.

"Tell him the rest of it," Burke insisted.

When she had finally finished explaining the reasons she had come to Whitechapel, there was still one more unexplained detail.

"Then I may assume that Mary Kelly is not your sister's true name," Abberline concluded. It was the one detail she had not elaborated upon to Burke during their hasty ride back to Whitechapel.

"No. It was a name of someone — a friend — from our childhood." She didn't elaborate that Mary had been an imaginary friend. "When I received the letter signed with that name, I knew it was from my sister. I also knew she must be in terrible trouble. She would never have used another name unless she was badly frightened."

"Is everything else you've told us the truth?"

"Yes. The letter was posted from Whitechapel three days before I received it. In it my sister mentioned that she was staying with a young woman by the name of Annie Chapman. She asked that I not try to find her, and that I not tell anyone of the letter.

"I love my sister very much. I have to find her. No matter what it takes. Something has happened and I intend to find out what it is and take her home."

"Where precisely is home? And what about your family? Or, are you and your sister alone?"

"My family knows nothing of this. I thought it best that way. I had tried to persuade them to make inquiries through a private individual, but they refused."

"Who did you contact?"

She looked briefly at Burke. "I spoke with Mr. Sherlock Holmes about making discreet inquiries. My brother-in-law discovered what I had done and dismissed him."

"Then I assume your sister's name is no longer Forsythe? And what about her husband? Surely he's been making inquiries into her disappearance, although there's been no word of such a disappearance through police headquarters."

"There wouldn't have been any notification. My brother-in-law chose to make discreet inquiries through his own sources."

"Not an inexpensive endeavor," Abberline remarked.

"No, but that was hardly the concern. Discretion was of utmost importance."

His eyes narrowed. He suspected what hadn't yet been said. "Discretion. A simple man would hardly be concerned about discretion. But for a member of society, discretion is everything."

She sensed Burke watching her. She didn't look at him. Instead she simply nodded.

Abberline understood. His tone had subtly changed.

"Who, precisely, is your sister?"

She felt Burke's intense blue gaze. There had been so many lies. She needed to explain to him why she'd done it. If they only had a few minutes of privacy. But there was no time for explanations, and she said simply, "Lenore Deverell." She added in a quiet voice, "Lady Rushmore."

"Good God," Abberline said under his breath. "The wife of Jason Deverell, Lord Rushmore, first cousin to Queen Victoria?" He was incredulous.

"Yes."

From across the office she felt Burke's unwavering stare. The room had suddenly grown very small. For a moment she allowed herself to look at him, hoping she would see some small shred of understanding in his eyes. That hope immediately vanished.

Abberline drew his fingers across his deeply furrowed brow. "A peer of the realm, practically a member of the Royal Family, for God's sake!"

She forced her gaze back to Abberline. It was as if Burke stared right through her. There was no understanding, no compassion or empathy, only that void of expression as if he suddenly despised her, or worse yet, felt absolutely nothing at all—not even anger.

"Surely you can understand why secrecy is absolutely imperative," she said to Abberline. "I was afraid what would happen if it were discovered that she had disappeared. I was certain it would only make matters worse. 1 had to be certain that no one discovered the truth."

"The thought of scandal must have been particularly painful for you," Burke added.

She looked at him. "I couldn't care less about scandal. I'm only concerned about my sister's welfare."

"Do you have any idea why your sister might have come to Whitechapel?" Abberline asked, bringing the conversation back to more important matters.

She shook her head. "I've been trying to think why she would

221

come here. She must have been very badly frightened. It's not the sort of place . . ."

"Not the sort of place where a lady of society would risk being seen," Burke suggested, the words tight with anger.

"Inspector." Abberline cautioned him. Burke turned and paced to the far side of the office.

Abberline swung about in his chair. "This changes everything. It would be disastrous if your sister's identity was revealed."

He pinched the bridge of his nose — an increasingly frequent gesture the past few weeks — and closed his eyes in concentration.

"Two more women were found dead last night," he finally said in a speculative voice. "From the description you've given us, neither was your sister."

She glanced over at Burke, stunned to realize that he obviously hadn't mentioned anything of her presence at Mitre Square the night before to Abberline. He still refused to look at her.

Weeks of frustration over the investigation came down to this moment. Abberline swung back around and slammed the palm of his hand down on the top of the desk.

"We have to find this murderer. If the home office steps in now, it will be a mass of confusion and ineptitude. We'll have no hope of finding him, or God help us, your sister."

"We've made remarkable progress, especially with the sketches you've provided. We could never have accomplished this much without them." His gaze narrowed thoughtfully.

"Why the secrecy about J.B. Dumont?" he suddenly asked.

He often did that, jumping about with seemingly unconnected questions that kept everyone slightly off balance, as if he were deliberately trying to confuse them.

"It's really quite simple," she answered very honestly. "Very few people are willing to take a woman seriously as an artist. It has absolutely nothing to do with talent, and everything to do with certain notions about who should be allowed to pursue certain endeavors. Therefore I assumed another name, one that didn't reveal the fact that I was a woman. Once clients were no longer concerned about that fact, they were willing to consider my work on its own merit."

He shook his head. "And I've been paying you a pittance for the sketches you've been making. Countless others have been thrown away. Which brings us to a more serious dilemma.

"Your work has been invaluable to us. Without it . . ." his voice trailed off. "Your work has provided the first accurate likenesses of possible suspects. And there is the matter of the *Times*. Cassidy is already cooling his heels in the outer office, wanting the latest information we have on the new murders. I've been instructed by Inspector Devoe to cooperate with him in whatever manner he wishes.

"I don't mind telling you that I don't like that. But I have to give Cassidy something or I'll have the home office down our throats over this." He gave her a long look.

"I need you. But the truth of the matter is that I should send you back to your family. No young woman of your position should be involved in such matters. Naturally, we shall continue to do whatever is necessary to find your sister."

He was going to send her away. Jess leaned across the desk toward him, more determined than she had ever been about anything in her life.

"It didn't bother you when you thought I was Jess Kelly," she pointed out to him. "You were perfectly willing to accept my assistance then. I still want to help in any way that I may."

"There could be dreadful repercussions," he pointed out. "It's simply out of the question."

"I'm sorry, Inspector Abberline, but that simply won't do," she told him emphatically. "I won't let you send me away. I've broken no laws, I've done nothing wrong. I'm of age and I have the means to support myself. I may come and go as I please. If you send me away, I shall continue on my own," she said quietly but leaving little doubt that she meant precisely what she said. "My sister is somewhere here in Whitechapel, and she's in danger. I won't leave until I find her. And there's nothing you can do to stop me."

She stepped back from the desk then. She'd said everything she intended to say and saw no point in discussing it any further. She glanced briefly at Burke, but he simply looked past her, his expression closed and unapproachable. Abberline's expression was contemplative, the circles deep beneath his eyes.

"Is there anything else about all of this that I haven't been told?"

he asked.

She thought of her sister's pin and felt Burke's gaze on her. He'd given no explanation as to why he'd taken the pin from Annie Chapman's flat. There'd been speculation in the newspapers that the police might somehow be covering up facts about the murders. Was there some basis for that speculation?

Silence drew out in the office. Abberline was waiting for an answer. She could tell him about the pin, but what would it gain? She looked at Burke then. He was also waiting for her answer, perhaps wondering if she would betray him.

She saw something behind his eyes — something behind that impenetrable wall that he'd put up between them, blocking out any emotion. She'd lied and deceived him, but it went beyond that. There was more that she didn't understand. It was almost as if he were mocking her, daring her to tell Abberline about it.

"There's nothing else," she said to Abberline. "I've told you everything I know." He watched her carefully. Then he, too, seemed to have arrived at a decision.

"You've put me in a very difficult position, Miss Kelly." He admitted, "I can't force you to leave. However I could always forcibly return you to your family." He smiled faintly then. "However, I somehow feel that would be pointless.

"You may of course remain as long as you are gainfully employed. And we have need of your talents. Therefore, I propose that we continue as before. Naturally, everything that we have discussed must not go beyond this office." When Burke came at him from across the desk and started to protest, he waved him back.

"I've made my decision. God help us all if it's the wrong one." He looked across the desk at Jess. "I want you to continue your work. There will be more need of it than ever now, with these two latest murders. It will mean long hours, and I refuse to pay you a farthing more. Is that understood?" he asked her with mock gruffness.

Jess smothered back a smile. "Yes, sir."

Then Abberline sobered once more. "You'll be in the thick of it, my dear. I believe it's safe to assume that your sister is somehow involved in this dangerous business. She may very well know the identity of the murderer, which makes it all the more imperative that we find her with all haste. And, my dear, that danger could also find you." His expression was grave as he seemed to arrive at another decision.

"Therefore, Mr. Burke, you are to stay with Miss Kelly at all times." He waved a finger at Jess. You are not to go about alone, under any circumstances. Is that clear?"

"Yes, but what about Toby Gill? He knew both Liz Stride and Catherine Eddowes, as well as Annie Chapman." He glanced at her suspiciously. They had discussed the most recent murders, but no names had been mentioned. Once again he suspected that she knew far more than she was telling.

"I must have your word on this, Miss Forsythe, Kelly, or Dumont. I don't care which you choose to call yourself, but I want it perfectly understood that you're not to pursue this by yourself. Or, by God, I shall have you removed. Is that clear?"

"Yes."

"By combining our efforts, we will prevail. By acting independently of one another, we are at risk of jeopardizing everything. Is that perfectly clear?"

She nodded.

"We need each other very badly, Miss Kelly or Forsythe." He made a frustrated gesture. "I don't even know what the devil to call you."

"I think Kelly will do very well," she said. "And it will maintain my anonymity with everyone else."

He nodded. "Very well." Then he turned to Burke.

"We must move as quickly as possible. These latest murders will very likely set loose a panic on the streets when word gets out. It's as if this maniac knows our every move. I want him found. I'm not concerned with your misgivings or personal feelings in this matter, Burke. You're to make use of Miss Kelly's artistic talents. I am making you responsible for this situation. Is *that* understood?"

Burke started to protest.

"A simple *yes* will do very nicely," Abberline informed him, removing any argument or choice in the matter.

Burke's expression was murderous. "Yes!" he snapped, realizing that any other response would most likely find him removed from the case.

"Excellent." Abberline turned back to Jess. "You have a great deal

225

of work to do. Mr. Burke, you need to find Toby Gill."

The meeting was officially ended.

She followed Burke out of Abberline's office, walking rapidly to keep up with his furious strides. Jimmy Cassidy saw them immediately and latched on to Burke like a leech.

"What is the latest information on the double murders, Inspector?"

"We're following up on information." His expression and voice were carefully controlled, giving nothing away of the cold fury that had followed him out of the meeting with Abberline. It was remarkable, she thought, how easily he slipped behind that remote facade.

He went into his office. Uninvited, Jimmy followed, not the least put off that he and Jess obviously weren't invited. "My sources say that the murders were the same—throats cut, bodies slashed, and both women in their midtwenties, and both prostitutes. Can you verify that, Inspector?"

"Your sources?" Burke looked up briefly, only his eyes momentarily giving away any emotion at all—a brief flicker of contempt.

"That's right." Jimmy then turned to Jess. "What information do you have from descriptions given by witnesses?"

She felt Burke's warning glance. She smiled carefully. "I don't know much about any of that. I haven't been in all day. I caught a bit of the sniffles."

"But they'll have you workin' soon enough, right, luv?" He gave her a cheeky grin, but she wasn't fooled for a minute. He was clever and tenacious. It was how he earned his reputation as one of the most widely read writers for the *Times*.

"Your sources seem to be well-informed," he remarked. "Perhaps they would be willing to come into the station and give descriptions of what they've seen to Miss Kelly."

Jimmy laughed, incredulous. "Not likely, Inspector. They're my contacts on the street, just like you got. They're willin' to give me information on the condition that they remain anonymous. They wouldn't be anonymous anymore if they was to come here and speak with the police, now would they?"

"I see your dilemma," Burke nodded. He looked up only briefly as Endicott appeared in the doorway.

"What is it?"

Endicott looked from one to the other. He smiled at Jess, then looked to Burke. "That package you lost, sir?"

Burke's gaze narrowed. "What about it?"

"I think it's been found, sir."

His expression was carefully fixed with a smile. She wondered if Jimmy Cassidy sensed there was something more going on here.

"Excellent," Burke commented, then explained for everyone else's benefit, "My dear Aunt Agatha would have been terribly disappointed if it hadn't been found."

"Wot would you like me to do about it, sir?" Endicott asked, as if they were discussing a piece of wrapped cod or a jar of homemade jam.

Burke's dear Aunt Agatha, indeed. He'd never mentioned any family at all that she knew of. And why this sudden concern for a long-lost aunt? What was he up to?

Burke smiled charmingly, startling her with the amazing swiftness with which he manipulated moods when he wanted to.

"I'll be along in a minute. I want to take care of it personally." Then his expression changed again as he spotted someone else in the hallway beyond the office.

"Devoe. A minute of yer time, if you please."

Devoe had obviously just returned, his immaculate overcoat was damp across the shoulders, the finely worsted wool glistening with moisture. He must have forgotten something and returned for it, since he always managed to leave the police station promptly at five o'clock each day. He didn't consider himself bound by the long hours everyone else had been keeping, although it seemed he was always well-informed about everything that went on.

It was well past eight o'clock in the evening. Whatever it was that had brought him back this time of night must have been important.

He removed his hat and then his leather gloves, placing them inside the crown. There was a deep brim-line in the hair plastered down about his head. He smoothed his hair back with lean fingers.

"Good evening, Miss Kelly. I wasn't aware that you'd taken to working so late of an evening."

She felt Jimmy's speculative gaze on her.

"She was a bit under the weather today," he explained.

"I wasn't aware that you were ill, my dear," Devoe remarked, watching her carefully.

"It's nothing serious. Just a bit of congestion in my head. The weather I suppose." She met Devoe's gaze evenly. "It's been very cold out, wouldn't you say, Mr. Devoe?" He was pale, his hands waxy and stiff, as if he might have been out in the chill night air for several hours.

"Most dreadful weather, Miss Kelly."

Burke cut through their stilted pleasantries about the weather. "I need your assistance, Devoe." He gave the special inspector a brief smile. Anything more, given their coolness to one another over the past few weeks, would have roused suspicion.

"Jimmy needs the latest information on the murders of last night. I've been out most of the day, and I don't have all the details." He moved efficiently around his desk then, and grabbed Jess's arm, guiding her ahead of him toward the door. "In the interest of cooperation with the newspapers, I'm certain you can bring him up-to-date on all the latest information that we have."

"I have an engagement this evening," Devoe protested, and started to follow them.

Outside the office Endicott handed Burke a note. He grabbed it and maneuvered Jess across the station in quick strides. They were out the door and climbing into a hansom before Devoe was halfway across the crowded station.

"What are you doing?" she gasped breathlessly, as Burke practically threw her inside the hansom.

"Following up on that package from my dear Aunt Agatha," he said.

"Do you have an Aunt Agatha?"

He gave her an odd look then, his face suddenly hard. "I have no family."

He didn't bother to give instructions to the driver, but instead motioned for him to leave with all possible haste, even before he closed the doors over the compartment. He settled into the narrow seat beside her. The conversation wasn't exactly polite or even congenial, but at least he was talking to her.

"What about Jimmy? Was it wise to leave him with Devoe?" After Abberline's specific orders that Jimmy was only to be given the most basic information about the cases she couldn't believe that he would deliberately disobey. "Isn't that a bit like leaving the wolf to guard the sheep?"

"Only if the sheep is really a sheep."

"What are you talking about?"

His expression was grim. "An old saying about wolves in sheep's clothing."

"Jimmy?" She glanced at him, suddenly comprehending what he meant, that possibly he was providing information to Devoe. It would explain why Devoe always seemed to know everything almost as soon as it happened.

Was there more to Devoe than anyone suspected? And what about Devlin Burke?

"The same could be said of you." She felt those cold eyes on her, even though she couldn't see through the darkness that enveloped them in the tight, cramped compartment of the hansom.

He knew precisely what she meant by the remark. "To answer your question, I didn't mention the pin when I found it *because* of Devoe. Annie Chapman never had the means to own a pin like that, nor the opportunity to steal it from someone in Whitechapel. I knew another woman had been there. The pin was the only thing I knew about her, until you arrived. But none of it made any sense. A woman who came from the circumstances you described wouldn't own somethin' that valuable."

"You knew that I was lying all along."

There was a moment of silence between them that seemed to deepen the darkness inside the hansom.

"I knew there was a great deal more that you weren't telling me. But I didn't suspect the truth. At least not until last night."

She realized precisely what he was saying, that until that moment when he made love to her—if that was what it could be called—he had only suspected the lies she told. But in those frantic, dangerous moments when everything spun out of control, he had learned the truth because of her innocence.

She was silently grateful for the darkness so that he couldn't see her embarrassment and mortification.

He went on to explain. "For a moment back there, I considered the possibility that you might have enlisted Devoe's assistance in your search for your sister, or that he might have been sent at the request of Lord Rushmore."

"If you believe that, then why did you bring me with you? Why not simply leave me with Devoe and keep me out of whatever it is you're up to?" Once again she had that feeling of being watched.

"I said that I considered the possibility. I didn't say that I believed it. It was obvious that Devoe didn't know about Toby's involvement."

"How can you be certain?"

"I know Devoe. I know the way he thinks. He cares about one thing—himself—at the cost of everyone else. If he knew about Toby, he would already have gone after him. He hasn't, because he doesn't know about him. It's about power. People like Devoe will do anything to have it. And that makes them dangerous. I just pray we find Toby before it's too late."

And what would a man like Burke do for power? she wondered.

Once again, a silent truce settled between them. It was an uneasy alliance, that came more from mistrust and suspicion than any bond of what had passed between them the night before. She put it out of her mind. Finding her sister was the only thing that mattered to her.

"Where are we going?" she finally asked as she glanced out the hansom at the darkened shops and stores on one unfamiliar street after another.

"St. Katharine's Dock."

"Isn't that out of the district?"

"Aye, and we wouldn't usually bother with anything there. But the river patrol found something. They want us to have a look."

It was foggy, but she immediately sensed something when they drew close to the Thames River. The fog thickened, wrapping about everything, making even the horse that drew the hansom disappear those few feet ahead of the carriage. And it was achingly cold, with a dampness that penetrated everything as the fog rolled off the water.

Somewhere out over the water was the low, melancholy toll of ships' bells and the lapping sound of water moving along the quay. Street lamps glowed with halos, and over all loomed the massive stone edifice of the Tower, where Queen Elizabeth, along with several other notables of history, had once been imprisoned. They

230

passed under the Tower bridge, the horse's hooves making dull clopping sounds on the wood landing that rimmed the embankment along the river. Out of the mist a figure appeared, swinging a lantern back and forth.

"Inspector Burke?"

"Aye. Came as soon as I received yer message."

"Chief Quimby said yer was to be notified if we found anything. We was through here on our regular patrol earlier this afternoon and didn't find nothin'. Then the evenin' patrol found it a couple o' hours ago. Ain't been in the water long."

"Stay here, Jess." He turned and followed the uniformed constable, not giving her the opportunity for argument.

The fog seemed to swallow them so that there was only the soft glow of the lantern swinging back and forth, growing smaller in the distance. She stepped down from the hansom and followed the light.

Gradually it quit moving and the glow grew larger. It was joined by others and the soft murmur of voices. Then she saw several uniformed constables standing in a group. They parted as she approached. She caught a brief glimpse of Burke, distinguished by his wide shoulders and bare head with the unruly waves of dark hair.

He was crouched low, bending over some object. All conversation suddenly ceased. "Damn." She heard his softly muttered curse.

Then he looked up, saw her, and immediately came to his feet. "I told you to wait." He tried to pull her back to the waiting hansom.

"What is it? What have they found?"

"Dammit, Jess. For once, do as yer told." The anger sliced at her through the cold night air.

"What is it?"

She wrenched away and pushed past the other constables. Burke's fingers closed over her arm, trying to restrain her as she plunged through the tight circle of uniformed police.

"Oh, God!" she cried out, her hand at her mouth. Then she slowly knelt on the hard wood dock, and touched the pale bloodless hand that lay limp and lifeless.

* * *

231

In the thick fog that shrouded all of London with a heavy, vaporous mantle, shadows disappeared in the gray mist almost before they were seen.

A shadow separated from the others on the quay at St. Katharine's Dock near London Tower, a ghostly figure that slipped unseen along the side of a warehouse. He hesitated and watched the uniformed constables gathered around the limp body and the slender young woman who knelt on the dock. Then he slipped once more into the dark of night, shrouded by thick gray mist.

Chapter Seventeen

"Come away," Burke gently coaxed her, his hands at her shoulders. She shook her head, holding onto that limp hand.

"It's no good, lass. There's nothin' you can do for him now."

"I won't leave him like this," she said softly, holding onto the hand clasped between hers, trying to give some warmth to the cold flesh. "He wanted to be warm. He said he was always so cold. He was ill and wouldn't eat. He said that all he wanted was a mug of ale and a place to sleep. He didn't have to help me find my sister, but he did." She looked up at Burke then, her face pale, but there was no sign of the hysteria he'd expected. There were only tears.

"Why did he have to die? Who would do such a thing?" she asked, her voice filled with an unanswerable anguish that went straight to his heart.

He thought himself used to scenes like this, it happened so often. But, as much as he tried to ignore it, this affected him profoundly for he saw it as she must see it, a senseless waste of a man's life.

The tears filled her soft green eyes, creating twin emerald pools, then spilled over dark lashes in wet paths down her cheeks. He gently laid a hand on her shoulder, wanting to comfort her. It would have been futile to try to pull her away. He knew she wouldn't leave Toby.

Just when he was certain he had her all figured out, knew precisely how she would react, she surprised him, stunning him with her reaction to the death of a man who had survived off the streets with odd jobs, stealing, and thieving, and then died by the streets, without even the coin for ale in his pockets.

Charity—that's what it was, he thought—that benevolent attitude that well-heeled ladies of society affected to ease the guilt of their souls. They had their proper speech, proper manners, and fine clothes, and once a month they met in some proper part of London and gave a few coins, some cast-off clothes, perhaps a few hours of their time, and felt better about themselves.

They were righteous and looked down on everyone who didn't have the acceptable family lineage or great wealth, hiding their secrets behind perfect manners and fine clothes as if the circumstance they were born to made them somehow better than others less fortunate than they were.

He had no use for any of them, their airs of self-importance and haughtiness, or their stately homes and fine carriages. As a child put out on the streets, he'd learned just how false all the trappings of wealth were. The wealthy, titled, and nobility were no different from the most common man on the street. They lied, cheated, and thieved just the same. It was just that they covered their sins with a mantle of wealth and lofty titles.

A man in Whitechapel went to prison for stealing a loaf of bread. A gentleman in Kensington stole just the same only the stakes were higher and it was called business investment. Women on the streets of Whitechapel, forced to sell themselves in order to survive were called prostitutes and whores. Fashionable young women of society who sold themselves to advantageous marriages were called *ladies*.

He wanted to hate her for what she was, for the lies, and everything she represented. He'd had a lifetime storing it up inside, building a wall of it around his emotions, convincing himself that everything he'd believed since early childhood was true. But at that moment, with tears in her eyes, clinging to Toby Gill's lifeless hand, he felt only compassion and the need to take the pain away.

Her emotions were genuine, exposed for everyone to see. The tears that ran unchecked down her cheeks were just as real, her face pale and drawn, the expression behind her eyes stark and haunted, as it had been the night before, when the only thing he could offer her was comfort. Even now, when he knew the truth about her, he wanted to comfort her. He wanted to wipe away her tears and take away the pain. No one, his entire life, not even the woman who'd given him birth and then abandoned him, had ever wept for him as she wept for Toby.

Over the past weeks, she'd slowly chipped away at the protective wall he kept around his emotions. In spite of what he now knew her to be, another piece disintegrated like crumbling granite and slipped through his fingers.

"Please get a blanket, or a coat . . . something to cover him."

He took off his own coat and placed it over Toby's body. She looked up at him briefly, gratitude flickering into her wide green eyes. Then she bent over Toby's cold, stiff body and carefully tucked the coat about him.

"We'll take care of 'im now, miss," the constable said gently.

She nodded, gently patting Toby's hand. Then she finally stood and let the constables carry his body to the police wagon.

Burke escorted her back to the hansom. She waited while he spoke with the river patrol who'd found Toby's body and reported it to the Crescent District police station. She had no idea what time it was when he finally returned and climbed inside the hansom, giving the driver instructions to return to the Commercial Street station.

"I've got to make inquiries about this," he said quietly. "I'll have the driver take you back to the flat."

"No!" She shook her head adamantly. "I'm going with you to the station. There's work to be done. I want to get started on the latest reports. Someone may have seen something . . . last night."

Her voice quavered at mentioning the double murders of Liz Stride and Catherine Eddowes at Mitre Square. Emotions played across her face as she struggled to compose herself. Then her voice was once more steady and calm.

"Perhaps someone saw something that will match one of the other sketches. And, after all, time is of the essence. Isn't that correct, Mr. Burke?"

He knew it was pointless to argue. The driver called to the horse, and the hansom moved away from the quay.

Her shoulder curved into the niche between his shoulder and the back of the seat, the hard muscles molding against the curve of her breast. She was oddly comforted by that solid strength. She felt safe and protected, the darkness inside the hansom closing about them like a protective cocoon during the ride back.

In the silence of the lurching cab she asked, "How did he die?"

He could hear the tears in her voice. "There's no need discussin' it, Jess. Don't torment yourself."

She struggled with the mental images she carried away from the quay—the smallest details of color and texture that served her so well as an artist and now tormented her. She would never be able to forget any of their faces: Annie, Liz, or Toby, or any of the people in the dozens of sketches she'd made.

There was a poignancy in every expression that revealed their compelling stories with a wary glance, a furtive look, or simple mirth in the features of the men, women, and children. She'd lived among them and glimpsed their struggles and pain. She knew they would haunt her for the rest of her life.

"I need to know," she said, trying to make sense of it all. "I have to know, to try and understand why it happened."

Burke shifted in the seat beside her, his face averted, so that he was looking out at the passing street.

"There were several wounds about the body," he recited, almost dispassionately. "It's difficult to tell for certain which was the cause of death until the surgeon has examined him." He looked over at her then as they passed a street lamp. But she had pulled back into the shadows at the far corner of the cab, making it impossible to see her expression.

"Was it done with a knife?" There was a long moment of silence.

"It is a possibility."

She knew he was being deliberately vague.

"Oh, God. Just like Annie Chapman and the others." She whispered. He didn't bother to contradict her. They rode in silence for several more blocks when another thought occurred to her.

"St. Katharine's Dock is quite a distance from Whitechapel."

"Aye, it is."

She felt the reassuring strength of his shoulder pressing back against her, but still she shuddered at the possibilities that suggested.

"Do you have any idea how long ago it happened?"

In spite of his determination not to he felt a grudging admiration for her quiet strength in the midst of such horror that he often found almost overwhelming.

"Two, possibly three days. The surgeon will be able to better tell us that."

"Two or three days," she repeated softly, and in the pale light of a passing street lamp he saw the quiver of her lashes against her cheeks as she squeezed her eyes shut. He couldn't stop looking at her, the fragility in the soft curve of her mouth, the vulnerability in the slender curve of her chin as it trembled, the single tear that squeezed from the corner of one eye. It was several more minutes before she spoke again.

"Then he couldn't possibly have killed Liz Stride or Catherine Eddowes because he was already . . . dead."

He nodded grimly. "So it would seem."

"I knew he couldn't have done it, but that means that whoever killed Annie and the others is still out there."

"Aye, he's still out there, watchin' and waitin'."

"And you're certain he'll kill again."

His voice was grim. "Aye, that he will." He didn't voice another fear—that Toby's death was somehow connected.

It was almost midnight when they finally returned to the Commercial Street station. They worked through the night.

Every available constable and inspector continued questioning anyone who might have seen something out of the ordinary the night before at Mitre Square. Jess sat quietly in the corner of Burke's office, sketching the countless descriptions that were given.

Several times through the night and into the early morning, Burke pressed a cup of hot tea into her hands. She sipped the fortifying brew while she drew yet another sketch. She refused to stop for even a short rest.

Among the countless descriptions she occasionally heard some-

237

thing that was familiar. She made a note of it, the description to be added later to the composite she'd been working on for weeks. She worked on doggedly, losing track of time, submerging herself in the images she created, certain that somewhere among the myriad descriptions was the identity of Jack the Ripper.

Burke shook her gently.

She jerked awake. There were deep shadows behind the soft green eyes and a flash of uncertainty just before awareness returns, at waking in unfamiliar surroundings.

Then he saw recognition along with something else, a naked fear that he might have bad news, and something deep inside him twisted in response. She was like a small, frightened child.

He understood what it was to live with fear. He'd experienced it daily as a child, not knowing where his next meal would come from, or where he would sleep the next night, or who would try to beat him half to death for the simple sport of it.

"You fell asleep, lass," he said gently, when she finally awakened and sat up. She was immediately more alert.

She clutched at his hand. "Has something happened?"

"No, nothing's happened." He gestured out the window of the office where early morning light filled the streets. Just outside the station, street lamps dimmed. "It's past seven o'clock. I'm going over to the Crescent station. The physician may have information for me about Toby."

She stood up stiffly from the chair. "I'm going with you."

"No." His hand closed over her arm, stopping her. "There's no need of it. Stay and rest. There's a cot in the back room. You'll be more comfortable there."

"I've had more than enough rest."

"Jess, you're exhausted. You'll stay and rest. You'll not be of much good to anyone if you become ill."

"I'm perfectly healthy, and as capable as you are of doing without a little sleep. You haven't slept in two days."

He grinned at her then. "But I'm used to it, lass. It's the way of things for a police inspector."

After all the anger, his smile was stunning.

"I'm already acquainted with the cot," she reminded him, hastily looking away, unnerved by that smile.

"I would rather go with you."

"There's nothing you can do," he said firmly. "And it's not a sight you'd be wantin' to see."

"You forget, Inspector, that I've already seen such things."

"Aye, and as I recall you fainted dead away." He pulled her along out of the office and down the hallway to the small room at the back of the station.

The room was empty, recently vacated by one of the constables who'd worked through the night to the point of exhaustion. A rumpled blanket lay across the cot. He sat her down, leaving no room for argument in the matter.

"You are rude and overbearing."

"And you are more stubborn than is healthy for anyone. You'll stay here, or I'll set Hobbs on that door to make certain you do."

"Obviously, there's no point in discussing this further."

"None whatsoever." He buttoned the front of his overcoat, his gaze coming back to her. He'd been more harsh than he intended.

"I may be a while, these things take time."

She nodded. She'd seen Annie Chapman's body and the lengthy report the surgeon had made about her death. It wasn't necessary for him to go into detail.

"Burke?" He stopped at the doorway on his way out.

"I don't think Toby had any family. I would like to take care of whatever arrangements are necessary after . . ." Her hands were clasped tight together. "That is to say, I want him to have a decent funeral."

"It's not necessary, Jess. He was just a common thief. They all end up in a potter's grave." He saw the stubbornness flare in those green eyes.

"I want more than that for him. It's the least that I can do."

He shrugged. "It's your money. You seem to have enough of it."

She came to her feet then, the blanket puddling at her feet unnoticed. The stubbornness had gone to anger. Fresh tears pooled in those vivid eyes. "It has nothing to do with that. He was a friend who tried to help. He deserves that much. And if you won't help me see that it's done properly, then I'll do it myself."

She stood there, all defiant and ready for battle, her slender body rigid, daring him to argue with her. There was something in the stubbornness and defiance that reminded him of a skinny little kid who had to scrape just for the right to survive on the lonely streets of Dublin.

"All right, lass," he said, trying to gentle her. "There's no need to get yerself all worked up about it. If it's what you want, I'll see that it's done proper."

"Thank you," she said quietly, then turned to the cot and lay down on it. She turned to the wall, curling into a small ball, as if she could find some comfort within herself.

He was about to leave, when he turned back with a need to put something right that had been bothering him.

"About the other night . . ." but when he looked over at the cot, he saw that she was already asleep. He shook his head, not at all certain what it was that he had wanted to say. An apology? Or some expression of remorse or regret? After he had left the streets of Dublin, he never allowed himself to feel either. She made him feel both, deeply.

Less than an hour later he walked through the narrow corridor at the Crescent station to the adjoining rooms that provided a morgue and an office for the physician who examined all the bodies brought in. Chief Inspector Quimby nodded a greeting.

"I appreciate your cooperation," Burke said.

Quimby's expression was grim. "These murders are nasty business. We all want this madman caught."

"What did you find out about the body that was pulled out of the Thames last night?"

"My men made their report from the information given by the river patrol. You can look at it after we're finished. The physician is waiting for us now. Worked through the night, he did, on my orders. I knew you'd want every bit of information as soon as possible." They reached a door, and the chief inspector opened it for Burke.

MORE PASSION AND ADVENTURE AWAIT... YOUR TRIP TO A BIG ADVENTUROUS WORLD BEGINS WHEN YOU ACCEPT YOUR FIRST 4 NOVELS ABSOLUTELY *FREE* (AN $18.00 VALUE)

Accept your Free gift and start to experience more of the passion and adventure you like in a historical romance novel. Each Zebra novel is filled with proud men, spirited women and tempestuous love that you'll remember long after you turn the last page.

Zebra Historical Romances are the finest novels of their kind. They are written by authors who really know how to weave tales of romance and adventure in the historical settings you love. You'll feel like you've actually gone back in time with the thrilling stories that each Zebra novel offers.

GET YOUR FREE GIFT WITH THE START OF YOUR HOME SUBSCRIPTION

Our readers tell us that these books sell out very fast in book stores and often they miss the newest titles. So Zebra has made arrangements for you to receive the four newest novels published each month.

You'll be guaranteed that you'll never miss a title, and home delivery is so convenient. And to show you just how easy it is to get Zebra Historical Romances, we'll send you your first 4 books absolutely FREE! Our gift to you just for trying our home subscription service.

BIG SAVINGS AND FREE HOME DELIVERY

Each month, you'll receive the four newest titles as soon as they are published. You'll probably receive them even before the bookstores do. What's more, you may preview these exciting novels free for 10 days. If you like them as much as we think you will, just pay the low preferred subscriber's price of just $3.75 each. *You'll save $3.00 each month off the publisher's price.* AND, your savings are even greater because there are never any shipping, handling or other hidden charges—FREE Home Delivery. Of course you can return any shipment within 10 days for full credit, no questions asked. There is no minimum number of books you must buy.

4 FREE BOOKS

TO GET YOUR 4 FREE BOOKS WORTH $18.00 — MAIL IN THE FREE BOOK CERTIFICATE T O D A Y

Fill in the Free Book Certificate below, and we'll send your FREE BOOKS to you as soon as we receive it.

If the certificate is missing below, write to: Zebra Home Subscription Service, Inc., P.O. Box 5214, 120 Brighton Road, Clifton, New Jersey 07015-5214.

FREE BOOK CERTIFICATE

4 FREE BOOKS

ZEBRA HOME SUBSCRIPTION SERVICE, INC.

YES! Please start my subscription to Zebra Historical Romances and send me my first 4 books absolutely FREE. I understand that each month I may preview four new Zebra Historical Romances free for 10 days. If I'm not satisfied with them, I may return the four books within 10 days and owe nothing. Otherwise, I will pay the low preferred subscriber's price of just $3.75 each; a total of $15.00, *a savings off the publisher's price of $3.00.* I may return any shipment and I may cancel this subscription at any time. There is no obligation to buy any shipment and there are no shipping, handling or other hidden charges. Regardless of what I decide, the four free books are mine to keep.

NAME _____

ADDRESS _____ APT _____

CITY _____ STATE _____ ZIP _____

TELEPHONE ( ) _____

SIGNATURE _____
(if under 18, parent or guardian must sign)

The physician was waiting for them. He was a portly man, wearing a long white apron. The apron and his arms were smeared with the blood of his profession.

The introductions were made. His face was round and cherubic, which struck an odd contrast of good-humored gaiety with the gruesomeness of his work.

"Pleased to meet you, Inspector," he nodded. "Almost through here. Probably have everything you'd be interested in."

Burke nodded, mentally bracing himself for something he never got used to no matter how many times he saw it. There was always that first, momentary shock when he first saw a body that had gone through a physician's examination. Now, as always, he pushed himself quickly past it.

"Do you know the cause of death?"

"To the casual observer, drowning would be the obvious conclusion since he was found in the river. But then there is the matter of the knife wounds." The surgeon pointed out several wounds Burke had noticed the night before.

"Any of these is deep enough to eventually have caused death by bleeding. But they were not the immediate cause of death. Nor was it drowning. There was no water in the lungs."

"If he didn't bleed to death and he didn't drown, then what was the cause?" Burke demanded.

"A broken neck." The physician went on to explain his findings. "There is severe bruising about the body, and several broken bones, along with rope burns on the skin, suggesting that our friend here was probably tied up while bleeding from the lacerations. And back here," he rolled the head to the side to reveal several, deep purple bruises about the neck, "You can see the marks made by a pair of hands—gloved hands I would say, by the wide, blunt pattern of bruising. Whoever did this, took his time about it, wanting to be certain of the outcome."

Burke frowned. Last night he was ready to conclude that the man who'd committed the murders in Whitechapel and called himself Jack the Ripper might very well be responsible for Toby's death as well. On first glance the marks were strikingly similar.

"You said the lacerations were not serious enough to cause death?"

The physician shook his head. "Not immediately. No vital organs were damaged, although several veins were cut in the process, producing loss of a great deal of blood over a prolonged length of time, but all arteries are intact. Still, it's the same, basic manner as your Ripper murders."

Burke lifted the sheet that had been drawn over the body. He forced himself past any emotional reaction for Toby Gill, and saw only the wasted body, like so much refuse that had been tossed out.

"How would you say the wounds were inflicted? What sort of weapon?" He looked up then, saw the bemused expression on the physician's jovial face, and wondered why some people ended up in their chosen professions.

"Obviously with a sharp instrument, most probably a knife, but not so skillfully made as the wounds on the other victims." At Burke's look of surprise, he gave a small smile. The physician obviously knew the details of the Ripper murders.

"Physicians tend to compare their findings, Mr. Burke, in spite of the best efforts of the police to keep those details to themselves. It sometimes assists us in our work—a consensus of minds so to speak."

Burke smothered back his irritation. "How would you say the victim was attacked?"

"Oh, quite certainly from behind. You can see the bruising about his shoulders, separate from the pattern of rope burns on the rest of the body. It is my opinion that he was grabbed from behind and his neck snapped. The stab wounds were secondary wounds."

"After he was already dead."

"Quite."

"And completely unnecessary."

"So it would seem."

He put that disturbing thought away. "Then the attacker would have had to be of substantial size and strength to overpower him."

"Yes, even though this poor wretch wasn't in the best of health, still he had a fair amount of body strength, as you can see by the muscles in his arms and legs."

"Which was the first stab wound?" Burke asked.

The physician looked at him with some puzzlement. "I can hardly see how that is of any consequence, since he was already dead at the time."

"If you please, Doctor. Indulge my curiosity."

The physician sniffed with displeasure, the joviality somewhat bruised. When he continued, his tone was curt, officious.

"Most probably it would be the wound at the throat, a slash from right to left. But there again, it's very superficial, not enough to do serious damage. And unnecessary. The other wounds, low on the torso, were the more serious ones."

"Unnecessary as it was, still it's there," Burke murmured thoughtfully. "Would you say it was made from the back, when the victim was first attacked."

"Quite unlikely. There was no point since he was already dead, and there is the matter of the widespread bruising across the chest, as if the body were held in place with a heavy object while the attacker went about his work with the knife."

Burke had noticed the wide bruise, approximately the size of a man's fist. And the wound at the neck had been made from right to left. Unusual.

"How long has he been dead?"

"That's a bit difficult to say. The river is extremely cold this time of year. Temperature can be misleading when it comes to body tissue. But from the colorations about these bruises, the slight deterioration of tissue at the wounds in contrast with the extensive bloating, I would say three days, perhaps as long as five."

Three days, but not five, for Toby had been alive four days ago.

He asked several more questions, making notes in the small tablet he always carried, adding them to his own observations.

It was well past noon when he returned to the station. He frowned as he saw Jimmy Cassidy from the *London Times* and Devoe sitting inside Abberline's office. He didn't like Cassidy or the people he worked for. They were like carrion, preying on the misery and fears of other people in order to print sensationalized stories that sold more newspapers.

It hampered the investigation, spreading panic and fear. Those who knew anything about the murders were reluctant to speak of them, doubting the ability of the police to stop the killer. And all because of the half-truths and speculation written by the newspaper.

Toby Gill had been reluctant like the others, especially since he knew three of the dead women. He was the common thread that bound everything together. Now Toby was also dead.

Jess came out of his office. Evidently she'd sent for her things from the flat. Her hair was neatly twisted in thick satin coils atop her head, and she wore a clean shirtwaist and a plain skirt. She saw him then, and carefully slipped past Abberline's office.

"When did Cassidy return?" he asked.

"Almost two hours ago. He's demanding that Chief Abberline release all details about Liz Stride and Catherine Eddowes for the newspaper."

"And whose side has Devoe taken in all of this?"

"The home office is demanding full cooperation to assure the public that the police aren't holding anything back."

"Does Cassidy know about Toby?"

She shook her head and lowered her voice to a whisper. "I don't think so. He asked if I'd heard from Toby."

"Or perhaps he suspects that something may have happened, but simply hasn't been able to find out for certain. I didn't give them Toby's name over at Crescent station." He pulled her aside so that they could speak more discreetly.

"I don't want anyone to know about Toby just yet."

She nodded. "Why would anyone want to kill him? What was he doing at St. Katharine's Dock?"

His expression was grim. "He didn't go to the quay. He was already dead when he was taken there."

"I don't understand. If he was already dead, then why take him there?"

"He wasn't supposed to be found. Someone went to a great

244

deal of trouble so that he wouldn't be found."

"Was it the same as the others?" she asked.

"The cause of death was from a broken neck."

"But there was blood on the front of his coat."

"Aye, there were slashes," he admitted.

"Were they the same?"

He nodded, pushing back a suspicion that nagged at him ever since he saw Toby's body. "They were very similar. But not the immediate cause of death."

Her expression was puzzled. "Why would anyone kill Toby? And in the same manner as Annie and the others? Until now, it was only women."

"Aye, that's been the way of it until now."

Her eyes went dark with shadows. "Annie Chapman, Liz Stride, and Catherine Eddowes." She met his gaze then. "Is it possible that Toby knew the first two women who were killed?"

"That's what I have to find out." But she was already past that possibility and confronting another even more frightening one.

"My sister knew Annie, Liz Stride, and Catherine Eddowes. She might very well have known the others as well, just like Toby. And now Toby's dead . . ." The fear wouldn't let her say what her horrified thoughts had already articulated.

"Burke . . ."

"Your sister is alive, Jess. And for the time, she's safe."

"How can you be certain?"

He knew it was pointless to gloss over it with meaningless, placating words. She was smarter than that and would only hate him for it.

"She would have been found if she was dead. It's the nature of the man we're dealin' with to leave them for us to find, like it's a game he's playin'."

She clung to that hope. "What do we do now?"

"I'm going to find everyone Toby came into contact after he met with you. Someone has to have seen something, or perhaps someone he spoke with. And I'm going to find out if he knew the other two victims."

"I'm going with you."

"No!"

"I have every right . . ."

"No, Jess," he repeated, in a tone that said it would be pointless to argue.

"You can't go where I'm going," he explained. "It's too dangerous. Besides, I can move faster if I go alone."

"What you're saying is that I would be in the way, I'd slow you down, cause problems."

"Aye, you would. Unless you've a mind to put on a pair of pants and man's coat." Her face lit up as she latched on to the idea.

"No!" he said firmly, cutting her off before she could even open her mouth.

"Burke!" she protested.

"No! You're needed here. Somewhere in one of those reports is a description which could lead to this madman. We're working against time, Jess," he reminded her. "Five women have already died, and now Toby is dead as well. The sooner we come up with a description of the murderer the sooner your sister will be safe."

She knew he was right and reluctantly agreed. She grabbed the front of his coat, and stood toe-to-toe with him — all five feet three inches of her looking up at his six-foot-plus height.

"You're to let me know the instant you find out anything. Is that clear?"

He gently loosened her fingers from his coat. "Yer rather pushy for someone who probably weighs no more than a hundred pounds dripping wet."

"Someone I met recently impressed me that it's the only way to get what I want."

"Must be a pushy chap, with no respect for rules," he commented with a slight twinkle in those blue eyes.

"He is, and one of these days he's going to meet his match."

As he left the station, Burke ignored a tiny voice in his head that suggested perhaps he already had.

After he left the station, Jess went back to his office. She continued to work there since Devoe and Jimmy Cassidy were still with Abberline in his office. Endicott was busy questioning a witness who'd been on the street two nights before when Liz Stride died, and Hobbs had been gone for hours along with every available constable and inspector. So much for Burke's threats to have Hobbs put at her door.

Late in the afternoon there was still no word from Burke. The door to Abberline's office opened abruptly. He crossed the station to Burke's office, followed by Devoe and Jimmy Cassidy.

"I need your assistance with something, Miss Kelly," Abberline said in a carefully controlled tone that revealed none of the anger she'd heard through the closed door of his office only moments before.

She looked at him curiously, aware that he'd suddenly started calling her Miss Kelly again, and she wondered about the sudden change. She hastened a quick glance at Devoe and Jimmy Cassidy. Jimmy reminded her of a hunting hound, suddenly set loose on the trail of a hare or fox, with a sort of maddening persistence that made her uneasy, likeable though he was.

His freckle-faced charm was deliberately disarming. She wondered how many young girls had found it equally disarming. It undoubtedly accounted for his ability to acquire information others found difficult to obtain.

Devoe was far different. He was cold and remote, the sort of person who understood his power and used it, rather than any affectation of charm. Whereas Jimmy's approach was direct, even as he stood before the desk, Devoe was far more subtle, circling around to quietly stand just behind her so that it wasn't possible to see his face or the direction of his gaze. But she felt it.

"The *Times* newspaper is going to print articles about the most recent murders," Abberline explained. "They're most anxious to have sketches to accompany those articles."

"What about the composites you've been working on, Miss Kelly?" Devoe suggested, immediately taking control of the conversation.

"Composites?" Jimmy cut in. "What's this? Somethin' I wasn't told about?"

Abberline's expression was murderous as his gaze fixed on Devoe. Devoe pretended innocence. "I wasn't aware you hadn't told

Mr. Cassidy about the composites. Quite an ingenious concept actually. I'd like to see them myself."

Whether it was deliberate or a simple mistake, the damage was done. The cat was out of the bag, so to speak, and Jimmy Cassidy wasn't about to let it go — like a hound on a new scent.

Though his voice was calm, the expression behind Abberline's eyes was filled with fury at Devoe's blunder.

Abberline's voice was carefully controlled. "It was an idea Miss Kelly had about some additional sketches. It has some merit." She looked at him with surprise at the last remark.

Earlier that morning, before Jimmy came to the station, she had gone over her progress with Chief Abberline. He had been quite pleased. And just the previous evening, when he learned who she really was, he had insisted that her talents were still vitally necessary to the investigation. It was the only reason he'd been willing to allow her to remain in Whitechapel — that along with her threats that she would simply continue on her own.

But his remark now was completely opposite that of this morning and the previous evening, as if . . . It was then she realized what he was up to. He was deliberately trivializing the idea about the composites, to try and divert Jimmy's attention away from them.

He smiled at her congenially. "Perhaps you have something that might be of use to Mr. Cassidy, my dear."

"Yes, I believe that I do. There are several sketches that might do." She took out several of the earliest sketches, which had been greatly changed in the intervening weeks.

They were crude at best, merely preliminary sketches, and no longer of use, since they had been changed greatly. But Jimmy Cassidy and Devoe had no way of knowing that. Devoe took the sketches from her and studied them.

"The idea is brilliant, of course," he was saying. "It may very well yield some positive results. We must not overlook any possibility." Without consulting either her or Chief Abberline he handed the sketches over to Jimmy.

"Run these along with your latest article. And of course you must mention Miss Kelly's efforts in the matter." It was then that he glanced briefly at Abberline.

"I assume you have no objections."

Not that it would have mattered if he had. Chief Abberline smiled evenly. "Of course not. We are most anxious to cooperate in any way we can with the home office."

Devoe smiled at his small victory. "Excellent." Then he turned back to Jess.

"Naturally, you will let me know when you have something more substantial."

She glanced briefly at Abberline, then replied evenly, "Of course."

The following day the sketches appeared in the *Times*, along with several she'd made of the murder scene at Mitre Square and a detailed article about the double murders of Liz Stride and Catherine Eddowes.

Tightly wrapped bundles of the *London Times* were tossed from the back of the delivery wagon onto the sidewalk. The young boy who sold papers, swooped down on them, quickly cutting away the heavy twine that bound each bundle. He was immediately engulfed by passersby on the street, all anxious to see the latest story about the notorious murders.

Several sketches filled the front page below the headlines:

GHASTLY DOUBLE MURDER — JACK THE RIPPER STRIKES AGAIN.
FIVE WOMEN BRUTALLY SLAIN IN EAST END

The papers were all quickly sold.

Finally the crowd dispersed, some reading the terrible details of the two deaths silently to themselves, others reading the sensational story by Jimmy Cassidy aloud for those who clustered about.

In the flurry of activity, several papers had been trampled underfoot. Pages blew about, adding to the trash and refuse that congealed in the gutters, gusting across the street in the cold wind, spiraling down an adjacent alley like pale ghosts.

A black coach sat at the curb as the people went about their way, until the street was all but deserted, except for the boy counting money across the street.

Within, the glow of a coach light fell across the front page of the newspaper as it was held aloft. The passenger studied the sketches.

"Jess Kelly," he murmured, storing the name away in his memory. Then the light from the lamp glinted off the blade of a knife, and the article with those sketches was cut from the front page of the newspaper.

He held it aloft in the soft glow of light, his expression made all the more stark as light played across his features. It was a dangerous expression, completely void of all emotion, or any depth of feeling. There was only a cold grimness of purpose.

". . . And then there were six."

Chapter Eighteen

Burke left the doss house on Shoreditch High. It was Toby Gill's place of residence when he had enough coin in his pocket to pay for a cot in one of the several common lodging rooms, or when he wasn't staying over with one of the prostitutes at another flat. But the old crone who collected the nightly rents hadn't seen Toby for several days, since before his meeting with Jess four days earlier.

Toby's body lay in the Crescent morgue, waiting Burke's instructions, with the simple entry of name UNKNOWN, made on the official police docket. For the time being he wanted Toby to remain right where he was—anonymously tucked away where neither Devoe or anyone else could find him.

Time. He had to have more time, to track down precisely where Toby had gone the last few hours he was alive, and who he might have been seen with, or met along the way to his death.

It was past four o'clock in the afternoon. The circle of Toby's world had lain within a tight little area of Whitechapel bounded by the Rose and Thistle tavern four streets over, the doss house on Shoreditch, the Aldgate workhouse where he occasionally spent time working off a sentence for some minor infraction of the law, the textile factory where he worked when he was physically able, the hospital, and the Magpie and Stump pub where he had met with Jess that last time.

It was Friday. The physician at the Crescent police station insisted that Toby had been dead for three days. Jess had met with him at the Magpie early Monday evening—four days earlier. There was one day in between that was unaccounted for.

Burke had the hospital and the factory yet to visit, but he didn't hold out much hope for either. The factories were supposed to keep records of workers' hours but Toby worked there infrequently. His best hope lay with the hospital.

The attendant who signed all patients in and out on a daily basis remembered Toby, but hadn't seen him for at least two weeks. He was a skinny little fellow by the name of Peck who Burke remembered had been taken in for a series of petty thefts in the past. He had sallow skin and a thin mustache and an uncooperative attitude.

"Sorry," he said with remote indifference. "I ain't seen him."

"Tell me something, Peck," he asked. "Is the hospital administrator aware of the extra money you make stealing from patients and dead bodies before the family claims them?" His eyes narrowed as he grabbed the little weasel by the front of his dingy coat front.

In one efficient motion, acquired on the streets of Dublin, he cleaned out the man's pockets, producing a woman's thin gold wedding band, a battered gold pocket watch with the initials A.L. F. on the back, and several coins of various amounts—far more than a hospital clerk earned in a year.

"Bloody hell!" Peck screamed, dangling several inches off the ground from Burke's large fist.

"Rotten peelers!" he choked. "Yer got nothin' on me. Them's me own things. Put me down."

"Undoubtedly your pocket watch with the initials A.L.F." Burke observed.

"Right yer are. A gift from me brother, it was."

"And the wedding ring undoubtedly belonged to yer sainted mother, or perhaps you've taken a wife since the last time we met, and you carry the ring around for her."

"Right! It's married I am now, all nice and legal."

"And who's the blushing bride? Tommy Fisk, or perhaps Robbie, or is it one of the other young lads yer like to bugger? And what about all that money? An inheritance, perhaps? From yer long, lost, rich old uncle who lives in Kensington or Westminster?" Then Burke went on.

"You have no brother, Peck. Nor mother who would claim you, and no wife that any clergy would marry you to."

"All right!" Peck screamed, wriggling about, trying to free himself.

"So, I took them things. Them wot had 'em before had no more use for 'em, and no relatives ter claim the possessions. It would all go to the charity house anyway, an' I can't get by on wot I make here."

"So you decided to simply expedite charity along a bit, by taking these things."

"Right yer are."

"Not good enough, Peck. You'll have to do better than that to keep yerself out of the workhouse for pilferin'. Those in the workhouse have a code all their own. Do you know what would happen to someone like you in there?" he asked, his eyes dangerous slits.

"The guards won't even find as much as this pocket watch, or a piece of clothing off yer back. You'll simply disappear, Peck."

"I don't know nothin' 'bout Toby. I told yer that. Wot more can I tell you?"

"Think very hard, Peck. As if your life depended upon it, man."

Peck shuddered, his body shaking as Burke held him suspended. He knew what happened to people like him in the workhouse. It was the reason he always made it a point to avoid the workhouse, until now. He began crying and sniveling.

"I don't know nothin'."

"That is unfortunate. Because I sent an old *friend* of yours by the name of Tucker over a few weeks back on a six-month sentence. You remember Tucker, don't you? A special friend of yours?"

The sallow skin went a sickly shade of green as Peck remembered.

"He'll be waitin' for you," Burke went on to explain, "because I intend to put out the word that yer goin' in. Somethin' for you to look forward to, Peck."

"Mayb-b-e-e . . . maybe Philpot saw Toby come in," he suddenly began to babble hysterically, closing his eyes in fear. He shook uncontrollably.

"He runs the ap-p-pothec-c-cary upstairs. Toby s-s-sometimes comes in for m-m-medicine."

Burke released him. He dropped like a sack of grain, spilling onto the floor as his knees buckled under him.

"Thank you for your cooperation."

"Hey!" Peck cried out. "Wot about our deal?"

Burke stopped at the door. "What deal is that?"

"I gave yer the information yer wanted, and yer agreed not to say nothin' 'bout those things yer found in me pocket."

"A deal?" Burke shook his head. "That wouldn't be honest, now would it?" Then he smiled. "I'll tell Tucker you were askin' for him. I'm certain he'll be real anxious to see you."

He found Mr. Philpot on the second floor of the hospital. He remembered Toby.

"I gave him medication for his cough. Wasn't no point in seein' the physician 'bout it. The misery in his lungs is killin' him, and he knows it. He comes round often like that, when he has the coin."

"I was workin' late Tuesday. Musta been around six o'clock. I finished up and walked down to the street with him."

"Did he take a hansom when you parted? Or did he walk?"

"Neither."

"What do you mean, neither."

"Just that. Toby met a friend outside the hospital. Leastways I thought they was friends. Had a few strong words they did, which gave me pause, as if Toby was upset about somethin'. Then they seemed to come to some sort of agreement, and Toby went with him."

"Do you remember anything about the man?"

"It was dark and foggy. The only light was the street lamp at the corner. I just caught a glimpse of him fer a moment. I couldn't see much. He had on a cape," he stopped and corrected himself, "No, musta been a coat."

Burke took out the latest sketches Jess had made.

254

"Do any of these look like the man you saw with Toby that night?"

Philpot studied each sketch then shook his head. "It weren't none o' them, guv'ner."

"Are you certain? Before, you said you couldn't see much at all."

"I saw enough to tell you it ain't him."

"Could you describe anything about him?"

"He was average height, dark hair, I think, clean-shaven except for long sideburns, couldn't see his eyes or anythin' else about his face."

"Was he young or old?"

Philpot shrugged. "Could be young, could be old."

Vague details that described half the men in London. The frustration returned.

"Which direction did they walk when they left the hospital?"

"Didn't walk at all. They got into one of them closed carriages."

"A hansom?" Burke repeated, fighting back the frustration.

"No, not a hansom. Musta been a private rig, like yer see about once in a while."

Burke frowned. It didn't make sense. "Do you remember anything about it or the driver?"

"Just a plain hack, nothin' distinguishin' about it or the driver. He was all bundled up on accounta it was a bitter night out."

"Do you remember anything else? Anything about the man — even the smallest detail?"

Philpot shook his head. "There ain't nothin' more. Toby went with his friend, and I went home."

"And he hasn't been back since," Burke added thoughtfully, knowing full well that sometime within the next few hours after Toby had gone with his "friend," he had died.

"No, not since. But he'll be back round. Always does. The medicine helps ease the coughin' spells that come over him."

Burke didn't bother to explain that Toby wouldn't be back, ever. He folded the sketch and put it in his pocket.

It was early November. The sky was leaden overhead, casting the city into darkness so that the lamplighters had begun their rounds early, even though it was barely five o'clock. He pulled his coat more tightly about him and thought of Jess.

She hadn't left the station for two days, unable to sleep much at all since they found Toby, her face drawn and pale with worry for her sister. That morning as he left the station, she'd told him she intended to return to the flat that night and work on the composite sketches she kept in her drawing case. He'd told Endicott to escort her home and remain there until he arrived.

A young boy was selling copies of the afternoon edition of the *London Times* in front of the hospital. Over the past several weeks he quit reading the papers. They were filled with speculation, half-truths, and rumors that spread panic about the murders.

"Yer ought ter 'ave a copy o' today's paper, sir," the boy called out to him.

"Jack the Ripper sent another letter fer the police. Says he'll kill again."

Burke grabbed a paper from the boy and quickly scanned the front page article.

"Hey, yer gotta pay fer it first," the boy protested. "That'll be tuppence."

Burke ignored him as he quickly read through the article.

"I'll call the bloody peelers, I will. Yer can't steal me papers."

"Stop yer caterwallin!" Burke ordered. "I am the police."

The boy's eyes widened.

"No offense meant, sir." He gathered the remainder of his papers more firmly under his arm as he backed away. "Keep it, sir, with me compliments." Then he turned and dashed off down the street to another corner to sell the remainder of his papers.

Burke found the contents of the letter printed in Jimmy Cassidy's latest article.

It was in the form of a poem:

All your efforts are in vain;
I've killed five times and I'll kill again.
Pictures are for children who are silly;
Who will my next victim be? Perhaps a girl called Kelly.

A light snow had begun to fall. Traffic thickened and became congested. Everyone was trying to get home before the weather worsened. It took several minutes to find a vacant hansom. Burke barely gave the driver time to stop before he was climbing aboard.

"Commercial Street police station. And there's an extra half crown if you make it in less than twenty minutes."

At the station Burke sprinted up the steps and into the station. He burst into Abberline's office.

"Do you know about this?" He thrust the paper down on Abberline's desk.

"What is it?"

"The latest message from Jack the Ripper, in the afternoon edition of the paper."

Abberline quickly read it. "A girl named Kelly," he said thoughtfully. "Good heavens! Mary Kelly."

Burke nodded. He'd been afraid of something like this. He'd suspected all along that Jess's sister might know something about Annie Chapman's death. If she did, she was indeed in danger.

"Where's Jess? I don't want her to find out about this from someone else. Perhaps I can ease it a bit for her." His face was heavily lined as he considered the possibilities of that cryptic message. There had been dozens of them ever since the murders began—some credible, others completely outrageous and obviously the work of some poor demented souls who merely sought attention and recognition, and had absolutely nothing to do with the murders. But this one . . .

"She's already left for the day. She was about to collapse from exhaustion. I sent her home early."

"How long ago did she and Endicott leave?"

"Must have been at least a half hour ago," Abberline recalled. "But Endicott didn't go with her. He went to follow up on that information you wanted."

"What information? What the devil are you talking about?"

"It was about a woman who supposedly had some information

257

about that fellow Toby Gill. You sent instructions round that he was to follow it up."

"I did no such thing. I sent no message." Something about all of this was very wrong.

"And Jess went on alone."

The door to Abberline's office shuddered back on its hinges. Burke raced across the station and down the steps. Abberline was right behind him, shouting orders to Sweeney as he buttoned on a thick overcoat.

Snow had begun to come down heavily in thick, fat flakes sprinkling the cobbled stones on the streets with spiky whiteness, dusting everything with a pristine purity that was incongruous in Whitechapel.

Burke ran part of the way, finally waving down a hansom several blocks from the station. He hastily gave the driver the address on Abbington Road. As the cab swung through the streets, the wheels slipping on frozen cobblestones, an inexplicable urgency spread through him.

A girl called Kelly.

He and Abberline assumed that the line in the poem referred to Mary Kelly. After all, she had been a friend of Annie Chapman's and might very well be able to identify Jack the Ripper. And she was still out there, somewhere.

But what if they were mistaken. What if it meant someone else?

A girl called Kelly.

Burke thrust his head out the small opening at the door and shouted to the driver, "Hurry, man! Hurry!"

Jess thanked the driver and paid him an extra amount for the additional stops she had him make: first at the corner near the station to purchase a newspaper. A young flower girl had been on the corner as well, shivering in the cold, trying to sell her small wrapped bundles of late-blooming roses and Michaelmas daisies.

They were her sister's favorite flowers. The house at Deverell Hall was always filled with them this time of year. Somehow that chance encounter with the flower girl gave her an odd connection to her sister. She purchased every bundle the girl had, determined to make the biggest, most beautiful bouquet when she got back to the flat.

The girl had thought her quite mad, of course, and said so. Jess realized how ridiculous she must have looked, dressed in the poorest threadbare clothes, no better than what the girl wore, and handing over a queen's ransom in coins for flowers.

"Yer certain you want all of 'em?" the girl had asked, not quite believing her good fortune.

"Yes, every last one."

"Yer must be downright balmy, luv. Wot yer goin' ter do with all them flowers?"

"They're for someone," she answered simply, thinking of her sister and how much she loved flowers. Somehow just having the flowers made her feel closer to Linnie. The girl had looked at her skeptically.

"Whatever yer say, miss."

She shivered slightly, pulling the threadbare coat Mr. Spivey had sold her more tightly about her. It had begun to snow, and everything was quiet, softly muted by the large flakes which slowly drifted to the ground, joined by several others that clung to shrubs, the wood-rail gate, the bare limbs of the chestnut tree in the side yard.

It was only a little past five o'clock, yet dark and dreary outside. She'd left early, beyond exhaustion after spending the past two days at the police station working almost nonstop.

What day was this? she wondered, too tired to struggle with the thought. Was it two nights ago or three that Toby had been found dead down at the quay? How long was it since she'd last seen Burke?

For the first time in weeks she was on time for supper. She wondered with a small smile if Belle would find some other reason to be disagreeable.

The house seemed dark and forlorn. The lights had not yet been lit. Would Belle be displeased that she had returned early today? She felt a vague uneasiness, perhaps because Endicott had been forced to send her on alone at the last minute after another constable approached him at the curb in front of the police station, and informed him that Burke wanted him to speak with a woman who claimed to have seen Toby the night he died. She stopped him as he was about to leave.

"You must let me know if anything comes of it."

"That I will, Jess. You'll be the first to know right after Chief Abberline and Mr. Burke." Then he hesitated.

"I shouldn't be goin' off like this. Mr. Burke was very specific about seein' you home. I'll tell Sergeant Sweeney to get someone else to go round to this woman's place."

"You should go, and then you'll be able to tell me what you've learned. I'll be quite all right," she assured him. "The driver will see me safely home."

She climbed the steps to the house, seized by a sudden chill. She thought of poor Toby, Annie, and the others, and prayed her sister was warm and safe. She turned up the gaslight on the wall inside the foyer. It was just like Belle to skimp by leaving all the lights turned down until the last possible moment. Even then she constantly nagged all her tenants about using too much light, too much hot water, too much wood for heat.

Light pooled softly onto the faded wall covering and worn wood floors. It was unusually quiet and cold in the house, the fire had not yet been lit at the hearth in the small parlor. She frowned slightly as she called out, walking back to the kitchen.

It was warm, heat radiating from the oven, along with a thin spiral of smoke that puffed from the edge of the oven door. Something—undoubtedly supper—was burning.

Where was Belle?

In her limited experience with kitchens, Jess had never learned the appropriate operations of an oven. There had never been the need for it. And even though logic told her that there must be a knob or valve to turn the thing off, much like a regular coal stove, she hadn't the least notion how to go about it.

That left her two choices: let whatever was in the oven continue to burn, filling the entire house with smoke, or remove whatever was in there. The smoke burned at her eyes, and she quickly made her decision.

She found cotton towels and wrapped them thick about her hands. She opened the oven door, and carefully removed the metal roasting pan.

It was difficult to discern what had been intended for supper that night. It was reduced to a charred lump in the middle of the blackened pan.

"And I chose to have supper here this evening," she said to herself as she set the pan on the wood sideboard. She closed the oven, deciding that it was safe enough as it was for the time being, and went in search of Belle.

She knocked on the door to the ground floor flat. There was a thin sliver of light at the bottom of the door, but no answer. She tried the latch.

The flat had once been a formal sitting room. It was extravagantly decorated with a braided cotton rug on the floor, and a large bed at the far wall, and red velvet hangings at the windows. She wondered if this was where Burke had spent the night when he had said he was going *downstairs*.

There was a smaller, adjacent room that might have been a butler's pantry in another more affluent time. It now served as Belle's wardrobe, with several mended dresses hanging on hooks, along with a red satin dressing gown, lace undergarments, and several men's shirts that suggested that this indeed might have been where Burke spent the night.

It was obvious that Belle had been there recently. A bottle of Irish whiskey sat on the table with two cut-glass tumblers, one half-full, as if she might have been waiting for someone—Burke perhaps?—and then gone on to have that first drink alone. The second glass was unused.

She left Belle's room and walked to the staircase. There she found someone waiting for her.

"Melrose!" she smiled. "What are you doing, you old reprobate? Where's Belle?" she asked, as if it were perfectly normal to carry on a conversation with a cat. He tilted his head to one side and gave her a lopsided look.

"Is she about? Upstairs, perhaps?" She glanced past Melrose to the darkened second-floor landing and frowned. It wouldn't be the first time Belle had gone into the upstairs flat, unannounced and uninvited.

She and the cat had become close friends. He was in the habit of waiting on the landing for her each evening. However, as with most cats, his affection was not altogether altruistic. He was fully aware there would be scraps of food from the plate Belle prepared for her each evening. But now Melrose scuttled out of her reach, slinking up the darkened stairs ahead of her.

She turned up the gaslight at the top landing, illuminating the top of the stairs and the long hallway with several doors to the three largest rooms in the house, which had all been turned into separate flats and rented out to tenants. Early as it was, it seemed no one had yet arrived home for the evening.

"What is wrong with you?" she asked the cat. "Did you encounter a particularly vicious mouse today?"

He sat before the door to Burke's flat, tail snapping back and forth across the carpet in agitated sweeping motions.

"I suppose you may as well know," she told the cat. "Supper is beyond saving. I'm afraid we shall both go hungry tonight." She put the key in the lock, but before she could turn it the door slowly swung open.

"It looks as if your mistress has been calling again," she muttered as she walked into the darkened room. The gaslight glowed low at the wall. She turned it up, flooding the room with light and shadows. Jess gasped.

The small sitting room was in shambles. The two small tables had been overturned. Drawers had been pulled out of the desk and overturned on the floor. The area rug had been pushed aside. One of the chairs that sat before the hearth had also been overturned, the seat cushion dislodged and lost somewhere among the rubble. The other chair sat upright, but the worn, threadbare fabric as well as the cushion had been slashed to shreds, tufts of cotton padding hanging out like disheveled hair.

A pipe stand and a glass jar that was used as a vase had been knocked to the floor, as if someone had swept everything from the mantel in a fit of violence. There were slash marks in the faded wall covering near the hearth, as if someone had taken a knife and tried to cut the cloth away. As she stared at the destruction, Melrose swooped past her and darted into the adjacent bedroom.

She stepped carefully over broken furniture and scattered papers from the desk, then pushed the door to the bedchamber open. Light from the sitting room slanted across the wood floor, the crumbled braided rug, and the corner of the bed with the feather mattress slashed open, feathers scattered everywhere.

She stared in disbelief. Why would anyone do such a thing? *Who* would do such a thing?

The cat sat before the closet, the door slightly ajar. With typical feline curiosity he pawed at the door, trying to wedge it open further.

"What is it, Melrose?" she asked. "What have you found?"

She opened the door, but instead of diving in, Melrose stood uncertainly in the black gap of the doorway. Then he abruptly turned and fled in the opposite direction, out the bedroom door to the sitting room.

"Damn cat," she softly cursed—something she was given to doing a great deal lately.

"If I find a mouse in here, I refuse to share it with you." Then she opened the door wider, light slanting in. She saw no sudden movement, and slowly let out a sigh of relief. From what she'd seen of rodents in Whitechapel, she had no interest encountering one in the closet.

The light played over the other clothes she'd acquired since she arrived in Whitechapel: a clean shirtwaist, a brown stuff skirt, a wool neck scarf, a nightgown, and several undergarments, including well-worn petticoats and men's long woolen underwear that she'd purchased new and discovered were marvelously warm. There was an umbrella with far too many holes to be effective, and the empty valise that had carried all her clothes when she first came to Whitechapel.

All of the clothes had been torn from the hooks, and scattered into piles across the floor of the closet. Then the light from the lantern played across something else—a badly worn, woman's button-top shoe.

Puzzled, Jess pushed the pile of garments aside. Her hand froze in midair as the light flooded across the body of Belle Rossi. She was pale and completely still, staring straight up at Jess. Her skin was white as wax, with an almost translucent quality, except for the contrast of the bloody, gaping wound across her throat.

Jess stumbled out of the closet, terror sliding across every nerve ending, her thoughts frozen, except for the horrible image of Belle's mutilated body and the blood. And then she was running, bruising her leg as she fell against the sharp corner of the table, stumbling against the post of the bed.

There was no pain, only the terror. She ran from it and the dark shadows in the bedroom, dragging deep gulps of air into her frozen lungs, and then she was screaming.

Burke took the stairs three at a time and burst into the flat. He found her in the bedroom.

"Jess!" He grabbed her, pulling her into his arms. "I've got you, lass."

Her face was pressed against his shoulder, and still she screamed, hysterical, struggling like a frightened and wounded animal.

"Jess!" he growled fiercely. "Yer all right, lass! I'm here! No one is going to harm you."

He held her face between his hands, his strong fingers pressing against her skin so hard they left marks. She stared back at him with wide, stark eyes. He shook her hard, and she finally blinked, a small flicker of recognition sparking behind the cold, vacant expression of terror.

"Aye, lass. It's me." His voice was strong, like those fingers, pressing into her, slicing through the terror, stripping it away, until she finally felt the warm pressure of his fingers against her skin, and she focused on that lifeline of pure sensation in the midst of the horror. And then he was pulling her into his arms.

"I've got you," he quietly soothed. "No one is going to hurt you. Do you understand?" Finally, he felt her slow, hesitant nod beneath his chin. She clasped him tightly about the waist. Her voice was muffled against the front of his coat.

"Belle . . ."

"What is it?"

"In there . . . Oh God . . . She's dead!"

"Burke!" The shout came from downstairs. It was Abberline, followed by Hobbs and several other uniformed constables.

"Why Belle Rossi?" Abberline asked, when they had returned to the police station. "It doesn't fit the pattern he's established. All the other women were prostitutes."

"Why Toby Gill?" Burke shot back at him, and then answered his own question.

"Somehow they both got in the way. Toby because he knew each of the murdered women, including Mary Kelly. Perhaps the murderer was afraid one of them might have said something to Toby and he might be able to identify the killer, or in the very least knew something significant."

"But you questioned him. He didn't know anything."

"Aye. But it could be he wasn't telling me everything. It could also be that he didn't realize what it was that he knew."

"What about Belle Rossi? She was no prostitute," Abberline pointed out.

"Perhaps the killer made a mistake."

"What are you talking about?"

Burke's expression was grim. "I didn't send that message round for Endicott. But someone did, someone who knew that Jess would go on alone to the flat. Only she didn't go directly to the flat. She made two stops. The extra time it took for those two stops saved her life."

"Are you saying the killer mistook Belle for Jess?"

"It was dark in the flat. Jess turned up the lights when she arrived. Either that or Belle disturbed the murderer while he was tearing apart the flat and he was forced to kill her."

"The damage to your flat doesn't fit the pattern of our murderer either," Abberline pointed out. "To the contrary. Each time before he has been almost fanatically neat, everything in its place, nothing disturbed, even to the extent of carefully covering his victims so that nothing seems amiss. Why tear the flat apart? What the devil is that all about?"

"He was looking for something."

"What could he possibly have been looking for?"

"He was looking for these," Jess said as she stood in the doorway that separated the two offices. She was holding a thick portfolio of sketches in her hands.

She was deathly pale, her voice carefully controlled as if the hysteria might return at any moment. Abberline crossed the office and escorted her to a chair before the desk.

"Are you all right, my dear?"

She nodded, trying to compose herself. Her green eyes were like wide dark pools, filled with the shadows of what she had seen.

Jess kept seeing Belle's body on the floor of that closet, sightless eyes staring back at her, that slash in her throat like an evil leering grin.

Belle, Toby, Liz Stride, Annie Chapman.

She closed her eyes briefly, trying to block out those images, but it was impossible. They followed her into the safe darkness behind her eyes until it wasn't safe any longer. There was no safe place from the horror of the past few weeks. And superimposed over all those sad images was the image of her sister.

She sat in the high-backed chair, her back rigid, shoulders stiff, as if holding herself tightly so that she wouldn't break into a thousand pieces. She haltingly handed Abberline the portfolio. Her voice was a ragged whisper, but the words were tightly controlled.

"Those are the newest composite sketches I've been working on from the descriptions taken after Liz Stride and Catherine Eddowes were killed—the ones you wanted me to hold back from Jimmy Cassidy." Abberline took the envelope and opened it. There were four sketches all somewhat similar, yet with distinctive differences.

He looked across at Burke. "Do you believe he was after these?"

Burke's expression was grim. "Aye. It's the reason he sent that poem to Cassidy. He feels threatened because of the sketches that were printed. The poem was his warning to us. We assumed that he meant Mary Kelly in the poem, but it was Jess he was givin' the warnin' about."

Abberline was thoughtful. "It is possible that one of these sketches bears a much closer resemblance to the killer than we guessed. Unfortunately our "friend," Cassidy gave the murderer all the information he needed about the person who drew the sketches. He knows who Jess is and he knows where to find her."

"I'd like to get my hands on Jimmy Cassidy," Burke muttered. "If he shows his face around here again . . ."

"Cassidy is a pain in the backside, but he's not the important issue here. The damage has already been done. She is obviously in great danger and we must do everything to keep her safe."

They were speaking about her as if she weren't in the same room. Jess suddenly stood. In a quiet but firm voice she said, "You need me to help you find him."

She looked at Burke, her expression calm, the look behind her eyes somber but also perfectly calm after the hysteria at the flat.

"He's afraid of the sketches. They're the key to finding him. All you have to do is draw him out into the open, and you'll have him."

"What the devil are you talking about?"

Abberline held up his hand at Burke's angry response. "Go on, my dear."

She looked from one to the other, felt Burke's disapproval, and went on to explain anyway.

"What if we were able to draw him out at a prearranged time and place? You could have your men waiting, and when he makes his appearance, you apprehend him."

"Are you suggesting we set a trap for him?"

"Yes, I suppose it would be something like that."

"He's proved to be a most elusive fellow, and very clever. In order to draw him out it would have to be something of tremendous value to him."

"Yes, it would," she said quietly. Then as he suddenly realized precisely what it was that she was proposing, Burke cut them both off.

"No! It's out of the question. It's too dangerous."

She looked at him, trying to understand the emotion behind his vehement refusal.

"It's not for you to decide."

"It is for me to decide, and I say no."

"It's the only way, and you know it," she said, as if they were the only two people in the room.

"Since this is abundantly clear to everyone else would you please explain it to me?" Abberline demanded.

"She proposes to set herself and the sketches up as the lure for the trap," Burke explained, his dark blue gaze fastened on her, trying to see beneath the perfectly composed facade of the well-bred lady—trying to understand why she was doing this.

He went on. "It would be impossible for the murderer to resist if he thought she had a sketch which could identify him to all the world as the killer. He would be forced to stop her and destroy the sketch to protect himself, just as he tried tonight."

Abberline had been listening intently, saying nothing. Now he shook his head. "It would be impossible to control such a situation. It would be extremely dangerous for you."

"It would be possible if the identity of the killer was to be revealed at a specific time and place, such as an art gallery where several paintings were to be exhibited."

Abberline's gaze narrowed. "Please go on, my dear. What, precisely, are you suggesting?"

"I suggest that you use Jimmy Cassidy to set the trap by announcing the time and location in the newspaper."

"It would never work."

"It will work if it is revealed that J.B. Dumont is the artist."

Abberline sat in the chair behind his desk. His elbow was braced on the arm of the chair, his chin propped thoughtfully in his fingers. His expression was grave.

"You would be willing to reveal the identity of J.B. Dumont in order to do this?"

She looked at him, eyes clear. "I would do anything to stop this madman before he kills again." Then her voice broke softly. "It's the only way I can save my sister."

"The risk would be enormous. It would be very dangerous."

"As dangerous as it was for Belle, Toby, or Annie Chapman? As dangerous as it is for my sister?"

Abberline looked at Burke. "It may be the only hope we have of catching this madman. It might work."

"No! It's too dangerous!"

She looked at Burke beseechingly. "I want to do this."

But it was Abberline who made the final decision. "We'll need time to make the necessary arrangements. How much time will you need to complete the composite sketches?"

"I need copies of the latest reports taken after Toby died, and anything you may be able to learn about Belle's death." She was thoughtful. "And it will take time to make arrangements with the gallery. Everything could be in readiness within a fortnight."

He nodded grimly. "We will give Cassidy another sketch as soon as possible. Any of the others you've been working on will do. Perhaps it will deter this fellow from killing again, until we can make the necessary arrangements. Then we'll give Cassidy just enough information so that he will print the date and location of the announcement to be made by J.B. Dumont." He frowned.

"We'll have to find another place for you to stay, some place that is absolutely safe. You cannot return to Burke's flat. It must be a place no one knows of in order to guarantee complete safety."

Burke turned to Jess, trying to reason with her. "Do you know the chance you're takin'? That fiend went to the flat tonight for the sketches, and you. He has no conscience. You won't be able to stop him with fancy manners or polite words. He's a brutal murderer, and he'll kill again."

He saw the wounded expression behind her eyes, and hated that he was the cause of it.

"I know the risk," she said in a quiet but determined voice. "I won't change my mind on this."

His hands were planted on his hips, his expression somewhere between anger and frustration. He looked from her to Abberline.

"You're both mad!"

"Perhaps it requires a little madness to catch a madman," Abberline suggested.

Burke could see there was no arguing with either of them. Logically, he knew the plan had merit. It could work. But a cold, naked fear edged around the logic, and settled somewhere in the pit of his stomach.

What if he couldn't keep her safe?

A safe place . . .

He slowly, reluctantly nodded. "I know of a place," he finally said with resignation. "We must leave as soon as possible. And no one outside this room must know of it."

"Agreed," Abberline acknowledged. "It's the only way we can guarantee her safety. I'll make the necessary explanations about your absence, Inspector. We'll keep everyone at bay for as long as possible."

Burke nodded. "She'll need witness statements from the files on the latest victims, including anyone who might have seen something at Abbington Road."

"I'll handle it myself and see that it's forwarded to you as soon as it's available. The fewer people involved in this, the greater our chances of maintaining secrecy." Abberline looked at her then. "What about the arrangements with the gallery?"

She took a paper and pen from the top of his desk and hastily wrote a note, signing it J.B. Dumont.

"Give this to the curator at the Gilot Gallery. He'll make the necessary arrangements." Abberline nodded, looking from Jess to Inspector Burke.

"Then it seems everything is in order."

"We should leave tonight," Burke suddenly decided.

When he started to explain, Abberline held up his hand.

"I don't want to know the details. It's better that way."

"All right, then. I'll make the necessary arrangements," Burke said, buttoning the thick coat he'd acquired after donating his previous coat that night on the quay.

"I'll be back as soon as I can." He looked at Jess. "Is there anythin' you'd be wantin' from the flat? We can't take a lot. It can't look as if either of us has left permanently, just in case he pays a return call."

She thought of the clothes in the closet and Belle's blood splattered over the walls and floor. She shook her head, her hands folded tightly against a sudden coldness.

"No, there's nothing that I need," she said in a quiet voice. Then she looked up as a sudden thought occurred to her.

"Melrose!"

Abberline looked from one to the other. "Who is Melrose?"

Burke shook his head. "It's not *who*, it's *what*." Then he informed her, "We're not takin' the cat."

Abberline was slightly bemused. "A cat?"

"We can't just leave him," Jess protested.

"He'll do just fine," Burke assured her. "One of the other tenants will feed him, or he can live off the streets, which is where he came from in the first place."

"No!" she informed him bluntly. "I won't leave him."

"He's a stray. A mangy, good-for-nothin' . . . Belle took a likin' to him. God know's why. He's like a dozen cats in any alley, on any road in Whitechapel."

"I'm not leaving without him," Jess insisted.

"We're not takin' him with us. There's no way round it, Jess. It won't work." His accent had grown perceptively thicker as he became more adamant. "And that's my final word on the matter."

271

Chapter Nineteen

They took a hansom across London, arriving outside the Theatre Royal on Drury Lane, shortly before eight o'clock in the evening. The performance had not yet begun. Patrons were still arriving in private coaches and carriages.

They were out of place, Burke in his well-made but simple suit of clothes, she in the common clothes a flower girl might wear, mingling with theater patrons dressed in their finest silk and satin gowns, men with their elegant hats, satin-lined capes, and walking sticks. Jess kept her head down, her face shielded, lest someone recognize her.

Finally, they unobtrusively climbed aboard a second hansom and continued their journey. They sped through the streets of London, the few possessions she was allowed to take with her in the small valise, including her charcoal pencils and paper. Burke carried a small leather case that contained the most recent information from the files on the murders that she needed to continue working on the composite sketches.

Burke had offered the driver an extra crown if he could reach Paddington Station before the last train departed at nine o'clock. They arrived at eight fifty-five. The final call for boarding had already gone out.

At the ticket window Burke explained to the agent, "We must have a private compartment. My wife is expecting a child and she needs her rest." Jess's mouth dropped open. Then she quickly shut it. The ticket agent gave her a brief look. She gave him what she hoped was a convincing expectant-mother smile. Then they hurried aboard, tickets in hand.

"The next time you decide to make me an expectant mother, would you please give me a little warning," she muttered under her breath as they slipped down the aisle of the coach behind the conductor.

"It was necessary. He wasn't going to give us a private compartment," he snapped, irritated that she found the situation so amusing. "It was all I could think of at the moment to convince him."

At the door to the compartment she hesitated, lifting a delicate brow as she looked up at him. The heated conversation contained more words than he'd said to her the entire ride across the whole of London. And even though he was clearly still angry with her over some matter which he hadn't bothered to explain, it was an improvement over silence.

She knew he didn't want her to be involved in the case, but like it or not she was. Somehow she sensed that it was more than that. He'd been remote and unapproachable ever since that night he followed her to the gallery.

At first she thought he was angry because she'd lied, but now she suspected that it was something more. He was keeping her at a distance and making no attempt to disguise his displeasure. He stood aside, with a sort of mocking grace, to allow her to enter the compartment first.

"Thank you," she said with mock sweetness as she stepped through the compartment. She was immediately rewarded with a look as cold as ice.

She sat in the wide cushioned seat that filled one end of the compartment. Burke closed the door securely then took the seat opposite, setting distance between them. Her heavy cloth valise sat on the floor.

"It's a long trip. Try to get some sleep," he said impersonally, then settled himself more comfortably in the seat, his long legs stretched before him, his gaze fixed out the window as the lights of Paddington Station slowly slipped past.

He couldn't sleep, so he watched her sleep. Occasionally they passed through a small station, and light played across her features. She didn't have a delicate beauty like other ladies of society of his experience; she had strong, dramatic features—dark winged brows, long dark lashes over vivid green eyes, and a full, sensual mouth that fascinated him in spite of all his intentions not to be fascinated.

The dark lashes quivered, her breathing suddenly went uneven, and her lower lip trembled with unspoken words.

What are your dreams? he thought silently. In those moments between waking and sleeping, what is it that you wish for and want more than anything?

To find her sister. He knew it as certainly as he watched her. But it made no sense. She had wealth and position. She could have almost anything she wanted, by simply wanting it. He suspected just one of her gowns cost more than what he made in a month on a police inspector's pay. And yet, dressed in rags she had disguised herself and gone into one of the worst parts of London to find her sister. Her love and fierce loyalty were stunning.

It didn't fit what he knew about ladies of society with their rules and manners and pretty words that hid their cruel lies and even crueler hearts beneath a facade of satin and lace.

She represented everything he hated, but it was hard to hate her—harder still to forget that he'd made love to her and even now wanted to hold and protect her, and touch her.

He jerked his gaze away and stared out at the dark night that seemed to envelop the train as it sped southward away from London, trying to escape, but her image was there on the glass, impossible to ignore just as she had been impossible to ignore over the past weeks.

She stirred, curling more tightly into herself on the narrow seat, and he remembered the feel of her slender body curled naked against him. She murmured something in her sleep, her lips moving, and he remembered the feel of them moving against his, rousing sensations and feelings that he'd thought long dead.

He took off his coat and covered her. Without waking, she snuggled more deeply into the upholstered seat, her face almost disappearing beneath the coat. She looked like a child with an innocence that slipped beneath the anger. And briefly, he wondered what it could have been like between them, if they were different people—if she hadn't been to the manor born, and he hadn't been born to the streets. If . . .

"Wake up, lass," he gently shook her shoulder. She slowly roused from sleep.

"What is it? Are we there?" she murmured groggily, having no idea where *there* was.

"Aye, lass, as far as the train will take us."

She finally sat up. She looked at his coat with momentary confusion then handed it to him. Her hair was quickly smoothed back into place, the wrinkles smoothed out of her skirt and shirtwaist as the porter announced their arrival in Exeter. She grabbed her valise and wearily followed the porter. Burke escorted her into the train station.

"Wait here. I've got to find us a wagon. It's another hour by road."

"Couldn't we find a room at an inn and continue in the morning?" She sat down on a bench seat inside the station. She was so small and slender that she looked like a forlorn child waiting for her mother to return for her. She was exhausted and slightly cranky—something no refined lady of society would have dared reveal to anyone.

The corner of his mouth twitched with amusement. "It would draw more attention if we were to stay in town till morning. We'll go on tonight. The cart should be outside."

Outside. As if it were waiting for them. She tried to think about that, but she was too tired.

She jerked awake at the touch of his hand on her shoulder. She had no idea how long she'd been dozing.

"Come along, lass. Let's be on our way."

The road turned out to be a deeply rutted path that no four-legged creature was meant to travel, much less a two-wheeled cart that seemed to find its way into every rut, hole, and abyss. Then to make matters worse, it started to rain. Burke pulled out a heavy canvas tarp that looked as if it might once have been part of a sail and made a tent of it over them.

She huddled against him, warmed by his strong body, and dozed between ruts. It seemed they went on forever. Her body ached and her head ached. But even that faded into a sort of numbed oblivion so that even the ruts in the road and the creaking cart couldn't keep her awake.

Her first immediate sensation was warmth, quickly followed by incredible softness as if floating on a cloud. Except that this cloud seemed very firmly grounded and her along with it. She wriggled her toes, savoring that delicious warmth. Then as she came slightly more awake, she instinctively braced herself for the next jarring lurch of the cart. When it didn't come, she snuggled more deeply into the warmth.

Slowly she became aware of voices.

"What is it?" a child's voice asked.

"It's a person, you twit."

"I know that, but wot kind o' person."

"Must be a girl. She's got long hair."

"Jordy gots long hair an' he's a he."

"It's a girl all right," an older, more authoritative voice announced.

"How do you know?"

"On accounta I sneaked a look last night when Moira was undressin' her. She was wearin' a corset. She's even got tits."

"Like Jillie?" the small voice asked incredulously. "She must be at least fifteen then."

"She's older I think on accounta Moira made us all leave."

Older? Corset?

Jess suddenly jerked upright and found herself staring, with eyes that felt as if they were filled with sand, at a dozen pairs of eyes all staring back at her.

"All right now!" an older, feminine voice called out from somewhere below. "Where 'ave you urchins gone off to now?" A woman a few years older than Jess appeared in the doorway of the bedroom.

"Thought I might find yer up here. Out with the lot of you. See wot you've done now. You woke her up."

276

"She was already awake," one small voice piped up. "We came up to say good mornin'."

"You can say it later. Out with ye." With a swish of her apron, the woman rounded up the children who varied in age from hardly out of nappies to the oldest of about nine or ten, and sent them all scurrying out of the room.

Jess stared after them, strangely certain that one of those faces seemed very familiar.

"Sorry 'bout that. They's just curious, that's all."

"Are they all yours?"

"In a manner of speaking."

"There must be a dozen of them." Jess was incredulous. Several of the children looked to be the same age, although they bore no resemblance to each other, except for two that might have been brother and sister. They had that unmistakable gold-as-wheat hair as the woman who crossed the room to open the window.

"Oh, more 'an a dozen," she said as casually as if she were counting puppies or eggs.

"There's twenty-three altogether."

"Twenty-three?" Jess was stunned.

"Aye. The oldest boy is eighteen. The youngest, little Nellie yer saw just then, is eleven months. With just about every age in between, sometimes two of the same age." She grinned then as she turned from the window, pressing a hand into the small of her back. "And this one is due next month. Might even make it fer Nellie's birthday." As Jess's mouth dropped open, the woman smiled, revealing a small dimple at one corner of her mouth and dancing blue eyes.

"I'm Moira. You'll meet my husband, Robbie, later. He's out with Dev checking the damage from the storm last night. That chicken house needs to be rebuilt. Hope we didn't lose any hens. The wind gets a mite fierce when it comes whippin' down from the high country. Lost the dovecote last week, but most of the doves is roostin' in the henhouse."

"It was about time Dev got back home for a visit. He's been gone too long this time. The work started pilin' up round here," she went on, as if everything she said made perfect sense.

"There's always plenty of work to be done round here. And he gets back so seldom. 'Course, it's often as he can, I s'pose."

"Home?" Jess asked with some bewilderment. Everything, including a dozen moppets, was coming at her a bit fast.

"Well, I suppose he didn't explain much to you. That's his way. Got his reasons, I s'pose. I'd better let him tell what he sees fit." She crossed the room in a flurry of activity in spite of her well-rounded stomach beneath the spotless apron, straightening linens and a lace doily at the small bedside table as she went, laying a neatly folded stack of clothes on the edge of the bed.

"Yer clothes was a mite soiled. I put them in the wash. Yer can wear these. I can't fit into them right now anyway."

"I can't take your clothes," Jess protested. In spite of the cleanliness of everything, including the children and their robust health, which confirmed that they were undoubtedly well-fed, it was obvious these people lived a simple life and possessions were few.

Moira's expression shifted. "I know they're not very fine, but yer welcome to them," she said, suddenly remote.

"They're clean and warm. You'll need warm clothes with winter settin' in hard in these parts."

It was obvious that she'd hurt Moira's feelings. "I didn't mean it the way it sounded," Jess apologized.

She looked at the fine-quality stitching on the sleeves, as fine as any seamstress in London. "These are very fine clothes. But you'll need them again. And I don't want to impose."

"Impose?" Moira laughed then, the uneasiness gone. "We've got plenty for everyone, and don't go frettin' about imposing. Every-thin' washes, Jess. It's all right if I call you that, isn't it? Burke said as how that was yer name."

"Yes, of course. And I deeply appreciate the use of the clothes. I'll be very careful with them."

"That's all right, m'dear. You'll have yer own in no time. In the winter, we have lotsa time to sew."

"Sew?" Jess was stunned, and thought briefly of all the countless hours she'd spent poking the tips of her fingers bloody over some bit of finery because her stepmother insisted it was expected of young ladies. Vivian had finally given up on her when she succeeded in sewing together all four corners of at least a dozen of her father's finest linen handkerchiefs into bundles that resembled miniature choir robes with large sleeves that a doll might wear.

"That will be very interesting," Jess confessed.

"You'll fit right in. We can always use someone with your skills."

Jess wondered precisely what skills Burke had mentioned to her.

"We don't have a fancy privy," Moira informed her on her way to the door.

"The bathtub is downstairs off the kitchen. Everybody takes a turn. There's an outdoor convenience when the weather is decent, and a water closet at the end of the hall that Devlin built for us last year." She grinned good-naturedly.

"There's a latch on the door. Best use it. Yer never know who's gonna come right in on you without a bye or leave. I'm tryin' to teach the kids manners about things like that, but with twenty-three of them, someone is bound to get caught in a pinch and forget about knockin' first."

"I'll try to remember."

"I've got a pot on and some cakes and ham warmin' on the stove."

"Thank you, I'll be down as soon as I've dressed. And thank you again for the clothes."

"See you downstairs," Moira called out. "Don't trip over one of the wee ones on yer way down."

Jess dressed quickly, made the bed, which she suspected by the man's clothes on the chair might belong to Moira and her husband, and made a quick trip down the hall to the water closet.

The cold water that came through the faucet helped waken her. She quickly washed with a large bar of soap that smelled faintly of roses and was smoothing back the plaits of hair that she'd made the day before when there was a muffled knock at the door.

"Hurry!" came an urgent cry through the door.

Jess immediately opened it and found a child who couldn't have been more than two or three by her limited experience and whose face she recalled from over the foot of the bed, standing cross-legged in the doorway, a look of desperation on his or her face—it wasn't readily apparent—and clutching the front of the gown at approximately crotch level.

"I gotta pee!" the child announced, hopping frantically from one bare foot to the other, an intense expression pinching the small face.

"I'm sorry," Jess apologized. "You may have it all to yourself." She started to leave when a wail stopped her.

"Can't do it by myself!" the child cried helplessly, tears filling large brown eyes.

"Good heavens!" Jess exclaimed, then whirled about. "I'll get Moira."

"Noooooo!" the frantic youngster cried. "You gotta help me."

"You don't understand," Jess tried to reason with the child. "I don't know how . . ."

Any further excuses were drowned in a flood of new tears.

"Dear God!" Jess muttered as she tried to decide how best to go about this.

"You poor child. You don't know what you're asking."

Logic prevailed. It seemed the best rule in a situation like this was *what went on, had to come off.* Jess scooped up the hem of the child's gown.

"What is your name?"

"Jamie?"

"Hold on to this, Jamie," she instructed and the child held the hem up high at the chest.

"Wot's yers?"

"Jessie," she answered with a smile at her success coaxing the child from tears. She found small snug pants and tugged them down.

Jamie—like her own name, a bit different for a girl . . . She suddenly stopped and stared. All right, she thought, a very fine name for a boy, and succeeded in pulling the small pants down to his ankles while she smothered back a smile at the mistake she'd made.

She'd never given it any thought before, but it seemed that boys came in all sorts of sizes. Then she felt her cheeks

280

go warm and she concentrated on the task at hand.

She started to lift him to set him on the commode, which seemed perfectly natural from her point of view. He protested with a loud wail and insisted on standing.

"I can do it," he announced, holding the hem of his gown with one hand and taking precarious aim with the other.

Jess's instinct was to offer some advice or assistance, but she decided that this part was definitely out of her realm of experience.

"I'll just wait outside until you're finished," she said. "Call me, if you need any help." Although for the life of her, she had no idea how she would help if Jamie needed it, save to help pull his pants back up.

"Good mornin', Jess."

She whirled around. Devlin Burke was leaning one shoulder against the wall at the landing, a slightly bemused expression on his face.

"What might little Jamie need help with?"

"His aim. It's a bit high and to the right." Then, she felt color flood into her cheeks, and she said offhandedly, "I'm afraid I wasn't much help."

"You seem to have done just fine. It takes a bit of gettin' used to. They come with all sorts of built-in problems and shortcomings."

She looked at him then, laughter bubbling into her throat, at their ridiculous conversation—a conversation she could never have imagined having with *Inspector* Devlin Burke.

"At any rate, he might make a very good artist one day. He has a free-spirited sort of . . . creativity."

"I'll tell Moira," he said, grinning at her. Then his expression changed.

"You look very pretty, Jess."

"Thank you. Moira let me borrow some of her things."

"Well, it's for certain she won't have any use for them for quite a while." He reached out and touched the edge of her sleeve.

"You look different."

"Well it's a bit of a change from brown linsey skirts and a black wool coat."

"I'm ready," Jamie's small voice piped up through the door.

"You go downstairs and meet the others," Burke insisted. "I'll give the lad a hand."

As she was walking down the stairs she heard Jamie's excited voice chirping, "Da! Da! Look wot I can do." And Burke's proud response.

"Aye, I can see that, Jamie. What a big boy you are, too. A fine lad and growin' so fast. I'm very proud of you."

Da? Father in Gaelic, if she wasn't mistaken.

Jess hurried down the stairs to the kitchen below, grateful for the confusion of dozens of introductions and questions that helped block out her uncertainty over what she'd overheard. Surely the child wasn't his.

Or, was he?

"This is me husband, Robbie Callahan," Moira said. He had sandy brown hair, warm dark eyes, and a ready smile. He had a compact, hard-muscled body and was hardly taller than Moira. His legs were slightly bowed and he walked with a slight limp. It must have been an old injury, for it didn't seem to cause him any pain.

He juggled several children on his shoulders, one hanging from an arm, another wrapped about one leg as he helped Moira set out breakfast cakes, a pot of tea, and several cups.

"Jillie," he called out to an older girl Jess had briefly met. "Take the older ones on over to the school. Ethan will be here shortly."

Jillie, probably about fifteen, slender as a reed with delicate features, blue eyes, and raven-dark hair that hung down about her shoulders, rounded up the older children.

She hardly said more than two words as they were introduced. Her expression as she glanced at Jess was dark, speculative, and slightly sullen. Then her gaze slipped past Jess to the staircase and her expression changed completely.

Burke came down the stairs with Jamie. The child's small arms were wrapped tightly about his neck. Jillie's face was filled with adoration, and hardly for the toddler he carried.

"Hello, Devlin," she said with amazing sweetness, the sudden light in her eyes transforming all her features into a promising prettiness.

"Hello, Slats," he said with a good-natured smile, tugging on a long tendril of hair at her shoulder. "Although, maybe I shouldn't be callin' ya that no more. You're practically all grown up." He looked at Jess then.

"The boys nicknamed her that, on accounta she's always been a skinny little thing, with no more than wood slats for legs."

"I'm not little no more, an' I'm not skinny. I got me a figure, and I was fifteen last month," she informed him with a proud and adoring smile.

"Aye, 'tis true. And she got even with the boys long ago by beatin' 'em soundly at footraces. Not a one could catch her."

"I don't race the boys no more," she said, as if to remind him how very grown-up she was. "I'm wearin' long skirts now. And Moira says I can have a special gown for the fair next week, with fancy lace."

"If I can finish it in time," Moira said. Burke gave her a wink. "Maybe ya should put that off a bit. Every laddie for miles about will be sniffin' round the door once they see our fine Jillie."

"I'm certain you and Robbie can keep the local pups at bay," she returned the wink.

"I don't care about any of them," Jillie informed all of them. "They're silly and childish, as if they was no older than Mick."

Mick, a familiar face in a crowd of new faces. Jess silently wondered how he came to be with them. She would have asked, but there was no opportunity. She was quickly learning that with a dozen children, and more unaccounted for, conversation was perhaps an inaccurate word for what was going on. It was more like a lively public debate with everyone joining in at once.

One had to speak up quickly or be left behind. She wanted to ask about Melrose and how he had fared the wet ride from the train station, but it was safer simply to listen. She'd always found it an invaluable way to learn about people.

"Perhaps there will be some older fellas at the fair," Robbie suggested. "But we'll have to watch them for entirely different reasons."

Jillie ignored them. "I've been practicin' my dancin'. I can do the waltz now." Her gaze fastened on Burke. "You said if I learned them, you'd dance with me at the fair."

"Aye, that I did. I suppose that means I'd better do some practicin' of me own. A promise made is a promise kept. I'd be honored to have the first dance with Jillie. Then I expect Robbie and I will have our hands full the rest o' the evenin' keeping the young bucks in line."

Jess had noticed several things. Moira and Robbie were both Irish. Their accents were thick and rich, wrapping around words with stops and starts and lost letters, in a sort of musical rhythm. In their company, with their easy camaraderie, Burke's accent slipped through more readily with a sort of spontaneity, as if some sort of barrier had come down when they left London behind. It was obvious that he felt at home here. And Moira had said that it was good to have him *home*.

What was his connection to these people? They seemed almost like a family, yet there was no familial resemblance. And Burke had never once spoken of having any brothers or sisters. No, it was something else—something that fit all of them so easily that they felt no need to explain it.

Jess had thought of the flat on Abbington Road as his home. But as she thought more about it she realized there was a sort of stark emptiness to the two rooms there, in spite of what had obviously been Belle's attempt to make them seem comfortable.

The rooms were simply walls, without adornment, no pictures or photographs set about, no mementos that gave anything of his past away. There were clothes in drawers, an umbrella in the stand by the door, warm blankets on the bed, all very functional and necessary. Except for that finely made quilt that she'd noticed, there was absolutely nothing personal or private that gave away anything about the man himself or any details of his personal life.

But this place was different. The kitchen was bright and warm and crowded. The oven radiated heat and scents of wondrous things already cooking for the midday meal. Several loaves of bread sat on the wood sideboard cooling. Shelves were decoratively lined with colorful jars of jams and jellies, tied with ribbons for decoration.

Sprigs of long-stemmed herbs had been tied about with more ribbons and hung over the stove where the heat dried them and filled the kitchen with pungent scents. A chipped crockery vase was filled with a chaotic mixture of Michaelmas daisies, late-blooming roses, spiky snapdragons with their round little faces, and stalks of dried heather.

By the door were boots of various sizes set on a wood rack inside a square box to catch water and dirt brought in on the boots and prevent them from muddying the floor. Nearby in the corner children's wood blocks were scattered about, along with a top, a yarn doll that had lost most of its yarn, a ball, and jax.

One end of the large kitchen was filled with an oak refectory table that was freshly scrubbed, with a long bench seat on either side. It was at this table that all the children were clustered about, talking excitedly.

She loved all of it. It was lived in with the sound of voices, laughter, even arguments, but with a pervading sense of love and warmth wrapping about all of it, that somehow said You are welcome, you are safe. We accept you.

She helped Moira pour tea and set out the late breakfast of ham and cakes, which she realized must have been prepared on her behalf and kept warming in the oven until she awakened.

From what little she had seen of the house the night before when they arrived and the fact that Moira had mentioned hens, she realized this was a farm. And from what little she knew about farms from summers spent in the country and in the Provence area of France, everyone rose early, for there was endless work to be done.

Moira tried to persuade her to sit with the others, but she refused, wanting to somehow repay their hospitality. She set out plates and utensils for everyone, drawing curious stares as she neatly arranged knives, forks, and spoons in their proper places.

"We always put them to the right of the plate where you can get at 'em," Jillie remarked with a frown.

"I'm sorry," she apologized, and quickly began to change the arrangement. Moira stopped her.

"Don't matter where they is, long as we can get at 'em. They're jus' fine the way they are. Kinda' fancy and special. I like it."

Jess glanced briefly at Jillian. The girl's expression had been smug earlier. Now it was once more sullen. It was obvious that she'd made an enemy without even knowing the girl.

"Here," Moira said from the stove. "Take this pan of cakes and put them on the table."

Jess took the flat pan, carefully fitting her hands over the thick pot holders so that she wouldn't burn herself. The pan was heavy and awkward, loaded down with fat cinnamon-scented cakes. It wobbled slightly and two cakes spilled to the floor before Jess could balance it.

"Yer'd think she'd never been in a kitchen before," Jillie remarked for all to hear, her voice dripping with criticism.

"Mind yer manners, miss," Moira snapped. "Take enough cakes for the others in a basket and be off with yer to school. And don't forget a cake for Ethan. I'll see all of you at the midday meal."

Jillie gathered up the younger children, including Mick, who darted away and rounded the table toward Jess. He winked at her.

"Hello, Miss Jess."

"Hello, Mick. It's so good to see you. I didn't know you would be here."

"Aye, Mr. Burke arranged it. Learnin' me letters, I am, and a trade."

"Oh, that's very good, Mick. I'm so glad to hear of it."

"Yeah, Mr. Burke said as wot I should get me arse off the streets."

"Mick!" Burke reprimanded him. The boy blushed, which was remarkable considering it had always seemed there was nothing that could embarrass the streetwise lad.

"Sorry," he apologized with a chagrined expression.

"That's quite all right," she said with a hidden smile. "It seems we both have a great deal to learn." He grinned up at her.

"Come along, Mick," Jillie reminded him impatiently.

He winked at Jess and leaned close to whisper. "She's a bit of a nag and likes to boss everyone around on accounta' she's older. But I can handle her."

Jess forced a stern expression. "I'm certain that you can."

"Yer goin' ter be stayin' with us a while then, Miss Jess?" he asked with open curiosity.

"For a little while, if it's all right."

"They got more than enough room," he assured her without even looking to either Moira or Robbie. "It's the way they do things round here."

She wasn't at all certain what he meant by that. She leaned down closer to Mick. "Who is the little girl, sitting beside Robbie? Moira didn't introduce her."

"That's on accounta she's real shy. She probably would have run and hid if Moira had made introductions. Her name is Mary Margaret."

Mary Margaret was a beautiful child, probably five or six. It wasn't just the resemblance of name that reminded Jess of her sister. Mary Margaret had flaxen hair and soft blue eyes and a delicate porcelain loveliness. But it was the poignant sadness in her eyes that pulled at Jess's heart.

It was as if she'd found the imaginary childhood friend that she and Linnie had invented, embodied in the form of this shy, skinny child. And the sadness in her eyes seemed to reflect Jess's own sadness of the past weeks. She immediately felt a kinship with Mary Margaret.

Beside her, Mick was saying, "Every one calls her Maggot. 'Cept o' course Moira and Robbie."

"That's dreadful! Mary Margaret is such a lovely name. How could anyone be so cruel to call her that horrible name?"

Mick gave her a good-natured smile. "They don't mean nothin' by it, and she don't mind none. She sorta' likes it. It makes her feel special to be the center of attention, although she never says so. She never says nothin'."

"Why not?"

"On accounta the Maggot don't talk."

"What do you mean she doesn't talk?"

"Just that, Miss Jess, she can't talk. No sounds come out."

"Mick!" Jillie repeated, all patience gone. "Come on along or I'll box yer ears."

"I'd like to see you try!" he flung back at her with all the swaggering street bravado that Jess remembered.

"You had better get along now," she suggested.

He nodded. "Right. Oh, by the way, I put yer cat in the barn."

"Melrose? Is he all right? I was very concerned for him riding all the way from London in that small bag."

"He's right enough." Mick grinned. "Caught himself a giant mouse in the corn crib this mornin'. He'll fit in right nice round here."

"Mick!"

As Jillie held the door open, he sauntered out at his own deliberately slow, slightly swaggering pace. He stopped at the doorway and looked up at Jillie.

"Thanks, luv," he said to her, and then to twist her tail just a little more, "You hold that door open right fine. Me thinks maybe you found your place in life as a door jock."

Then he quickly raced out the door and beyond range of her foot as she swung it at his backside.

"We can always use another cat," Moira was saying without missing a beat, the complete calm in the center of the storm, as if there weren't a dozen noisy children racing out the door.

"Your Melrose seems to have taken a fancy to our Lucy."

Was this another child Jess hadn't yet met?

"Lucy is the dog," Moira went on to explain. "A sheepdog to be more precise. She's out with two of the older boys and the herd this morning."

She looked from Moira to Burke. "Melrose can be somewhat difficult. I'm not at all certain how he will react to dogs."

"The cat?" Moira laughed. "It's Lucy we was worried about. That is one very assertive feline. Burke let him out of that bag yer was carryin' last night, and he went right on over and curled up right on top of Lucy, as if she was a big blanket.

There was a bit of fur flyin' at first, and a lot of hissin' and spittin'. But the cat soon got the upper hand."

"Good heavens!" Jess couldn't quite believe what she was hearing. On the other hand, this was Melrose they were discussing.

"I'm very sorry. I never intended to cause any harm. But I couldn't simply leave him."

Moira made an unconcerned wave through the air with one hand. "There's no harm. I'm glad to have a good mouser about the place."

"Damned cat," Burke muttered. "Probably has fleas."

"I have an herb powder that will take care of that," Moira informed him. "Same one I use on Robbie and the boys when they shear them sheep. Works every time. We'll use it on you as well if you come down with any of them critters." She pointed to the platter of food.

"Eat them cakes and ham. There's a full day's work waitin'," she informed him sternly from across a fresh platter of cakes she'd just removed from the oven. The others had quickly disappeared into the hands and pockets of several children on their way out the door.

"Mean woman," Robbie remarked about his wife, as he swallowed back a mouthful of cake. "She gets meaner the closer it gets to her time."

"Yer lucky, Robbie," Jess overheard Burke telling him. "All that matters in life is right here."

Robbie grunted, with a grin and careful look to see if Moira was also listening. At that particular moment she was carving more ham off a huge roast on the sideboard.

"I give ya three days, tops, and yer'll be high-tailin' it back ter London. She has that way about her when she gets near."

"I heard that, Robbie Callahan," Moira called over her shoulder. "If yer want yer supper tonight and me to warm yer bed, yer better sweeten yer words."

"I was just tellin' Devlin that the cider will be set in about three days, me luv."

"And pigs can fly, me luv," she retorted. "Now, how was it yer wanted this coffee you like so much? In yer lap perhaps, darlin'?"

289

"In the cup will be jus' fine, darlin'," he responded with a wink and huge grin, convincing Jess that their banter was all in good jest. "Then I think Devlin and me will go down to the old farm. He said somethin' 'bout checkin' the thatch on the roof."

"You be careful on that roof, Robbie Callahan, with that crooked leg o' yours. I won't be havin' a new babe and a crippled husband to take care of."

"Yes, luv." Robbie and Devlin slammed out of the kitchen, cups of thick, dark coffee in hand.

Jess could have sworn she heard them both laughing. She envied all of them their easy camaraderie and friendship. They were obviously very close, as she and her sister had once been, but with a sort of lighthearted easiness that one never experienced at Carrington Square.

She sat down at the long table, and took a sip of the strong brew, unaware until she had swallowed it that it was coffee and not tea. Then she took another bracing sip and frowned at the strong, bitter taste.

"It takes a bit o' gettin' used to," Moira said as she sat down opposite.

"The coffee or them?"

Moira laughed. "You're a smart one. Dev said yer were. You'll fit in fine around here."

"Where exactly is *here?*" Jess asked, since she hadn't any precise notion after that jouncing, rain-soaked ride from the train station in the middle of the night.

"This is Old Orchard farm. And just over the hill a wee bit is the village of Farway."

Jess thought she had heard wrong. "I beg your pardon."

Moira grinned at her. "Most folks react that way when they first hear it."

"When Dev found this place, he knew it was where we needed to be—*far way* enough from the life we left behind in Dublin and any other city for that matter. And the people in these parts don't hold it against any man where he's from. It seemed the best place to be."

She took another sip and went on to explain. "Dev came here

290

fifteen years ago. Me and Robbie followed a year later. We've been here ever since—farmers and sheep people. A *far way* from the streets of Dublin. And lucky we are Devlin bought this place."

Jess was stunned. "This is his farm?"

Moira nodded. "This is his house as well. But you'd never hear him tell it. The farm has two houses. There's a smaller cottage over the hill. Devlin said as how we should take the big house because of the kids. 'Course we didn't have any then, but I think he knew we would."

"What about all the children?"

Moira's brows lifted and her eyes widened. "I can see there's a great deal he didn't bother to explain. You thought they were all my own natural children?"

When Jess nodded, she laughed softly.

"In a way I suppose they are, and seven or eight more that are older and gone on their way now. And there's always a new one Dev brings along or sends to us." She refilled both their cups and put fresh cakes on their plates, even though they had both already had two each.

Moira grinned wickedly. "I'll worry about me figure when the babe is born. For now I can eat whatever I like, and this is definitely a three-cake story. Devlin should have told you, bringing you here like this and all. But since he didn't," she shrugged, "I'll tell you what I can, which is just enough to make you curious enough to pester the livin' daylights out of him to tell you the rest." She winked.

"It's a dark and dastardly story about thieves, cutthroats, and a wicked old witch."

Chapter Twenty

Thieves, cutthroats, and wicked witches.

It was an intriguing and poignantly sad story of Burke's youth.

She turned it all over in her mind as she walked down the dirt lane that connected the big house to the cottage, past the barn, the corn crib where Melrose was now in ecstatic residence, and open fields where hillsides were covered with late fall colors, and a distant flock of sheep looked like a large puffy cloud caught between the horizon and the sky.

She stopped and watched the herd. It shifted, one moment round and full, the next strung along the horizon. Then it grew fat once more as a black and white object darted and streaked at the fringes, obviously Lucy, the sheepdog, hard at work.

Occasionally there was a shout or a piercing whistle from two young men who watched the herd, calling out commands to the dog. They must be two of the older boys Moira had spoken of, she thought.

The sun was warm with that last brightness of fall that makes false promises. The breeze lifted the edges of her skirt, slipping cold underneath, reminding her that it was November. They'd arrived in a rainstorm that had washed everything clean. But there was an expectancy in the crisp air, an urgency that had tinged the grass and colored the leaves of trees in bright oranges and reds. Winter was only a breath away.

She looked back at the big house, nestled in a copse of trees. It was rather untidily built and seemed to follow the contour of the ground, haphazard and rambling. The whitewashed upright walls gave the appearance of being at odd angles, making it a wonder the whole thing didn't shift in the wind and suddenly angle forward into the yard in front.

Windows appeared at odd intervals without any grand design or plan, peeking out from under the eaves of the thatched roof over the second story like surprised, lopsided eyes under equally surprised, thatch eyebrows.

The farm rested in the curve of the earth, intimately a part of the trees, hedgerows, orchards, and sun that surrounded it, as if that particular place on earth would somehow seem lacking if the house were not there.

Down the lane in the opposite direction was the *school,* and something referred to as the workshop. She had overheard two of the children talking about it.

When she first came downstairs that morning, the house seemed overgrown with children. And if numbers were to be believed, only half of them were present at the time. The others that made up the total of twenty-three were off and about on various chores.

From the vague explanations that Moira provided, she concluded that only three of the children were actually Moira and Robbie's, and then of course the baby that was due in December. The others were an odd lot of various ages, descriptions, and accents, right down to little Jamie whom she'd overheard calling Devlin Burke his *da.*

After the children left for lessons, she helped clean up the kitchen while Moira explained about Old Orchard. Moira good-naturedly but firmly threw her out after she succeeded in breaking two crockery dishes, scalding her hand in hot dishwater, and spilling a sack of flour all over herself. She spent the next half hour sifting flour out of her hair and clothes.

Surviving on her own in Whitechapel with all its dangers was nothing compared to survival in a kitchen. She brushed more flour from her skirt and kept on walking, hoping that Moira hadn't misinformed her when she told her to just keep walking until she found the small cottage. Although considering what she did to Moira's kitchen, she wouldn't have blamed her.

She rounded a bend in the road, the distant hillside obscured by deepening foliage. Then she found it, set apart from the surrounding heavily wooded hillside by the meticulous, precise woven line of roof thatching.

As she walked closer over the uneven rise in the road she discovered more of the cottage. Thick white plaster walls emerged with dark wood window casements, the lower level visible, the second-story windows barely visible beneath the dipping overhang of thatch.

A flagstone walk surrounded it, or at least attempted to, when it wasn't interrupted by a crumbling break in the pathway, riotously overgrown gardens, scraggy trees that were out of control and in desperate need of pruning shears.

At the front there was a small outthrust enclosed entry with a lopsided door that appeared stout enough except that it hung precariously by only one hinge. The entry was like a small attached guardhouse with its own thatching, a small window in the door to inspect callers, and an oil lamp mounted on the side wall.

The first-floor windows were dirty and smudged with an accumulation of filth that could only be acquired over several seasons of neglect. Two small panes were broken out of the second-story windows. But like the big house, the cottage appeared to be stout and solid. It had undoubtedly been here for at least two hundred years and seemed in no danger of going anywhere for at least two hundred more, given care and attention.

In a flight of fancy that she preferred to acknowledge as artistic creativity, she imagined lace curtains at the windows, gleaming polished panes of glass, gardens manicured just enough to gently restrain a riot of columbine, hollyhocks, wisteria, and snapdragons, and at night, that lamp beside the door, glowing with welcoming light.

It was as enchanting with its quaint snugness as the big house was in its rambling chaos, and inexplicably filled her with a poignant longing for things she couldn't quite understand.

"Wouldn't try the door if I were you," a voice called out. She immediately recognized the deep, resonant tones. Moira had said she would probably find him here. Except that she wasn't quite certain where he was. "It might come off the other hinge and fall on you. I'll fix that next."

She looked up. Devlin Burke was illuminated against the early afternoon sky at the top of the roof. A section of thatching had been peeled away. Clumps of new thatching lay on another section of solid roof nearby.

"Moira said I might find you here."

"Decided I'd better get at this section before the next storm. We get a lot of rain and some snow. It's leaked the last two seasons but I didn't have the time to get to it."

"Good at that, are you?" she asked, tilting her head back and shielding her eyes from the glare of the sun with her hand.

He shrugged. "Fair. I learned thatching and other necessary skills when I first came to Devon."

"Was that after your career as a thief?"

He stood, hands firmly planted on hips, his face in shadow with the sun at his back as he stared down at her.

"Moira's been tellin' stories again. She does that now and then. I think it's being round children all the time. Her mind's gone to mush and she starts spinnin' yarns and fairy tales."

Jess went around to the back of the cottage and found the rough-hewn but stout ladder propped against the roofline. She stepped onto the bottom rung.

"The only thing mushy about Moira is her kitchen floor with all the flour I spilled."

He shifted several more bundles of thatching within easy reach. It was hard work, the bundles were obviously heavy. He'd removed his shirt in the warm afternoon sun. His skin glistened with a fine sheen of moisture over strongly corded muscles. She should have looked away, but instead found herself staring at the movement of those muscles, equally unable to forget the memory of his skin bare against hers, their bodies intimately close the night they made love.

He was dark even where the shirt usually covered, something she hadn't discovered that night they'd been together. Fine dark hair spread across his chest in delicate strokes as if an artist had feathered a brush across the hard muscles, then tapered to a narrow line down his belly. His pants rode low on his hips, revealing his navel, and the whorl of dark hair there that disappeared lower. She jerked her gaze back to his shoulders. They were wide, emphasizing the narrow taper of his lean hips that even at that moment she remembered pressed so intimately against hers.

His arms were long and heavily sinewed with a strength that wasn't readily apparent beneath the linen shirt and the plain suit of clothes he usually wore. There was a wild, raw power about him that said he was equally at ease atop a roof laying down fresh thatch as he was moving through the streets and back alleys of Whitechapel. Both impressions exuded a dangerous recklessness in a lean, physical grace that she longed to capture on canvas.

The clothes that represented who he was in London were gone now, replaced by nubby woven pants that hugged his hips and molded his legs, stuffed into the tops of high sturdy boots that reached just below each knee. He didn't look like a police inspector now, but rather a man used to hard physical labor and the sun beating down on his bare back. His hair, as dark as a raven's wing, waved about his head and lifted gently in the breeze. She ached to touch it.

But there was a difference about him that had nothing to do with the difference in clothes. She noticed it in the relaxed line of his body, the easy shift of shoulders that had none of the familiar tension of movement, his easy stance atop the roof, feet planted on exposed heavy wood beams.

He moved with catlike grace and agility that accounted for some truth to the stories Moira had told her. She wondered if she painted him, would she know him even then?

"I'm coming up," she suddenly announced, reaching for the next rung and stepping up.

"You'd be safer on the ground," Burke warned as she climbed higher and closer, his head momentarily disappearing from view as she climbed up under the eave of the roof. Then she reached the top rung and looked over the edge.

"Somehow I think Moira would disagree with you."

"Threw you out, did she?" he asked, extending a hand to her.

"I'm afraid she'll be mopping flour out of the floorboards for weeks."

He shrugged. "Mix it with water, and it makes a good glue. The walls may crumble but that floor will stand forever."

"Moira suggested that I take a walk. She said I was dangerous."

"Not suited to farm life?"

She could have sworn there was a smile at the corner of his mouth. "Let's just say that I'm not quite prepared for work in a kitchen."

"No, I don't suppose you are. People like you usually have someone else to do that for them."

Her gaze came back to his. So, they were back to that.

She thought they had reached some sort of truce about his resentment of her. She discovered she was wrong.

She also discovered that his anger hurt far more than she wanted to admit.

"I like Moira very much," she said, struggling past the unexpected feelings his anger roused, trying some other emotional balance with him. "She's very easy to be with, she doesn't require anything from anyone. She just simply lets you know that she's there to care and talk to."

"Aye, she's as good as they come. Robbie's a lucky man. And he knows it."

"Does he?" she asked, because in the short space of time since she'd met everyone, Moira was the only one she actually felt she knew anything about. Robbie, as well as everyone else, including twenty-three children, seemed to take Moira for granted.

He agreed. "She makes him complete, gives him balance, and truth—even if he doesn't want it all the time."

Truth, as opposed to lies. It was a subtle reminder of the lies that she'd told him and gotten caught at. It also accounted for his anger.

He doesn't hold with cheats or liars. It came back unexpectedly, and she thought how ironic it seemed, considering what she now knew about his past.

"Moira told me that the three of you all came from Dublin. You first, then she and Robbie."

"Aye, a long time ago."

He kept on working, seizing the next bundle of thatch, weav-

297

ing it into the previous row with a surprising agility for such large hands. She remembered how those hands felt on her body and quickly looked away.

"Moira and Robbie must have been very young." There was a moment of silence, broken only by the rustling sound of the heavy thatch as it was secured into place.

"Moira was fourteen, Robbie was seventeen."

"How old were you?"

He looked at her then, briefly, with measuring eyes, then seized another bit of thatch and began to work it into the row.

"I was eighteen when I left Dublin and came here."

"And purchased Old Orchard," she prompted.

"I worked here for two years, for the previous owner. He was old, there was no family to pass the farm on to. I bought it from him before he died. Then I sent for Moira and Robbie."

"All this land, two houses, the barn, and the school. That's a great deal for a lad of twenty who grew up on the streets of Dublin."

"The school came later," he deliberately avoided giving a direct answer that had anything to do with how he'd purchased it.

"Robbie and I built the school."

Short, direct answers. It seemed it was all she was going to get out of him.

"You don't like me very much do you?"

He looked at her then, those cobalt eyes filled with bright light and dark shadows—questions that went unasked.

He should have expected the bluntness, that direct way she had of confronting an issue without any reservations. He imagined it caused problems within circles of society where ladies told lies more easily. It was one of the many incongruities about her, that made all his easily made assumptions evaporate into thin air. He didn't like not being certain about her. It kept his emotions off balance.

Defensively, and just as bluntly as she'd asked, he said, "I don't like what you are, or what you represent."

She'd asked because she wanted to know, but deep down inside, after what had happened between them, she really hadn't expected him to say he disliked her.

"At least *you* don't have any difficulty being completely honest." She felt his gaze on her, but she couldn't look up, afraid of what she might see, more afraid of what he would see in her eyes.

"What do you assume I am?" she asked, as she moved a clump of thatching within his reach.

"Be careful there, lass," he warned. "Put your foot in the wrong place and you could well find yourself in the kitchen."

"Answer my question," she demanded, moving about more carefully to what she hoped was a solid perch.

His eyes narrowed. "For one thing, you're wealthy," he stated flatly.

"A circumstance of birth that I neither chose nor asked for."

"It's not the fact of how much money, it's what it represents."

"What does it represent, according to your experienced observations?"

"Privilege for one thing."

"Oh, my yes," she answered derisively. "That is indeed a quality to hate a person for. Go on. There must be more. You've obviously given this a great deal of thought."

Those penetrating blue eyes fixed on her, the blue all but disappearing into thick bands of black. "Power, and the cold-blooded ruthlessness that goes with it."

"Of course, you speak from practical experience about this as well. No doubt in your work as a police inspector," she said with more than a little sarcasm.

He handled the heavy thatching tool as if it were no more than a needle pulling through silk. The muscles stood out on his arms as he plunged it into the heavy thatch, weaving through the thick mass with heavy hemp. Then he plunged it in again as if thrusting a knife. His gaze met hers.

"No, Jess. It comes from knowing firsthand how those with money treat those without, from experiencing the pain of poverty, starvation, and depravity because a high-born lady chose wealth, privilege, and power over the life of an innocent child."

She thought then of one particular part of the story Moira had left untold.

"I'll leave that to others," she had said. "It's not my place. It's not my pain."

Burke's pain and hatred didn't come from the difference of their circumstances in life. It was more. They came from deep wounds because of something that had happened in his life—something that she represented to him.

"The witch," she said in a quiet voice.

"What?" His hard gaze snapped back to hers.

"Moira said it was a tale of thieves, cutthroats, with a wicked witch thrown in for good measure."

"Did she now?" His expression was intense. This was no fairy tale. "Did she also tell you who they were?"

"No, she said that was for you to tell. But she did talk about Dublin, and how she met Robbie, and how the four of you fought to survive."

His gaze sharpened then. "So, she told you about Megan."

Again he plunged the thatching tool hard into the bound thatch, as if he were exorcising demons, or perhaps stabbing at some imaginary target. The cold fury with which he did it made her suddenly go cold inside. She wrapped her arms about herself.

"She talked about four young people trying to survive on the streets."

"Did she tell you that Megan was fifteen when she died, stabbed to death by a man who thought he owned her?"

"No," she answered in a small voice.

"Did she tell you that Megan was forced into prostitution at the age of ten?"

"No."

The fury had a dangerous edge. "Did she tell you how she died?"

"Please don't say any more. Moira didn't tell me anything about that. I shouldn't hear it. It's private. I'm sorry."

"You're wrong, Jess. You do need to hear it. Because it's part of who and what I am. And perhaps then you'll understand what it is that I hate about what you represent—people who think they can have anything so long as they have enough money. They buy elegant carriages, fancy homes, fancy clothes, and human souls.

And it means nothin'—thrown out like so much garbage when they're through with it."

"You're wrong!"

"Am I? Then let me tell you about Megan."

She moved away from him toward the ladder. "No, I don't want to talk to you when you're like this." He grabbed her by the arm and jerked her back.

"You wanted to know. Now by God you'll listen."

"She was eight when I first found her, all skin and bones, and soft gold hair. She was the finest thing I ever saw, my Meggie."

His voice had gone gentle and thick with memories. She wanted to leave. She didn't want to hear this. But she couldn't seem to leave, as if compelled to hear about this secret part of his past that was so inherently a part of who and what he was.

"We survived together, the four of us. Friends, pals, comrades. We vowed to stay together no matter what happened, and dreamed of leaving one day." As if he somehow couldn't bear to sit there and simply say the words, he began working again, his strong hands weaving the thatch, securing it, then reaching for another bundle.

"Robbie was always the daredevil. That's wot got him a broken leg, crushed beneath the wagon wheel of a swell whose pocket he picked. A high price it was to pay, too. There was no chance of gettin' him to a physician. So me, Meggie, and Moira cared for him. We held him at nights when the pain was so bad he would pass out.

"We leeched the infection out when gangrene set in. I carried him on me back so we could move around, on accounta the constables constantly checked the rookeries where we lived. And Meggie and Moira took to pinchin' and shillin' on accounta he couldn't thieve no more to help feed the four of us. His leg healed but it was all bent up crooked like it is now.

"Moira was always the tough one. Tougher than either me or Robbie, tougher than Meggie. She had somethin' inside her that just wouldn't quit, not ever. She used to say it was all the hope she had stored up."

"Me and Robbie didn't have no more hope by then. The streets had killed that in us. There was only survival. It was Meggie who had dreams of a better life—a small cottage with a garden, chickens, some sheep, a warm fire in the winter, and the warm earth in the summer. The only other thing she wanted was a fine blue dress with satin ribbons."

Jess thought then of the cottage and Old Orchard. Was it Meggie's dream he'd tried to fulfill by coming here? He'd obviously loved Megan very much. She had never loved anyone like that, not even with the infatuations of youth. At least he'd had that much. In a sad way she envied him that, and the pain he'd carried all these years because of it.

"I tried to keep her safe," he went on to explain. "But the streets take everything away from you. And in the end they took her away as well, brutally used by a man of wealth and power who bought her, and then threw her away when he'd finished with her."

"I'm sorry," she whispered, unable to find words that would somehow ease his pain and anger.

"What? No coins, Jess, to ease my pain and make things a little easier?"

She winced as if she'd been physically struck. "I'm sorry for your pain and loss," she said in a voice that ached with so much sadness that he looked up.

Her eyes were like forest moss, dark green and glistening with moisture, and there was a disquieting catch in her voice that had suddenly gone whisper quiet.

Without understanding why she said it, she went on, "I wish I could take it all away. I wish I could give you peace and happiness. But you have to find it within yourself."

"Pretty words, Jess. You use them, like you use people, to your own end. A few coins to buy hand-down clothes to use as a disguise, a few more to buy information and perhaps ease someone's plight for a few hours or a few days. You used Maude and Toby to help find your sister."

His words were meant to cut and wound. They succeeded.

She came to her feet, her body rigid with fury. But her voice was achingly calm. "Precisely the same way you have used me to help find your murderer. Perhaps, Mr. Burke, we're not that different from one another." She moved back a step, intent on leaving as quickly and expeditiously as possible.

"Jess! Don't move."

Her head snapped around. "And give you the opportunity to say something more hurtful? I think not!"

"No, you little fool!" He came out of the crouched stance and moved toward her. "So that you don't fall."

But he said it too late. She had instinctively backed away, stepping onto an adjacent section of thatching.

Too late, she heard a snap, her foot sinking down between layers of broken thatch. Light as she was, the weakened area of roof gave way beneath her weight. She plummeted down through the heavy thatching.

He dove for her, grabbing her wrist. "Jess!"

Her first thought was that she'd sooner be grabbed by a snake. Her second thought was to hold on. She screamed.

"I've got ya, lass. Hold on."

"I can't. My hand is slipping." There was a jarring movement as he suddenly relaxed his hold. She screamed as he then took firmer hold.

"Don't squirm or twist about," he warned. "I'll try to pull you back through."

"No!" she cried out, as he began to pull her up. "Don't! My other arm is caught. I can't move at all."

"What's goin' on up there?"

Jess heard Robbie call out from the yard below. Above her, Burke shifted his weight and called out.

"She fell through the roof, and she's caught. I can't lower her or bring her back up."

The blood completely drained from her hand, and her fingers went numb as she dangled below the new opening she'd made in the roof when she fell through.

She was suspended only by Burke's hold on her. After what she'd said to him, she dared not contemplate how easy it would be for him to simply let go and let gravity take its course.

Then, just when she felt as if her arm were about to be torn out of her shoulder socket, the shadows over the opening above shifted, and she saw Robbie's face above her.

"Pitched her into the roof, did ya?" he looked up at Burke. He clucked his tongue.

"Moira feared as much and suggested I come over and see if either one of ye was still alive."

"She fell," Burke informed him tightly. "Had no place bein' up here as it was."

"Now, who do you imagine let her come up in the first place?"

Burke cursed his friend. "Shut up, and take a hold of her. I'll go below and we'll see if you can lower her to me."

His curses and foul temper had absolutely no effect on Robbie, who'd obviously heard it all countless times before. Then he peered down through the hole in the roof.

"Take it easy, lass. I'm goin' to take hold of yer arm, and then Devlin is goin' to catch you from down there. Don't wiggle about now, I'm not as thick in the arms as he is. 'Course I'm not as thick in the head either."

In spite of her predicament and the fact that she was dependent on Devlin Burke to help her, she giggled.

"And if you've a mind to, you can kick him in the gullet on the way down. Would serve him right." Robbie shifted his position as he took hold of her, then held tight about her already bruised arm as Devlin quickly descended the ladder.

"I've got you, girl. If you go, we both go. I wouldn't dare go back to Moira and tell her that I dropped you."

"I'm very glad you're up there," she called out. "I'm afraid he isn't of the same opinion."

She hung suspended for several more seconds, which were measured by the rapid thudding of her pulse through her aching arm. Finally she heard movement below, through the house. She looked back over her aching shoulder and saw Burke take the last steps of the stairs two at a time and then quickly cross the room below her.

She dangled through the rafters of the ceiling in the upstairs bedroom. Low as it was, she was still several feet above the floor and caught by her other arm wedged between two cross timbers of the roof.

There was a scraping of wood against wood, as Burke moved a piece of furniture, then she felt his hand on her knee.

"I'm goin' to hold her up," Burke called up to Robbie. "You lean through and see if you can free her arm." His arms went round her legs and he held her, immediately taking the dragging weight off both arms. Robbie leaned through the opening above, feeling around for her other arm. His hand brushed hers.

"I found her other arm. She's soundly wedged. Boost her up just a wee bit higher, lad." She clamped her eyes tight against the pain as Robbie gently pulled on her other hand. Then she felt movement and her arm was free.

"That's it," Robbie called out below. "Take her down slow. That arm might be broken."

Burke lowered her, letting her slowly slip down through his strong arms. She braced her one hand at his shoulder, then at his bare chest as her body slid down the length of his.

His arms were about her, holding her. She was safe, but there was another danger.

On the roof she'd noticed the fine sheen of moisture that glistened on his skin. His hair was too long, disheveled, and dark as midnight. She'd wanted to brush it back from his forehead and feel the crispness of the dark waves tangling about her fingers. And those eyes — they were deep blue, filled with dark shadows and pinpoints of dangerous light.

Suddenly he pulled her against the length of his body. What had begun as merely intimate became needy and demanding. His fingers bruised her upper arms, one thickly muscled thigh thrust between hers, as his mouth came down over hers. The contact was intimate: thigh against thigh, her breasts pressed against the hard shift of muscles at his bare chest, her hips flattened against his, and the sudden pressure of hard maleness molded into the cleft of her body.

She closed her eyes, stunned by the sensations of memory that poured through her — his naked body entwined with hers, his hands and mouth moving over her with slow invasion, then another more intimate invasion and the startling presence of him

305

deep inside her—just as it had when they made love.

It was an invasion of the senses as much as the body, his tongue slipped past her parted lips, he swallowed her startled gasp, and plunged further still, until he found the soft, warm velvet of her tongue. Her fingers clung to the damp flesh at his arms, then dug into the heavy muscles, her nails leaving pale half-moons in the dark skin.

Then just as suddenly at it began, he jerked her away from him. Her eyes were wide and dark, her breathing heavy as she looked at him with confusion and a naked, dangerous desire.

His face held myriad expressions—an uncertainty that shifted to something very near pain, then quickly disguised by anger. It darkened his eyes to black, thinned those sensual lips to a hard line, and emphasized the wariness that seemed to reflect her own confusion.

"Moira was right," he finally said, dragging air into his lungs as if he'd just run a very great distance. "You're dangerous. You could have killed yourself fallin' through that roof."

He moved away from her then, taking firm hold of one arm and gently lowering her the rest of the way to the floor from the top of the chest of drawers they'd both been standing upon. Then he jumped down beside her with that catlike agility, surprising for someone of his size.

"I'm comin' down," Robbie called down to them, from his perch at the edge of the gaping hole in the roof. Then he disappeared, to find his way back down the ladder.

Burke took hold of her arm, from the safe distance of several inches. He carefully examined the small, fine bones, hardly bigger than a child's.

"Nothing seems to be broken. You'll be a bit bruised. You'd best get back to the main house. Robbie and I will finish patching that new hole you created."

"It'll take the better part of the afternoon," he added with a tone very near disgust, as if the damaged roof were entirely her fault. Robbie had climbed down from the roof and joined them, preventing her from telling Devlin Burke precisely what she thought of him and his idea to come to Devon in the first place.

"Aye," Robbie added as he came through the doorway, stepping over the door that hung from a single hinge. "And we'll need to find something else for you to do round here lass, other than fixin' leaky roofs," he said with a good-natured grin. "It's dangerous enough for a city lad who tries to act the part of the gentleman farmer every few months when he has the time to pay us a visit."

"And irresponsible females who know nothin' more than how to pour tea and gossip," Burke bit off furiously, as he kicked aside some sections of rotted thatching that had given way and fallen through to the floor.

Robbie's eyes widened. He glanced from her to Burke and sensed that it was probably wisest not to pursue the conversation. He coughed behind his hand, and made some comment about the repair of the roof.

Jess hitched up the skirt of the dress Moira had loaned to her. There was a three-inch tear in the skirt, the bodice was smudged with dirt, and one underarm seam had split open. All in all, she'd had a perfectly wretched morning. She glared at both of them.

"I'd say the city lad acts more like the farmer's braying ass," she informed them both.

Then with as much dignity as she could possibly summon under the circumstances, she stalked past both of them, silently hoping the entire roof fell in on that one arrogant head.

Chapter Twenty-one

"Students," Ethan Podewell, instructor at Old Orchard school announced, "This morning Miss Kelly will be joining our class. She's going to be with us for a few weeks. She'll be assisting us at the school."

He was a bright-faced young man full of energy and enthusiasm, with equal doses of patience and humor thrown in, and bore absolutely no resemblance whatsoever to the conventional notion of what an English headmaster should be.

He was slender with sandy blond hair that was forever falling over his forehead in disarray and stood no taller than several of his older students. But along with the humor and patience was a gentle discipline and a precise knowledge of where each of the children had come from, which made him seem head and shoulders above them all.

There was no trick or prank that he wasn't familiar with or hadn't tried before himself. He could read an expression, or lack of one, with uncanny accuracy. The students could hide nothing from him, because he came from precisely the same place they had—the cold, hard streets. And because he had lived as they had—cheating and stealing in order to survive.

It was when Moira explained about Ethan Podewell that Jess gained a deeper understanding of the children of Old Orchard.

Other than Moira's three children, the others, including little Jamie, Mick, and Jillie had all come from the streets of London.

Some were orphans, but in every instance they were the cast-offs of society, left to manage as best they could in a world where they had no hope of survival beyond eight or nine years of age due to starvation, disease, or some other misfortune.

They had once been pickpockets, thieves, and prostitutes, male as well as female. But no more. They'd been rescued from the streets and brought to Old Orchard where they were given a home, an education, and—as Moira had casually mentioned—an apprenticeship at a trade so that they would have a better life than the ones they'd been born to.

There hadn't been time for further explanation that morning over steaming hot porridge, cakes, and fresh herb tea. School began promptly at seven o'clock, which seemed an ungodly time of the morning for studies, until she learned that the children attended school until noon each day, then worked in the fields, tended the animals, and spent several more hours in apprenticeship.

That first day in Ethan's class a small hand raised from the back of the classroom, the face that went with it blocked by the heads of several taller children.

"Yes, Caroline," Ethan called out.

"What does she do?"

"Roof mendin'," another voice responded, sending the entire classroom into gales of laughter.

It was obvious that everyone was well-informed about her previous afternoon at the cottage, by way of rumor that would have rivaled any of polite society for its speed.

"And kissin' Mr. Burke," another added with an obvious smirk in the tone.

Jess felt her face go warm. It seemed nothing went on at Old Orchard farm that everyone wasn't aware of. She was aware of the sullen expression on Jillie's face from the second row.

Then little Caroline grew bolder, stood up and stepped into the aisle beside her desk. "But what does she do besides fallin' through the roof and kissin'?" she insisted, hands planted firmly on thin hips. Ethan glanced over at Jess.

"I warned you about them," he said with a grin. "This isn't for the faint of heart or the weak in spirit."

"Good," she announced in a quiet but firm voice. "Since I am

309

neither." Then she turned to the class. They were far more intimidating than any headmistress she had ever encountered.

"Since you seem to know so much about me, then I think it is only fair that you tell me about yourselves. I'd wager that a good number of you have tumbled from a roof before."

"And been kissed," Caroline insisted, smothering a giggle behind her hand as she sat in her chair.

And so her first several days at Old Orchard were spent with the students at Ethan's school. She learned all about young Paul, who had been badly burned in a doss house fire, that killed his mother and sister, when an oil lamp overturned. He was apprenticed to be an apothecary.

Little Perry's feet were crippled from birth. He moved about on a small wheeled platform much the same as the one she'd seen on the street in Whitechapel, but in this case he was pulled about the farm by Ralph, a huge moth-eaten mastiff who looked as if he could just as easily eat the boy in one bite, but had the heart of a lamb.

The boy had an uncanny affinity for animals. The pigeons that now roosted with the chickens belonged to him. It seemed every animal on the farm at one time or another owed its life and health to Perry.

Caroline had been thrown in the river as an infant because her mother, who was a prostitute, could not provide for her. She'd been rescued and cared for at Old Orchard ever since, but she was small and frail, her growth impaired by the damage to the brain that she'd suffered in that icy river.

Jess learned that it was only by some miracle that Caroline could speak and articulate at all. Yet the child had a marvelous sense of humor and was very mischievous. Her spirit spoke of the resilience of children in the midst of deprivation. She loved to write stories, her imagination somehow escaping the bonds of her shrunken little body.

At first she decided she wanted to be an actress in the theater. Then, at the age of ten, perhaps sensing that she must set her goals a little more realistically, she decided to become a writer. "I don't care if only men become famous writers, I'll be a famous writer, too," she announced stubbornly with an obstinacy that Jess admired.

Some had more practical but no less important goals. Several young girls studied their subjects hard, with the desire to be governesses.

The boys studied harness making, masonry, farming, in addition to their regular studies. Others intended to become lawyers and doctors, including two of the girls.

To Jess's wonder and amazement they had all been taught that education was the only way to tear down the barriers imposed by society.

Jillie was pretty and clever, if more than a little sullen and resentful toward Jess. She refused to talk about her goals, but Jess learned that she had an affinity for helping injured and wounded animals and people alike. She often helped Perry with his "patients," but seemed inclined to focus more on the impossibilities of her life than the possibilities.

She had come to the farm three years earlier, sold into prostitution by her father when she was eight years old. Burke had rescued her from the doss houses with the help of Maude. Together they snatched Jillie away from the Mudger.

Not too surprising, several of the boys were intent on becoming police inspectors, others wanted to be teachers. Several of the girls were very accomplished as seamstresses and milliners, their work rivaling any that Jess had seen bring exorbitant sums in the finest London shops.

Diverse as their endeavors were, they had a common goal—to better their lot, to make something of their lives, to gain an education and have a measure of pride in themselves. They worked hard: five hours each day in school six days a week, then another six hours at their apprenticeship, and somewhere in between another four or five hours at farm chores.

It brought tears to her eyes to listen to their goals, hopes, and dreams, to see their hard work, their struggles against the adversity they'd been born to or handicapped with, and to compare it with many of her friends and acquaintances who took their privileged lives for granted, never knowing the true measure of struggle, hard work, or life itself.

While she discovered all these things about the children, she also discovered they were extremely curious about her.

One day Perry asked, "How old are you?" When she had sufficiently recovered enough to realize it was the same question any of the children would ask each other, she was flattered. Insignificant as it was, it meant that they'd accepted her.

"I'm twenty-four years old."

"That's very old. Ain't you married?" another asked.

One of the older boys answered for her. "Not bloody likely if she's been kissin' Mr. Burke. We know he ain't married."

"That ain't rightly so. In the rookeries and doss houses, it don't mean nothin' fer a man and woman to be kissin' and carryin' on when they ain't married."

"She's different."

"How do you know?"

"Because I do. Listen to the way she talks. And she even speaks French, and knows all the things Ethan knows."

"That don't mean she's any better." This from Jillie who said it with an angry snap, prompting Jess to answer the question as straightforwardly as it had been asked.

"I'm not married."

"Are you an old maid?" This from Caroline, who was surprisingly observant. "Don't nobody want you?"

"Well, I don't think that I'm an old maid," she answered truthfully. "I have received several proposals of marriage."

"From the same man?"

"No, from different men." That brought a uniform raising of eyebrows in the classroom, which brought a disconcerting reaction. She wondered if it was the quantity or even the possibility that surprised them. She decided not to ask that question, afraid of the brutally honest answer she might get.

"Why didn't you marry any of 'em?"

She could feel all of them, especially Jillie, waiting expectantly. She thought her answer through very carefully, sensing that it was important that she make these young people understand her reasons.

"I had a very specific dream that I wanted to accomplish," she began hesitantly, hoping that they, more than any she had ever known, would be able to understand. "They didn't understand my dream. They wanted me to fit into what they believed I should be." The small one-room school had suddenly gone completely quiet. "I wasn't willing to give up my dream."

"Did you try to make 'em understand?" asked Perry, the boy with the crippled feet who wanted desperately to be a doctor for animals.

"Yes, but they wouldn't listen. I was told I shouldn't try to be more. That I should be satisfied with my life the way it was."

"What was your dream?" Hannah asked with wide eyes. Until that moment the only person they'd ever known who'd told them they could be anything they wanted was Devlin Burke. He intimidated some of the children, but they all respected him. Now someone else was telling them they could believe in themselves.

"I wanted to paint pictures. I wanted to be very good, so that everyone would come from faraway places to see them. There were feelings inside me that I wanted to express. There were pictures only I could see, and I wanted others to be able to see them as well."

There were varied reactions from the children, as if they didn't know whether to believe her or not, from all, that is, except Mary Margaret.

She sat in a corner of the schoolhouse at her desk, her pale, scraggly hair hanging in disarrayed tangles about her face, as if she were trying to hide behind each strand, her large eyes like saucers in the thin oval of her face. Her skin was translucent, like pale silk drawn over blue veins, sharp bones, and tiny haunted features.

She stared out the window, without the slightest change of expression, even the blink of an eye, one foot curled under her, the other swinging back and forth several inches off the floor beneath the desk.

The thumb of one hand was stuck in her mouth, the other was twisted in a tendril of matted hair as she constantly rubbed it between thumb and forefinger.

313

"Is she always like that?" Jess had asked Ethan that first day, her heart breaking at the sad, vacant expression on the child's face.

"Aye, most of the time. We include her in everything, but mostly she just sits and stares out the window. She's been here almost a year. Her father, or at least the bastard who called himself that—beg your pardon—used to burn her with hot coals if she cried too much when she was hungry or cold."

"Devlin found her in the gutter tryin' to put cold water on the burns one day. That's when he brought her here. Her back is a mass of scars. But there's deeper ones on her soul. God knows if they'll ever heal."

It was then that Jess learned that Burke was the one who had brought the children to Old Orchard farm. It gave her a new and unexpected insight into him. But she discovered that the more she learned about him, the less she knew.

He had been angry with her for the secrets she had kept from him. He gave no explanation or excuses for the ones he had kept. He was a complex man, not easily defined or understood, neither black nor white but shadings in between. As an artist, she at least understood the inherent value of those subtle shadows and everything that might be discovered in their depths.

"Is she interested in anything?" she found herself asking Ethan.

He shook his head. "If she is, we haven't found it. Most of the ones who are really bad off respond to the animals. Like Perry, Hannah, or even little Jamie. But not our little Mary. She just sits and swings that foot back and forth, suckin' her thumb, and twistin' her hair, hour after hour."

"What about her letters and numbers?"

"I'm not sure," he said. "She picks up on things. Every once in a while she'll look interested in something we're discussin' in the class. But the minute I try to join her in, she pulls back, goin' wherever it is in her head that she feels safe."

Jess nodded sadly. "A world only she can see."

"Aye, and not about to let any of the rest of us in. But we keep tryin'."

Mary Margaret became a personal challenge for Jess.

Perhaps it was the coincidence of her name, the name her sister had used when she disappeared—a name that linked them to their own innocent childhood. Or perhaps it was her resemblance to her sister; she had that same pale gold hair and those beautiful blue eyes. There was an immediate bond even if Mary Margaret chose to ignore her and every effort she made to try and reach her—until the day Jess discovered that Mary loved bright red colors, as she was showing the class the powdered pigments she'd brought with her. It was the briefest reaction, but Jess was determined to find out what lay behind it.

She helped with all the school subjects, and even began teaching some basic lessons in French. But her particular expertise was, of course, art. All children, young or old, loved to draw, sketch, and paint. It was a creative form of expression where there were no restrictions. For one hour every day they were allowed absolute freedom. They produced pictures of flowers, cows, pigs, puppies, and Ethan Podewell, as well as Moira, Robbie, and, of course, Devlin Burke, who it seemed held a rather heroic status with the children.

She taught them how to hold pencils and brushes, how to make bold strokes and subtle shadings. She understood how easily Ethan, who was one of the first "children" taken from the streets, had found himself drawn back here.

"It's my way of paying back something of what I got here," he explained to her one afternoon over a cup of tea, after the children had left for their apprenticeship lessons. "Young Jeremy and Allison will make fine teachers as well. Allison has spoken of coming back here. The last few days have proven we have a need for more than one teacher."

"How does the school pay for itself and for your position as well?" Jess found herself asking.

He laughed. "I don't exactly make a lot of money. But it's enough, and I've been given the use of a small cottage for me own. In addition I have an interest in the profits of Old Orchard."

"Profits?"

"There's not much, mind you. Feedin' and clothin' two dozen children plus adults requires sizable revenues. The farm produces

315

enough food for everyone and a great deal more that goes to market. The apple orchards produce a great deal, along with the wool from the sheep. Then there are the goods the students produce through their apprenticeships.

"There are harnesses—some of the finest work in all England—and dress goods. The girls sell what they don't need. Those that apprentice to a trade earn a small portion in addition to their apprenticeship. They're allowed to keep half for themselves which they're required to save so that they'll have a small sum to get started when they leave Old Orchard. The other half goes to the farm to pay expenses." He said it all matter-of-factly, as if such an enterprising system were the most common thing in the world.

"Mr. Burke is a right fine businessman when it comes to turning a coin. He's the one who's made Old Orchard what it is."

"But I thought Moira and Robbie owned most of Old Orchard."

"Did you now?" Ethan asked with a faint smile. "Well, I suppose that is what Devlin would like everyone to think. He takes credit for very little. But he was the one who bought the farm. And it was his ideas Moira and Robbie set in motion for making Old Orchard a profitable community that everyone had a share in for as long as they contributed."

"What about the school?"

"The expenses for the school come from the profits of the farm. It was the first thing Devlin and Robbie built, even before they made repairs to the big house. Robbie didn't have much of a care for education, but Devlin insisted it was the only way the children had of making their way in the world."

She frowned. "But even without the school, all of this must have cost a substantial amount of money. How did he ever have enough to buy the farm?"

Ethan gave her a long, contemplative look. There was a faint twinkle in his eye. "Well, that's another story. Leave it to say that Mr. Burke wasn't always on the side of the law that he is now. He's done a goodly amount of thievin' himself." Then he quickly changed the subject by informing her that the children were being excused from class for the next several days.

316

"The village fair is next week. It's an annual event at Farway. Everyone has been picking apples for weeks. The crush will begin tomorrow and go on for several days."

"The crush?"

"Aye," he said with a huge grin and a bit of accent that reminded her of Burke. "The best cider in all Devonshire. We sell it every year at the fair. It was a good crop this season. Those old trees keep surprising us.

"Everyone joins in the crush, then we all go to the fair. It lasts for three days. The girls sell their stitchery. The boys sell their harnesses. There is cider, apple pies, tarts, even apple scones."

She laughed. "It's a good thing I like apples."

"Very good," he agreed. "It's the one thing we have in abundance. That and children. You'll have time to yourself then, what with the children busy with the crush."

"What about Mary?" she asked, with a sudden thought. "Could I keep her here and work with her?"

Ethan gave her a sympathetic look. "You may do whatever you like, Jess. But don't go setting your heart on getting any results from her. Moira has tried, and God knows the woman has the patience of a saint when it comes to children. There have been times when I thought she *was* a saint. But even she hasn't been able to reach Mary. She's locked away inside herself, and I doubt that anyone will ever reach her. Perhaps it's enough that she's safe and loved here."

"Perhaps, but I would like to try. I'm not very good with things about the farm." She thought of her experience with roof thatching. It brought back memories of Burke. The past weeks they'd hardly spoken to one another except to discuss the sketches she was still working on for Chief Abberline.

"Do as you like. The school is always open."

Two days later the crush began, and she saw even less of Burke, Moira, and the others. They were busy in the crushing sheds from first light to last.

That first morning, as everyone left the huge refectory table in the main house after breakfast, Mary—whom Jess forbade anyone to call Maggot—also got up and started to trudge off silently

317

after the other children. Jess stopped her with a gentle hand on her shoulder.

"I thought we would go to the school today, just you and I. Ethan said it was all right. Perhaps we can find something new to do together."

Mary looked at her with that vague indifferent expression with which she responded to everything, and then let Jess lead her along down the wagon path that connected the farm to the school. It was a bright, warm November day, rare enough in Devon that time of year, or so Moira had told her. Jess opened the windows and let the warm sunlight pour into the classroom. Then she pulled several of the heavy wood desks out of the way and picked a spot in the middle of the floor where sunlight poured in on the smooth wood flooring.

Routine had made up the boundaries of Mary's life since she had first come to Old Orchard. Perhaps it was the routine and order that had saved her from the chaos of her young tortured life. She seemed to cling to it, holding herself tightly composed, except for that one foot that dangled and swung back and forth as it did now, as she sat at a nearby desk and watched.

For days Jess had tried to persuade Mary to join in during the time the class spent drawing, sketching, or painting. She had noticed a certain amount of interest in the sad blue eyes, but Mary always held back, as if afraid to express her ideas, which Jess was certain lurked somewhere behind the sadness, if only she could draw them out of the little girl.

Now, Jess spread a huge piece of butcher paper across the bare spot on the floor. She smoothed it out on the floor and then set out several bowls of oil paints all in different colors. She glanced up and caught Mary watching her with curiosity. But once she sensed that Jess was watching her, the curiosity was gone, hidden behind her sad eyes.

So, my little friend, Jess thought, with a small thrill of satisfaction. You are curious. Let's see how curious.

She dipped a thick, fat brush in one bowl and made the vague outline of a tree on the canvas.

"I thought I would paint a picture about the apple harvest," she explained, not expecting any response in return. She made the trunk of the tree tall, smooth, and skinny. She caught the slightest movement out of the corner of her eye as Mary shifted at her desk, craning her small neck to watch more closely. Appearing to ignore her, Jess took another brush and began drawing in a black, furry creature sitting beside the tree. "This is Ralph," she said, deliberately painting the mastiff the wrong color.

There was another movement, and she was aware that the foot-swinging had stopped. As she often had in class, Mary got out of her desk and slowly approached her, to stand just a little distance away and watch.

Jess seized another brush, and dipped it into bright purple paint. On hands and knees she crawled over to the far edge of the paper and began painting the tree. Mary followed, like a small, silent shadow.

"And these, of course, are apples." She painted several in, making quick deft strokes, creating huge luscious orbs that greatly resembled plums, instead of apples.

A quick sideways glance caught the frown on Mary's tiny face. She dipped the brush again and started to paint another apple.

Mary slapped the brush out of her hand. It clattered across the floor, dribbling droplets of purple paint as it rolled.

Jess didn't scold her. From what she had heard from Ethan there had been too much scolding early in Mary's life.

"Did I do it wrong?" she asked, still expecting no answer. "I'm not very good about this sort of thing, since I've lived my whole life in the city. But I thought that is what an apple looked like." She pretended not to notice as Mary walked back around to the bowls of paint. Then she held her breath as Mary seized a clean brush.

The child contemplated the painting for several moments, then dipped the brush in the bowl of bright, red paint. Her movements were halting, jerky, as if there were some great conflict within her. Then she came over beside Jess and painted a crudely shaped *red* apple.

Jess watched in silent fascination, not daring to respond, or hardly breathe, sensing in the frozen gestures the child made the great effort these small movements required. When she had finished the apple, Mary returned the brush to the bowl as she had seen Jess do. Then she found another brush, a much skinnier one, and dipped it in the bowl of green paint.

Silently, wordlessly, Mary had watched, and understood the difference in brushes that Jess had explained to the other children. She had deliberately chosen one small and fine bristled enough to make the tiny, deft strokes required to make the stem that attached her apple to the tree. She painted it in, the finer, more precise movements, taking greater concentration. Again, Jess, dared not breathe.

When Mary was finished with her apple, she stood back, and looked up at Jess as if to say, "There, that is what an apple looks like. They're not purple, they're red. Anyone should know that."

Watching the child, seeing her own inner struggle, Jess sensed that more than one small barrier had come down. Mary had reached out to her, if only to take the brushes. She couldn't bear to lose her again behind that safe protective wall.

Keeping her voice carefully modulated, she asked, "Are you certain that they're red? Perry told me they were purple." It was a small lie, but one she was certain Perry would forgive.

The foot that before had only swung back and forth in monotonous rhythm now firmly stomped the floor with impatience. Then Mary returned for more paint. This time she seized the bowl of red paint and brought it back with her. She knelt on hands and knees imitating Jess, and began painting dozens of apples—in all sizes, big ones, small ones—glorious apples, hanging brilliant red from the branches of the tree she and Jess created together.

No words were exchanged. None were needed. There was simply the silent communication of creation. It was as if a floodgate had opened.

When Mary was finished with as many apples as she could cluster on every branch of the tree, she painted Ralph the color he truly was—a great patchwork of gray, brown, with white tufts of thick fur—not the black that Jess had painted.

Midday came and went. Neither of them noticed. They

crouched together over the huge picture, paint smeared over their skirts, hands, and faces. Each time Jess painted in the crude outline of an object, Mary took over, voraciously filling in color and texture. Not all of it was perfect, for her experience was limited. But she accurately painted the objects she was familiar with.

The light began to fade with late afternoon, and Jess wanted to hold it back. Don't let this day end, she thought. Not yet.

They worked on, partners, collaborators, friends bound by the brush, paper, and the colorful images they created. Time swept by them unnoticed, until it fell in deep shadows, the light almost gone.

That was how Burke found them, crawling about the floor of the classroom, as much paint on them as the paper, working over and around each other, as if they couldn't work fast enough, as if the images might escape like real live dogs, cats, pigeons, chickens, and sheep, if they didn't capture them on the canvas.

It was a hodgepodge, a riot of color, almost chaotic as one image crowded another, all shaded under the umbrella canopy of that odd-looking tree—obviously apple, where the red color had been painted over several pieces of purple fruit.

"Moira sent me down to fetch Mary for the evenin' meal," he said quietly, hating to interrupt. For days, ever since the encounter at the small cottage when the rotted thatching had collapsed under her, he'd stayed away from Jess, except for meals at the big house. But Moira had refused to send anyone else to remind them of supper. She looked up then, stunning him with the emotion in her face.

She was smeared from head to foot with paint. Paint was smudged across the wood floor of the schoolhouse. He doubted it would ever be the same. But the expression on her face was so compelling it took his breath away, reminding him of what he'd discovered weeks ago in small moments—she *was* beautiful.

It was there in the soft, breathless smile at her mouth, the bright green eyes that glistened, the vivid color that had nothing to do with paint, across high cheekbones, emphasizing the stunning angles of her face, and made each expression a new discovery.

Her expression now was one of wonderment and sheer joy, banishing the haunted shadows from behind her eyes for the first time in weeks. With that same unabashed joy, she smiled up at him, a heart-stopping smile that he'd glimpsed before but lost somewhere in the anger and wariness that had become so familiar between them.

"We've been painting," she said with a ripple of laughter. "Mary's been showing me how to paint apples."

He watched them with disbelief. He knew precisely what she'd done. On her own, she'd taken a small child, so closed away within herself that she responded to no one, and painted a world of pictures that she could respond to.

"So she has," Burke remarked with a sense of wonderment at what she had accomplished. This wasn't a cool, remote lady of society. No proper lady of his experience would get down on a floor and wallow about in paint, much less allow it on her clothes, to emotionally reach out to a small child whose only world until that day had been darkness and pain. She was someone he didn't know, but found he wanted to know.

Jess grabbed his hand, pulling him down beside them, and he immediately understood that as well, when he saw the surprise in Mary's eyes. All her young life, she'd been dominated by people who stood over her and beat and tortured her into submission.

He and Jess crouched down, allowing Mary to stand taller than they. While Jess explained the picture, Mary actually pointed out the specific images on canvas.

"You've painted Ralph," he remarked with obvious pride and a slight catch in his voice. They discovered that Mary was capable of yet another expression as her face brightened with the satisfaction at his recognizing the dog. She said nothing, but words weren't necessary.

For another hour they remained together, the three of them, until the light had completely faded through the opened windows and darkness forced them to quit. The entire time Burke sat cross-legged on the floor beside them, mud from the orchards clinging to his heavy boots. He sat as quietly and attentively as any student, while Mary painted and dabbled, all the while holding Jess's hand lightly in his.

When the light was gone and Mary seemed to have finished, Jess reluctantly stood up. Her muscles complained about the cramped position she'd sat in for several hours, but she wouldn't have traded it for anything in the world.

She carefully watched Mary's expression as Burke also stood, once more setting a physical distance, for she, too, had been aware of Mary's change of attitude when they all crouched together about the painting. But there was no retreat or blank expression, instead Mary came over and stood beside Jess. She took her hand and tugged at it, pointing at the painting with her other hand, of which the thumb was usually firmly rooted in her small mouth.

Jess wasn't at all certain what she meant, but had discovered that any communication at all was usually effective.

"Yes, we can work on it again tomorrow if you like. We'll mix new colors together. If you like we can fingerpaint, too." Mary's pale brows lifted.

"It's marvelous fun. We can get as messy as we like, and it makes wonderful pictures. Your finger becomes the brush." Mary held up her index finger. Jess knelt in front of her and kissed it.

"Yes, that finger, and all the rest as well. We'll have great fun, and when we're finished we can show the others what beautiful pictures we've made." She wanted desperately to take Mary in her arms and hug her, but sensed that perhaps might yet be unwise, for the child had always avoided physical contact.

"I don't know about you, but painting always makes me very hungry." She looked up at Burke then. The expression on his face was filled with emotions she'd never seen before. There was a poignancy in the slight frown at his handsome mouth. The lines about his eyes, usually so deeply etched, had all but disappeared. And those blue eyes, usually so closed and hard, for a moment, exposed something deep inside—pain, so naked and raw that it made her ache inside to hold him, as she had wanted to hold Mary.

"The two of you go along now," he said, his voice suddenly low. "I'll clean up the paint and soak the brushes."

"But I need to . . ." she started to protest.

"I've watched you often enough, lass." Suddenly his voice had gone softer still, with other emotions that reached out to her, even as he bent down and picked up the brushes and bowls. "I can manage well enough. And I want to spend more time lookin' at Mary's marvelous painting."

Mary had touched something deep inside her with her woeful eyes and sad silence. She had suffered great pain in her brief life, but a door had opened today, and Jess was hopeful that the pain could eventually be assuaged and replaced with love, kindness, and hopefully some understanding.

But in that moment, she had seen the child within Devlin Burke—in many ways the same child. A child of pain and sadness that no one had ever reached. And she wanted to open that door as well.

"Thank you," she said softly, her gaze fastened on his. She felt an inexplicable bond between them.

The entire week of the crushing, Burke came to the schoolhouse at the end of each day to inspect Mary's new paintings, help them clean up, and then escort them up to the main house for supper. One evening he stunned Jess by holding her back and allowing Mary to go on ahead to the washhouse to clean up before going inside.

"You've done marvelous things with her, Jess."

"It's not so much. She's done most of it. I suspect it took great courage for her to reach out at all. She still won't speak. I don't know if she ever will."

Then she said in a quiet, broken voice, "I can't bear to even think of what she's suffered."

"But look at what you've given her," he said softly. "You've given her color, light, and beauty. Look at her paintings."

"I give her the images, and then she paints them. She gives them color and even adds images to them. But they're not really hers. I keep hoping she'll draw her own pictures."

"She will, lass. I'm certain of it. She'll open up. It was just a matter of findin' the key to unlock what she was holding inside."

"You saw it, too?"

"Aye, we all knew it was there. But you provided the key—you and the marvelous pictures you make. Moira believes it's there in everyone. It's just a matter of findin' what it takes to bring it out."

"What is the key for you?"

"There's no key, lass," he said quietly and his expression changed. "Because there's nothin' inside."

"You're wrong. There's a great deal inside of you, I think."

"Perhaps you think that you can provide the key." It was said teasingly, but behind it there was a question that went unasked. Before either of them could acknowledge or confront it, Jillie stepped out onto the flagstone walk.

"Moira says to tell ya that supper is gettin' cold." She turned specifically to Jess then.

"Them that can't get to the table on time go without."

"That rule is for the children, Jillie," Burke reminded her.

"Well, she's not like you and Moira and the rest, who do their fair share of work. All she does is paint pictures."

"Jillie . . ." Burke started to reprimand her. Jess laid a hand on his arm.

"She's quite right. I should be on time, like everyone else. Thank you for reminding me, Jillie."

Burke started after her, but Jillie stopped him and inserted her arm through his.

"I kept a plate warm on the stove for you, Devlin. I know how hard yer been working with the crushin' and all. The fair is only two days away. I got somethin' I wanted to ask you."

"What is it, Jillie?"

"Would you ask me to dance at the fair? I'm older now, and I don't want to dance with Paul or Joey, or the others."

"What about Ethan? You should save a dance for him."

"And one for you, Devlin?" she insisted.

"Aye," he finally agreed. "I'd be honored to dance with you, lass."

The following day Jess decided her relationship with Mary was firmly established enough to try something different. She placed a blank paper on the floor, set out the paints and brushes, but didn't proceed any further.

325

Until then they'd drawn everything imaginable about Old Orchard and the surrounding countryside with Jess providing the outline images and Mary filling in the colors. Today she sat back on her heels, with a perplexed expression on her face. Mary waited expectantly.

Jess shrugged. "I can't think of anything to paint. We've painted everything that I can think of. What else is there?" Silence.

Mary sat beside her, mimicking the same position, hunched forward over the canvas, tiny chin propped on one hand, her straggly hair swinging forward and obscuring her face.

"I just don't know what to paint," Jess said.

Mary tugged at her sleeve and motioned through the opened window at the cart horse in the nearby pasture.

"We already painted horses."

Mary then pointed to the main house off in the distance.

"We've painted Moira's house twice. Perhaps you can think of something." Mary shook her head adamantly and again pointed to the house.

Jess stood. "I can't think of a thing." She busied herself at the chalkboard, writing out several words in French. It wasn't necessary. The fair began the following day. The other children wouldn't return for classes for several more days. But it was something that she pretended to be very busy with so that Mary was forced to confront the blank paper on the floor by herself—something Jess had always discovered to be both intimidating and irresistible.

It was like a new world waiting to be discovered, created, painted, expressed any way that she chose. Mary had opened the door. Now Jess opened it a little further and waited to see if Mary would step through.

The child began tentatively. When she saw that no amount of gesturing or waiting would persuade Jess, she finally picked up a brush and began making a few lines—thick ones, fat ones—outlining as she had seen Jess do dozens of times.

She stopped several times. Occasionally she sat back on her heels and contemplated the blank paper before her. Once she put

326

down the brush and held herself very tightly. Jess held her breath, certain she had pushed Mary too far. Then just as she was about to tell the child that she didn't need to go any further, Mary picked the brush up again and began making more lines with the black paint.

She concentrated very hard. At first her movements were jerky and hesitant, recalling her first efforts days earlier. But then each stroke became more certain, until it seemed they gathered a momentum of their own. Her images were untrained and unskilled, but she had a keen eye and understood basic form. Occasionally Jess stole a glance at the picture as it began to emerge, not wanting to disturb Mary by appearing too interested. But as the afternoon wore on, the images became more distinct—stick figures of people, buildings, streets—all in shades of black.

Jess sat beside Mary. Hours passed. Images emerged clearly—the horrible creatures of a child's nightmares—monsters who took the form of an angry man, a woman, obvious by the outline of a bosom beneath ragged clothes, who screamed open-mouthed.

They were horrible pictures that came from the horror locked away in Mary's soul. Several times, Jess tried to persuade her to draw something else, but each time the child adamantly refused, as if compelled to finish.

A haphazard scene began to emerge, childish in its images of a man and woman and a little girl, yet perhaps all the more compelling because of that simplistic style. And it was all black, as black as the nightmares that must have still haunted Mary and wouldn't let her go. The only color she finally allowed was bright fiery red, as the man held the child and burned her. Crude as the stick figures were, the images were unmistakable.

Finally, Mary simply sat there, the brush dangling from her tiny fingers, her small body trembling from the force of what she had drawn out of her soul. Jess felt as if her heart had been crushed. She struggled to hold back her own tears, damning herself for the pain she had caused. She reached out and gently brushed back a scraggly tendril of hair.

"Mary?" she said softly. Her fingers, as they came away, were damp. The child turned to her then, her eyes wide, deep pools of

327

pain and anger. They spilled over with tears that coursed down both cheeks.

"The fire hurts," Mary said haltingly with a soft trembling sob that seemed to shudder through her frail body.

Those first words stunned Jess. Of everything that she had tried to imagine, the last thing she expected was that Mary would finally speak.

"It won't ever hurt again, my darling. It's gone now. You've put it here on the canvas. It can't harm you ever again." Then, going on pure instinct, Jess gathered little Mary in her arms. She expected resistance, instead the little girl, whom everyone had once called Maggot, snuggled tightly and clung to her.

When Jess looked up, she found Burke standing in the doorway watching them, his eyes bright with tears.

"Don't remember, guv'ner," the hansom driver said with a vague shake of his head.

"Think! The woman has dark hair. She's small and slender and plainly dressed. The man would have been wearing a suit of clothes, plain as well. He's tall, with black hair and blue eyes. You'd not likely forget him. You might even have heard him speak, with a bit of accent."

"I sees plenty of folks like that. They all look the same."

A heavy gold coin was held aloft. It glinted in the lamplight that gleamed dully through the heavy London fog.

"Might remember somethin'," the driver hinted, his eyes gleaming as brightly as the coin.

"Try a bit harder," a harsh voice rasped.

"Seem to remember some folks that might have looked somethin' like that. The woman was real pretty. Not a stunner, all made up with powders and paint like yer usually sees on the streets, but she had a way about her. Real refined. Come ter think on it, she spoke real refined, too."

"Where did they go?"

"Ah, c'mon, guv'ner. How should I recall somethin' like that?"

"Was it an unusual address? Possibly the train station?"

"Nothin' like that."

A fist tightened in the heavy, well-tailored coat the man wore. It would be so easy to snap the fool's neck, or open it with the quick thrust of a knife. But he needed him, and the information he was certain he could provide, if only he would remember. . . .

Another coin was quickly added to the first. They were both held aloft, just beyond the driver's greedy reach.

"As a matter o' fact, I do remember now. There was something unusual 'bout the address. It weren't no address at all. It was the opera house."

"The opera house?"

"Right yer are, guv'ner. Thought it was strange at the time, the way they was dressed. But that's what the man said."

"Thank you. You've been most helpful."

The driver turned away for a moment to adjust the harness on his horse. "Can I give yer a lift, guv'ner?" he asked thinking to add more to the two gold coins he was about to collect.

But when he turned back around the stranger was gone.

"Hey! What's goin' on? Where's me coins?" he shouted into the swirling gray fog that draped the lamp, the hansom, and the horse that pulled it. He thought he heard the distant tread of a man's heavy footsteps on the sidewalk, and started to follow.

Having taken no more than a dozen steps, he stopped. His hansom was no longer in sight. The footsteps had disappeared. All he could see was the dull glow of the lamplight. He started after the man again, then turned back.

He found his hack and quickly climbed atop the hansom. But even as he whistled to the horse and felt the reassuring tug on the harness, an uncontrollable shiver slipped down his back.

There was still a murderer on the streets of Whitechapel.

Chapter Twenty-two

The country fair at Farway was held each time this year, immediately following the apple crush.

It lasted three days, and everyone from miles around brought their apples, baked goods, ciders, and handmade goods to sell or trade. It was a celebration of the end of the harvest that went back to the time of the Celts, and it was filled with traditions from those ancient times, including games, contests, and competitions.

It was a festive affair, the last celebration of the season before winter set in, and the Michaelmas holidays. Moira and all the smaller children had been preparing for weeks, ever since the first of the harvest began. She had put up various fruits in the cellar, and baked countless pies and pastries.

The older girls had worked on their finest stitchery, which would be sold at the fair, while the younger girls were busy in kitchens preparing the finest Devonshire cream, along with butter and cheese, which also would be sold.

The older boys had put the finishing touches to gleaming leather harnesses. The smaller boys, including Mick, prepared the animals that would be sold for market.

Everyone was involved in the apple crushing, the most lucrative of the farm's enterprises. They carried baskets of the gleaming fruit from the orchards to the wagons, which were then driven to the crushing sheds. There, Robbie and Burke operated the huge presses. The three varieties of apples grown at Old Orchard were poured in, in specific proportions according to a traditional blend, the huge wheels set in motion, lowering the presses within huge vats. Eventually, pale golden liquid drained out through a sieve at the bottom into smaller barrels.

As each small barrel was filled, it was capped and sealed. It was sold, as it had been for several centuries. Through the long winter, the barrels of cider that weren't sold were opened and enjoyed.

"It's apple juice," Jess had said with surprise as Robbie held a cup under the sieve spout, caught some of the golden liquid, and then handed her the cup.

"Now it is. But in a few weeks it will be cider. It's a combination of the blend of apples and the standin' time that turns it into cider. Old Orchard farm has a reputation of producing the finest cider around. We've won competitions with our cider. People come to the fair from Exeter just for the cider. We ship barrels of our cider as far away as London and the north country."

"I had no idea this was such an important enterprise."

"Most of our income comes from the orchards. That, and the wool, and what the children produce in their apprentice work."

Again, she was awed by the complexity of the small community at Old Orchard. It was like a large extended family involved in various business enterprises, all of which benefited the children, their education, and futures.

More often than she wished to admit, she found herself looking at Devlin Burke through different eyes. He wasn't the man she had first thought him to be. He was a contradiction to everything she had assumed about him.

He was complex and difficult to know, driven by the secrets in his past to make a better world for these children. He couldn't make it better for all the children of London, but he could save a handful. And he was doing it. It was a side of him that fascinated and intrigued her, like the layers of a painting slowly being stripped away one by one, to reveal an entirely different painting underneath.

He was made up of colors and facets, values, and hues, and shadings in between. The artist in her was drawn to the emerging picture. The woman in her wanted to understand all the layers of emotions that were gradually exposed.

331

She had never seen him like this—relaxed, the edge of anger gone from the lines in his face, the gentleness in his smile, the tenderness with which he treated each child and every young man or woman at Old Orchard. There was a peacefulness about him, and suddenly an exposed vulnerability.

She saw it that afternoon when she looked up to find him standing in the doorway of the schoolhouse watching her with Mary. More than any words the tears she'd seen revealed far more about Devlin Burke.

These children were his renewal, a last, best hope to make something right out of the secret pain and loss of his own life.

And then she discovered another layer to Devlin Burke—laughter.

"C'mon, lass. Move yer arse, big as it is," Burke teased, as Moira shuffled out the door of the main house and waddled over to the large wagon. Jillie and the older ones had taken the younger ones on ahead in two smaller wagons. Robbie, Burke, Jess, Mary Margaret and Mick, all waited for Moira as she slowly lumbered down the flagstone walk.

"You just try movin' fast with this in front of you," she grumbled with a good-natured smile, hands clasped over the protruding bulge of her unborn child nestled safe and warm within her belly.

She was out of breath when she reached the wagon, and it took Burke and Robbie's combined efforts—one pulling, the other pushing—to assist her atop the wagon seat.

"This is the last one!" she announced emphatically. "Four is enough."

"Ah, but it's such fun makin' em', love," Robbie teased, leaning across to kiss her on the mouth as he seized the harness firmly in hand. She turned to make a comment to Jess, and the kiss landed somewhere west of its intended target.

"Fun for them, work for us. Look at me, all swelled up like one of Jeremy's pigs and fit for nothin' more than rollin' about in the yard."

"Fit fer rollin' in the hay any day," Robbie grinned, then

grunted sharply as an elbow—one of her less rounded body parts—connected with his ribs.

"That's wot got me in this condition in the first place." At Jess's look of dismay, she blushed slightly.

"With twenty-three youngins and not all of them so young, it's a little difficult to find some privacy. So Robbie and me went up to the hayloft one day."

"Spent the entire afternoon up there," Robbie grinned foolishly and rolled his eyes.

"I was pickin' straw out of me hair and clothes for days. Not much longer than that and I knew I'd gotten more than straw up in that loft. He's been grinnin' like a fool ever since."

"Ah, c'mon, luv. Didn't hear you complainin' none at the time. Come to think on it, yer weren't sayin' much at all, jus' makin' them woman sounds I like so much."

"Robbie Callahan! I don't see the need to go discussin' such private matters. Not in front of the wee ones and Jess."

Jess looked over and caught the bemused expression on Burke's face as he checked the ropes on the cider barrels one last time. He made a coughing sound behind his hand that was very suspicious, especially with his wide smile.

The fair was held in a park in the middle of town. Wagons, carts, and carriages gathered under the spreading canopy of chestnut and oak trees, turned bright yellow, gold, and orange by the crisp fall nights and pungent conifers.

Barrels of cider formed the legs of tables set up beside wagons and carts. Various foods, pies, pastries, including tarts—everything that could be made from apples—were displayed in tantalizing abundance along with handcrafted wares that all the families from miles around had brought to sell.

There were intricately woven laces, delicate stitchery on skirts, gowns, bodices, hats, and shawls. The rich smell of leather blended with the fragrance of cider, baked goods, and overall the dusky pungence of fresh wood smoke from fires over which warmed hot cider, a side of beef, a leg of lamb or roasting pig.

The competitions began early, with the judging of farm animals. The children had several lambs, goats, calves, and chickens they'd brought along to enter. The animals were kept tethered behind the wagons until each competition began. Then they were paraded about before a panel of judges.

Jess suppressed a giggle at the sight of Devlin Burke, inspector of police, calmly and efficiently, running his hands over a goat. Moira explained that the judges looked for flaws, subtracting points when they found any, from a beginning total of ten points for each animal.

He circled the goat, an ornery animal, firmly held in check by a small girl. Each time he moved, the goat moved, clearly not at all pleased with being inspected. With amazing patience Burke quietly instructed the girl on how to calm the animal and keep it from moving about with a firm downward pull on the rope about its neck.

The girl was obviously very upset by the goat's behavior. At one point she seemed close to tears, and Jess overheard her explain to Burke in a quavering voice, "Freddie's usually well-mannered. Don't know wot's got into him."

Burke smiled gently. "He's probably just a wee bit excited with all these other animals about. Don't worry about it, lass. He's a fine animal."

"But they judge on manners, too. Freddie won't get nothin' if the others think he's mean-spirited." As if Freddie sought to prove precisely that point, he turned his head, stretched his neck, and quicker than it would take to tell about it, he took a nip at Burke's arm.

For a policeman who spent most of his time chasing down robbers and thieves, he was surprisingly attuned to the habits of a temperamental goat. With a quick motion, he jerked Freddie's head down and smacked him right between the eyes.

The little girl and Jess both stared in amazement. Freddie tried once more to take a nip out of Burke and was rewarded in precisely the same manner. He didn't try again, but instead became very cooperative, yet keeping a wary eye on Burke.

"There you are. You see, Freddie has to know who's boss. When he gets a bit devilish like that, you have to remind him.

Not a hard smack, mind you. It's the surprise more than anything."

"Thank you, sir."

"You're welcome, lass."

The judging was soon over. Freddie's owner stood, disconsolate, as if she already knew their decision. Her head jerked up in amazement when she was awarded the purple ribbon for Freddie, who obviously considered it in his best interest to maintain good behavior as he was led forward to have his ribbon pinned on his lead rope.

"Oh, thank you, sir," the little girl beamed happily at Burke as she accepted the ribbon. Once the judging of the prize goat class was over, he looked up, found Jess watching him, and joined her.

"That was a fierce competition," he said with a wink and a widening smile as he folded his long legs beneath him and sat down on the grass beside her. Jess sat with her legs curled under her, leaning on one hand. Mary Margaret was sitting in the curve of her body, drawing.

Ever since that day when she'd painted that revealing picture on paper, there didn't seem to be enough paper or pencils. She was constantly sketching everything about her. Jess suspected there might be a young artist inside the young girl.

She smiled at Burke, amazed at how easily it happened now. "You seem to be at your best when you're charming young ladies," she remarked.

"Or goats," his mouth twisted in a wry grin. "I had to do somethin'. He tried to bite me in the . . ." he hesitated and gave a quick glance at Mary Margaret. "Well, let's just say that it seemed preferable to impress him with the fact that I didn't care much about havin' his teeth marks on me. . . ."

"Arse?" Mary looked up with an innocent expression. Ever since that day, she often did this—speaking up, joining in a conversation when everyone else assumed she was still off somewhere in her own little world. She spent less time each day in that world, and more in the real world. Jess could have sworn she saw a glint of mischief in the little girl's eyes. She had a feeling they'd all been had. Mary understood far more than she liked for any of them to know.

"I think *backside* might be a more appropriate word," Burke suggested.

"Robbie says *arse*," she said with that same innocent expression.

"He probably meant backside." Jess tried very hard not to smile.

"No," Mary said insistently, with the outspokenness only a child can possess. "He said Mr. Burke was a horse's arse because he couldn't see what was right under his nose."

His gaze met hers over the child's head. "Did he now, Mary?"

"Aye, he did." She looked up then. "How could you not see wot's under yer nose? Have you got problems with yer eyes, like Mr. Peabody?"

Mr. Peabody was the town vicar, who was pathetically myopic. He wore thick glasses that were very heavy and continually slipping down his wretchedly thin nose. He was constantly pushing them back up. He always looked down the length of his nose at everyone, his eyes slightly crossed as if a bug had perched on the end of his nose and he was staring at it.

The smaller children in the parish of Farway mimicked him when he wasn't looking, throwing their heads back, shoving imaginary spectacles back up their noses, and looking cross-eyed at each other.

"No, I don't, Mary," Burke said with infinite patience.

"Then what's under yer nose that yer can't see?"

He looked at Jess then with a thoughtful expression, as if trying to decide how he should answer, or perhaps searching for the answer. But before he could say anything Jillie came running across the green.

"Dance with me, Devlin," she said breathlessly as she seized his hand.

"Perhaps later, Jillie," he said gently.

"You promised, and I've learned real well. Moira showed me how. The musicians have already played three tunes. Please, Devlin. It's the last day of the fair, and you promised." She tugged insistently, and her lower lip protruded in a soft pout.

She was a pretty girl and would undoubtedly break several local hearts. But at the moment her own heart was very obviously set on Devlin Burke.

The musicians she spoke of were more like medieval minstrels, the sounds of a mandolin, a tambourine, and a lute, sparkling in the cool afternoon air.

"I'm not very good at that sort of thing, Jillie," he explained with a pained expression. "It's all I can do to keep from trippin' over me own feet, let alone yers."

It had become a contest of wills that Jillie was determined to win. She gave Jess a sly glance, as if to say, "He will dance with me, just you wait and see."

"Please, Devlin. Robbie says there was no one finer on his feet than you, when you was lads in Dublin."

He winced. "Somehow I think Robbie had somethin' else in mind when he told you that."

"Go ahead," Moira called out as she joined them. She slowly sat down beside Jess, taking Mary Margaret onto what remained of her lap and snuggling her close, as she did constantly with whatever child happened to be within reach. It was one of those special qualities about her—her ability to love any child.

Knowing that she'd won, Jillie smiled prettily. "Come along. They're just beginning a jig." But Jess saw the brief, cold glint of victory that sparkled in the girl's eyes. Then it was gone, hidden behind a coy smile.

"One dance," Burke said firmly.

"Two, and if you complain it will be three." Jillie's laughter mixed with the sounds of the music, an old ballad that hadn't changed in several hundred years. Burke reluctantly allowed himself to be pulled across the green.

"It was better to get it done with than to have her moping about for the next two days," Moira explained as she stroked Mary's hair. "It's harmless enough, I suppose. She's young, full of emotions and uncertain feelings—not a little girl anymore but not yet a woman." She stroked a hand over her distended belly and laughed. "If she only knew what lustin' after a man can get you."

"Somehow I think she knows," Jess said with a smile.

"Ah, that she does, or at least thinks she does. But she's safe enough with Burke. He'd not let any harm come to her. Brought her to us when she was not much older than Mary. Pitiful little thing she was—called him Da."

"Jamie calls him that. I thought . . ." her voice trailed off.

"That perhaps Jamie was his own?" Moira shook her head. "He's done a lot of things, most of them I probably don't know about, nor would I want to. To be sure, there's been a fair share of women in his life. But none that he's cared enough to have a child with. And certainly none that he's left breedin'."

"Some men are that way," she went on. "But not Devlin Burke. He's not Jamie's father. But he's the only one the lad has ever known. It comes easily enough to a wee child like that, and Burke doesn't mind. At one time or another I suppose all of them have called him that, even me own children."

"What about Megan? He loved her very much, didn't he?"

"Told you about her, did he?"

"Just that she meant a great deal to him."

"Aye, that she did, the way it always is the first time. We were all young, alone, and livin' on the streets." Moira looked out across the green, watching the circle of couples who danced.

"There's some that is survivors, and then there's others who can't no matter what you do for them. Burke is a survivor. I guess me and Robbie are, too."

"But she wasn't?"

"Megan was fragile, like a small flower. Delicate and pretty, the kind of flower that comes first in the spring, and quickly fades away." She looked at Jess then. "Robbie told me that Dev couldn't see what was right under his nose. You've lain with him, haven't you?"

Jess was so taken aback by the bluntness of Moira's question that she could only stare at her.

"There's no need to answer. I can see it in his eyes. The last time I saw it, it was with her."

"You don't understand . . ." Jess started to explain, all the old rules of propriety that she'd been raised with rising to the surface. "It was an accident." Her skin went hot with embarrassment. She looked away. Thankfully, Mary seemed oblivious to their conver-

338

sation, concentrating on the picture she was drawing.

"It should never have happened. He thought that I was . . . He didn't realize that I . . ." she stopped.

Why was she trying to explain any of this?

Moira was wrong, Burke didn't feel anything for her. It was only in the past few days that he'd even smiled at her, and that was because of what had happened with Mary.

"You're mistaken about what you think you've seen," she said in a quiet voice.

"Is that right?" There was challenge in Moira's voice. "I know what it is to want a man, Jess. I know the feelins that start low inside and burn till you think there's no help for it. It's a wantin' so bad that it's like hunger, except it never goes away.

"You might be a proper-bred lady," she continued, smiling softly at Jess's startled look. "Yeah, he told me all about you bein' that famous artist, and a wealthy society lady at that. It's wot feeds the anger inside him. Now the anger is all tied up with the wantin', and he doesn't know what to do about it."

"What does that have to do with anything?"

"So he hasn't told you about that yet. Well, I suppose I should let him be the one to tell it. Robbie would tell me to keep me mouth shut." Moira gave her a long look. Then she slowly smiled. "But I'm Irish to me very bones, and there's just two problems with that." The smile deepened. "The Irish love to gossip. The second is that we're very romantic. So, I don't suppose there's much hope of me not tellin' this story.

"You see, his mother," she looked out at the couples dancing, her gaze resting fondly on Devlin Burke, "she was a highborn lady to the manor born and wealthy, too."

Over the next hour, Moira explained about Burke's mother, the daughter of a wealthy English gentleman, who owned a family estate in Ireland. Young and impetuous, she fell with her father's Irish groomsman.

"According to the story Burke told me and Robbie, she was given a choice—give up the child and never speak of the matter again, or give up her family and all that went with it."

Jess was stunned. She felt cold and hollow inside. "She gave up her child."

"Aye, sold him to the streets. He was raised by an old crone of a woman who raised children to support her with thieving and shilling."

"That's what you meant when you said the story included a wicked witch."

"Aye, and that she was. Beat him twice a day just to remind him that she could, until the day he took the leather strap away from her and threatened to kill her if she ever laid a hand on him or any other child again. He left after that, supportin' himself on the streets at the tender age of nine."

"Did he ever see his mother?"

"Only once. He saved up his money and went back to the family estate. The master of the house had him taken to the stables and horsewhipped for daring to come onto the property without permission. You see, the young lady had married, and her husband wasn't exactly pleased to find a young whelp on his doorstep askin' ter see his mother—the lady of the house.

"Said he looked up and saw her watchin' from a window on the second floor. She just watched and never did nothin' to stop the whippin'. Somehow he made it back to Dublin, but he almost died from the fever that set in." Moira's expression was filled with pain and sorrow. "To this day, I believe the only thing that kept him alive was his hatred for her. He swore that he would make her pay for what she'd done to him."

Hatred.

It explained so much about him. The pain, the haunted shadows behind his eyes, and finally, the rage at discovering her own secret. It must have seemed as if she were no different from his mother.

"And yet, he has such love and compassion for the children."

Moira agreed. "It's focused on the children. It's safe to love them. They love simply and completely, because they need it so desperately. He's given them what was lacking in his own life, and in theirs."

Mary reached for a clean piece of paper. She smiled shyly up at Jess, crawling back into her lap. Jess gathered her close, snuggling the small, thin body against her own, and feeling a stirring of tenderness. It had become an automatic gesture over the past several days.

"And he thinks that I'm the same as she was."

Moira had seen the way she tucked Mary against her. She smiled softly. "Aye, it's what he thinks. It's up to you to make him believe the truth, if it's important to you." Then suddenly her eyes widened.

She grabbed Jess's hand as if it were the most natural thing to do, and flattened it under hers, over the hardened swell of her belly.

"Do you feel it?"

Jess's expression was even more surprised. Beneath her flattened hand she felt the shift of movement beneath taut skin and the padding of oversized petticoats and dress. It was like movement through water, that slow swell of hardness that seemed to reshape Moira's stomach.

"It's the babe," Moira beamed. "That's probably an elbow. Or it might be a fist."

"Does it do that all the time?"

"Sometimes. Other times, it's quiet, like it's restin', saving up its strength for the birthin'. Other times it's like it's turnin' somersaults inside me." Moira clasped Jess's hand, and made small circular motions on the hard, distended knot. Soon it eased, as if moving in another direction. Moira smiled.

"Sometimes, it's like holdin' hands with it, the babe still inside me. We've gotten to know each other real well by now."

Jess stared in wonder at the movement of Moira's stomach beneath the pale blue dress. "What does it feel like inside?"

Moira's expression softened. "It's like bein' able to touch yer own soul, feel it movin' in you, givin' it life. There's no other feelin' like it in the world." Then her smile deepened into a grin.

"Except of course, for feelin' yer man movin' inside you. I wouldn't know about that lately." She shrugged. "When my time is this near, Robbie gets scared he might hurt the baby. And this belly of mine does make lovin' a bit difficult."

The music had ended. Jess looked up as Burke crossed the

341

green toward them. Jillie clung to his arm. He wasn't the man she had first come to know in Whitechapel. That was Inspector Burke. This man walking toward her was someone different.

He gently unwound Jillie's arm from his and turned to Jess and Mary. He bent low at the waist, like a cavalier, or some medieval nobleman.

"Mistress Mary, would you do me the honor of this next dance?"

"But she's just a child," Jillie protested.

"There's a first time for each lady to dance," Moira diplomatically intervened. "You've had your turn, Miss Jillie."

Mary looked hesitantly at Jess, then shook her head, burying it in the curve of Jess's arm. Burke suddenly clasped his hand against his chest as if he'd been mortally wounded.

"You must dance with me," he cried out with exaggerated pain. "If you don't, I'll die of a broken heart, Mistress Mary." He staggered about, as if he were about to collapse, hand over his heart, his head thrown back, his eyes closed. "Please, save a dying man."

Mary giggled, peeking out at him from under Jess's arm.

"You should save him," Jess agreed. "Think how badly you would feel if he died of a broken heart."

"Can't die from a broken heart," Mary announced, almost believing it was true. Burke gasped and went down to his knees.

"I can't breathe. It's breaking in two. I can feel it. Please, have mercy, Mary." He collapsed at her feet, like a lovesick swain.

Mary's giggles went to peals of laughter that were a joy to hear after so much silence. Finally, she nodded her head, and crawled off Jess's lap. Burke scooped her up in his arms and whirled away, her stockinged legs and small feet dangling high off the ground as they joined the circle of dancers.

"He seems so different," Jess murmured, watching them. "Is he always like this?"

"Like a child?" Moira suggested, and Jess nodded.

Moira agreed. "Aye, when he's with them, but he can also be very strong and assertive with them, thank the Lord. They need a strong hand sometimes. But at times like this, it's as if he's tryin' to give them back their childhood that was stolen from

342

them, like a priceless gift."

"Or perhaps trying to recapture something of his own childhood?" Jess suggested.

Moira shook her head. "He was always old, that one. It was as if there was an old man inside him from the beginning. And me and Robbie have known him since we were all runnin' around with wet noses and skinned knees.

"No," she shook her head again firmly. "Devlin was always older and wiser in ways that none of us understood, as if he come from the womb an old man who understood even before he first drew air that he had to make his way alone in the world. Worldly wise, he is, with not a breath of innocence or wonder about him. He's always been that way. And as long as I've known him, I've never seen him shed a tear, not even when Megan died. And she was full along with child." At Jess's startled look, she nodded.

"Neglected to tell you about that, did he?" She shifted her position, arching her back against the fatigue of carrying the unborn child.

"I know what yer thinkin' but it weren't his child she carried. It was a rich, highborn man wot got her with child and then left her when he was finished pleasin' himself on her.

"Megan was devastated, 'cause she was afraid of what Devlin would think of her. She was only tryin' to better herself, even though Devlin tried to tell her countless times not to do it. In the end the man left her, with his child in her belly. When she went after him, askin' only that he provide for the child, he denied that it was his and beat her badly. Devlin found her. She and the babe died in his arms. Then he went after the babe's father."

Jess turned her startled gaze across the green, and stared at the tall dark-haired man who had haunted her dreams and her sketches since she'd first set eyes on him. He was lean with the grace and precision of a stalking cat. He whirled about, with Mary in his arms, executing the intricate steps of the ancient Celtic dance, his head thrown back in laughter.

From that distance she couldn't see his eyes, but she knew the look of them—intense blue that took the breath away, haunted by deep, darkening shadows of the past that he could never escape.

343

She knew all the hard planes and lines of his face, the sensual fullness of his mouth—a mouth capable of smiles, as she'd learned in the past week. Not an easy face. She had sketched it countless times as they worked together, seeing him through an artist's eyes and trying to understand him.

There were layers to him, as there were to any painting that conveyed emotion. But as she'd learned today, far more layers than she'd ever guessed. The more she discovered, the more there was yet to be discovered. And without asking the question she already knew the answer.

"Aye," Moira said, sensing that she knew. "He went after him. There are those that called it murder, and others wot called it justice. If Meggie had been a lady born, he would have been a hero. But she was born to the gutters, and that made her a whore, and him a murderin' thief. He was fifteen years old, with more years on his soul than any three men, and he ran until Dublin and Megan were far behind him."

"And came to a place that was Farway," Jess repeated what he had told her only days earlier.

"Now you know the whole of it. He's told you more than he's ever told another livin' soul except me and Robbie. He came here and apprenticed to the old man who owned Old Orchard. Then he purchased the farm, with money he took from that highborn gentleman, brought me and Robbie here with the two oldest boys also from the streets of Dublin, and started the home for the children, and the school. Said it was a way of givin' back what the streets had taken away from kids like us."

There were tears in Jess's eyes as she stared out across the green. That tall man with the young girl in his arms slowly strode toward them. She blinked her tears back. She knew a great deal more about him now, but would she ever know him?

He grinned as he came toward them. "I'd ask Moira to dance, but I fear for my feet as well as me back," he grinned wickedly as he set Mary down.

Moira gave him a sharp look. "When I get me girlish figure back, I'll show you what you have to fear," she threatened good-naturedly. "As it is, it would take me too long to get to me feet, which I haven't seen in weeks." Then she suggested, "You haven't danced with Jess yet."

"I'll dance with you," Jillie spoke up as she came back to stand beside him. She'd disappeared right after he swept Mary away. Now she looped her arm through his possessively.

"You have too much energy, lass," he smiled down at her. "Tommy Noonan was askin' about you. Said you promised him a dance."

"Tommy Noonan is a boy, and he's got bad manners. He doesn't know how to treat a girl."

"Perhaps you should explain that to him," Moira suggested as she looked past Jillie to the freckle-faced young man who quickly pushed through the crowd toward them. Jillie groaned.

"Moira! Do something!"

"I will," she assured the stricken girl, and waved her arm aloft like a signaling beacon.

"Tommy! Jillie's been waitin' for you to claim yer dance."

Jillie's expression wavered between horror and panic.

"What am I to do now?"

"I suggest that you dance with him."

As she was led helplessly away by the smitten Tommy, Burke bowed low as he had with Mary, and extended his hand toward Jess.

"M'lady," he said with an enigmatic expression. Mary clapped her hands together with delight.

"Dance with him, Jessie. It's great fun."

"Yes, Jessie," he said softly, turning his head slightly so that he looked at her from under the fall of dark wavy hair that spilled across his forehead.

M'lady. It was fraught with subtle, hidden meanings. Before when he'd called her a lady, the word had been laced with anger and a bitter irony.

"Dance with me," he repeated.

She slowly placed her hand in his.

Chapter Twenty-three

He pulled her with him into the circle of dancers. They were given masks, the traditional masks of Celtic lore—the falcon, the fox, owl, squirrel, and countless other woodland creatures.

They were made from feathers, pieces of bark, stalks of grain, seeds for eyes, anything that came from the forest, and exquisitely crafted so that they looked like the animals they represented.

Her mask was the fox, made of gray-and-white feathers created to look like animal fur. His was the falcon—the hunter—also made of feathers. The masks concealed features and added an air of mystery and magic to the dance that had once been part of the ancient rituals of the Celts.

Slowly, they joined in the steps and movements that celebrated the end of the harvest and the changing seasons.

Her fingers slipped through his, then her palm brushed against his palm. She felt the warmth of his fingertips against her wrist, sliding along the bones until they clasped her with gentle strength, then slipped around, enclosing her hand in his larger one. She followed the steps of the other dancers, in patterns of steps, half steps, and turns. And at each turn the fox encountered the falcon.

"Your hand is trembling," he said as his fingers clasped hers, the words softly muffled behind the mask. Then they moved apart once more, and she was grateful that she didn't have to answer.

Strength. It was there in the power of those long fingers lacing with hers, clasping, holding her, like the hunter, then slipping away, freeing her, only to return again with the gestures and movements of the dance.

Safety. It wrapped about her with only the lightest pressure of his fingers on her arm, her shoulder, then pulling away almost before she was aware of it, only to return again as his hands clasped her shoulders and gently turned her first to the right then to the left.

Then facing each other once more, he slipped his left arm about her waist, and they slowly moved in a circle.

Power. It was alive, like a raw energy that moved between them with each gentle touch, the graze of his hand, the brush of his shoulder against hers, so that she could no longer look at him as they moved about each other, afraid he would see the emotions that she sensed were naked in her eyes.

Danger. She felt it in his touch—an awakening of sensual danger that slipped beneath her senses, reminding her of a night many nights ago, amidst the horror and pain of death on the streets of Whitechapel when he'd made love to her.

That night, she sensed it was far more dangerous to let go of him—dangerous to her soul. She discovered it all over again now as they moved together, their bodies lightly brushing, then moving apart, joined only by their hands. It was a powerful sensual awareness.

And there was another danger that came from what Moira had revealed about him. *Some called it murder.*

He'd killed a man. Did it make him any different from the killer that stalked Whitechapel and killed those poor women, and had sworn to kill her?

But he was different.

He was the man who'd helped Jamie that first morning after they arrived, taking such care and showing such tenderness.

He was the man who patiently instructed the older children how to handle the animals at Old Orchard, the same man who read to Moira's children at night, and the same man who'd brought Moira and Robbie out of Ireland to a new life, and made a home and school for other cast-off children the world no longer wanted.

And he was the same man Moira had said never shed a tear, not even when Megan and her unborn child died in his arms. Yet she had seen tears in his eyes that day he arrived at the school unexpectedly and heard Mary Margaret utter the first words anyone had heard her speak.

As if he had read her thoughts that day he'd said, "It's a special gift you've given Mary." He had turned to her then and unexpectedly took her hand between his. He turned it over, tracing the lines in the palm of her hand, extending the touch down the length of each finger.

"You gave it to her with your pictures. Nobody else could do that." The look in his eyes had changed, deepening to almost black.

"You gave yourself to her, and that's a wondrous, rare thing." He looked at her then, and said softly. "You're trembling."

Suddenly, she felt like the fox, trapped by the falcon, without the safety of the mask to hide behind that concealed the emotions that churned through her.

Falcons were dangerous. They were predators, graceful, elegant, winged hunters who killed swiftly and without mercy. She suddenly broke free of the chain of dancers and like the fox, sought refuge in the shelter of chestnut and birch trees that lined the green, their leaves drifting like snowflakes on the brisk afternoon breeze.

The day was wrapped in a hazy glow of sunshine, lengthening shadows, the pungent fragrance of woodsmoke, changing seasons, and a sensual awareness of the man who walked beside her, like none other she'd ever experienced—not even in the dreams, illusions, and visions she created on canvas.

The masks were removed, returning them to the familiarity of who they were. They climbed a distant knoll that rose above the village in silence. The ancient music of the lute drifted after them. She stopped and looked back. The scene that spread below them seemed almost magical.

The thatched cottages, plaster, and wood-beam buildings, the wagons and carts on the green, might have been out of a scene of three hundred years ago, so unchanged were they that it seemed impossible that they were part of a modern world of trains, steamships, and telephones.

Sheep and goats were tethered at the edge of the green. Men, women, and children strolled about, sampling the foods that had been prepared. An archery contest had just begun. In another part of the green children were bobbing for apples, floating in an oak barrel, celebrating the last day of the festival.

Everywhere was the gaiety of laughter, the excited squeals of children, the piney wood smoke from the cookfires, and the soft glow of late-afternoon light as the night fast ran down the day.

It was as if she had stepped into another world, far removed from the pain and horror of Whitechapel, as if she had only imagined it, like one of her paintings, as if there were no other place except this one.

At the top of the knoll, she discovered it wasn't a knoll at all but a small plateau, surrounded by forest.

"Come along, lass," he grabbed her hand before she could protest. "I'll show you a special place."

The thought sprang unbidden that this was already a special place, but before she could say it, he was pulling her after him through the thickly wooded copse.

For moments the sun and blue sky was obliterated, as they plunged into the deepening darkness of the forest that lived beneath that evergreen canopy. Then it seemed almost as if the forest fell away, or as if it were drawn back by some unseen hand, and they emerged into the soft gray afternoon at the center.

The stones were taller than any man, seven of them, some upright, others lying on their sides, forming a peculiar cluster, as if a child had very carefully laid them in precise order—a very large child.

"What is this place?"

"According to local legend, it's a place of worship, dating back to the time of the ancient Celts. The stones are sarsen sandstone, smoothed to a perfect roundness and unlike any other found in this region. They're called the Rune stones."

"But how did they get here?"

"That is the mystery. No one seems to know, except that they came from outside the region. There's no others like them about for hundreds of miles. But that is another mystery as well. It's guessed that they weigh several tons each, not easily moved about with a horse and cart."

"Or even several horses and carts," she mused as she walked around the stones, lightly running her hands across the smooth surface.

"Listen," she said, as they moved into the center of the ring of stones. "You can hear the wind."

"It's the voices yer hear, lass."

"Voices?"

"Aye, the voices in the stones—the whispers of the young lovers who were to meet here and be wed."

"According to ancient legend," she speculated with a wry grin.

He raised his hands in supplication. "I don't make the legends, I just tell them."

"What happened to them?"

As he told the story it seemed that his accent, often unnoticed except when he became angry, suddenly thickened and deepened, wrapping softly about each word.

"Ah, well, that's the tragedy of it," he said. "They pledged their love to each other and intended to wed. They planned to meet at the stones to seal their vows with one another. But it was not meant to be." His voice deepened with an appropriate tone of sadness.

"Their families kept them apart?" she guessed, having read her share of Shakespeare and the classics.

"No. The young lad fell into a bog and died."

"He fell into a bog? What, no balcony from which to declare his undying love? Or at least a crypt where they made their impassioned vows to be together always, even in death? That doesn't seem very romantic."

"In these parts a soggy bog was about as good as they could do for the legend."

She shook her head, smothering back a giggle.

"T'was a very soggy bog," he reminded her with mock seriousness. "Claimed all manner of animals, wagons, carts, that sort of thing."

"A very dangerous bog, I think."

He nodded, his expression grim as he continued telling the story. "When the girl discovered what had happened, she came alone to the stones. And the story is that she gave her soul to the night wind that stays close to the earth so that she could remain near the lad for all eternity. And the sound yer hearin' is her pitiful, mournful cryin' trying to find . . ."

"That soggy bog?" she guessed.

"Aye, 'cause the wind can't see nor hear. So the poor thing wanders about, cryin' because she can't find her lover."

"That is a very interesting story. And, of course, you believe every word of it."

He laid a hand over his heart with an expression of incredulity. "Of course. It's a grand story. No Irishman could have told it better except perhaps with a pint of ale."

"And of course the story improves with more ale."

He grinned at her. "Well, it is an aging process of sorts." Then he gave her a long look with a somewhat rueful smile. "The tellin' doesn't necessarily get better, but it does get longer." Then his expression changed again.

He came to stand before her, so close that all she had to do was reach up and touch him. Instead, she wrapped her arms about her against the cold, or perhaps the sudden, uncertain emotions that filled her in this ancient place, or because of a sad, Celtic tale.

"Can you hear it?" his voice was like the whisper of the wind, weaving through the sounds that came from the rocks so that it seemed as if the lovers voices did speak to her.

His fingers lightly brushed her cheek, gentle as a breath of wind.

"Can you feel it, Jessie?"

He'd called her that before. Even so, the sound of it was new, stunning in its intensity, filled with memories of that other time when her name had been a sigh from his lips. He cradled her face in his cupped hands.

351

His touch was feather-soft, so that it seemed he wasn't touching her at all, his fingers whispering across her skin. Then it seemed that his fingers trembled as they grazed her cheekbones. His mouth lowered over hers, and she felt the trembling of his lips.

The kiss was tentative, a faint brush of warm against warm, like those whispered voices his lips whispered against hers—the words, the rush of breath unintelligible and timeless, in this ancient place.

Uncertainty, fear, an unspoken warning. They echoed through her tangled thoughts and then slipped away to disappear among those gray monolithic stones. Then his mouth hovered over hers, a breath away, the silent question asked in the waiting. Her eyes closed and she lifted her mouth to his, drawn by the heat. Her lips parted against his and she breathed him in, even as she curved her mouth against his, drawn by some emotion of the soul that lay waiting to be discovered.

"Jessie." He breathed her name and then deepened the kiss, his mouth moving in tender strokes against hers as his hands slowly closed over her arms, pulling her closer.

Wet heat. She felt the gently probing velvet of his tongue against her lips, and an answering heat spread low inside her. Then she felt the brush of his fingers against her bodice, and wordless sounds escaped her lips.

One arm encircled her waist, while his other hand opened, those long, warm fingers fanning across the swell of her breast, and Jess felt the world spin away, even as the wind whirled around them.

Lore or legend, reality or unreality. Whatever it was it built around them in that ancient place, surrounding them with ancient whispers carried on the wind. It whirled and built around them, even as his hands moved over her; cupping her breast through the fabric of her bodice, his thumb grazing over the nipple that grew taut, the other moving low at her back, closing over the curve of her hip and pulling her against the hardness of him with intimate hunger.

She clung to him, her fingers cutting into the hard flesh at his shoulders, the breath shuddering out of her in tiny sobs and end-

352

less sounds. They were small sounds; a gasp as he caught her mouth with his, a whimper as he broke away and then changed the angle of the kiss, a fragile, needy sound as a sigh trembled from her swollen lips, and then a soft cry deep in her throat.

"Devlin?"

"Are you there?" a feminine voice called out.

The kiss ended abruptly.

"Damn," he swore under his breath, and then whispered against her cheek. "It's Jillian."

She pulled away from him. Her cheeks were flushed with vivid color, her mouth softly swollen. Her eyes were a bright shade of green, the expression behind them a little desperate as she looked about for some route of escape.

Her hand instinctively went to her hair that had come partially undone. He smiled a little at the transformation. One moment she had been wild, all restless heat in his hands, her mouth hungry beneath his, as wanton as any woman he'd ever kissed. Now her fingers shook as she fussed with her hair.

His fingers wrapped about hers, warm, strong, reassuring. "I'll take Jillie back down to the village. Take a few minutes and then follow."

Her eyes were filled with relief and an expression of gratitude only a lady would feel at being caught in such a compromising situation.

"Do I look that bad?" she asked with a small, hesitant laugh.

His gaze met hers, with an unexpected expression she'd seen that day at the school with Mary. He reached out and touched her cheek.

"You're beautiful, Jessie." Then he turned and quickly retraced their steps out of the circle of stones, in the direction they'd heard Jillie's voice.

When her skin had cooled and she'd restored some order to her hair, Jess followed them back down the hill. She let them return to the green, Jillie clinging to his arm, then she slipped through the circle of wagons at the edge of the green and rejoined the revelers.

Since it was the last day of the fair, almost all the pies, scones, cider, and baskets of apples had been sold, along with delicate laces, harnesses, fine woolen coats, skirts, and other garments.

Several of the children from Old Orchard had received purple ribbons for their fine animals. The last of the games were underway while cookfires smoked with whole pigs, racks of lamb, and kettles of fine stewed briskets and potatoes.

Mary found her and pulled her along by the hand to the center of the green where a game of blindman's bluff was about to get underway. Jess was chosen to be the "blind man."

A scarf was securely tied about her head, making it impossible for her to see. Then she was spun about by the shoulders, until it was almost impossible to stand.

It was a game for the smaller children, ten and under. Out of the thirty-odd children who giggled, teased, and ran about her, she was supposed to find the red-haired, freckle-faced lad.

She made several attempts, guided by the voices who called out to her, coming close several times, and she made sweeping gestures with her arms, first in one direction and then another. Several times she whirled completely about, sensing someone standing directly behind her.

Shrill laughter and wild giggles filled the air. "You'll never find me," the lad called out from her right. She quickly spun about, her hand closing over nothing but air. She followed the sound of movement and quickly grabbed again. This time her hand brushed against the soft, spun cotton of a workshirt. Then she felt a tap on her shoulder and whirled in the opposite direction.

"I'm not there, I'm over here."

She whirled around again, bumping into a slender body that was dressed in skirts and petticoats. There was a muffled giggle as she held onto her prey, and carefully felt the long braids of hair that twined over the shoulders. She released her captive and continued her search. There was another tap on her shoulder.

She turned, and there was another, accompanied by several complaints from the other children. Something wasn't quite right with the way the game was going. It seemed someone was having a bit of fun with her, taking advantage of her sightlessness to play a prank by leading her in the wrong direction.

Again there was a tap on her arm and more urgent outcries from the smaller children urging her forward. She took several more hesitant steps wondering what hazard loomed in front of her. Suddenly she was grabbed by the shoulders, pulled back, and turned around. The blindfold was quickly stripped away and she stared up at Devlin Burke.

"What are you doing?" she laughed up at him. "Now see what you've done. We shall have to start over again, and I'm already quite dizzy."

"I think it's enough blindman's bluff for one afternoon." He gestured behind her at the brightly leaping fire that only moments before lay directly in her path. If he hadn't stopped her, she would have walked right into it. The small children had gathered about them, their small, worried faces upturned.

"It's all right," she quickly assured them. "I'm quite safe. No harm has been done."

She had heard the warning in their confused voices. Her gaze met his in silent question, then she saw Jillian slipping away through the cluster of wagons. It was obvious that she had been the one luring Jess on.

"It was just a harmless prank, nothing more," she insisted. But the expression on Burke's face was skeptical. Then Mary was tugging at her hand insistently.

"Can we bob for apples?" she implored in a small voice for which so many of the words were still new and uncertain. Jess knelt down in front of her.

"Of course we can bob for apples," she remarked with all the confidence of someone who'd actually done this before, which she hadn't. But she'd always considered herself a quick learner. They walked off together, hand-in-hand toward the huge half-barrels that had been filled with water, apples floating and bobbing about with carefree, elusive abandon.

The other children scattered to various activities, the frightening incident during blindman's bluff already forgotten.

Watch and learn, she told herself as she observed the other kids and their various techniques for apple-bobbing. When it was her turn, she stepped up to the edge of the barrel, hands tied with a scarf behind her back—no hands allowed—and flashed Burke a confident smile that all but said out loud, "there's nothing to this."

Ten minutes later she revised her opinion, as she stood at the edge of the barrel, face dripping with water, tendrils of wet hair plastered against her cheeks, the front of her bodice soaked through to the skin, stubbornly refusing to give up or give in.

Cheers went up for both sides, as she and her opponent furiously nudged apples about the barrel. Finally she was able to pin an apple into place against her opponent's apple. She quickly bit into it, triumphantly clenching it between her teeth as she stood up.

Everyone who had been watching the contest cheered loudly and then swarmed around the barrel in wild laughter and excited chatter. At the edge of the crowd Burke grinned at her. Then she felt the strong push of a hand at the middle of her back and she toppled forward into the barrel.

Strong hands pulled her out of the water. She came up sputtering and coughing, holding only a piece of apple between her teeth.

"Are you all right?" Burke asked. The grin was gone, replaced by a worried frown.

"Of course I'm all right. It's just a little water." Hands untied, she wiped the water from her face.

"I lost my apple."

"You could have lost a great deal more."

"I'm a good swimmer."

"Good heavens!" Moira joined them. She gave Jess a long look. "What happened?"

"It was Jillian," Burke said in a quiet voice.

"She did this?" Moira asked, looking about them.

"Aye, she was here. I saw her standing only a few feet away. I'm going to have a talk with her."

Moira stopped him with a hand at his arm.

"I'll talk with her."

Jess protested. "There's no need for anyone to talk to anyone else. No harm has been done. It was just an innocent prank."

"Not so innocent," he muttered.

"I'll deal with Jillian," Moira said. When he started to protest, she held up a hand. "The lass has strong feelins for you. I should have done something about it before now. I'll talk to her. She just needs a bit of a firm hand and a clear understandin' about what's proper and what isn't."

"She's a child," Burke protested.

"That's the problem, darlin'," Moira smiled at him and laid a hand against his cheek. "She's no child, and her feelins aren't the feelins of a child. She's quite taken with you. And it has to be handled properly so that she isn't made to feel ashamed for it."

He looked at Moira as if he thought her quite daft. "But she's too young. She's only a child. She's only . . ."

"Fifteen years old," Moira said softly. "The same age as Megan."

Chapter Twenty-four

The apple festival was over.

It had been a big success. They sold enough cider apples and goods to ensure a comfortable winter for those who lived at Old Orchard farm. Now, it was time to go home.

The first few miles the children chatted excitedly about the past three days, calling back and forth between the wagons and carts as they lumbered down the road. But the smaller children soon fell asleep, completely exhausted.

The night air had taken on a bitter chill. Soon even the older children were fast asleep, huddled under thick blankets in the back of the wagon — except for Jillie who had chosen to stay over at a neighboring farm after a lengthy conversation with Moira that afternoon.

Now Moira sat in front of the first wagon with Robbie. Jess sat behind them with Mary Margaret snuggled in her arms, and a thick wool shawl bundled tightly about them. Burke drove the second wagon, the two oldest boys drove two carts that followed with the animals.

A light rain began to fall when they were still more than an hour away from the farm. Jess quickly pulled a heavy canvas over the sleeping children. Robbie and Moira huddled together the last few miles, wrapped in a thick wool blanket.

Instead of going on down to the barn to bed down the animals, Robbie pulled the wagon around to the house first. Moira and Jess climbed down, gently rousing the sleeping children.

There were groans and softly murmured complaints. The older

ones helped with the smaller children. Soon everyone was inside, and Robbie was guiding the wagon down the road toward the barn to tend to the animals. Burke and the two older boys, driving the other wagons, turned down the road to the barn and followed.

It was over an hour later when the children were all finally in bed, warm and dry in nightshirts and nightgowns, filling the third-floor rooms that had been converted into dormitories—one for the older boys and one for the older girls.

The smaller children slept in two rooms on the second floor near Moira and Robbie's bedroom. The older boys bedded down in rooms over the barn. Jess had been sleeping in the room across the hall on the second floor.

It was small, hardly more than a closet, actually. But it was cozy with just enough room for a narrow bed and a small table. When she first saw it, it reminded her of the room at the back of Annie Chapman's flat, where she was certain her sister had been staying prior to Annie's death. Somehow it had given her a connection to her sister that wasn't exactly comforting, but at least reassuring.

She had to believe that her sister was safe. She had to be, and she would find her. But the key to finding her sister was the identity of man who called himself, Jack the Ripper.

Incredible and impossible as it seemed, Linnie was involved. And once Jess was able to finish the composites for the gallery show that Abberline was arranging with Monsieur Gilot, the murderer would be exposed and caught. It was the only hope any of them had at the moment of stopping the senseless and tragic deaths.

She'd been working on the composite sketches since they first arrived at Old Orchard. Burke had picked up a thick envelope from Abberline, at the post in Farway. First thing in the morning she would go through everything with him and resume her work, which had been set aside to attend the festival.

Mary Margaret had insisted on one more story about her life in London. She tucked the child in and then finally went downstairs, looking forward to the cup of tea Moira had promised when she had gone down almost a half hour earlier.

"You live like a princess," Mary had said with childlike awe as she told her about her home, family, and the servants at Carrington Square. "How wonderful your life there must be."

She hadn't the heart to tell Mary, who had been through so much, of the fear and horror she'd lived with the past few months, the uncertainty that she would ever see her sister alive again, the hard lessons she'd learned daily—that pain, sadness, and uncertainty didn't magically disappear because one lived like a princess. But she couldn't tell Mary that. A child needed to have wishes, hopes, and dreams. Children needed to feel loved and safe and protected from those harsh realities. God knows, from what she'd learned of Mary Margaret's short life, there'd been very little of any of that.

The kitchen was warm and cozy, glowing with the fire at the huge cook oven, capable of warming the entire house. Moira had lit it the moment they arrived and set a kettle to boil. It popped and hissed, steam shooting into the air as Jess came down the stairs.

"Well, that's the last of them. They were so tired I was certain all of them would drop right off, but Mary and one of the other girls insisted on a story."

"That's the way of it," Moira said as she stood before the stove. "There's always some wee one who just won't settle down for the night even though they're daft with fatigue.

"Robbie and Devlin should be along soon. They'll be in sore need of something hot. I'd wager even Devlin will take some of this tea, provided it's liberally laced with some good Irish whiskey."

Four cups were set on the long refectory table. As the kettle finally sent up a shrill whistle, she grabbed a thick stove pad and started to remove it from the stove top.

Jess smothered a yawn behind her hand. The warmth of the kitchen had made her drowsy. It had been an exciting three days at the festival. She thought longingly of the small bed upstairs. She looked up as Moira stood for the longest time before the big, wide stove.

"Do you need some help?"

Moira's shoulders shifted as she let out a very long sigh. She took hold of the kettle once more and then turned about.

"No, I've got it."

Jess watched her. Her voice sounded different, and her face was pale.

"Are you all right?" She immediately came to her feet. "Here let me take that kettle. Sit down. It's been a long day, you probably shouldn't be lifting anything so heavy."

Moira laughed. "I've been lifting children all day, Jess. A wee kettle is nothin' compared to wiggly, energetic bodies."

Jess knew absolutely nothing about the advanced state of being with child. Certainly such things were never discussed among ladies of society. And although her sister longed for a child, she had not yet conceived. And then she had disappeared. Therefore Jess's entire experience was somewhat limited to rumor and innuendo.

"Please sit and rest. I shall pour the tea," she firmly instructed. "Would you like the footstool for your feet?" Over the past few weeks, she'd often seen Moira propping her feet up on the small stool. It seemed to make her more comfortable.

"Please, don't bother, Jess."

"It's no bother at all." She whirled around and went into the adjacent room. It was small and tidy, with two rather threadbare overstuffed chairs, tables, and lamps. It was here that all the children were encouraged to read each evening. She heard a clatter of breaking china and raced back into the kitchen.

"What is it?"

The broken cup and saucer lay scattered across the floor where they had fallen and shattered. Moira sat at the table, leaning heavily on bent arms, head bowed and eyes closed.

"Moira!" She ran across the kitchen and knelt beside the woman, who was in considerable pain.

"It will pass. Just give me another minute."

Jess watched helplessly, holding onto Moira's hand, gently stroking it, trying to offer what comfort she could. Finally Moira's expression eased. The thin line of her mouth softened, she breathed out a deep sigh, and her eyes slowly opened.

"Are you all right?"

"Right enough, now." Moira smiled up at her and squeezed her hand gently. "Thank you for not getting upset."

Jess smiled tentatively. "Does this happen often?" she asked.

"Well, it's happened three times before."

"When was the last time?"

"About a year ago."

"It doesn't happen very frequently then."

Moira's bemused gaze met hers. "Not very often. Just when I'm about to have a baby."

"Oh, I see." Then Jess's eyes widened. "A baby? Now? Tonight?"

Moira nodded. "Probably more toward mornin'. It usually takes that long."

"But how?" Jess asked, stunned almost to speechlessness. "When?"

"Are you askin' how I got the babe?" Moira's amusement deepened.

Jess's mouth dropped open. Her cheeks grew hot.

"What I meant is how did this happen tonight?"

"Babies have a habit of doin' the unexpected. Actually it started up during the ride home."

"Does Robbie know?"

Moira shook her head. "I didn't want to alarm him." She patted Jess's hand reassuringly. "There's plenty enough time, Jess, to tell him when he comes in from the barn. Havin' babies takes a long time. And on a night like this the animals come first."

"Well if you're absolutely certain."

"Certain I am."

Jess looked at her dubiously. "Shouldn't you be in bed?"

"I understand some women prefer it. But when I have my babies, I get the worse pain low across me back. Layin' in bed is murderous. I'm more comfortable stayin' upright as long as I can. That way I can move around, and sorta' walk me way through the worst of it."

From a practical point of view that brought up a very interesting question about babies dropping on their heads on the floor, but Jess wasn't about to ask it. Obviously Moira had a great deal more experience in the matter, and if she wasn't concerned about walking about while she was about to have a baby, then it certainly wasn't Jess's place to question her choice.

Moira was doing precisely that — walking slowly about the kitchen, one hand pressed into the small of her back, the other gently massaging the roundness of her stomach, breathing in slowly and deeply — when Robbie and Burke finally came up from the barn.

"Beastly night out there," Robbie said over his shoulder to Burke as they stamped mud off their boots at the back step, and then came into the warm kitchen. He rubbed his red, chapped hands together, then finally turned. He saw Moira slowly pacing back and forth across the kitchen.

"What is it? What's happened?"

Moira gave him a calm smile. "It's your son, or perhaps another daughter." She slowly smoothed her hands down over her distended belly. Robbie blinked as comprehension slowly sunk in. He crossed the kitchen, and laid his larger hand over Moira's.

"Are you certain, luv?"

"As certain as I can be, after birthin' three other babes."

They stood like that for several moments. Then his fingers seemed to contract over hers for several long moments. He looked at Moira with love and tenderness in his eyes.

"That was a strong one."

"Aye, they've been like that for the past two hours. But they're quite a bit apart in time."

"Are ye hurtin' bad, darlin'?"

She touched her hand to his cheek. "It feels like it did with little Tammy. Not so bad that I can't bear it. It will be several hours."

Tammy was their four-year-old, a bright, impish, dark-eyed little girl, who resembled her mother.

Their words for each other, their loving gestures were almost intimate. Jess felt as if she and Burke were intruding on something very private, and should leave.

"I'll get old Gert hitched up and go fetch Sarah," Robbie was saying.

"There's no hurry, luv," Moira insisted. "This will take hours. It's dreadful out and yer as tired as the rest of us."

363

He kissed his wife then. "It may take a little longer to get over to her place, it's started to rain. I want to get over and back just in case this is more than a light storm."

"I'll go with you." Burke was already at the door putting on a thick woolen coat and stepping into high boots. Robbie stopped him.

"A house full of kids can be a handful. You'd best stay here to lend a hand should they awaken."

"Then let me go for the midwife."

Robbie grinned. "This farm may be half yours, but you spend so little time here that you'd get yerself lost and then where would we be—in a storm, no midwife, and a baby on the way, although I'm certain Moira could practically do this in her sleep.

"You must stay, me friend, and mind the women and children. I'll make the trip faster alone." He took the coat as Burke slipped out of it. Then he crossed the kitchen and kissed Moira again.

"Have a care, luv. I'll be back soon with Sarah."

She grinned at him. "I'm not goin' anywhere, Robbie Callahan. At least not very fast, at the pace I'm capable of these days."

Jess checked on the children again just after midnight. The wind had come up with a dreadful howl that gusted around the heavy beamed roof, making the rafters and walls creak. Rain pelted the windows, creating dozens of watery rivulets that merged until the glass ran with water. But they were all snug and warm inside, the stout old farmhouse sheltered from the worst of the storm in the niche of a hillside.

Burke went out and checked on the animals, and returned soaking wet, arms piled high with wood. It was bitterly cold out. Water dripped from his coat, muffler, and the edge of his hat into icy spikes. The rain had turned to sleet.

"Will Robbie be all right?" she whispered under her breath as she helped him out of his coat.

"He knows the countryside better than anyone." He nodded. "He'll be all right. How's Moira?"

"She's tired. I finally persuaded her to let me take her up to bed."

She frowned slightly but said nothing.

As if he read her thoughts, he said, "I know, lass." He squeezed her shoulder reassuringly. "He'll get back in time."

While he put more wood on the stove, she went upstairs to check on Moira.

She lay pale and quiet against the muslin sheets in the large bed. Her lashes were half-moons against her cheeks as she rested. Beads of perspiration appeared on her forehead and her upper lip, even though the room was quite cool. Jess wiped her face with a wet cloth. Her breathing was even and steady. Thinking that she might have dozed off, Jess got up to leave.

Moira's hand closed gently over hers. "Stay with me."

She took hold and sat down at the edge of the bed.

"He's not back," Moira said. It wasn't a question, but a simple statement of fact.

"He'll make it back in time," Jess reassured her. Instead of replying, Moira shook her head. Then her expression contorted as her fingers constricted over Jess's hand and her entire body convulsed. She panted short, shallow breaths, her eyes squeezed shut, as her shoulders came up off the bed, and her other hand clutched at her belly. It seemed to last much longer than anything that had happened downstairs.

Jess's hand felt as if the bones were being crushed, but she refused to let go. She held on tightly, mentally giving Moira her strength as she panted, grunted, and groaned her way through pain that seemed to crest through her prostrate body like a gathering wave.

Then it was receding, and Moira's body seemed to relax a bit. Her fingers eased about Jess's, her shoulders relaxed back against the pillow. Finally she opened her eyes and then slowly turned her gaze to Jess.

"That one was much stronger, and closer."

Jess wiped her forehead with the cloth. "You'll be fine. Robbie will get here with the midwife." She spoke rapidly. Even to herself it sounded as if she were chattering hysterically. Moira gently took her hand.

"It's all right, Jess. It's the most natural thing in the world."

"But you're in so much pain."

"Aye, there's pain. But in the pain you know that your body is struggling to bring a new life into the world, a life that you and your man have created out of love. It's a wondrous thing."

"Even with the pain?"

Moira nodded with a small smile. "Aye, even then. I've often thought it's like the first time with a man." She seemed not to notice the stunned look on Jess's face, or if she noticed, she said nothing of it.

"That sharp pain deep inside ye, like you've never experienced before. Except with birthin', it goes on a bit longer. And then there's that same feelin' of completeness like when yer joinin' with the man you love, that moment of holdin' life inside you, when it seems to burst all through you.

"And then when the babe is born, and you feel it pushin' out, leavin' you, there's that moment of aloneness, as if you've lost part of yerself, just like when yer finished joinin' with yer man. But you know that one is part of the other, and there is this little miracle of life that the two of you share."

Jess rinsed the cloth. "You should save your strength."

"Does it embarrass you, to hear me talk this way, Jess? I know yer not used to such unrefined manners." There was no criticism in the words, merely a simple question.

"It's just that I don't know anything about . . ."

"Aye, you know," Moira said quietly. "I've seen it in yer eyes. And in Devlin's eyes as well."

Their gazes met then, briefly.

"It's no business of mine, Jess Kelly," she said softly. "But anyone at all can see that it's unfinished between you."

"It never began," Jess said resolutely.

"Yer almost as poor a liar about that as yer are about Robbie gettin' back in time."

"What do you mean?"

"I mean this baby is comin' and it's not about to wait for its da to greet it properly."

"Do you mean, right now? This minute?"

"Very close to it, m'dear," Moira groaned as another pain began, fast on the heels of the previous one. "I've soaked the bedclothes. The baby will come fast now."

"What shall I do?"

It was several seconds as Moira doubled up, pulling her knees up, and grunted her way through the crest of the pain. Then, breathlessly, she relaxed against the pillows.

"Fresh bed linens, scissors, yarn from the knitting box, and a basin of hot water," she called out the list of items. "Oh, and get Devlin up here."

When Jess ran down the stairs, Burke looked up. "What is it?"

"The baby is coming now. Moira is asking for you."

He took the stairs two at a time while she raced about the kitchen, gathering up everything Moira had asked for. When she returned to the second-floor bedroom, he was sitting at the edge of the bed. Moira's hands were clutched in his. Her knuckles shone white over his tanned and callused hands.

"Scream if you have to, lass," he said.

"The children!" she protested through clenched teeth.

"They've heard worse when you and Robbie go at each other, and probably worse still when you make up afterward."

Her muffled groans broke into choked laughter. "Damn you, Devlin. Don't make me laugh. It hurts too much."

"It can't possibly hurt that much," he informed her, causing Jess's mouth to tighten.

Moira's expression was murderous as she worked through the pain. "If yer such a damn expert, Devlin Burke, then we'll trade places and see how ya do."

"Nah!" he exclaimed. "I'd be no good at birthin'. I've not got the right equipment, lass."

She panted as she lay still once more. "You'll have to be good at it tonight, m'dear. The baby is comin'."

"I know. And yer not to worry. Everythin' will be just fine, luv. I won't let anythin' happen to you or the babe."

"I trust you," she said, and Jess had the feeling that she was hearing words that had been said before between these old friends.

It went that way for the next two hours.

367

Moira's body labored to deliver the child, her muscles contorting, and spasmed painfully, so that she was drawn up almost double by the dreadful pain that seemed to come endlessly.

Together, they removed the wet sheets from beneath Moira and replaced them with clean ones. The room was kept warm. Jess rinsed the cloth countless times, bathing Moira's perspiring body, occasionally coaxing small sips of water between her parched lips.

In the beginning Moira had been the self-confident, reassuring one. Then as the hours wore on the roles changed, and Jess was the one who quietly offered words of encouragement.

Burke watched them. Two women from vastly different worlds. One born and raised in the gutters of Dublin, who'd whored herself in order to survive, with an inner strength that no amount of horror or degradation could destroy. The other, sheltered, privileged, raised with every advantage, who had undoubtedly never known a moment of hunger or cold, and yet with a fierce inner strength that was unexpected and stunning.

For hours he watched as Jessamyn Forsythe, also known in the circles of polite society as J.B. Dumont, stayed with this woman, who had become one of her dearest friends.

Her sleeves were pushed up to her elbows. Moisture showed dark at her bodice where beads of perspiration broke out on her pale skin. Wisps of long dark hair curled about her face. There were circles of fatigue beneath those incomparable green eyes. If ever there was a moment when she seemed farthest from that polite world she'd been raised in, it was now.

Her mouth was determined, her words soothing, her hand sure as she eased Moira's pain.

Strength. It was as much a part of her as breathing. And it occurred to Burke that in those humble surroundings, without the satins and laces and fine trappings of wealth that were so inherently a part of her, she was at that moment the most stunningly beautiful woman he'd ever known.

Moira was weak. It had been hours since the labor had begun. Almost as long that Robbie had been gone, and still not returned. Jess had been momentarily stunned when Burke announced that he had to check Moira to see if the baby's head had appeared yet.

It was the most intimate thing she had ever experienced. But she wasn't in the least horrified or offended. He was gentle and caring and Moira obviously did trust him beyond question. She lay quietly and held onto Jess's hand.

"It's not so bad, Jess," she smiled slightly. "He's helped with his share of lambs, goats, and a foal or two. It's all pretty much the same."

Jess looked questioningly at Burke. He smiled down at Moira as he finished and pulled the sheet back over her.

"That it is, lass." Then he looked over at Jess.

"I'll help you with more hot water. The baby is close now."

They walked out of the room together as Moira tried to relax between the spasms of pain. Jess started down the hallway. He stopped her. She immediately knew something was wrong. Fear was cold around her heart.

"What is it?"

"Her fluid broke and the baby should have started down, but it didn't. I couldn't feel the head. The baby isn't turned down like it should be."

"I don't understand."

He quickly explained. "Sometimes they don't come out the right away. Most babies are born headfirst, so that they can breathe right away until the mother can get the rest of the baby out. Moira's ready to have the baby, but the head isn't down." There was no need for him to explain more. The fear deepened.

"Her baby might die."

"Aye. I've seen it happen with animals. Sometimes comin' feet first like that, the cord inside that binds the babe to the mother is wrapped about its neck."

"Dear God!" she whispered, unable to bear the thought of the baby dying. She had felt it alive, moving in Moira's belly.

"There has to be something we can do."

He looked at her sharply, wondering if she even sensed what she was suggesting. Likely as not, he thought. And likely as not, she wouldn't have the courage for it when she knew.

"There's something that might work. It's been done before with lambs that sometimes come the same way." He watched her with intense, blue eyes. "We could turn the baby inside her so that the head is down and goin' in the right direction."

She swallowed hard. "Is that possible?"

"Aye, it's possible, but not without risk as well.

Her gaze broke from his, and he fully expected her to give all manner of excuses why it shouldn't be done — that it wasn't proper or dignified — or even possibly faint at such a suggestion.

"How would you do such a thing?"

"Animals are bigger. Most times it can be done by reachin' up inside and workin' the wee one about. It's a bit different with a woman, even though Moira has birthed babies before.

"It would have to be done by gently working the baby around until it's goin in the right direction. It will be very painful for Moira since the laborin' has already started."

"And if we do nothing?"

"Then they baby will die for certain, and probably Moira along with it."

Her chin lifted slightly. "Then I don't see that we have any choice. I'll get more hot water and a clean cloth."

With that she turned her back and quickly descended the stairs. He heard her moving about the kitchen below, unable to confront the emotions he felt inside at the amazing strength she had shown. He went back into the bedroom and spoke with Moira.

Jess found them talking quietly when she returned with the water and clean sheets.

"I checked on the children. They're all asleep," she announced, then turned at the answering silence. Burke was staring at the wall behind the headboard of the large bed. Moira was looking at her with soft, intelligent eyes.

"I know what has to be done," she said softly. "I want you to know that whatever happens, I trust the both of you." She reached out a hand to Jess.

"My new friend, and my dearest old friend." Then she was seized by a new pain and Burke called out instructions.

"We have to do it right away, before the baby starts down. It has to be done between pains, when the muscles are relaxed. It's easier to move the baby." Then he bent over Moira.

"It'll hurt fierce, lass. I have to tie your hands." She nodded in answer. He gently bound her wrists with soft muslin cloth and tied them to the bedposts. Moira eased her fingers around each post and took hold. Then he took out a small wooden mouth pipe one of the younger boys had made to sell at the festival. He placed it between her teeth.

"When the pain gets bad, bite down on this so you won't harm yourself."

"Bet you never thought we'd come to this, Devlin," she grinned weakly up at him, before taking the piece of wood between her teeth.

He smoothed the damp hair back from her forehead, and gently teased, "Sometimes, lass, yer more trouble than yer worth."

A new pain began, and he quickly lifted her gown. He gently placed his large hands over the mound of the child in her belly, and as the pain receded, he massaged the shape of the mound about, easing it with painstaking slowness into a new direction. Each time a new pain began, he stopped and waited to continue until they once more receded.

It went on like that for what seemed hours, but in truth barely more than minutes passed.

It was painful. Jess could see it in the expression on Moira's face each time he forcefully shifted the mass of the child by small degrees. Perspiration poured off Moira. Jess wiped it from her face and neck, all the while speaking soft encouraging words at her head, stroking her strained muscles when the pains took hold, rubbing her taut shoulders.

"I can't do this no more!" Moira gasped. She was pale, barely able to hold onto the bedpost.

"It's almost done, luv," Burke softly encouraged her. "The baby's head is movin' down in the right direction."

"I can't do it." Her head rolled from side-to-side. "I can't. And I can't feel the baby movin' no more."

Burke's alarmed gaze met Jess's over the bed. He sat beside Moira on the bed and leaned over her.

"It's because the baby is ready to be born now, darlin'. You can

371

do this!" There was a fierceness in his voice Jess had never heard before. It bordered on desperation, and she recalled when he'd told her about Megan—how he'd looked when he talked about her death, the tone of his voice, the anguish and pain in his face. It was there now, as if he were reliving it.

A new pain took hold. Before, Moira had breathed her way through them, drawing her legs up, trying to force the child from her body. But now she had no strength left. She groaned softly as the flesh over her belly contorted, the spasmed muscles trying to respond to the instinctive process of birth.

Jess felt completely helpless. She didn't know what to do. Nothing in her life had prepared her for this. It was an echo of the desperate helplessness she'd carried around inside for weeks over her sister.

A rage built inside her—a rage that came from the impotence of fear and helplessness. There was nothing she could do to help her sister at that moment. The entire world as it existed had been reduced down to the four walls of that small room in a remote farmhouse at Old Orchard. But inside those four walls were three people, and a child wanting very much to be born.

Not one more death! she thought as tears of fury filled her eyes. Not one more! She rounded the bed and knelt on the floor beside it, her face very close to Moira's.

Moira was pale, her face filled with dark shadows, her breathing shallow and faint. Burke sat at the edge of the bed, an agonized expression on his face.

She didn't whisper, but spoke in a firm voice, jarring Moira from her stupor. "There's life inside you! You said it was the most wondrous thing of all." She took hold of Moira by the shoulders and shook her. "If you give up now, your baby will die."

"Jess, what are you doin'?" he grabbed her arm, alarmed at the anger in her voice. She jerked away, shaking Moira again.

"You created that life. You made a promise to that child. You don't have the right to give up now. You have to fight to do this."

Moira's eyes were open. Behind the pain was a lucidity neither of them had seen in hours.

"I'll help you," Jess promised. "We'll both help you, but you have

372

to help, too. Because I don't know how to do this by myself."

She spoke more rapidly now, logic giving way to the edge of hysteria. "I don't know how to light a kitchen stove. I can't even boil water. And you know how perfectly hopeless I am with stitchery." There was a ghost of a smile on Moira's dry lips. "But you can do all of that so well. And you can do this! You're too close to the end now to quit. Damn you! If I'm willing to try, you have to try."

Burke stared at her as it began to sink in what she was doing. She begged, badgered, and argued, breaking through Moira's stupor with threats and old-fashioned bullying. There was a fierce strength in her that he'd glimpsed, but never knew the depth of.

"Quit squawkin' at me," Moira whispered weakly, but there was a smile gleaming in her eyes. Then she said, "God help us all, but if you're willin' to do this, then I can't be the one to quit first."

Jess looked up at Burke. "What do we do now?"

"I'll hold her hands," he said, gently untying Moira's wrists. "You'll have to tend to the baby. I'll talk you through it."

They worked together. In spite of her exhaustion, when the next pain took hold Moira was possessed of a fierce strength as if it were the last assault in a great battle.

Burke sat behind her on the bed, cradling her back against his chest. When the pains came, he held her tight, arms wrapped about her, holding her so that it was possible for her to draw her legs up.

Propriety and delicate manners were forgotten. The sheet had been pulled back once more. The gown rode high about Moira's hips. Several more minutes passed by, filled with Moira's determined grunts and groans as the pain came unceasingly.

"You'll have to help the baby out when it starts to come, Jess. It's probably as exhausted as Moira is."

Without even thinking if it was the proper or right thing to do, Jess simply nodded and quickly gathered several towels at the foot of the bed. Everything seemed to happen very quickly after that.

Moira screamed painfully, her body convulsed, knees drawn up. It was then Jess saw the dark dome of the baby's head emerge.

"I see the baby," she announced, oblivious to the blood that accompanied the infant's arrival, aware only of a sense of awe at what was happening.

Moira cried out again as another pain came very quickly and Burke urged her to push hard. The baby's head was fully emerged.

"The shoulders will come next, lass," Burke called out to Jess. "You may have to take hold, and help the wee one along."

At the next pain, Moira once more bore down. Her knuckles went white, and her nails cut into Burke's dark hand. She cried out as one little shoulder appeared.

Without a second thought, Jess carefully slipped a towel under the small head and shoulder.

"What should I do now. I only see one shoulder."

"Turn the babe face down to ease the other shoulder out," Burke instructed.

As if it were the most natural thing in the world, Jess took hold of the slippery baby and gently turned the head and one shoulder a few centimeters. The other shoulder eased out, quickly followed by tiny arms, chest, hips, bottom, and legs, and a sudden burst of squalling as the newest member of the Callahan family finally made a complete arrival.

Moira's baby cried, tiny arms quivering in the sudden cool air of the room as Jess held the newborn in her hands. She looked up at Burke, quite well covered with blood, a radiant smile on her face.

"It's a boy," she announced with a joyous laugh, then looked up. Her eyes glistened as she looked at Burke, and tears were streaming down her cheeks. She held the baby close, mindless of the blood, aware only of the perfection of him.

"My God, he's beautiful," she whispered.

Chapter Twenty-five

The kitchen was warm and silent, except for the low whisper of the kettle that simmered on the stove. A single oil lamp glowed at the long refectory table, creating fingers of soft light on the white plaster walls. Splinters of gray appeared at the windows, shuttered from the inside to keep out the cold. It was dawn.

Burke leaned wearily against one of the heavy timbers that framed the low-beamed passage from the stairs into the kitchen. For long moments he let the comforting silence wrap about him — safe, secure . . . home.

Then his gaze rested on the slender young woman sitting in the rocking chair before the stove, where the heat wrapped about her like a warm cocoon.

Her head was bent forward, exhaustion obvious in the slump of her shoulders, the twin crescents of dark lashes that lay against her cheeks, the slow rise and fall of her breasts as she breathed.

She was asleep, yet even so, she protectively cradled the sleeping newborn child carefully against her breast, the soft downy head curved at her neck, the small bow of pink mouth slightly open, as the baby's own breathing fell strong and even.

They were both asleep. And upstairs in that first bedroom where they had all struggled to bring her baby safe into the world, Moira lay sleeping as well, exhausted from the ordeal that could have ended so tragically for both mother and baby. But it hadn't. And in those quiet, safe, and silent moments, Burke knew it was mostly because of the young woman who sat cradling Moira's son in her arms.

She had shown a rare and surprising courage and selflessness

375

that he was still trying to understand. It undermined everything he was so certain he knew about her.

He crossed the kitchen with weary steps, unwilling to accept until that moment how very close he had come to losing Moira and her child, unwilling to confront how those desperate hours had taken him back over the years to those equally desperate hours when he had lost Megan and her unborn child.

In the night, as the storm raged around them, he had relived that night, as if all the years in between had never existed. The pain and fear he felt were the same. He had refused to accept it. But in those worst moments, when Moira's strength was gone and he felt the life going out of her, someone had unselfishly given back her strength, her life, and that of her unborn baby.

He gazed down at Jess and felt a stirring of emotions that he'd buried so long ago he hardly recognized them now. For twenty years they had lain beneath the pain and loss of that other night when he chose to close out everyone and every other emotion except for Moira and Robbie, and what they had built together here at Old Orchard—a haven for unwanted children as they had been unwanted themselves.

The irony was that Jess Kelly represented everything he had spent the past twenty years hating, but hate was the last thing he felt at that moment.

His fingers gently touched her disheveled hair that no proper lady would have allowed to come undone, then grazed her skin, like warm satin, and soft as the newborn infant's. He crouched beside the chair, one arm resting along the back.

He stroked the sleeping infant's downy head. Then his fingers lightly brushed her cheek, and he felt some long lost need expand and take hold deep inside, like a huge hand closing around his heart, and he kissed them both tenderly.

A thought lay half formed in the debris of those shattered emotions: this could be our child—my son—safe, protected, and wanted, in her arms, if only . . .

She stirred then, those dark lashes slowly lifting over sea-green eyes filled with sleepiness and such stirring tenderness that he felt himself wanting desperately to believe in what could be. Her mouth curved in a soft, welcoming, and intimate smile, as if there were no other world beyond the warmth of the kitchen. He stroked her cheek.

"It's morning, lass," he said softly, so as not to wake the baby.

"Moira?"

"Sleeping . . . like a baby, " he smiled, allowing himself to feel the warm glow of the moments they shared, banishing the cold ache of despair he'd carried for so long.

There was a sudden noise from the yard outside, and Jess looked up.

"No doubt it's Robbie, returned with the midwife," he concluded.

"Just a bit late, wouldn't you say?" she smiled over the head of the sleeping infant.

"Just a wee bit."

"What is a wee bit?" Robbie asked as he abruptly came through the door, followed by a cold blast of air, and a stout woman bundled thickly in heavy clothes who no doubt was Sarah, the midwife.

The sudden noise and the cold air awakened the sleeping baby in Jess's arms with a startled jerk of tiny arms. Burke stood, no longer blocking Jess and the infant from view.

"This is the wee bit we were speaking of," he said with a grin.

Robbie blinked, uncomprehending for a few seconds. His face was heavily lined with fatigue and worry. The thick wool coat was crusted over with ice, as were his cap and the heavy gloves he wore. His skin above the roughened outgrowth of beard was chapped raw from the cold, and his eyes, which usually sparkled with a wry humor, were bloodshot and glazed.

Then, as if the warmth of the kitchen or the reality of the scene before him suddenly sank in, he blinked uncertainly. The fatigue and confusion seemed to melt along with the ice on his coat as he stared at the baby.

"About two hours ago," Burke answered the question his friend couldn't quite seem to move his mouth enough to ask.

"Moira?" Robbie asked anxiously from between chapped and frozen lips.

377

"She's fine enough and asleep upstairs."

The midwife, Sarah, ignored until this moment, quickly moved around Robbie's immobile form.

"I'll check on her, then," she announced, unwinding heavy woolen wraps as she climbed the stairs.

"The bridge was out . . ." Robbie made a muffled sound then, and a helpless gesture with his hands. Burke wrapped an arm about his friend's shoulders.

"They're both all right, man," Burke assured him. "Moira is a stout lass, and you've the son you always wanted. Although he's a mite stubborn about things, like his father." He didn't elaborate, or explain how desperate the situation had been those few hours when Moira lay completely exhausted with the baby turned the wrong way inside her. There would be time enough for that later when everyone was rested.

Robbie briefly inspected his new son and then went upstairs to assure himself that Moira was truly all right. The midwife came back down to check the baby, declaring that Jess and Burke had done a fine job.

"There's nothin' to it," she said jovially as she changed the baby's nappies. "Especially for them wot has already had youngins. They just slip right out."

They exchanged weary glances and secretive smiles. There was no point in telling her that young Jesse Devlin Callahan — as Moira had wearily insisted her new son was to be called — had done everything but slip right out.

Everything became very frantic and noisy after that, as the other children awakened. As soon as word spread from floor to floor that Moira had her baby, they all clamored excitedly down to the second-floor bedroom and the kitchen, anxious to see Moira and the new baby.

By midmorning, Jess felt as if she were about to collapse. Moira had nursed the baby earlier. They both lay sleeping, miraculously, with a house full of children of varying ages and several adults swarming over them.

Jess longed to crawl into the small bed in the room across the hall, convinced she could sleep if cannons were being set off across the farmhouse, but she discovered that Sarah had moved into the room. With the foul weather and the new baby, the midwife had declared that she would stay for the next few days, to help out and make certain that Moira regained her strength.

Before Jess left the bedroom so that Moira could get some much needed sleep, they had spoken briefly of the long, frightening hours during the night.

"I know nothin' about you," Moira had said to her. "Except that Devlin says yer lookin' for your sister who disappeared. Yer a rare, kind person. I hope you find yer sister. And I want you to know that you always have friends and a home here. I thank you for my son, and meself, and I'm glad to call you me special friend."

It had been a touching moment, unlike any she had ever experienced with her school friends or the daughters of society patrons chosen to be her friends. Except for her sister, she'd never felt that special bond. Because Linnie might well be lost to her, the words and the sincerity behind them were all the more poignant and meaningful.

"Thank you." She had stood to leave then, but Moira had stopped her with a hand around hers.

"He loves you, Jess." The words startled her. She shook her head. "You're wrong."

"I'm not wrong. With everythin' else that was goin' on last night, I saw it. And, I felt it."

"It's not likely that he can admit to it, himself. It's been too long that he's locked all those feelins up inside him, except for the children he brings here. There's a safety in lovin' a child, because they love ye back unconditionally.

"But the pain he learned as a child has stayed with him. Only once did he ever allow himself to feel anythin' more."

"With Megan."

"Aye, and then he lost her, too. He's never allowed himself to love since then. It's closed so deep away inside him, just achin' to get out."

"It's not that simple," Jess said in a quiet voice. There were so many other things that Moira didn't know about her—all the secrets that Burke had discovered and hated her for.

"Sometimes you have to let it be that simple."

Jess's gaze locked with Moira's at the profound simplicity of those words. Then Moira let out a sigh, closed her eyes, and fell asleep once more.

Jess turned to leave. Burke was standing at the doorway of the bedroom. His eyes were a dark, piercing blue, looking at her as if he were trying to see inside her thoughts.

"Yer tired, lass," he said gently, as silence drew out between them. "You've hardly slept at all."

"And you've slept even less."

He shrugged. "I'm used to it."

"On the streets of London?"

"Aye, and Dublin. You should try to rest. Sarah has things well in hand."

"Sarah also has my room," she said with a small smile. "Actually I was contemplating the barn."

The thought of Jessamyn Forsythe, lady of society and also the celebrated artist, J.B. Dumont, sleeping in a barn in Devonshire with goats, sheep, and chickens, brought a wry smile to his lips that eased the lines of fatigue, softening them to a breathtaking handsomeness. Then the smile also softened and all but disappeared. His gaze moved away from hers, as if he didn't want to see the answer he might find there at his next suggestion.

"There's more than enough room at the cottage." He looked up then.

"Stay with me, Jessie, for whatever time we have left."

She sensed the fear, heard it in the soft timber of his voice, barely more than a whisper, saw it in the frown that began at one corner of his mouth, and in the shadows that waited behind those penetrating eyes.

Everything he was, had been, survived as a boy, and knew to be true in life, all but waited for her to refuse, to reject the man and the lonely little boy who ached inside of him.

Sometimes you have to let it be that simple.

Even before Moira's words leaped back into her thoughts, the answer was already there.

"Yes," she whispered.

They left, quietly, unobtrusively. Robbie was the only one to see them go and he said nothing, except to thank them both once more.

The yard beyond the farmhouse was a sea of mud, leaves, and downed tree branches. It wasn't difficult to see why it had been impossible for Robbie to get back any sooner. And it was bitter cold, the previous night's rain gone to sleet and hanging from the trees in silvery icicles.

Burke carried her to the barn where he hitched one of the horses to a small cart. They would never have made it to the cottage otherwise, for the road from the main house was almost impassable except for the hard-muscled draft horse who plowed steadily through the thick, clinging ooze.

At the cottage, Burke unhitched the horse and secured it inside the shed at the back. Then he carried Jess to the back door of the cottage.

He set her down to the floor just inside the door. The cottage was dark and icy, the stove unlit for the past several days since before the apple festival. Their breath shivered between them in a pale, shimmery cloud. Without a word Burke moved past her and quickly lit the stove.

"Jess?" There was an unspoken question behind the sound of her name—that if she chose it, he would take her back to the main house.

She turned, her gaze meeting his, hearing the question and the uncertainty that went with it in spite of the answer that had brought them this far. His face was in shadow. His eyes were watching her, waiting. She reached up and touched his beard-roughened cheek with her fingers, the tips grazing the hardened muscles along his set jaw, the deep lines at the edge of his mouth. Then she reached up and gave him the only answer there was.

Her mouth found his, molding to his lips, cold from the chilled air, finding the warmth waiting inside. Everything she might have said became the kiss, opening the door of her own emotions and flooding out to him in answer.

"Touch me," she whispered against his mouth, as he had once said to her. "Please, touch me . . . Devlin."

The sound of his name echoed out of his past, spun past him taking with it the pain of years and tears as his hands came up to her back and spread to hold her against him, welcoming the wet heat of her mouth as it banished the cold shadows of his life.

He slipped an arm beneath her legs and lifted her once more. He turned and carried her into the room at the back of the cottage. There he slowly lowered her until her feet touched to the floor. More slowly, her mouth came away from his.

"Love me, Devlin," she murmured against his lips, stroking her own across the harsh scrape of beard at his chin, closing her eyes as she tasted the textures of him.

The small stove stood silent and momentarily forgotten in the corner of the room as they built the fire with the slow stroke of hand against hand and mouth against skin. The barriers of clothes were slowly drawn away. Then his hand came up to her hair pulled back in one long braid down the middle of her back.

"I want to see it loose about yer shoulders, so that it's the only thing coverin' you," he said with a sudden thickness in his voice.

He untied the ribbon that bound it, then slowly untwined the heavy, thick strands, pulling them through one at a time, unwinding the intricate weave, until it lay thick and shimmering in his hands, like heavy dark satin.

"So many times I've thought of what it would feel like to have it windin' about me, to feel it in my hands, to smell it." He lifted the heavy strands to his face, his eyes closing as he stroked it against his lips.

"You've taught me to see things, Jessie," he whispered, his gaze fastening on hers. "And made me feel . . . some things . . . I never thought I'd feel again . . . afraid to feel more."

Her fingers gently pressed against his lips, silencing the doubts and fears that she knew tore at him.

"Love me, Devlin. Love me now, for the time that we have left."

He lifted her again, holding the slender length of her body high against his. The contrast of the slender hollows and soft fullness of her body smoothed against his, skin against skin, heat against heat.

Then slowly he lowered her over the length of the bed, one knee slipping between her thighs, as his body eased hers down in the waiting softness of the downy mattress. His mouth found hers as she arched up against him, her slender arms wrapping about his neck, pulling him intimately closer, then closer still. Her slender hips pressed against him. The next moment she opened to him, molding the hot fullness of him tight into the cleft of her body.

"Jessie," he whispered. "Make me feel safe. Let me feel you lovin' me. Make me whole again."

Then he drew her taut nipple into the dark, wet heat of his mouth. Her fingers scraped back through his dark hair holding him tight within her as his words wrapped around her.

Sometimes it is that simple.

The heat that built low inside her was anything but simple. It expanded and contracted at the gentle, persistent tugging at her breast, then simmered breathlessly as his tongue slowly stroked over her breast as if he intended to taste every inch of her. She gasped and then shivered at the strange, animal sound she made.

"Aye, lass," he whispered against her skin that now glistened with a fine sheen of dampness in spite of the chilled air that surrounded them. "I want to hear the little sounds you make when I'm kissin' you." His mouth moved low over her, his tongue tracing wet heat across her shivered skin, then lower still.

"I want to taste when you make the sounds," his own voice quivered as he explored intimately, his hands holding her hips as she felt the hot tip of his tongue slip intimately between soft folds of skin. A small, strangled sound escaped her lips.

Bewilderment, confusion, fascination. Images slipped behind her closed lids at the sensations that built inside her.

Inspector Burke—angry, stubborn, then coldly remote at his discovery of the lies she'd told. Burke—the man who'd cut her stays and intimately undressed her, who first made love to her, coldly, impersonally, and then left her. Devlin—a man tormented by the past, and a little boy who'd been betrayed.

He was all of those things and more—complex, uncompromising in things he believed in passionately, driven by pain and loss, yet infinitely tender as his hands cradled her, and his mouth moved over her with a soul-robbing tenderness.

383

Then she discovered the passion as he slipped inside, the velvet heat of his mouth shattering her fragile hold on that self-imposed control she'd been bred and raised to.

She felt exposed, helpless, with a sweet penetrating invasion as though all of her would splinter into a thousand shards of glass each time his tongue stroked, his breath warm against her cool skin.

"Devlin!" she cried out, except that his name and the actual sound of it were oddly different. It was a low, frantic sound in her throat. His response was a feral murmur as he rose over her.

He kissed her then, pressing her down into the gathering softness of the bed at her back, his body over hers hard by contrast, his full, strong mouth sweet with her wetness.

It was a startling awareness, her taste on his lips. And then the only awareness was of heat — the heat of his mouth against hers, silencing any other sound, and the heat of his thick flesh burning through her as she took him deep inside her.

Completeness, rightness, a feeling as if she were only emptiness waiting for him to fill her.

Moira had spoken of it in quiet words as one who knew what it was to join with a man intimately and feel the wholeness of it. She had likened it to the feel of a child inside, like life itself — the strength, promise, and hope of it.

But it was more.

She felt it low inside, as he built it along every nerve ending. It was a breathlessness as their bodies moved together, and he moved deeper still within her until it seemed they ceased to exist and became one breath, one heart, one pulse moving between them like the frantic beating of a drum.

His hand moved up over her thigh, then stroked over her hip as his hard flesh filled her again and again with a stroking rhythm that obliterated all other sensations.

"Devlin! I can't . . ." her breath shuddered out of her paralyzed lungs.

"Aye, you can, lass. Feel it. Let me feel it with you."

"I'm afraid," she gasped. "I've never . . ."

"Aye but you have, lass," he murmured thickly. "You create it with colors and images. You've seen it. Now let yerself feel it."

Then his hands closed over both of hers, his body slick and hard against and within hers. She was afraid she would die from the sensations that poured through her—*certain* she would die if it all ended now.

His fingers laced through hers, and his mouth closed over hers. His breath became hers, and the pulse that beat between them became one pulse of sensation so intense that it was like living and dying all at once.

She quivered beneath him, her hips taking him deep with a shuddering innocence and completeness that stole through him. He heard her startled gasp, felt the sudden clench of her fingers around him even as the muscles deep inside her clenched and spasmed around him, and in the sweetness of pleasing her, he found safety, hope, and his own lost soul.

He moved within her as she held him tight against her, the hard length of him snuggled inside, and the fullness of him clasped within her body. Then he cried out, shuddering into her, and she felt the powerful contractions of his body, and the warm flood that spread inside her.

For long moments afterward, they lay together, his body warm and secure within hers, the need within them both momentarily at rest. His forehead rested against hers. Their breathing slowed along with the double beat of strong pulses. His lips moved against hers in tender strokes and whispers. In the cool air of the silent cottage he said simply, "I love you, Jessie."

They made love again, slowly, with discovery, and tender exploration, learning about each other in the language of senses rather than words.

Much later, when the fire had been built at the stove, he brought them slices of bread, cheese, and mugs of steaming cider laced with Irish whiskey. They made love lustily, as the hunger still raged within them, slipping to the woven rug at the floor, as she slipped over him, taking him inside in one powerful thrust that left them both shattered by the strength in her lithe body wrapping about his.

And in the first light of dawn the following day, with leaden clouds and the first new snow falling in a heavy curtain to blanket the earth, he cradled her face in his hands, stroking the high arch of bones at her cheeks with his fingers, studying all the curves and planes, the wide sweep of dark satin brows, the brush of thick sooty lashes.

She was fragile and strong, like porcelain and steel. There was an openness and honesty he'd never known before with any human being, and secrets he wanted to discover forever. She was innocence and youth, child and woman, and she had found the hurting child within him and drawn him outside of himself, freeing him to want something for the first time in his life. She gave him strength and innocence, and took away the pain of his own secrets.

"My God, you're so beautiful," he whispered against her mouth.

Her lips trembled beneath his. No one had ever said that to her before, and she knew that she would never want or need to hear it from another living soul. Her fingers brushed against his cheek, and she felt the sudden wetness of tears. She cradled his face between her slender hands as she pulled him down to her, her mouth seeking his as her body slowly joined once more with his.

Chapter Twenty-six

Jess looked up from the sketch she was working on. The cottage was like a warm, safe cocoon, while winter descended over the land outside. Devlin had explained that so much snow was unusual even though they were well into winter, with Christmas only a little more than two weeks away. Neither of them complained about the weather.

They sat in the small, warm kitchen. He had taken over the responsibility of preparing the evening meal after the disaster of the evening before when they were forced to open all the doors and windows in spite of the freezing cold outside, because of smoke that filled the cottage from her attempt at cooking. He was preparing a lamb stew with the last of the fresh vegetables from Moira's garden, and fresh bread.

"Tell me about your mother," Jess asked. She wanted to hear it from him.

"Old Hattie, the crone who owned me, told me about her, and where she was from. I saw her only once," he said with a sudden coldness in his voice. "I was nine at the time."

She shuddered at his choice of words, and the thought of one human being owning another. Moira had told her stories of how they survived on the streets of Dublin as children, and how they all came to Old Orchard, but the buying and selling of children was abhorrent and incomprehensible to her. And yet it was a painful reality in his life.

Devlin, as she now thought of him, had told her little else about his young life, perhaps choosing to keep it closed away with other painful reminders of the past.

"I walked all the way to Kilkenny," he finally went on to explain. "Her family estate was there. Lady of the manor, she was. With her fine clothes, gleaming coach and horses, and her fine, cold manners. Spent every last coin I had for as fine a piece of clothes as I could find for meetin' her. But the footman wouldn't let me in."

"Did you return to Dublin?"

For a brief moment there was a flash of a grin. "I picked the lock and stole inside the manor."

Somehow that didn't surprise her. "And that was when you saw her?"

"Aye. With the lord of the manor yellin' orders to throw the *filthy, heathen trash* back to the gutters when I was found out. Looked right through me, she did, even when I shouted out my name loud enough for the dead to hear."

"Perhaps she didn't recognize it."

He looked over at her then and the expression on his face was so contorted, so filled with pain that it made her ache inside, and she went to him. His voice was low, echoing the remembered pain of a little boy confronting the painful rejection of the mother who had sold him to the streets of Dublin to spare herself the disgrace of her affair.

"She recognized it well enough. I saw it in her eyes, for it was my father's same name, the groomsman she shamed herself with, and then had sent away."

Jess went to him and laid her hands on his arms, trying to comfort him. He jerked his tormented gaze away from hers.

"She knew, and just stood there and watched while her husband ordered me horsewhipped for daring to enter their fine house and embarrass such a fine lady. Just as easily as she got rid of me nine years before that for a few coins to old Hattie on the streets of Dublin."

"It's ended," she whispered softly. "Let it go. It has nothing to do with you anymore."

He pulled her into his arms and held her tight, as if he could banish the cold ache of that old pain with the feel of her in his arms, warm, soft, and giving. But the expression in his eyes as he held her was stark.

"I pray God yer right lass," he whispered against her hair. There was a sadness in his voice that filled her with uneasiness. An acrid, burning smell pulled them apart. He flung open the door of the oven and pulled out the blackened loaf of bread, with several colorful curses.

"It's all right," she said, smothering back a smile as she peeked at the badly singed loaf. "It scrapes off very nicely," she reassured him. "I've had some experience with that sort of thing."

"Is that right?" There was a wicked gleam in his blue eyes as he turned and looked at her. He reached out and grabbed her by the wrist. He slowly pulled her to him.

She looked at him warily and tried to resist. "It was merely a suggestion."

"I have another suggestion," he said softly with a new, far more subtle, and infinitely charming threat. She was no match for him, and he pulled her against his body. "I've an appetite for somethin' other than burned bread." His head bent to hers, his mouth grazing the hollow beneath her slender jaw. That brief warm caress sent tremors through her.

"Devlin!" she whispered as his mouth wandered lower and she guessed at his intention.

"It's not decent. It's still . . . light . . . outside."

The last words shuddered out of her as his fingers released the buttons at the front of her bodice and his warm hand closed over her flesh.

"It was light at noon," he reminded her, his warm breath moving over the shivered flesh at her throat. "I heard no objections then." He kissed her, temporarily silencing any further objection.

Then he lifted her, one arm about her waist. Instead of carrying her into the bedroom as he had at noon, he slowly lowered her to the heavy oak table. There was a flicker of confusion in her seagreen eyes, then the flash of comprehension followed by the sudden flush of heat that spread across her cheeks.

"You can't mean . . . !" she stammered, unable to articulate the scandalous thought that finally registered.

"It's not possible . . ."

His mouth moved down her throat, forcing her head back. She

ached with a sudden expectancy, then shuddered as his fingers pushed the bodice aside and his mouth closed over her.

"Aye, lass. It's very possible. I'll show you."

"We shouldn't . . ." the fragmented whisper splintered out of her and brought the gentle reprimand of his teeth.

Somewhere in the tumult of sensations she heard the whisper of clothing being drawn away, then felt his hands brush her thighs as he pushed back her petticoats. Then he was lifting her and pulling away the soft flannel bloomers she wore since it had grown so cold.

"Look at me." The command was whispered, with an abrupt harshness that emphasized the sudden need. She opened her eyes and looked up at him as he leaned over her. Their breathing was labored, mingling as his mouth hovered over hers, and the heat in the cottage seemed to radiate between them, glistening across his forearms and the dark V of exposed chest at the neck of his shirt.

It was almost oppressive, weighting her down, moving through her in dark pulses. His hands clasped her hips. She could feel the heat of his fingers burning into her flesh.

Breathlessly, she looked at him, wondering how it was possible that she could want him again, unable to comprehend that it could be more than what they'd already shared. He lifted her slowly and brought her to him, guiding her legs about his waist.

"Look at me now, Jessie," he whispered tenderly. "I've a need to see your face when I'm fillin' you with myself."

She gasped as he slipped inside, firm and hard. Her slender body clung to his, her arms wrapped about his neck as he supported her. Her breath came in sharp, hard gasps that struggled out of her lungs.

"Have I hurt you lass?" he asked, his voice low and caring. Her head moved back and forth. She breathed slowly and deeply, her muscles easing about him. Then she looked up, her eyes dark and smoky green, her mouth softly swollen. Her arms tightened about his neck, and she moved her hips against his, so that his thick, hard flesh buried deep inside her.

"Jessie."

She loved the sound of her name in his throat, that one moment when every last ounce of control shattered and disintegrated.

390

He laid her back over the table, time and place forgotten.

As he had watched her that first moment when they joined, she now watched him with a stunned fascination of the senses. Color and texture coalesced into myriad images and sensations—bold patterns, soft shades of light and dark, the dryness at her mouth, the wetness of her body gliding over his, then gloving him firmly inside her.

One last ridiculous thought intruded.

"Devlin, the supper," she whispered. His tongue slipped between her lips.

"Let it burn."

She looked up from the sketch she'd been working on from the recent information Abberline had sent. The soft frown at her mouth deepened.

"I can't seem to get it right."

"How do you mean? You've never had any trouble before. Perhaps the information in those latest descriptions after Belle was killed aren't accurate."

She shook her head. "No, that's not it. I'm certain they're quite accurate. They were taken by Endicott, Sergeant Hobbs, and Chief Abberline himself."

"It's just that the descriptions don't match with the earlier ones. It's as if . . ."

"What?"

Again she shook her head, mentally dismissing an absurd thought. "It's nothing."

"I've come to value your thoughts, lass. And your talent. If you have an idea about this, I want to hear it."

There was no way he could possibly know how much those words meant to her, after having her work so easily dismissed by her family and friends—with the exception of her sister. She brought the sketches over to the table where he was working on a piece of harness.

On the streets of Whitechapel tracking down an illusive, brutal murderer, at Old Orchard gently bringing a new life into the world, or sitting at a cottage table mending a piece of harness, he seemed comfortable, at ease, sure of himself. Yet in the quiet moments of the past few days since they had come to the cottage she had discovered the silent torment he carried deep, yet kept carefully at bay.

She spread the sketches before him, knowing that he would see it before she pointed it out.

"I've made four sketches from the descriptions taken in all the murders."

He set the harness aside. "And all quite different."

"Even though they're incomplete you can see that the eyes are different, and the shape of the head and faces as well. Other details are less accurate, probably because either a hat was worn, or possibly a scarf concealing the lower part of the face.

He continued to study the sketches. "These two might possibly match," he suggested, rearranging them so that they were laid side by side.

"It could be just a difference of expression."

Then he laid one over the other, imposing the image of one on the other. There was a resemblance in the shape of the faces.

She smiled. "I had thought that as well. But the other two are very different from either of these."

He looked at her then, once more Inspector Burke of the metropolitan police of London, his expression scrutinizing.

She took a breath, and made a wild, improbable suggestion, "More than one man?"

His eyes narrowed. "The police surgeon confirmed that the murders were all committed by the same person, in the same manner."

She let out a long, disappointed sigh. "But why is there so much discrepancy among the descriptions?"

"That's been the dilemma from the beginning. At least you've been able to narrow it down this far." He smiled at her gently.

"It helps, lass."

"But it's not enough. And the gallery show is only ten days away."

"I know."

There was a subtle change in his voice that she hadn't noticed before, a reminder that their time together was short.

His hand covered hers. "I know you're frustrated by this lass, especially since it somehow involves your sister. But your sketches have helped, and may yet be of more value to us."

A loud knock at the door, the first sound from the outside world since they had come to the cottage.

It was Robbie. He had finally ventured outside the farmhouse during a lull in the weather.

"Moira was havin' a fit and fallin' in the middle of it, worried that yer might have come to some harm out here all alone," he said as he stamped fresh snow from his feet and went to warm his hands before the stove. His eyes crinkled with a grin above the thick wool scarf that was wrapped about the lower part of his face. He looked from one to the other.

"I can see you survived well enough."

"Aye," Devlin acknowledged, turning away from Jesse so that she couldn't see the expression on his face. "Well enough."

Their interlude at the cottage was gone even though the weather remained uncertain. Sarah was no longer needed at Old Orchard. Robbie drove her home the same day he came calling on them at the cottage. That left the small room at the big house vacant once more.

Amid the younger children's inquisitive looks and innocent questions about where she'd been for the past several days, Jess decided it was best that she move back to the farmhouse until it was time to return to London.

She assumed that Devlin would understand her reasons, but it was impossible to know for certain with the careful distance he set between them. It wasn't anger, she would had recognized that. It was something else—an acceptance, as if he had expected it of her all along.

That calm acceptance wounded her more deeply than anything he could have said or done, but it pleased Jillian enormously, who had returned a few days earlier from the neighboring farm. Now the girl went about the house with a smug expression on her face whenever Jess was about, and turned to open flirtation for Devlin.

393

"I don't care how old that girl is, I'm goin' to take her 'cross my knee and thrash the livin' daylights out of her," Moira announced one morning as she finished nursing the baby.

All of the other children were finally able to go outside, unleashing frustration, boredom, and stored-up energy from being housebound the last several days. Robbie promptly put them all to work, mucking out the stables and feeding the animals. School was to resume the following day. For the past hour the old farmhouse was blessedly silent.

"She's got a bee in her bonnet, and I won't tolerate it. Makes life miserable for everyone. Just because she's all moony-faced over Devlin. She's just a child, for heaven's sakes."

"A rather well-developed child, wouldn't you say," Jess pointed out with a small smile, as she took the baby and cradled him against her shoulder.

"It means nothin' to him, Jess. Dev has known her since she was four years old. But somethin' is botherin' him right enough."

Jess busied herself with the baby, walking with him across the kitchen to the windows where they stood in the feeble warmth of the sunlight that struggled through the gathering clouds, and trying to avoid the unspoken question behind Moira's observation.

"I'm not one to pry, Jess. I figure most of us have enough things in the past that are best left in the past and not for talkin' about. But Robbie told me how it was between you two that first day he went to the cottage when the storm broke. And it's plain enough to see something is real wrong between you now. I know him, and I know his feelins. You got inside, Jess, for the first time. Whatever it is, it can be fixed."

Jess closed her eyes as she pressed her face against the sweetness of the baby's neck, closing out the misery and uncertainty that she'd been fighting for days since she'd returned to the big house. She looked up then, silence filling the kitchen.

"I have to leave very soon." The words ached out of her throat. "Perhaps it's better this way. It's too complicated."

"Is it?" Moira demanded.

In the silence that gathered about them, she remembered something else Moira had said—sometimes it is simple—and pushed it back into the shadows of the memory of what she had shared with him at the cottage. The babe stirred against her shoulder, making soft gurgling sounds, followed by an impossibly loud burp.

"Well, at least the wee lad knows what he's about. And that's simple enough. I'm not certain you know what yer about, lass." She took the baby from Jess and laid him in a thickly cushioned basket on the table.

It was then that Mary Margaret burst through the door and wrapped her arms joyously about Jess's legs.

"Devlin says that people in London put trees in their parlors for Christmas. Is it true, Jess? Trees in the parlor? Do they grow there?"

She laughed, welcoming the child's innocent exuberance and joy that helped banish her uncertain emotions at Moira's questions. She knelt down before Mary and held her within the circle of her arms. How could she leave this place? This child who needed her? This family? But most of all, him?

She blinked back the tears that suddenly appeared and gave Mary Margaret a smile filled with all the love and joy she had discovered there.

"Yes, it's true."

"What sort of trees? Apple trees?"

"No, they would be much too large, and there would be apples all over the floor."

"It would be a mess," Mary concluded.

"A very big mess. Usually, it's an evergreen tree, and it makes the entire house smell woodsy and spicy."

"What sort of decorations do they put on them?"

"Oh, all sorts. There are soldiers and horses made of carved wood, some of cloth and yarn, small pieces of fruit, and cinnamon sticks all tied with ribbons. And there are glass ones shaped like bubbles and stars, and even some made from dough decorated with bits of candy." Mary Margaret's eyes were huge, as she imagined all the things Jess described.

"But the very prettiest decoration of all are the candles."

If it was at all possible, Mary's eyes grew rounder. "Real candles?" she asked with a squeak.

"Real ones. And on Christmas night, we light them. Then we sing the Michaelmas songs, and have delicious hot drinks."

"Hot cider," Mary piped up.

"Yes, of course, it would have to be hot cider," Jess agreed. "And then we sit down to a very special Christmas dinner, and afterward there are games and music, and mistletoe."

"What is mistletoe?" Mary asked, her small tongue twisting about this strange, new word.

"According to ancient custom, when a lad kisses a lassie under the mistletoe it means they shall marry."

They all looked up. Devlin stood just inside the opened doorway. For a moment his gaze fastened on Jess. Mary seemed oblivious that anything was amiss, as her eyes widened further.

"If I kiss Mick under the mistletoe, does that mean that we'll marry one day?"

"It doesn't work the same for children," Jillian announced as she came in immediately behind Devlin. She stopped beside him, looping her arm through his.

"Just for grown-up people," she clarified with a soft smile.

"Like Jess and Devlin?"

Jess glanced at him, then away. It seemed Mary was far more observant than any of them had suspected.

"Like me and Robbie," Moira informed her, sparing an answer from Jess. "He kissed me under the mistletoe and we got married."

Mary clapped her hands together with delight. For her, everything was so simple. "Then we must find some mistletoe, and a Michaelmas tree." She dove back across the kitchen and took Jess's hand.

"Jess and I will find just the right one," she announced.

"What is it you'll be findin' in this weather?" Robbie asked as he came in, his breath steamy on the frosted air.

"Mary has been findin' out all about Michaelmas trees and mistletoe," Moira informed him. "It seems you'll be out cuttin' down a tree once she finds the right one." That brought a groan.

"In this weather?"

"It will be wonderful," Mary declared, her eyes dancing with merriment and visions of candles, stars, and cookie decorations.

"And we can all help decorate it, and have a special dinner with hot cider, songs, and mistletoe."

Moira seized her opportunity. "We'll have a grand party on Christmas Eve night. But first we need a tree. Robbie, sharpen yer ax. You'll be needin' it as soon as Mary and Jess find the perfect tree."

Jess had never considered what went into finding the *perfect* tree. Always, before, for Christmas at Carrington Square, the footman purchased a tree from a man who went door-to-door, trees piled high in a horse-drawn cart.

Once the tree was set up in the formal parlor, she and her sister and the household staff spent the next several days making decorations, adding them to the ones that were kept from year to year and brought down from the attic.

Mary asked her to draw pictures of different trees, and then they set about finding the perfect one. They tramped about the woods at the edge of the farm when the weather allowed, trying to find just the right one.

Each tree was somehow flawed in Mary's opinion. They were either too short or too tall or lopsided with gaping holes between the branches. Jess tried to explain to Mary that it wasn't the tree, but the decorations that made it beautiful.

But, with a child's sort of unflagging determination, Mary was adamant that they would eventually find the perfect one that matched the pictures Jess had drawn.

"We'll find it, Jess. I know we will." Mary clutched at her hand, drawing her on a little further to the next shelter of trees they'd not yet explored. Snow, newly fallen from the night before, squeaked softly under their booted feet. "I promise we'll find it today. And it will be perfect. Just like the pictures."

Jess laughed. The child's joy was contagious. "And we'll have candles for every branch. Moira will help us make them. But we mustn't go too far. We should keep the farm in sight."

"Just a little further, Jess. I can see the trees now. I know our tree is there."

* * *

"Good day, Jillian."

Jillian turned abruptly, frowning slightly at the sight of the open cart on the road after the recent snow. She immediately recognized it as one of the carts old Hamish Potter sometimes rented out in Farway. It was the same one Freddie Simkins brought over from the village last summer when he came calling and took her for an evening ride. She recognized the driver as well, old Amory Stebbins.

"Good day, Mr. Stebbins. It's a mite cold to be out and about."

"Could say the same for you as well."

"I'm to Sarah's farm, for to takin' this basket of food as payment for her midwifin' to Moira."

"Ah, then there's a new wee one at Old Orchard farm," he guessed.

"A fine boy. Robbie and Moira are right proud, and both are fit as can be now."

There was an abrupt signal from his passenger. She didn't like him, in his fine worsted wool coat, matching gray gloves, and tall hat. He wasn't the usual sort that came callin' at Old Orchard, or any of the other farms about. She pulled the heavy woolen shawl more tightly about her. It was difficult to see anything of his features in the narrow slit between the hat brim and the heavy scarf.

"The gentleman just arrived from London," Mr. Stebbins informed her. "He's lookin' for that young woman, wot has been stayin' with Robbie and Moira."

Jillian was immediately more alert. "Jess Kelly?"

"That be her," Mr. Stebbins nodded. "Is she about?"

"Right enough," she answered hesitantly. It was then that the stranger leaned forward, the scarf pulling low over his face. It was a handsome face, and he looked every inch a gentleman.

"Do you know where I might find her?"

She hesitated again, a faint hope lighting up her eyes. "You down from London?" she asked.

"Yes, that's right."

Jess Kelly had come from London with Devlin. He had mentioned briefly that she would soon have to go back. Perhaps this man had come for her. That faint flicker of hope burned brighter.

"Come for her, have you?"

"That's right. Now if you would be so good as to tell me where I might find her?"

Jillian pointed back up the hill. "Old Orchard farm is where she's been stayin', but she's not there this mornin'." She thought she heard the slightest trace of irritation in the stranger's voice, muffled behind the neck scarf.

"Where is she this morning?"

She frowned slightly, but decided there was nothing wrong in telling him. The sooner Jess Kelly was gone, the sooner Jillian would have Devlin all to herself.

"She went to the woods beyond the farm. The road goes past the way over to Shoscombe Place." It seemed odd that he wanted to know precisely where she was. "She should be back soon enough. You can wait for her at the house."

"Thank you, my dear," he said in a clipped, educated voice. Jillian stepped back from the cart as he signaled for Mr. Stebbins to be on his way. Snow churned from beneath the wheels, and the cart slid sideways before straightening out behind the swift gait of the horse.

Jillian watched as the cart sped up the road toward Old Orchard. Then she turned in the opposite direction, toward the midwife's place.

The cart sped up the hill to the main house, and then past it along the road toward the woods.

Chapter Twenty-seven

Jess held back a low-hanging tree limb to let Mary pass by; then she followed.

They inspected one tree after another, yet none was quite right according to Mary's expectation. Jess was about to call her back. It was getting late, the sky had gone from dazzling blue to cold gray. Suddenly, Mary squealed with excitement.

"I found it, Jess. It's perfect!"

She had scooted on ahead with that boundless energy Jess had discovered that all children seemed to possess in abundant quantities. She could barely make out the red of her woolen scarf as she darted about, dancing from one foot to the other. The rest of her, dressed in the drab brown coat, blended in with the tree trunks and branches. The scarf was the beacon that Jess followed.

"What have you found?" she asked as she finally pushed into the small clearing.

"Look! Isn't it beautiful? It's the most perfect tree!" Mary clapped her hands together with unbridled joy. "I knew if we looked hard enough we would find it."

"You certainly have found it," Jess said, laughing and tilting her head back to gaze up the length of it, shaking her head in dismay, and wondering how they could possibly make it fit into Moira's small parlor.

"It's rather large," she said skeptically. "Do you think it will fit through the doorway?"

"Of course it will fit," Mary informed her with absolute conviction. "It must. It's *our* tree. Can't you see that it is, Jess?"

She realized, of course, that it was a dilemma of her own making. She had told stories about Christmases past at Carrington Square, not realizing how special it must all seem to a child like Mary who'd had so little joy in her life.

Jess scooped her up, burying her face in the sweet warmth of the child's neck.

"Of course, it's our tree. And it will fit very nicely. Robbie will see that it does."

"And Devlin."

"Yes, of course, and Devlin."

"Will you have a tree with Devlin at the cottage?"

It was the first anyone had mentioned of the time she had spent with him there, and it caught her slightly off balance for she had no idea how to answer the child. Yet, Mary asked it with such acceptance and innocence, as if it were the most natural thing in the world for Jess to be there with him.

"I think this tree is quite enough. It's a grand tree, and will take a great many ornaments. There wouldn't be enough for a second tree."

"Then we'll make more decorations." The solution was as easy as that for Mary. Jess wished it were that easy in reality, for Devlin had barely spoken to her since the day she'd moved back into her room at the farmhouse. And they had such little time left at Old Orchard. Before Christmas, before the Michaelmas tree would be decorated on Christmas Eve, she had to return to London.

She tried to push it from her thoughts. Moira and Robbie knew they must leave soon, but none of the children had been told. There was no point in telling them before it was time. As it was, she fretted over telling Mary. Each day it seemed the child became more attached to her.

From the first moment she had held Mary in her arms it had been impossible to keep an emotional distance from the child. No matter how unwise it was, she cared deeply for her. With each passing day she wondered how she would explain that she had to leave.

"She's stronger than you think," Moira had reassured her. "It will be difficult, but when the time comes, she'll be all right.

Would you withhold your love from her now, to make the parting that much easier for yourself?"

She had known the answer then as she knew it now. And as if to reassure both herself and Mary that everything really would be all right, she swung the child high and held her tight as they inspected the tree.

"How shall we know it from the others so that we can find it again when we bring Robbie to cut it down?" Mary asked with a child's pragmatism.

Jess looked about them, trying to memorize any unusual landmarks. There were mostly trees, and they all looked alike.

"We shall have to mark it," she announced.

"What shall we mark it with?"

"Something bright so that Robbie will see it easily among the other trees." Mary's eyes widened and her mouth formed a large O.

"I know! We can use my scarf. Then we'll surely be able to find it, and the birds won't eat it like they ate the bread crumbs in the story."

"You're very clever, Mary." The child squirmed out of her arms and ran to the tree. She busied herself unwinding the knitted wool scarf from about her neck and then secured it tightly about one of the branches so that it wouldn't get blown off in the wind.

"That should do very nicely," Jess announced, praising the child. But instead of that gap-toothed grin she had become so used to over the past weeks, Mary frowned as she looked past her.

"What is it?"

She turned around then, to see what it was that had brought about such a dramatic change in the child.

A man was standing several feet away, watching them.

He was dressed in a gray wool overcoat, with a gray hat, gloves, and a finely made matching gray scarf wrapped about the lower part of his face.

From that distance, with the fading light and the concealment of the scarf, it was impossible to see him clearly. But the fine cut of his clothes set him apart from the people who lived nearby or in the village of Farway. And she couldn't begin to imagine how he might have gotten there, unless he'd come by carriage or cart from the village.

He was a stranger, yet there was something vaguely familiar about his appearance, something that stirred in her memory.

"Jess?"

"It's all right, darling," she said automatically, not wanting to alarm the child, not even fully understanding why she felt it herself, except that she did—that vague sense of uneasiness at seeing someone out there so far from the farm, as if . . .

He started to walk toward them, his finely made boots making soft squeaking noises in the fresh snow, and Jess inexplicably felt an instinctive warning that sent fear tingling along her nerve endings.

The people of Farway and the surrounding farms and villages were friendly people, given to calling out a hearty greeting to people they met. She had grown accustomed to the warmth and open friendliness that was in such contrast to stiff, sometimes overbearing reserve and formality of manner in the people she knew in London.

There was no such friendliness in this man. Instead there was a silent menace that seemed to envelop him as he walked steadily toward them, his head bent forward, holding his coat about him as if he were very cold . . .

It was then that she remembered.

That night at Mitre Square! The man she'd encountered at the edge of the crowd.

He walked that same way, with the same angle of his shoulders, his head forward as if he didn't want anyone to see his face, and his coat clutched against him as if he were very cold or . . . concealed something!

They were subtleties no one else might have noticed, but she had noticed them that night with that rare attention to detail and gesture.

The man at Mitre Square had bumped into her. She remembered the stunning blow of his shoulder. She would have staggered off balance if not for the press of the crowd around them.

In fragments of seconds as he approached, she saw his eyes and knew it was the same man. Then, loosened by his exertions, the scarf dropped away from the lower part of his face.

"Mr. Devoe!" she said softly, her breath making a vaporous plume in the cold air.

"Miss Kelly."

He was standing no more than a half-dozen yards away. His gaze lowered briefly to Mary, and then returned.

"You were at Mitre Square that night."

He inclined his head slightly. "A chance encounter that has proven most unfortunate. I knew it was only a matter of time until you recalled it, as unerring as you are with details."

"I don't understand. . . ."

But suddenly she did understand. He was at Mitre Square, not arriving to aid in the investigation, but leaving.

"Oh, I think you do understand."

She drew in a sharp breath. The air was cold as it filled her lungs, and became the sudden coldness of a fear that spread.

"It was you . . . you killed Liz Stride and Catherine Eddowes!"

"If you would prefer to believe that, then by all means, Miss Kelly. Very shortly, it will no longer matter what you believe."

She moved ever so slightly, maneuvering Mary behind her. "What about Toby?" She asked with a sort of stunned curiosity. "Did you kill him as well?"

"Ah, yes, Toby Gill. He shouldn't have interfered. It would all have gone according to plan if he'd stayed out of it, and if you hadn't become involved, with those ridiculous sketches, and so determined to find your sister."

"And Belle Rossi? Was her death *necessary* as well?"

"Alas, an unfortunate accident. Certainly you must know, it was supposed to have been you, my dear. Then we would be done with all of this. But once again you eluded us."

Us? What was he talking about?

He had admitted killing Toby, but not Liz Stride or Catherine Eddowes. Was it possible that he wasn't acting alone?

There had been suspicions of police involvement from the beginning. God help her, for a time she had even suspected that Devlin might be part of it. But all along it had been Devoe, with his superciliousness and obsession for efficiency, delivering orders from the home office. And, of course, he had access to a great deal of information about the ongoing investigation of the murders, which kept him several steps ahead of the police at all times.

But if he didn't kill Liz Stride and Catherine Eddowes, then who did?

She carefully moved back a few steps. As she did, the angle of his head changed, like an animal catching a scent.

"Let the child go," she demanded. "She can't harm you or anyone else."

"I'm afraid that's impossible, my dear. She's seen my face She could identify me. You saw far less that night at Mitre Square, and yet you finally recognized me. I cannot take that risk again."

She was stalling for time. In her frantic thoughts she tried to guess how long she and Mary had been gone. It was growing dark. How long would it be before someone from the farm became concerned and looked for them?

She also realized the futility of it. They'd been gone longer than this before. It might be another half hour or more before anyone became alarmed, and in that length of time . . .

"Jessie!" She heard the alarm in Mary's small voice at her side and slightly behind her. Devoe was still several feet away.

"Don't be frightened, darling," she tried to reassure her, squeezing her shoulder gently. "Everything will be all right. I promise you."

If they had any hope at all of getting out of this alive, Jess knew that it was up to her to find it. It was then that she saw Devoe's left hand move down from the opening of his coat, and also saw the knife that glinted in his gloved hand.

Mary saw it, too. "Jessie!"

She whispered, keeping her gaze fastened on Devoe. "When I tell you, you must run, quick like a bunny, darling, and find Robbie."

"But, Jessie . . ." the small voice protested from behind her.

"Do as I say, Mary," she whispered vehemently. From the corner of her eye she saw Mary's head come up. She'd never spoken to her that harshly before.

It was then that Devoe lunged toward them. There was no time for kind words. She shoved Mary away from her with a hard push.

"Run, Mary!" she screamed. "Run!"

The child stumbled, fell, then scampered to her feet. She looked wild-eyed over her shoulder.

"Run!" Jess shouted after her.

It happened in fractions of seconds, less than a heartbeat, for she knew that the moment she moved, Devoe would be on her.

She had fallen to her knees as she turned and shoved Mary away from her. In brief flashes of thought, she realized that she was probably going to die. Oddly enough there was no fear, only a grim determination to save Mary.

She heard the child lunging wildly through the brush and low-hanging branches, heard the uneven lunging thud of heavy footsteps behind her as Devoe closed in on her. Too late, she tried to push to her feet, the skirt of her dress — wet from the clinging snow — weighting her down, making her movements clumsy and slow.

Devoe grabbed at the back of her coat.

She scrambled in the knee-deep snow to get away. Her right hand closed over a length of broken tree branch buried in the snow. She expected to feel that cold blade against her throat any second.

She clutched the branch in both hands and brought it up with all her strength just as Devoe whirled her around.

The blow smashed into the side of his head, staggering him backward. His hold was momentarily broken, the knife falling from his stunned fingers as his hands went to the torn flesh at his temple. He collapsed to his knees.

Jess had also fallen. She scrambled to her feet, gathered her skirts high about her knees, and ran, not daring to look back.

Devlin turned the team of lathered horses up the road to the farmhouse from the post road. They labored up a slight incline, their heavily muscled legs churning through the knee-deep snow. Steam rose from their thick coats and jetted out in frosty plumes as they dragged the wide platform that scraped the snow from the road, making it once more passable.

This was the last stretch of road to be cleared. It was rarely necessary, but the storms had been unusually cold this winter, the snows unusually deep.

The sun was low on the horizon. It was getting colder, time to return to the barns so that the older boys could rub down the horses while he cleaned and put away harness. Robbie would be finished bringing in more cut firewood from the south orchard.

The setting sun reminded him that time was short. In three days he and Jess had to return to London. Abberline had made all the arrangements for the gallery showing with Monsieur Gilot. Just the day before, the announcement was to have run in the *London Times* that the artist, Jess Kelly, who had been assisting the police in the investigation in the Whitechapel murders was none other than the reclusive, celebrated artist, J.B. Dumont.

That same article went on to announce the show at the Gilot gallery, at which the composite sketches by J.B. Dumont were to be made public for the first time, revealing the likeness of Jack the Ripper.

The closer it came, the more uneasy he was. He didn't want her to go back. But he could find no way to tell her, or to explain his feelings. Then she had moved back to the big house, and he rarely had a moment alone with her. He retreated to silence, waiting out the days, the fear inside him turning into a dark anger that lashed out at everyone, especially her.

Robbie usually scraped the road. But that morning, Devlin slammed out of the house before anyone was about. He'd been at it most of the day, clearing the road to the barn, the cottage, school, and then down to the post road, painfully aware that he wasn't as skillful as Robbie with a team of horses. Nevertheless he took a sort of furious and perverse satisfaction in the blisters that raised across his hands from the harness, and the ache of straining muscles across his shoulders as he guided the team back and forth on the road, aware that Robbie would've had it cleared in half the time.

He didn't want to be at the house. He didn't want to see Jess, and be forced to confront the fact that time was fast running out for them. Their time at the cottage was gone. Soon she would be gone from Old Orchard, returned to London. What then?

He snapped the harness over the horses' rumps as he turned them back to the barns. His gaze wandered out across the open fields, where sheep could usually be found grazing in the spring and summer. What remained of the herd, after the lambs had been sold, had been moved to the barn. The fields were now bare.

Then he looked toward the woods where Jess and Mary had gone earlier in the afternoon. Unwilling as he had been to watch them, he had been powerless not to as they set off to look for the Michaelmas tree. He had wanted to go with them. But he had held back. Just as he held back each evening when all the children were gathered about in the big house and begged her to tell stories of the Christmas celebrations she remembered.

Yet, like an enraptured child, he had listened, fascinated with a sort of profound, sad longing by the sound of her voice, and watched the joy on her face as she had told about shared Christmases with her sister and family. He had no such memories and like a starving beggar he had listened for hours, seeing the bright ornaments and decorations, as she described them down to the smallest detail. And as he watched and listened, he had been confronted with something even more profound — he had fallen in love with Jess Kelly.

Jess Kelly, not Jessamyn Forsythe, or J.B. Dumont, but the poignantly beautiful young woman who had fainted in his arms that day so long ago. She had lied to him, and kept her secrets. She represented everything he'd spent a lifetime hating. In spite of everything, he'd fallen in love with her, and he didn't know what the devil to do about it.

Now, in frustration he slapped the harness again, urging the tired team onward. Sensing they were returning to the barns, their ears pricked up and their pace quickened. It was then he saw it — what appeared to be an animal in the distance, lunging out at the edge of the woods and scampering across the field.

He frowned as he watched it, perplexed as it stumbled, then picked itself up and kept running, oddly clumsy for a fox. Then his gaze narrowed, and something inside him went cold with dread, as he realized it was no animal at all, but a child. Mary. And she was alone.

He shouted at the team, sending them churning down the road toward the main house then past, and further, past the barns. He dragged back on the heavy reins, the leather cutting into the blistered flesh at his palms. He flung himself from the seat of the cart and plunged across the open field.

She was soaking wet and sobbing hysterically when he reached her. He scooped her into his arms and held her against his chest, murmuring soothing words over and over to her.

"It's all right, Mary. I've got you lass. Nothin' can harm you."

His first shouts had been heard. Answering voices from the barn, orchard, and main house filled the crystal clear air. Moira was the first to reach them, her wet skirts wrapped about her legs, her breath coming in sharp, hard gasps.

"What is it?" Then she saw the child in his arms. "My God! Mary! What's happened?"

She reached for her with the natural instinct of a mother to comfort, and gathered the child against her breast, crooning softly to her in Gaelic. The words were unintelligible but the comfort they offered was unmistakable.

"What is it, darlin'?" she asked softly, stroking the child's head nestled at the curve of her neck. "What is it that's frightened you so badly? Tell, Moira." Over Mary's head, she looked desperately at Devlin for some answer.

"I saw her coming out of the woods like a frightened animal," he said in a soft whisper.

"The woods? She and Jess went there to look for the Michaelmas tree." She gently eased the child far enough away on her lap as she sat in the snow so that she could cradle her face.

"What happened, Mary?" she asked calmly but firmly. "You must tell us. Where's Jess?"

It seemed hopeless. The child was completely overwhelmed and hysterical. Her small shoulders convulsed with uncontrollable sobbing, and tears streamed down her cheeks. Her eyes were wide and filled with fear. Moira tried again but without success as others finally reached them, including Jillian from the main house, the older boys, and Robbie.

"Let me try again," Devlin urged. He took the child's small hands between his.

"It's very important, Mary. I know how you love Jessie. If something's happened I want to help her. But I can't do it unless you tell me where she is."

The breath shuddered out of her in small, sharp gasps. For the longest time, it seemed Mary was incapable of answering. Then she finally uttered a small word—"Man."

Moira looked at Devlin with confusion. "What man? What is she talking about. We saw no man. No one came to the house."

"There was a man," a small hesitant voice broke through their confused questions. Devlin looked over at Jillian. She twisted her hands together as she glanced uneasily from him to Moira, and then Robbie.

"What man?" Devlin demanded.

"There was a man on the road. He'd come from the village."

"What did he want?" Moira demanded, trying to keep the alarm from her voice so as not to further frighten Mary.

"He said he came from London to see her. He asked where he could find her."

"What did you tell him?"

Jillian slowly began to back away, sensing the horrible thing she'd done.

"I showed him where Jessie had taken Mary to look for the Michaelmas tree . . ." her voice trailed off. Her face was filled with the misery that spread through her.

"Oh, Jillian," Moira said heavily. "What have you done, girl?"

"I didn't know," the young girl protested. "I just thought he'd come to take her back to London." She gulped down a sob. "I just wanted her to go back to London so that she wouldn't be here no more." She burst into tears, burying her face in the hem of her apron.

Moira nodded to one of the older boys. "Take her back to the house, Simon." Then she looked helplessly at Devlin.

He felt no anger for what Jillian had done, only a smothering fear for Jess. He gently spoke to Mary again, trying to keep the urgency out of his voice.

"Mary, sweetheart. You have to help me find Jessie. If you help me, then I can help her." He gently stroked the child's hair, hating that he had to push at her like this, fearful of what this might do to her fragile hold on reality. "Please help me, darlin."

She looked up at him then, and the wildness of hysteria seemed to clear from her eyes.

"My scarf. The tree has my scarf."

At his questioning look, Moira explained, "She was wearing a bright red scarf when they left this morning. She must have lost it."

"Or left it behind." Devlin lunged to his feet. "I'm going after her."

"I'm coming with you," Robbie announced.

"No!" Devlin snarled at him. "Whoever it is, he's killed before. Get back to the house and keep everyone inside. Send one of the boys for the constable at Farway."

"Take this," Robbie thrust a small wood ax into his hands. Devlin turned and set off across the field toward the woods.

Jess lunged through the thick cover of trees. She could hear Devoe's labored breathing, the furious curses, the frantic lunges through heavy low-hanging branches. As much as the thick tree cover hindered her, she knew it also slowed him down. It was her only hope of escape.

Snow filled her boots and weighted them down on her feet. She plunged on, trying to guess which direction would lead her toward Old Orchard, disoriented by the fading light without the sun.

She'd lost one of her gloves. Her fingers were raw and bleeding from pushing her way through gnarly pine branches. She quickly dropped the hem of her skirt needing both her hands to hold back more boughs and limbs. Those same branches and the heavy snow, snagged at her clothing and dragged her down, hampering her escape. And always behind her she heard him following.

He was stronger, better able to move through the snow in pants and tall boots. She refused to accept it, crashing through the trees as the edge of hysteria clawed its way into her brain.

He'd killed Toby, and then he'd killed Belle Rossi. It was supposed to have been her. It would be her if she stopped, and so she

411

forced herself onward, half running, stumbling, falling, and then scrambling back to her feet.

Then, abruptly she stumbled from the cover of trees and partially tumbled down a small knoll. She crawled to her knees, gasping for air. Then she saw the cart, the driver sitting in the seat. She pushed to her feet and ran toward it.

She collapsed against the side of the small hack, her lungs aching, the cold dry in her throat.

"You have to help me. Please! There's a man . . ." When he didn't immediately answer or acknowledge, she jerked at his sleeve. He tumbled from the seat of the cart and fell to the snow at her feet. He stared up at her with wide, lifeless eyes. There were ghastly bruises about his neck, and his coat lay open, revealing gaping slash wounds.

She screamed, terror filling her frozen lungs. There was blood on her hands, blood everywhere. And then she felt those brutal hands closing about her throat. The pain jolted through her. She tried to scream again as she was jerked around, and discovered that it was impossible as his gloved fingers cut into her throat. Then darkness swirled about her, closing out the terror, leaving just one thought . . . Devlin.

He forced himself to think logically. Frightened as she was, Mary wouldn't have run about trying to be clever about eluding the man who had gone after her and Jess.

With a child's simplistic way of things she would have taken the most direct path out of the woods, and she knew them well. Therefore it made sense that the best way to find out where she had separated from Jess was to enter the woods where he had seen her come out.

He found the location where he had first seen Mary. Her trail was easy enough to follow, the marks frantic and frenzied in the new snow.

She had said that the tree had her scarf. He quickly found it, securely tied about a huge tree that had undoubtedly been chosen for the Michaelmas tree. Then he found the marks in the snow nearby were there had obviously been a struggle, crimson droplets of fresh blood stark on the snow, and the bloodied piece of wood.

He'd never known a fear so terrifying—that he might already be too late . . . that she might already be dead.

It was then he heard her scream.

He ran through the stand of trees, following that horrifying sound. Jillian had said the man came to Old Orchard in a cart. The post road bordered the far side of the woods.

He lunged and half fell through the tree line. He saw the cart and horse and a body sprawled on the ground amid a spreading stain of blood. Then he saw Sinjin Devoe bending over Jess. He plunged toward them, throwing his weight against Devoe, catching him at the back of his legs. They rolled together in the soft drifts of snow.

Both struggled to their feet, stumbling and falling over uneven footing concealed beneath the white blanket. From the corner of his eye, Devlin was aware that Jess hadn't moved. Filled with an animal rage, he went after Devoe.

They fell again, clawed and fought each other, Devoe's heavy coat whipping about them. Burke plowed his fist into Devoe's body several times, the blows landing dully against the thick padding of several layers of clothes. Devoe's gloved fist came up and caught him at the jaw, staggering him back. Devoe lunged away, then whirled back, gasping for breath. The steel blade of a knife gleamed in his hand.

Dozens of questions raced through Devlin's thoughts, beginning with—Why?

There would be time for it later, for he had no intention of allowing Devoe to escape. This was a dangerous game, but one that Devlin understood. He'd been raised on the streets where a man would just as soon cut you to pieces as look at you, and he'd learned to survive there by the same rules.

"Put down the knife, Devoe. It ends here."

Devoe slowly shook his head. "No, Inspector. I can't do that. There's too much at stake."

Slowly, Devlin circled him, trying to draw Devoe around where his footing would be less sure. It was then Devoe lunged at him.

They came together, muscles straining, Devlin's hand clamped around his wrist as Devoe struggled to turn the knife toward him. The blade quivered between them. Their labored breathing created a single blast of steam in the chilled air as they leveraged their bodies against one another. Their boots dug into the snow, scrabbled frantically for a better foothold, and then held.

Devlin Burke had often looked death in the face. He saw it now, as that blade slowly quivered closer to his throat. His muscles ached and strained as he held fast, refusing to weaken, knowing that it meant death if he did.

His foothold gave way, he shifted, going down on one knee. In the space of a heartbeat, the angle of the knife altered. Devoe countered a fraction of a second too slowly. Devlin brought the knife up hard under Devoe's ribs.

For a moment neither of them moved. Devoe stared at him with wide-eyed disbelief. Then the air scraped out of his paralyzed lungs, and he rolled away, dead.

Devlin collapsed on his hands and knees. Then his head came up, and he looked across at Jess. She wasn't moving. Like a half-crazed animal, he lunged through the snow to her, falling, stumbling, going down on his knees, then lunging back to his feet. He fell to the snow beside her and quickly turned her over.

Her pale eyelids were tinged with purple as were her lips, and there were horrible bruises at her throat. Her head hung limp against his shoulder. She wasn't breathing. He shook her violently. She was like a broken, lifeless doll.

"I won't let you die! Damn you! You can't die!" he screamed hoarsely, but there was still no response. His expression was contorted by disbelief and the beginnings of grief. He shook her again. Then pulled her to him, clasping her against his chest, as if he could hold on to her life and hold back death.

Tormented and sobbing, he threw back his head and screamed her name into the gathering darkness.

"Jessie!"

Chapter Twenty-eight

He sat there, rocking back and forth, as if she were a small child that he was trying to comfort. His head was buried in her hair that had fallen about her shoulders, her body was cradled across his lap. He tried to warm her, rubbing her hands and her arms through the wet fabric of her clothes. And then he just rocked and rocked, too numbed to think, or feel, except for her slender body held tight against his.

It was a small shuddering sound, part gasp, part sigh, as the air escaped. Then her lips moved against his cheek, like the brush of butterfly wings, so fragile and faint that his frozen skin didn't feel it. Her lashes slowly fluttered open. She tried to whisper something, then swallowed painfully. The only sound that came out was a soft whisper.

At the sound of his name, his head came up. His hand shook as he brushed his fingers against her cold cheek. The expression on his face was tortured, his eyes gone black with grief.

"Aye, lass. I'm here." Then he laid his forehead against hers. "You're safe."

"Devoe?" Her voice failed, coming out in a ragged, painful gasp.

"He'll not hurt you again. He won't ever hurt anyone again."

"Is he . . ."

"Shhhh, lass," he quieted her. "He's dead."

It seemed the last bit of strength—that instinct to fight off Devoe on first rousing—drained from her. She was small and fragile in his arms. The frightening pallor of her skin was gone as she

415

breathed evenly once more. Her fingers clasped the front of his shirt.

"I'm glad he's dead," she whispered from pale lips.

He slipped one arm beneath her legs, tucking her against him to keep her warm.

He refused to put her in the cart. It was covered with the driver's blood, and he'd left the team of Robbie's horses far behind. Instead he turned and carried her.

There was the sound of muffled hooves on the snow-covered road. Robbie jerked hard on the reins, slowing the frantic horses, the cart skidding a stop. He leapt down.

"My, God! What happened?"

His friend said nothing, but continued walking as if he hadn't heard. Robbie shouted at him but still there was no response. He went after him.

Robbie laid a hand on his shoulder. He instinctively jerked back as Devlin turned. The expression on his friend's face was stark, his features cold as death.

He looked down at Jess and noticed the shallow rise and fall of her breathing. He also noticed the band of bruises at her throat. She was alive, but deathly cold.

"Let me take her, Dev," he said gently, his hand on his friend's arm. For long moments Devlin just stared at him, the look behind his eyes void of any comprehension.

"She's as dear to me as my own. I'll not harm her, lad."

Slowly there was a shift in that cold expression, a faint recognition. Devlin looked down at her, held tight against his damp coat. Finally he looked up at his friend. His voice agonized.

"She's so cold."

"Aye, my friend. I've a thick blanket in the cart. Let me take her now," he said again. Devlin slowly nodded. Carefully, as if she were a newborn babe, he allowed Robbie to take her.

When they were all in the cart, Robbie turned the team and whipped them into a frantic pace that churned the snow in the road.

He reined the team in at the yard before the main house. The door opened immediately and Moira came out.

416

"Dear God! Is she . . . ?"

"She's alive," Robbie answered tersely as he swung down from the cart. Burke was already out of the cart, carrying her, the thick blanket wrapped about her.

Moira quickly called out instructions to the older children. A path was made to the stairway, and Devlin carried Jess upstairs. At the top of the stairs, Moira directed him to her own bedroom.

She asked for a basin of warm water from the kitchen, fresh towels, and more blankets, instructing a somber-faced Jillian to tend the younger children.

Devlin stood, hollow-eyed, at the foot of the bed while Moira bustled about the room with amazing ease for a women who had given birth less than two weeks earlier. She laid a hand on his arm.

"Come away, darlin', and let me do what must be done for her."

He shook his head. "I brought her to this."

Blood stained his shirt, but she knew from what Robbie had hastily whispered downstairs that it wasn't his. Whoever the man was who'd gone after Jess, he was dead.

She'd known Devlin Burke since they were children. She owed her life to him many times over, including that of her newborn son. It wasn't likely that she would ever question his reasons for anything, not even killing a man. But now she realized he needed help as much as the young woman lying in her bed did.

She gentled her voice. "She's a rare, fine lass, with a strong spirit. I don't s'pose there's anyone who can force her to do much of anythin' once she has her mind made up about somethin'. Not even you, Devlin Burke." He looked at her then, and she smiled with compassion.

"It's the same as with Mary Margaret when everyone else gave up on the child. And it's like the night you and she brought little Jesse into the world. When she wants somethin', she keeps at it, until she gets it." Her heart started to break at the tears that she saw in his eyes. But she went on, saying what needed to be said.

"She has a rare strength, a fierceness in her that won't ever let her give up. Not with Mary, not with me, and not now."

His gaze bore into hers, as if he needed very much to believe her. She patted his arm.

"Now go, and let me do for her. You look as if you could use some hot tea." She laughed softly. "Your own special blend, of course. There's a fine bottle in the cupboard by the stove. Now, go. And then you and Robbie can tend to matters with the local constable."

Moira could feel the eyes that watched her as she carefully pulled off Jess's wet clothes. Then he was gone.

She checked for broken bones. There were none, but it hardly made the severity of the attack any less frightening. Horrible bruises spread around her throat, shoulders, and across one cheekbone where she had obviously been struck. In addition there were bruises on her arms, and scratches on her legs and ankles where she had probably scraped herself on brush.

She dropped the clothes into a wet pile on the floor, and looked up. A pair of eyes watched her intently from the doorway.

Mary Margaret was pale, frightened, and silent, her bottom lip sucked into her mouth. Her eyes were stark and haunted, with an expression that had disappeared in the past few weeks, but had now returned. Jillian stood behind her just outside the doorway, as if uncertain whether she dare go in. Her face was drawn, her shoulders slumped, and when Moira looked at her, her gaze shriveled away. Moira held out a hand to Mary.

"Come along, child. See for yourself. Our Jessie is alive and well, if a bit bruised. She'll be right as rain in a few days."

Mary hesitated, then finally tiptoed into the room. Hesitantly she went to stand beside Moira, her somber gaze fastened on the young woman in the bed.

"Give me your hand," Moira said softly. When Mary hesitated, she gently took the girl's hand and wrapped the small fingers about Jess's hand where it lay on the coverlet.

"There now, you see? She's just a mite cool from bein' out in the snow, and she needs rest. You must stay and keep her warm. Hold on to her hand and give her your warmth, lass."

Mary looked up hesitantly, as if uncertain whether to hold on or turn and run. No words were exchanged. None would come,

418

and Moira could only weep inside for the pain the little girl must feel at seeing her special friend so badly bruised.

"Will you stay and watch over her, while I go downstairs to fetch some hot broth?" Mary looked up at her with large eyes.

Moira smiled. "I know she's in good hands. And when I return, you can help me give her the broth."

At the door, Jillian backed away, her hands twisting into hard knots.

"Please let me help," she said with a soft catch in her voice. "There must be something I can do."

Moira looked at her sharply. Then her gaze softened and she slowly shook her head. The girl was plainly suffering for what she'd done. At times like this, Moira knew a troubled conscience was the worst possible punishment.

"You can help by keepin' the smaller children cared for while I take care of matters up here, and bring me little Jesse when he starts frettin' to be fed."

Jillian nodded, her expression stricken, eyes downcast. "I never thought . . ."

"No, I don't suppose you did," Moira said softly. Jillian's gaze came up and met hers.

"I want to make up for what I did."

"It's not that easily done," Moira informed her. "It has to come in small ways, honest ways, straight from the heart. But for right now Mary Margaret has a need greater than yours. So let it be for now. Think on what you've done. Learn from it. That is the best way to make up for what you've done."

Jillian nodded somberly. "I'll take care of everything for the evenin' meal, and see that the children get to bed." Moira nodded and then went downstairs for the hot broth.

Jess slowly came awake.

The room was filled with vague shadows, and unfamiliar shapes, outlined by the soft glow of the bedside lantern.

It wasn't the small room she had occupied the past few days, nor the cottage bedroom she had shared with Devlin. Yet there was a familiarity that struggled out of sleep to register briefly in her sluggish brain—this was Moira and Robbie's bedroom.

She turned her head and winced at the pain that simple effort brought. And with the pain came a flood of memory: Mary and the Michaelmas tree, the snow in the forest, and Sinjin Devoe. Then the frightening truth that he had killed Toby and Belle Rossi, and had come to kill her.

She cried out, except that there was no sound.

It seemed she could still feel those brutal hands about her throat, choking, squeezing so that she couldn't breathe. . . .

"Jessie! It's all right, lass. You're safe."

Strong hands took hold of her, and then she was pulled into warm arms and held, one of those hands stroking back her hair. "I've got you. No one is goin' to harm you."

That voice eventually broke through the terror, and she clung to him.

Devlin held her gently against himself, mindful not to hurt her. There was no fever, her skin was cool to the touch.

Finally he reached over and turned up the lamp beside the bed. The soft glow of light played across her features, and his heart twisted. There was a purplish-black band of marks about her throat, bruises the size of a man's fingers, and he felt the rage all over again.

"Is it that bad?" she whispered with a faint smile, the terror gone from her eyes now. Her hand came up and she tenderly touched her fingers to her bruised cheek, and then her throat. She winced at the touch. His fingers closed with tender warmth over hers and drew them away.

"It will all be gone in a few days." When she tried to see around him to the small mirror that usually sat atop the chest of drawers, he gently restrained her.

"Moira removed it." Her gaze came back to his.

"I must look dreadful." Her hand trembled as she brought it up to shield her bruised cheek from him. He gently caught her hand. Then he turned it and brushed his lips against the bend of her wrist.

"You're beautiful," he said in a voice as quiet as the night that

420

surrounded them. He turned his head without lifting it. His mouth was very near hers. He tenderly kissed her.

He lifted his head then and looked at her. There was a question in her eyes.

"Devoe?" she asked, remembering little of what had happened.

"It's over, Jess."

She nodded, without asking anything more. Then she moved about in the bed, her foot brushing against the soft, warm mound of a body at the foot of the bed. She looked questioningly at Burke.

He gently pushed back the end of the coverlet, revealing Mary Margaret curled up in the covers.

"She hasn't left the room since I brought you here." Then he added gently, "And she hasn't spoken."

Even though her bruised body protested painfully, Jess gathered the small, exhausted child into her arms. Mary didn't waken, but some of the tension seemed to ease out of her small body as Jess held her close.

When Moira came up a short while later, she found all three of them on the bed, Devlin's arms wrapped about Jess, the child snuggled between them.

Two days later, Jess insisted on going downstairs over his protests.

"I won't be an invalid, and I won't have Moira and Robbie turned out of their bedroom another night," she told him vehemently, with some fierceness of temper.

She had been working on the composite sketches during her recovery, trying to make some sense of Devoe's involvement. She had made new sketches and then changed them again, for time was short. The gallery show was only a few days away.

Devlin finally compromised, agreeing to take her downstairs later that evening, if she allowed him to carry her—she was still weak and unsteady on her feet. She protested vehemently, but since it appeared she would accomplish it no other way, she finally agreed.

She dressed in a warm woolen dress she had bought at the fair. It was simply made, and the handwork was among the finest she had ever seen. It fit her well, although the rounded neckline did little to cover the vivid bruises at her throat.

For the first time in two days, Mary Margaret had left the room, and was nowhere to be seen when Devlin finally arrived to take Jess downstairs.

She had straightened up the room and made the bed, and quickly stood when he came through the door.

"I see you've been up and about already this afternoon."

She smiled. "I couldn't bear another moment in that bed."

"Well, you'll have to bear being carried downstairs and that's the way of it."

"Devlin . . ." she started to protest only to be cut off as he brought his hand up.

"Carried proper, or over my shoulder, that's the choice."

"I see. Very well, if that's the only way it can be done then I suppose I shall have to accept."

"Knew you'd see it my way."

"You did? Well, don't be so smug about it. I'm a desperate woman." She flashed him a smile that made him ache inside.

"By the way, where is Mary this morning? She's been like a shadow the past two days."

He was rather vague. "I saw her downstairs earlier. Most likely she'll be about soon enough. Supper is ready, and you know how Moira likes everyone to be on time." He carefully lifted her. Her arm went round his neck.

"I won't break," she informed him, with a tiny glint of the devil in her eyes. The lines about his mouth suddenly deepened.

"I feared it, Jess," his voice had gone thick. "When I went into the woods lookin' for you, I didn't know what I would find . . . if I would be in time . . ." She stopped him with her fingers against his lips.

"You found me."

"Aye," he said.

Wonderful, delicious aromas filled the house. On the way downstairs, Jess discovered that she was ravenous after two days' confinement with a steady but meager fare of broth, broth, and more broth.

"Everything smells wonderful," she said, craning her neck, eager as a child as he carried her downstairs. "Please put me down." She squirmed like a child as well. "I can walk the rest of the way."

"I have my orders," he informed her with mock severity.

"Yes, Inspector." They finally reached the last step.

With so many children, meals at Old Orchard, she had learned, were a noisy raucous affair. But supper was especially so.

Contrary to meals at her home in Carrington Square where everyone observed the rules of society, which called for quiet, polite conversation, the evening meal at the farm was punctuated with excited chatter as everyone joined in conversation about the way they'd spent their day, the lessons learned at the school, something new learned in apprentice studies, new additions to the farm stock, amid the usual petty squabbles that were bound to break out.

It was a loud, noisy affair that she savored, sitting back, letting the artist in her observe all the animated expressions and gestures of twenty-seven people all in motion at once. Overall was a warmth and a sense of love and safety that wrapped around each child.

It made her think of her sister, aching for the closeness they had shared their entire lives, and somehow lost when Linnie had married.

Seeing this family, sharing and being part of them the past few weeks, made her relationship with her own family all the more poignant for its lack of emotion.

There had once been that same special closeness with her mother, father, and Linnie. But all that had changed when her mother died. Grief made her father remote. The special closeness they had shared was changed. It seemed he no longer wanted to be part of their family. Out of necessity she and Linnie had become their own special family—with Mary, their pretend friend.

They trusted and relied on one another. Linnie had always

been her best, special friend as well as her sister. When Linnie married, they had promised one another that nothing would change. But everything had changed.

She saw Linnie only occasionally after that, usually at some society function, infrequently when they met for luncheon or at the gallery. And then, three months ago, her sister had disappeared.

As she watched this extended family of odd-assorted children at their meals, most of whom had no blood bond between them, but they were bound by a stronger bond of love, she felt that aching sense of loss for her sister all the more strongly.

But now as they arrived downstairs the kitchen was strangely empty except for pots which bubbled enticingly from the top of the stove.

"I thought you said everyone was waiting for us."

"Moira said something about the parlor."

"The parlor?"

She thought it an odd suggestion since the adjacent room which was designated the parlor, for lack of something more appropriate to call it, was quite small and hardly had room to accommodate that many people for supper.

Refusing to release her, Devlin swung through the warm, inviting kitchen and carried her into the parlor.

It was dark except for the glow of fire at the stone hearth, and like the rest of the house unusually quiet for so many children about.

Then there was the sound of several matches being struck, and the sudden flare of an equal number of flames, as several oil lamps were lit. The room glowed to life, amid the wild chorus, of all those children shouting at once, "Surprise! Happy Christmas!"

He finally set her to her feet. She stared in amazement at the roomful of people, the gaily decorated walls, and the huge evergreen tree that filled one corner, hiding various sized children who popped out of the branches like animated ornaments.

It was the Michaelmas tree Mary had picked out that day in the woods. She recognized the red knitted scarf that was still tied about a low branch. Mary came running forward and flung her arms about Jess's legs, hugging her tightly through the folds of skirt.

Since that day in the woods, Mary hadn't spoken. It was as if the terror of that day had plunged her back into her safe, silent world once more. But she had been Jess's constant companion, even sleeping with her at night, curled at the foot of the bed. Now, she gazed up at Jess with adoring, uncertain eyes.

Jess knelt and gathered Mary into her arms, holding her tight, breathing in the child's sweet innocence. She felt the trembling that went through the small body.

"Mary, it's your tree," she exclaimed happily, trying to give the child some of her joy. "You found it again."

At Mary's brisk nod, she asked, "Was it your idea to do this?" Again there was a quick nod, and a brief flash of uncertain smile.

"What a wonderful surprise. It's the most beautiful tree I've ever seen."

"It's the biggest tree I've ever seen," Moira said laughingly as she navigated her way through a sea of children. "Aye, it was Mary's idea. She kept at us until we went with her into the woods. Robbie and Devlin cut it down this morning and dragged it back with the team."

Jess lifted the child in her arms, carrying her with her to inspect the tree closer. "It's a grand tree, just perfect. Don't you think, Mary?" she asked trying to draw some sort of response from her, but again there was only a nod of the head.

Devlin stood beside them, looking at the tree with less than admiration, but with a more critical eye after having battled to get it through a somewhat unaccommodating doorway.

"She would have no other," he explained. "Since you and she found the tree, she insisted it had to be this one."

Robbie nodded over a cup of steaming amber liquid, that hardly looked like tea. "Since the two of you must leave for London in the mornin', she wanted to have the Michaelmas celebration tonight, even though Christmas is still several days away."

"She told you this?" Jess asked excitedly.

Moira stood with them, tucking her arm through Robbie's.

425

"She told us with her pictures. She painted the tree in the woods, then bedeviled all of us till we understood what it was that she wanted."

Jess squeezed Mary lovingly. "I should like to see your picture."

"There will be plenty of time for that," Moira said. "But first we'll have our Christmas supper, and then we shall decorate the tree, just like you told us." She quickly rounded up a half dozen children, boys and girls of various ages and herded them to the kitchen amid grumbling protests from the older boys about kitchen work not being proper work for men.

"Makes no difference to me whether you wear pants or skirts, m'dears," Moira told them. "As long as you have strong backs and quick hands. Besides, anyone who eats in this house, helps with the work, and that goes for the kitchen as well." There were more grumbles although not quite as loud as before.

"Keep it up boys, and you'll have yer hands in a bucket of dish water scrubbin' plates as well." Any further grumbling promptly ended.

Supper was a marvelous feast of roast goose with stuffing, ham, salmon, spiced apples, steamed garden vegetables, and potatoes with cream sauce, and for dessert, a traditional plum pudding, decorated with bits of holly and candy. Afterward, everyone helped clear and clean dishes so that they could return to the parlor to decorate the Michaelmas tree.

Once again Jess discovered a wonderful surprise.

Ever since she had told the children stories about the trees decorated at Carrington Square, they had busily been making decorations for their own tree.

There were small hand-carved rocking horses, with leather harnesses, tiny angels with yarn hair and satin dresses, garlands of colorful dried berries all strung together, woven satin ribbons, small cloth balls filled with pungent spices, sticks of cinnamon tied with bright red ribbons, a cutout garland of paper dolls joined at the hands, and eggshells that had been hollowed out and painted to make dozens of small candle-holders to be tied at the tips of the branches.

The children swarmed over the tree, like bees at a hive, darting about, placing their decorations on the tree. The larger children helped the smaller ones, holding them aloft to reach the higher boughs.

Jess chose to sit back and watch them. They needed no help from her, but relied on the stories she'd told, and their vivid imaginations.

Devlin brought her a cup of tea. She took a sip and looked up at him at her first taste of the particularly strong brew.

"The doctor said it wouldn't harm you."

"Which doctor is that? Dr. Callahan?"

"Aye," he said with smile. "A fine old family remedy. It'll soothe sore muscles."

"It is a beautiful Christmas tree, isn't it?"

"That it is, Jess. The children wanted you to have this before you left. They made everything themselves, even the candles. They gave Moira fits tryin' to make them small enough to put in those eggshells."

"It's the most beautiful tree I've ever seen," she said softly. She watched as the older children carefully set candles in each eggshell by first dripping melted wax from another candle into the base of the shell. Then they pressed a candle into the molten wax. As it dried, the candle held in place without danger of falling over.

They were finally finished, and the tree sat in radiant splendor like a grand lady all dressed in her finest gown and jewels.

Mick came over and handed Jess one last candle that was left over. His gaze angled away from hers and he seemed to be having great difficulty with something he wanted very much to say.

"This is to light the other candles with," he said, twisting his mouth around. "But yer not supposed to light 'em till Christmas night according to the story you told us. Ain't that right?"

"Yes, that's right."

"Well, seein' as how yer gettin' fixed to go back to London tomorrow, we wanted yer to take this candle with you. On accounta, then you'll have to come back to light the candles on the Michaelmas tree." He pushed the candle into her hand, then ran back to join the other children. Even Mary had finally joined them, watching quietly, occasionally darting a quick glance back at Jess to make certain she was still there.

Days earlier Abberline had sent word that all was in readiness for the gallery show. He had made the appropriate arrangements with Monsieur Gilot and publicized the event through Jimmy Cassidy at the *London Times*.

"You don't have to go back," Devlin said in a quiet voice. "Stay here where it's safe."

She looked down at the candle in her hand. She found that she had never wanted anything more.

"There's no need for it. Abberline and I will find whoever was involved with Devoe."

Devoe had been the element that didn't fit. They had spoken of it over the last two days, trying to find some logic to it.

Devoe had been desperate to stop her by any means, even murder. When he found Jess in the woods he had spoken of "us."

"I can't let you interfere with us."

They had to assume that someone else was involved—someone who might also know there was another woman in Annie Chapman's flat the night she died.

"How will you find him?" she asked.

"The same way we've been going about it all along. Please stay. It's too dangerous for you to go back to London."

As dangerous as it was for her sister?

She was convinced that Linnie had seen something the night Annie Chapman died and had fled for her life. If she had any hope of finding her sister, she had to go back.

She looked down at the candle once more, thinking of everything that it represented. Then her gaze found Mary in the crowd of children. Moira was standing beside her, gently stroking her hair as she cradled her newborn son. Robbie stood with them, a pipe clenched between his teeth, his head encircled by a plume of fragrant tobacco smoke.

Again she was filled with terrible conflict. In the space of a few short weeks these people had come to mean so much to her—more than she could ever have imagined. And she heard the

428

pleading in Devlin Burke's voice, as much as he might ever offer of his feelings.

"I have to go back," she said in a quiet voice, hardly audible amid the uproar of excitement. But he had heard. Her gaze met his then. "Please try to understand. It may be my last chance to find my sister."

"By offerin' yerself up to this murderin' animal?" His voice rose in anger.

She looked at him, wanting him to understand, needing him to understand. Surely he, more than anyone, with everything he'd been through in his own life, could understand how important this was. She would never forgive herself, or him, if she didn't return to London. And yet, it seemed, he didn't want to understand.

"Yes, even that," she said adamantly.

He rose abruptly, his body rigid with the anger that he struggled to control. But his face was deeply etched with it, the lines hard about his mouth.

"Then there's nothin' more to be said," he replied coldly. Just before he walked away to the other side of the room, he said, "We leave in the mornin'."

In that small parlor crowded with people, dozens of conversations, a warm fire at the hearth, and the glowing Michaelmas tree, she had never felt so alone.

"It's hard for him." She looked up as Moira joined her.

"He doesn't understand."

"Or perhaps he understands too well?" Moira suggested.

"No," Jess said. "He doesn't know what it is to . . ."

"To lose somethin' that you love fiercely?" Moira asked.

Jess looked away, remembering the stories of Megan. Her gaze came back to Moira then. "It's all the more reason why he *should* understand this."

"Understandin' with yer heart is not the same as understandin' somethin' with yer head."

It was then that Mary and Mick ran across the room. Mary seized Jess's hand and pulled her from the chair.

"You must come, Jess, and see our Michaelmas gift for

429

you," Mick announced, and the others joined in.

She knew it would be hopeless to refuse. She smiled. "Where is it I must come to see it?"

"First you must be blindfolded," one of the older boys informed her.

Remembering her previous experience at being blindfolded, Jess was hesitant.

"There are no barrels of water, are there?" she asked with a suspicious smile. Then she saw Devlin leaning against the doorway to the kitchen, standing apart from the celebration, watching her. Their gazes met briefly.

His expression was as hard and closed as it had been the day he discovered that she was Jessamyn Forsythe—not Jess Kelly—their worlds separated by circumstance of birth and by the bitterness of a lifetime.

He had looked away then, and left the room, as if he couldn't bear to even look at her.

"We promise not to push you into a water barrel," one of the other girls solemnly vowed, digging an elbow hard into Jillian's ribs as she stood beside her.

"All right then," Jess said. "Let's go see the Michaelmas gift."

The older boy, Andrew, stepped forward with Mary's red woolen scarf and tied it about her head. Then a coat was wrapped about her shoulders and she was led from the house blindfolded.

It was clear and cold outside, hardly the night for a walk. Then she heard the faint welcoming nicker of one of the horses. She was guided down the slate path to the gate, then passed along by several hands. Her hand brushed the side of the cart.

She was immediately swung up in strong, familiar arms, and lifted atop the wagon, amid cries that she mustn't remove the blindfold. She knew it was Devlin who settled her atop the wagon, with as much care as if she were a child. Then there was a scrambling of bodies aboard the wagon as the smaller children climbed in back.

Then he released her, and with the blindfold that prevented her from seeing him, she felt an even greater sense of abandonment. She wanted to reach out, physically hold on and end the distance that he'd put between them. But he was gone, and then the wagon was lumbering down the road, taking them to her special gift.

The distance they traveled wasn't far from the main house. She guessed that they were at the school. Robbie lifted her down, she smelled the sweet pipe smoke about him. And then she was being rushed down the slate walk and into the school.

There was a sliver of light and then the blindfold was removed to another chorus of, "Surprise."

She blinked, her eyes slowly adjusting to the flood of light from several lanterns that glowed off the walls of the classroom, revealing panels of dozens of paintings.

There were large ones, small ones, all in a vivid array of oil colors, each portraying a scene she'd shared with the children over the past weeks.

There were pictures of sheep in the fields, the barn, the older boys milking the cows and goats, the apple orchards rolling across the hills, the dogs, Ralph and Lucy, the big house, the millpond, the village fair at Farway. And in all the pictures, were the children, Moira, Robbie, the new baby, Mick, Jillian, Devlin Burke, and herself with her face dunked in the barrel of apples.

Some were detailed with exceptional skill, and showed promising talent. Others were almost caricatures of people, showing humor. Others were no more than stick people picking apples from trees.

It was a beautiful, priceless collage of images of the days and weeks she had lived with them, like a memory of the time they'd shared.

"They're beautiful . . ." she said with tears in her voice. "The most beautiful paintings I've ever seen. And the most wondrous gift anyone could give me." She turned, looking at every face that went with the pictures, memorizing them as well.

"Thank you, from the bottom of my heart." Then there was a tugging at her hand. She looked down at Mary Margaret, who stood silently, with a painting held in her hand. She knelt beside the child.

"What have you got, my darling?"

Mary opened the picture and held it for her to see. It was a painting of the Michalemas tree, decorated with all the wonderful ornaments they had all made for it. She gathered the fragile child close and hugged her hard.

"Thank you, Mary. It's beautiful. I shall always keep it with me."

There were tears in Mary's eyes when she let go of her, and she spoke the first words anyone had heard since that day in the woods.

"Don't go away."

Jess felt as if her heart were breaking. She pulled Mary to her once more and as her eyes filled with tears, she saw Devlin standing just inside the doorway of the classroom. So, he had come after all.

"Mary, I . . ." words failed her. How could she possibly explain to this child that she had to leave?

Simply enough, it was the child's name that focused her emotions and thoughts. She knelt before her, holding both her small hands between her own.

"Mary is a very special name—a very beautiful name. Someone that I love very much . . . also has that name." She thought of her sister and the childhood name she had taken when she disappeared. "I once made a promise to her that I would always take care of her."

"Just like you made the promise to me in the woods?" Mary asked.

"Yes, exactly so. I made that promise because I love you very much. But now the other Mary needs me."

The child's expression was no longer blank or void of emotion as it was when Jess had first come to Old Orchard. It was filled with a terrible sadness.

"And you have to keep your promise to her, just as you kept your promise to me."

The wisdom of a child was always unexpected and poignant.

"Yes, I have to keep my promise." It was then Mary looked up, a new expression pushing through the sadness.

432

"Then make me another promise. Promise that you'll come back."

It was stunning in its simplicity, and she should have expected it. Over the child's head, her gaze briefly met Moira's. There was understanding and compassion in her eyes.

"Do you want me to come back?"

"Oh, yes, we all want you to come back. Even Jillian." In the crowd that had gathered inside the schoolroom, Jillian was obvious by the sudden redness in her face.

Jess started to look at Devlin, but she hadn't the courage to confront what she might find in his eyes — that he might not want her to come back.

"I shall try to come back, Mary."

"Promise?"

"Yes, I promise."

"And you must take my picture with you to remind you of the Michaelmas tree."

"Of course I will take it with me."

They had to leave early the following morning in order to reach Exeter in time for the afternoon train to London. Good-byes were said that night.

The children were all in bed, including Mary Margaret, who had clung to Jess until she finally fell asleep, completely exhausted. Moira and Robbie had gone upstairs a short while earlier with the baby.

The house was silent except for the occasional pop and hiss at the stove. Light from the oil lamp cast a soft glow over everything in the cozy kitchen, and glinted off the sparkling ornaments of the Michaelmas tree in the adjacent room.

Unable to sleep, Jess had stolen back down to the kitchen for a cup of tea. She moved around the kitchen confidently after the past few weeks at Old Orchard. At least she could prepare water for tea without filling the entire house with smoke.

The house was quiet and cozy with a peaceful silence. It smelled faintly of wood smoke, the lingering aroma of the fresh

433

apple tarts Moira had baked earlier in the day, and the pungence of the Michaelmas tree.

They were simple pleasures that she had never noticed before, nor had the opportunity with the life she lived in London. She stood before the stove, watching steam from the kettle shoot into the air, her thoughts filled with poignant memories of the past weeks.

She heard a floorboard creak underfoot and looked up. Devlin stood in the doorway. She thought he had already gone back to the cottage. Evidently he had been kept overlong upstairs with stories for the boys.

"I couldn't sleep . . ." she made an uncertain gesture at the teapot. "I know you don't care much for tea . . ."

His gaze was fastened on her, inscrutable, as he leaned against the doorway, his face concealed in shadows.

"I'd like to share a cup of tea with you," he said quietly coming away from the shadows. "Do you need help, lass?"

She smiled. "I think I can manage well enough. It's the one thing I can do without setting the house afire."

There was a shadow of a smile at his lips. "We can only hope."

Then he moved past her, setting out cups and saucers that Moira had acquired here and there. Everything was different— the plates, utensils, cups, and saucers, with a sort of mismatched charm that seemed inherently a part of Old Orchard farm and its odd assortment of animals, children, and love.

Silence settled once more around them as she went to the cupboard where Moira kept Robbie's special *blend* of tea—a good, stout Irish whiskey. She poured a liberal amount in his cup, and then a lesser amount in her own cup.

He leaned against the wall behind the opposite bench as he sat across from her at the long table. The light from the oil lamp played across his features, shifting with the occasional flicker of the flame so that it was impossible to guess what he was thinking.

"You've changed," he said, his voice low as the whisper from the tea kettle.

"How could I not be changed? This place has changed me.

434

And Moira, Robbie, the children." She felt him watching her from the shadows.

"And Mary Margaret?"

"Especially Mary, She has a very special gift."

"And you as well, lass," he said from the shadows where he leaned back and contemplated her. "A gift for reachin' out to the children, for findin' things inside them, for helpin' them look at things in a different way. It's a rare gift you've given them. You've changed them as well. They'll never forget you."

The silence expanded once more. Then he said in a quiet, thoughtful voice, "The Irish have a saying 'No matter how far you travel, no matter where the road may take you, you always leave a part of yourself behind in the places you've known'. "

"Do you believe it?" she asked.

"That I do. I left a part of myself behind when I left Dublin, a part that I know I can never get back."

"What part was that?"

"My childhood, shattered innocence, dreams . . . and hope."

"And what of Old Orchard? What do you leave behind when you leave here?"

"Old Orchard is a place for comin' to. It always will be, and I'll always come back because of what I left behind in Dublin."

"A place for leaving, and a place for going to," she repeated softly, staring out the window at the pale moonlight that made shadows over the white landscape beyond. His voice brought her back, quiet, yet filled with a sort of waiting sadness.

"Don't go back, Jess."

She looked into those shadows where he'd retreated.

Why couldn't he understand? Hadn't he ever wanted something so badly that the risk didn't matter? Wasn't even important?

"Please don't ask it of me," she said, her voice gone to a whisper.

"I have to ask it, lass." He leaned across the table then and took her hands between his large, strong ones. "It's too dangerous. There are others involved. We don't know for certain who they are. But it's safe to assume they'll do anything to stop you."

435

There was a desperate strength in those powerful hands as he tried to make her understand. She finally pulled her hands from his, moving away from the table as she pulled away from him. She wrapped her arms tightly about her.

"I have to go back." She said, her voice low and filled with anguish. "My sister's life depends on it."

"For God's sake, Jess! Devoe was sent here to kill you. He failed. Whoever he was connected with will try again."

"I have to take that chance!" she whispered angrily, tears glistening in her green eyes. "How can I do anything less, when my sister's life is in danger? You wouldn't have done less for Megan."

There was no way to call the words back, even if she could. The expression on his face stunned her. It was cold, the lines deeply etched. She'd touched a pain so deep within him, and so profound, that for long moments he said nothing. When he finally did speak, it was a voice she didn't know. He stood and slowly walked to the door. He didn't turn around, wouldn't look at her.

"Aye, Jess, I wouldn't have done less. But it made no difference in the end, for she died anyway."

And then he was gone, the stout door slamming after him, leaving her with the echoing loneliness of his anger in the silent house.

Chapter Twenty-nine

Chief Inspector Abberline met them at Paddington Station when they arrived in London the following evening.

According to Devlin's instructions, she wore a thick woolen scarf about her head and the lower part of her face as she left the train. They walked quickly, Devlin's arm firm beneath hers.

They were escorted to a waiting coach — the driver was a police constable wearing plain clothes — for the remainder of the trip to a private residence in the center of London.

"It's good to see you again, my dear," Abberline said gently. Then he looked over at Burke.

"I received your wire. I'll have Devoe's body removed to a separate location."

She glanced briefly over her shoulder at the two post cars at the back of the train, aware that Devoe's body had been put aboard at Exeter. The remainder of the ride was made in silence.

It was an inconspicuous house on a quiet street in an affluent section of London, with a high wall all about and an iron gate at the entrance from the street. They passed through, then the gate was closed behind them.

"I took these precautions after I received your wire about Devoe's involvement," Abberline explained as the coach came to a stop. "The house belongs to my wife's cousin and her husband. They're currently away. I appropriated it for our use." They stepped down and were quickly led through the back service entry, into the kitchen, and through to the main part of the house where they were met by a somewhat dignified-looking Sergeant Hobbs, dressed in the formal livery of a footman.

437

"Good evenin', Miss Kelly," he said in greeting, stretching his neck against the starched stiffness of the tight collar.

She gave him a quizzical smile. "Good evening, Sergeant. Have you also been appropriated?"

He grinned then. "We all have, miss. Me, Endicott, and a half-dozen lads wot could be trusted. None of 'em had much fondness for Inspector Devoe."

Abberline cleared his throat. "I'm certain Mr. Burke and Miss Kelly are hungry. Perhaps you could have Endicott bring some of the supper he's kept warm in the kitchen."

"That I will, sir." Hobbs gave Jess a wink. "Not the boy's cookin' mind yer. Wouldn't give it to a stray dog. Had his sister come over as well. She's got everything straight away in the kitchen."

"And I was so looking forward to tasting Endicott's cooking," she remarked. He shook his head.

"No yer weren't, Miss Jess. The lad could burn water given half a chance."

She said nothing in reply, certain it would have been inappropriate given her own abilities in the kitchen. She sat down wearily in a high-backed chair before the hearth.

"If you would like to rest, my dear, there will plenty of time to go over everything later," Abberline suggested.

She shook her head. "If it's quite all right, I would like to get it over with now."

He nodded. "Very well."

For the next half hour and through late supper, he went over the latest developments in the investigation and the plans that had been made for the gallery exhibition.

"I've arranged everything myself. I personally contacted Monsieur Gilot and took care of the details of the show as you requested. It will begin promptly at ten o'clock tomorrow morning."

"What about Jimmy Cassidy?" Devlin asked, joining the conversation for the first time.

"When I received your wire about Devoe, I determined that it might be necessary for Mr. Cassidy to take a small *vacation* for a few days, to relieve him of the necessity of following up on the gallery show and perhaps jeopardizing our secrecy."

"Another of your appropriations?" Jess asked.

"A necessary appropriation. We couldn't take the risk of Cassidy interfering."

Devlin went on to explain. "He killed Toby and Belle, but he didn't kill Liz Stride, Catherine Eddowes, Annie Chapman, or any of the others. Someone else killed them."

She stared at him. The change was dramatic and complete. In that long train ride from Devonshire to London he had changed. It was more than the coat and suit, more than the hat he wore and the polished boots that replaced the knee-high work boots he'd worn at Old Orchard.

It was a look about him, a coldness in his features, and the dark shadows behind those piercing blue eyes. The man she had come to know — the man who helped a tiny boy that first morning at Old Orchard, the man who wept for Mary Margaret and fought to save Moira and her newborn son — no longer existed. Or if he did, he was carefully hidden away.

He was gone, replaced by someone she hardly knew — Inspector Devlin Burke of the London metropolitan police, the man sworn to hunt down the murderous fiend who had stalked London for months, Jack the Ripper.

She shivered at the profound sense of loss. Whatever they had found together at Old Orchard was gone. It was gone from the moment he had begged her to stay and she had refused.

"How can you be certain . . . ?" she faltered as she thought of her sister, still out there somewhere, then quickly recovered. "How do you know that he didn't kill the others?"

He stood before the fire at the hearth, much as he had stood before the hearth at the cottage countless times. For a brief moment when he turned to look at her she felt a deep, intense longing to see what she had seen in him then.

"I realized it the moment I saw Devoe standing over you at the edge of the woods."

At the memory, her own hand went to her throat, as it had that day when she had tried to break his hold. The bruises were still vivid beneath the high lace collar.

439

"Annie Chapman and the other women were killed by a right-handed person. It was part of the evidence given by the surgeon after his examination of each body. The marks at the neck and on the body were made from the left to the right side of the body."

Her hand lay protectively over her bruised throat. Suddenly she knew.

"Devoe was left-handed."

"Aye, and the marks on Toby and Belle were made by a left-handed man as well. Devoe had access to a great deal of information about the investigation. It wasn't too difficult for him to discover that Toby knew all of the murdered women, including your sister. That made Toby a threat. And when you learned of it, it made you a threat as well. As we already guessed, Belle was in the wrong place at the wrong time."

Abberline went on to explain. "Devoe undoubtedly went to Abbington Road that night, expecting to find you there. He had no way of knowing that you had been delayed when he found a woman in the flat." His voice was even, in that controlled manner she had become familiar with as they sat across the desk from each other in his office at the Commercial Street station, going over police reports together.

"It's possible that he discovered the mistake he made almost immediately, or perhaps he learned of it later through his access to information about the investigation. By then you and Burke had left London."

Abberline continued. "When we learned of his involvement through that wire from Inspector Burke, we found people that he had spoken with—the driver who took you across London to Drury Lane, and the second driver who took you on to Paddington Station. From there it was easy enough for him to learn your destination."

The late supper was long over. She had eaten very little. They sat before the fire in the formal parlor.

"What arrangements have been made for the gallery show?"

She was aware of a look that passed between Devlin and Chief Abberline.

"Monsieur Gilot has been very cooperative. He's made his patrons aware of the show. A second announcement appeared in today's newspaper as well. In addition, there was a formal announcement about the tragic death of Inspector Sinjin Devoe, while in the line of duty."

"You announced his death?"

Abberline nodded. "A most tragic affair—run down by a coal truck while crossing a street here in London."

She turned to Devlin. "I don't understand."

"Whoever is involved in this mustn't suspect that we know of Devoe's involvement."

Abberline concurred. "If they thought for a moment that we suspected a conspiracy, all our efforts would be for naught. They must believe that you are alive, and the show will go forth as planned. They will only come forward if they believe they are in danger of being exposed."

"And what about my sister? What about the risk to her?"

"We have no idea what her involvement may be in this, except that she lived for a time with one of the victims. What she may or may not have seen is merely speculation. All our efforts to find her have been in vain."

For the next hour Chief Abberline explained the plans that had been made for the gallery show the following morning.

It was past midnight. His expression reflected all the sleepless nights and months of work that had brought them to this point.

"The plan is not without great risk to you," he concluded. "If you chose at this time not to go forward with it, I would understand. Whoever is behind this will not hesitate to kill again."

"No," she said in a quiet but firm voice. The room was equally quiet, except for the hiss of the fire and the rhythmic ticking of the large clock.

"My dear, we might still pull this off without necessitating your involvement."

"No!" she said more emphatically. Then she looked up from where she had been sitting the past hour listening to all the possibilities and probabilities. The entire time, Devlin remained silent. He had said the very same things himself, and a great deal more, trying to dissuade her.

"I appreciate your concern," she told Abberline. "But it appears this may be the one chance to capture the murderer. You've set a trap. You must have the bait for that trap. I have to go through with this." She saw that he understood or in the very least accepted that she would not change her mind.

"Very well, my dear," he finally said, his expression grave. "I trust you have the composite sketches with you."

"Yes. After the information you sent to Devonshire, I came up with four possibilities. Two were very similar, which may mean they are the same man. One is quite clear from several descriptions. The fourth one is not complete. There were only vague descriptions."

She said nothing more about the fourth sketch—that it was the one she had the most trouble with, changing it several times, always coming back to one of the first sketches she'd made, unable to say precisely why she kept coming back to it.

It was a look about the eyes, that matched vague descriptions given by three different people, even though the other features were unknown.

In her own mind she had named all the subjects in the sketches, as she did her paintings. After weeks of work, changes, refinement, and more changes they were as familiar to her as her own face.

The first two sketches that greatly resembled one another when laid one over the other she had called the Twins, the man in the third sketch she called the Watcher, because that was the look about him, that of someone watching intently. The fourth sketch she called Shadow, because most of the features were obscured. Only the eyes were seen with that horrible, deadly expression.

Devlin laid her sketch case on the side table and opened it. He took out the finished sketches. Abberline leaned over the table, studying them carefully.

"Quite remarkable, my dear." Then he came to a more recent sketch, made on the train as they returned to London. He looked up at her with some surprise.

"Devoe?"

"I thought it appropriate to add it to the collection. I call it The Traitor." He nodded.

"By all means, we shall include it then."

She slept fitfully, tossing and turning for what remained of the night. The unfamiliarity of the house made her restless. She woke several times with that first panic of the senses at waking in a strange place.

She must have cried out. There was a sudden urgent knock at her door, and then it was opened. Devlin stood in the doorway, his lean, muscular body outlined in the soft glow of light from the gaslight in the hallway.

She pushed her hair back as her senses cleared. He came into the room, momentarily lost in the shadows between the door and bed. Then there was the faint scrape as the valve on the wall fixture was turned up and light pooled into the room.

He wore pants and boots, nothing more, except the revolver clutched in his right hand. She stared fixedly at it, black and shiny in the dull light. She had never considered that he knew how to use a gun, much less that he had one. It startled her, for she was aware that police inspectors rarely had the need for firearms.

He first checked the window latches behind the heavy drapes, then the adjoining door that led to another room on that floor.

"I'm all right," she assured him. "It was just a bad dream."

He turned then and slowly walked to the bed. It dipped with his weight as he sat at the edge. In the muted light his eyes had gone black and watchful. His features were bathed in the shadows of the room, while the light played across the gleaming surfaces of skin at his shoulders, chest, and the flat plain of his stomach.

"Bad dreams, Jess?" he asked, his voice low in his throat.

"I keep seeing eyes."

"Eyes?"

"The eyes in the sketches." She brushed her long hair back, her

443

hand quivering with restlessness and a faint trembling of uncertainty.

"I've drawn them hundreds of times. I know I've drawn them right, it's just that . . ."

He reached out then. The gun was laid aside. He took her hand between his, soothing the restlessness with his fingers.

"What is it, lass?" he asked gently, stroking his fingers along the length of hers. "What is it that troubles your dreams?"

She gestured helplessly with her other hand, unable to explain what it was that troubled her. "I don't know. I just keep seeing these eyes—Shadow's eyes."

"Shadow?"

There was such gentleness and warmth in him, that part of him that she'd seen with Jamie and each of the children, and that had been so carefully hidden away from her ever since the attack. This was the man she had come to know at Old Orchard. This was the man who knew and understood her. She needed him to understand now all the reasons that she had to do this.

"I've named the sketches. The first and second ones are the Twins, because they're so similar. The third one I call Watcher, because that is the feeling I get about him. The fourth one is Shadow, because there are no accurate descriptions of him. No one has seen him clearly, except for his eyes."

"They all have eyes, Jess."

"I know, but it's *his* eyes that I keep remembering."

"Even in your dreams," he said thoughtfully. "There's still time to change your mind about this, Jess."

"I can't."

"It's too dangerous. This maniac has killed five times. He'll kill again if he can."

"I *can't*," she repeated.

His voice raised slightly. "He'll try to kill *you*."

"No."

"Jessie!" he hissed, taking her by the shoulders and shaking you. "What will it take to make you understand?"

"What will it take to make *you* understand?" she shot back at him. "This is my sister's life. I have to do this." He let go of her then, so abruptly that she fell back against the pillows. He turned and strode to the door. The anger that had come between them, exploded in the slamming of the door.

"What the devil?" Abberline shouted, coming out of the room across the hall, and face-to-face with Devlin Burke. "What's happened?" Hobbs appeared at the end of the hallway, in footman's pants and little else, a revolver dangling from his hand.

Devlin looked at both of them as he tucked his revolver into the waist of his pants. "Nothing's happened! Not a bloody thing." He pushed past Hobbs.

"If yer goin' to be running through hallways at night, put on some clothes, man! And take a care with that gun." Then he slammed into the room he was occupying for the night.

Hobbs gave the chief inspector a perplexed look. Abberline shook his head and motioned for Hobbs to return to his own bed.

Then he walked across the hall. He was about to knock on the door opposite, when he heard the sounds of soft weeping. He slowly lowered his hand and quietly returned to his own room.

Jess sat stiffly in the darkened coach the following morning. The shades had been drawn at the windows for privacy during the ride to the Gilot gallery. Mr. Abberline sat across from her, Devlin beside him. Hobbs and Endicott sat atop with the driver.

"Are you quite clear about everything, my dear?" Abberline asked.

"Yes, I'm to wait until ten-thirty. You will send Sergeant Hobbs to escort me to the main gallery."

"Quite right. I will have additional men, all completely loyal, posted throughout the gallery and at all the entrances. No one will be allowed to enter or leave without our knowing of it. We have taken every precaution," he assured her. "However there will be a great number of people in attendance. Monsieur Gilot has said the response has been extraordinary. The name J.B. Dumont has caused quite a stir throughout London."

Throughout the ride Devlin had remained silent. He didn't try to dissuade her again. He wouldn't even look at her.

Oh, why can't you understand? she thought, wanting desperately for him to say something, anything that would let her know that he understood.

He was different from every man she'd ever known. She thought that because of his past he would understand. She needed for him to tell her that everything would be all right.

He did look over at her then. But his expression was unreadable. He was Inspector Burke now—hard, cold, inscrutable, remote.

She sat perfectly composed, almost rigid in the seat across from him, dressed in an elegant, dark green silk gown that would have cost a month's pay for an inspector of police. It was hardly appropriate for J.B. Dumont to wear the simple wool dress that she had purchased at the fair in Devonshire.

She was so beautiful and remote, her head held high by the stiff, high collar that covered the ring of bruises about her neck. The silk rustled heavily, a reminder of wealth, breeding, and position that set them apart as surely as a stone wall.

Her gloved hands were tucked inside the warm fur muffler, and her lustrous dark hair, that he could almost feel heavy in his hands, was also tucked away inside the deep fur hat.

Her features were pale and drawn, her wide green eyes slightly red as she had looked at him briefly when she first came downstairs that morning. The plains and angles of her face seemed more sharply defined, her mouth somehow fuller with an almost poignant vulnerability.

But she hadn't changed her mind.

The coach lurched to a stop, slowly turned, and then came to a final stop. There was the double thump on the roof, given in a prearranged signal, then a shifting movement as Hobbs and the driver stepped down.

"We're at the gallery," Abberline informed them. "Are you ready, my dear?"

She nodded firmly. "Yes, I'm quite ready."

Hobbs opened the door. Abberline stepped out, followed by Devlin. He turned and held out his hand to her.

She hesitated, then accepted his assistance. Their gazes met briefly as she stepped down. For long moments he held on to her gloved hand, his eyes an intense shade of blue gone almost black in the gray morning air that was sharp and cold about them.

She thought she saw something in that moment—something of the man she had discovered at Old Orchard—it was a shadow of an expression stunningly like his expression that afternoon at the school when she found him watching her with Mary.

Then it was gone, amidst quickly snapped orders from Abberline, swirling away like the morning mists. In the cold morning air, their hastening footsteps, the sharp rustle of her silk gown, were sounds and images frozen in her mind, as she was escorted through the service entry and into the private gallery.

The warmth after the bone-chilling cold and the sudden familiarity of the ornately furnished surroundings stunned her at first. This place was as familiar to her as the house at Carrington Square.

She could recall to the smallest detail each room, the furnishings, the thick carpet underfoot, and the sweep of heavy wine-colored drapes fringed in satin at the entrance to the main salon. Yet, as familiar in detail as it all was, there was an unexpected sense of the unfamiliar, a feeling of detachment, as if she were removed from it all in a way that she had never experienced before.

Then it was gone, and she was quickly escorted along the service hallway used by the staff to an unobtrusive door across the hall from the kitchen. It opened onto a narrow service stairway used by servants when the house was a private residence.

"We shall use these stairs," Abberline informed her. "It is more discreet. I don't wish to announce your arrival, my dear." She was acutely aware of what had been left unsaid—that the fewer who knew of her arrival, the greater the chance of protecting her if they were successful in luring the man who called himself Jack the Ripper to the gallery.

The stairway had been built with the purpose of accommodating one person in the steep, twisting passage. Hobbs went first, followed by Abberline, then Jess, and Devlin followed last at some distance, lingering in the hallway below to make certain they weren't seen.

They emerged on the second floor at the end of what was once the long open hall with doors that led to private rooms now used for storage, except for two of them. What was once the large master bedroom was the gallery owner's private suite. The adjacent sitting room had been converted into his office.

The second room, nearest to the servant's stairway, was the room she used as her private atelier—the same room where Devlin had discovered the truth about her.

Abberline crossed the hall to her small studio.

"I believe you have the key, my dear."

She handed him the key. When they were all inside the small studio, he explained. "It is my understanding that only yourself and Monsieur Gilot know that this is your private studio."

"Yes," she answered, hesitantly. Her sister knew of the studio as well. "And perhaps some of his staff," she added. "Although Monsieur has always made every effort to protect my privacy."

"Excellent, the fewer who know of it, the easier it will be for us to maintain your safety." Then he went on to explain.

"Inspector Burke and I shall remain downstairs until the appointed time. Sergeant Hobbs will be at the bottom of the stairs to make certain that no one comes up. Another constable will be posted at the bottom of the servants' stairs. Hobbs will call for you at the appointed time and escort you down to the main salon where the exhibit is to take place." His expression was grave.

"Under no circumstances are you to open this door until Hobbs comes for you. I will give him the key. Is that understood?" When she nodded, he continued.

"The sketches shall remain with me. If you don't have them, then we shall reduce the threat to you."

"I understand."

"Very well, then we should get about our business." He took his watch from his vest pocket and checked the time. "It is approximately twenty minutes until the appointed time

448

for the exhibit." He looked up then and smiled reassuringly as he touched her hand.

"Everything will be all right, my dear. We've taken every precaution. If this fellow makes an appearance, we'll catch him." Then he turned to leave, handing Hobbs the key to the studio door. Devlin was the last to leave. As he pulled the door closed behind him, he hesitated.

His lean fingers were white-knuckled at the edge of the door. His features were stark, his mouth that she remembered hot and impassioned against hers was a thin, hard line, the muscles of his jaw like stone. The expression behind his eyes was intense and enigmatic.

"Jessie . . ." The sound of her name was equally intense, a harsh whisper in the still studio.

For long moments the silence hung heavy between them—filled with unspoken questions each was afraid to ask, answers each was afraid to give.

She ached inside. She wanted him to hold her, to give her strength and compassion, to take away the fear as he did so easily with a small child, but most of all to tell her that he understood what she must do. She waited impossibly long moments that came and went.

Finally his gaze broke from hers. His fingers seemed to cut into the wood at the door, and his voice was as harsh as the look behind his eyes.

"Lock the door behind me."

Then he was gone, the door clicking shut behind him. She went to the door, tears filling her eyes, and locked it.

Now she must wait.

She slowly walked about the small studio, familiarizing herself all over again with the brushes, paints, and canvas. The painting she had authorized Gilot to sell was gone, but the other two remained, the latest series by artist J.B. Dumont.

When this was over, she found herself thinking, she would begin a new series. Images and ideas already formed in her mind— the Devonshire series.

From the earliest days of her career, Monsieur Gilot had insisted on one thing—"Paint what is in your heart. Not what you see, but what you feel. To feel is to see."

Devonshire, the farm at Old Orchard, the children and the people of Farway, were in her heart. Even when she closed her eyes, she could see the images she had carried with her, she could feel them. Even if she never *saw* them again, they would always be with her.

At the window she gazed down at the street below. Coaches arrived, the occupants stepping down and entering the gallery. Soon it would begin. She would reveal to all of London the identity of J.B. Dumont, and within those three sketches—she was certain—the identity of Jack the Ripper.

Time passed agonizingly slowly.

She glanced at the small gold watch at the bodice of her gown—a gift from her sister that she had taken with her when she went to Whitechapel but had not worn until now. It was still several minutes before the exhibition was to begin. Each time she paced across the studio she came back to the door.

She rested her hand on the knob. Before she could change her mind, she turned the lock, and opened it. The hallway was empty as Abberline had said it would be.

She heard the excited buzz of activity and conversations that drifted up from the first floor where patrons were arriving.

Would the murderer come? drawn by the threat of exposure for all of London to know what he looked like?

Was he there even now?

Would she know him if she saw him, having drawn those sketches countless times?

She slowly walked to the balustrade at the open galleria at the second floor and peered down at the gathering crowd that was drawn by the notoriety of the brutal murders and the terror that had held the city in its grip for months.

Her gaze scanned the faces of the patrons who filled the gallery, dressed in their fine satins and brocades, fine worsted wools, and gleaming jewels. It was a world she was part of, yet she had never felt so apart from it.

It was then she saw them—her father and stepmother.

450

In all the time since she had left Carrington Square she'd had no contact with them, except the few, brief notes she had forwarded to the country and asked her dear friend to send back to London, to keep up the pretense of her visit.

She and her father had forever been at odds, even though she loved him. Linnie was the one who helped smooth the way between them. All that had changed when he married Vivian.

Difficult and lonely as the intervening years had been when they were sent off to school in France, she still loved him, or at least the man he had once been when their mother was alive and they were all happy.

It was that memory she always held in her thoughts, and as she and Linnie grew up there were occasional moments when she saw a look or a glance, that reminded her of the man her father had once been. Even now, he seemed unchanged, except that his hair was perhaps a little whiter, his features tired. He hated these affairs and attended only because Vivian insisted upon it, she was certain.

Was the fatigue because of worry for Linnie, who in all these months still had not been found? She wanted to believe it, even though he had adamantly opposed her involvement in finding her sister.

Vivian was beautiful in a rust-colored gown that matched the auburn glow of her hair. She smiled at acquaintances, chatting with great animation.

Then her breath caught. Behind them, walking several paces removed, resplendent in elegant waistcoat and pants, was Jason Deverell, Lord Rushmore. He was coolly handsome, with lean patrician features, golden hair that sleeked his head, and the remote self-possession that seemed so innately a part of those who belonged to society. She understood what Devlin had meant by it.

She immediately looked past him, in a futile, desperate hope that she would find Linnie walking beside him. He was alone.

Her gaze came back briefly to Jason. She wondered if he had learned anything of Linnie's whereabouts all these weeks.

There was an air of brave sadness about him as he turned and also spoke to acquaintances, nodded to friends nearby, bent his head in brief conversation. She reminded herself that in spite of his adamant objections to her involvement and his insistence that she leave well enough alone, he had been as devastated by Linnie's disappearance as she was. Yet he was calm, perfectly composed, controlled, maintaining the facade that everything was as it should be.

They passed below her, entering the main salon. Jess continued to watch the patrons who arrived or milled about in the foyer. Occasionally she glimpsed a familiar face—family acquaintances, friends, and police constables, dressed in fine suits of clothes that had obviously been acquired for the exhibition, blending in among the society patrons with surprising ease.

She looked for Devlin even though she knew she would never see him. He moved easily and unseen by everyone. Still she searched the faces of the patrons and realized the faces she looked for—The Twins, Watcher, and Shadow.

Were they there? Would she even know them if she saw one of them? Or was there not enough similarity of feature between those faces and her sketches?

Then as she leaned over the balustrade, she caught a glimpse of Chief Abberline. She quickly stepped back. He would be furious if he knew she had left the studio. She retraced her steps, locked the door behind her, and continued to wait.

It wouldn't be much longer now.

Even now she could imagine the attendants, employed by Monsieur Gilot, escorting the last of the guests to the chairs that filled the large salon, just as they had at the exhibit for the Provence series.

She had attended as an art patron, taking her seat with friends and family in the gallery, watching with a secret smile as the bidding began for her paintings, those who bid on them never aware that the artist sat among them.

Linnie had been with her that day, grasping her hand excitedly as the bids for each painting built to fever pitch. The paintings in the Provence series were quickly sold, as around them buzzed excited conversations about the "genius of the artist," "the exquisite attention to detail," the "extraordinary vision of the human quality" in each of the paintings.

It was all she and Linnie could do to not burst out laughing at the marvelous deception that had been accomplished. That day, five years earlier, the reputation of the reclusive—and it was rumored, slightly eccentric—artist, J.B. Dumont, was firmly established.

Time had passed so slowly the night before and the entire morning, now it seemed to gather momentum, the minutes and seconds slipping away. Her usually calm nerves were suddenly drawn taut.

That intense gaze had been drawn by a sudden movement at the second-floor galleria. His gaze narrowed at the shimmer of dark green silk, the slender, feminine figure, pale features, and glossy dark hair.

Then *he* noticed the heavy-set man at the foot of the stairs, with bulldog features, wearing a finely-tailored suit of clothes. Appearances were often deceiving, but the man's discomfort was obvious as he stretched his neck against the starched restraint of the stiff collar, and tugged at the satin vest drawn taut over his barrel chest with rough, callused hands.

For the second time in barely seconds, the heavy-set man glanced at his pocket watch. Then his heavy-lidded gaze came up as if he were looking across the room for someone, or something.

It was then *he* saw the man's brief nod of acknowledgment of a prearranged signal. Then the man turned and climbed the stairs.

That cold gaze came back to the second-floor galleria. The young woman was gone, but *he* was certain he had just discovered J.B. Dumont.

With cold, calculated detachment, he moved from the edge of the crowd, slipped down the hallway, and discovered the servants' stairs.

Jess replaced the cover cloth on one of her two remaining

453

paintings when she heard the key in the lock at the door.

"Is it time?" she asked, as she lowered the cloth.

"Long past time."

She turned around, with a smile at the familiar voice. Then her smile wavered uncertainly and disappeared as the terrifying reality of truth set in.

"Oh, my God," she whispered as she stared into those eyes that had haunted her dreams.

Chapter Thirty

She had called the man in the sketch Shadow because she had only the description of his eyes. The rest of his features had remained indistinct and so she had left them in shadow, as unknown as the man.

But now he had a face and a name.

"Jason?" she whispered incredulously.

She stared at him in disbelief, her stunned thoughts moving slowly as she tried to grasp the horrible revelation.

"I warned you not to interfere, my dear. You were foolish not to heed my advice."

"Why? How is it possible? . . . I don't understand." She felt a small bubble of laughter begin in her throat at the ridiculous impossibility of it. Jason the murderer?

It was too fantastic to believe, too . . . impossible . . . It must be some sort of prank or . . . foolish joke that he was trying to play.

She stared at him, waiting with almost impossible hope for him to suddenly laugh and tell her it was a prank. If it was a prank it was cruel, inhuman, completely unfeeling, depraved, the workings of a . . . maniacal mind.

Devlin had called the murderer a maniac, beyond reason or any human feeling, void of all compassion.

As her stunned thoughts fragmented into images out of the past weeks, she saw again Annie Chapman's mutilated body, with the horrible slash marks as if some crazed animal had torn her to pieces and then left her for them to find.

Left her for them . . .

"Your sister is alive," Devlin had insisted. "If she were dead, we would have found her. He always leaves them for us to find."

She stared at him, as moments seemed to hang suspended in the horrifying silence of the studio.

"What has this to do with Linnie?" she asked, equally stunned by the unreal sound of her voice. His expression changed then, the handsome features completely void of all expression, his eyes hooded.

"Ah, dear Lenore. She didn't understand."

"She knew?" The words were caught in her paralyzed throat.

"An unfortunate complication that must still be dealt with."

An unfortunate complication. Dear God, he spoke of Linnie as if she were no more important than an overcharge on the bill from his tailor.

That still must be dealt with.

Suddenly, Jess knew. "She's still alive." And if she was alive, it meant that he had not yet found her. It was one small fragile hope as all others died. At least for now Linnie was still safe, wherever she was.

His head angled toward her, those pale blue eyes almost transparent. She had once thought him handsome. She realized now, that it was a cruel handsomeness, a deceptive attraction, for there was nothing behind those eyes. They were cold as death.

Cold, remote, self-possessed, controlled. People admired Jason Deverell for those qualities. Whatever the reasons were, she now realized those qualities masked a horrible cruelty.

Then her gaze went to his hands. She saw the dull gleam of the key as he laid it on the table where her paints and brushes were kept.

"Hobbs?" she whispered, horrified at the thought that came with it as her brain finally began to accept it. Jason Deverell had killed those women. He was Jack the Ripper. He intended to kill Lenore.

"He won't interfere," he assured her in a casual, even voice as if they were discussing some recalcitrant servant who had been instructed not to interrupt.

She tried to make sense of it. It seemed like some horrible

dream. But it was no dream, not even a nightmare. It was real, as real as he was, standing there, perfectly controlled. Then, as if her thoughts had suddenly engaged, or perhaps terror provided the catalyst, countless questions tumbled chaotically over themselves.

How easy it must have been. A peer of the realm, a member of society, an art patron, a man completely beyond reproach or doubt, who easily slipped past the police, a stranger to Whitechapel that no one was able to identify.

"Why, Jason? All those women? What could they possibly have done to you? How could you do such a thing?"

"I really would like to discuss it with you, my dear Jessamyn. Perhaps then you could understand why you must die as well. But there simply isn't time to discuss the reasons."

He slowly walked toward her. She reacted instinctively and began to back away from him. Then she saw the blade that gleamed in his hand.

. . . The reasons you must die as well.

It jolted through her brain as she stared at that knife — perhaps the same knife he had used to kill Annie Chapman and those other women — and she knew that he intended to kill her. He had to. He had to stop her from revealing the sketches which held the identity of the Shadow. But what of the Twins, and the Watcher?

Was she wrong? Had she made a mistake with the other composite sketches? Were they some nameless men who were simply seen in Whitechapel at the approximate time of the murders and had nothing to do with them? She had to know, and she needed time to somehow distract him. She took a wild gamble.

"And the others? What is their involvement?"

His head came up slightly and that cold gaze narrowed with an intense expression.

"You're very clever with your little sketches, my dear. Our small group considered ourselves quite clever as well. A different murder, a different murderer, and each time minimal risk that anyone would see anything that they might remember."

"The Twins, The Watcher, and you. But there were five murders."

457

"A small discrepancy, my dear. Brothers, not twins. The Watcher?" he smiled faintly. "No need to reveal his identity. And myself. Our little club took care of . . . a difficult situation that could have proven most embarrassing if it were made known." Then his smile changed, his expression terrifyingly familiar, for she had seen that same charming, guileless expression countless times before at Carrington Square and Deverell Hall.

What could have possibly brought him to this madness?

My God, she thought, he is insane.

"And now, my dear. There really is no more time to discuss this. We must be going." It was then he came toward her in quick, powerful strides.

Jess lunged away from him, ducking behind a table, easels, a chair, putting anything between them, to hold him off as she desperately tried to reach the door. It was the only way out of the studio.

Devlin stood at the back of the formal salon. Every seat was taken, occupied by well-heeled members of society, art patrons, the merely curious, and at least a dozen plainly dressed constables and inspectors.

They all waited expectantly for Monsieur Gilot to present the artist, J.B. Dumont and the stunning sketches that were to reveal the identity of the notorious Whitechapel murderer, Jack the Ripper.

He moved restlessly out into the grand foyer and glanced toward the staircase at the end of the hall. A quick glance at his pocket watch told him what he already knew—it was past ten-thirty.

Hobbs was not at the foot of the stairs. He didn't expect to find him there. According to plan, he was to have gone upstairs to escort Jess down to the main salon at precisely ten-thirty.

It was now ten-thirty three. Instinct made him uneasy.

He looked for Abberline in the salon, saw his head bent in conversation with the gallery owner, and knew it would be impossible to draw his attention without going back into the salon.

458

He spotted several constables throughout the crowd, posted discreetly, blending in with the patrons who had no notion of what was about. It would take time to contact any one of them without rousing excitement among those in attendance.

He made his decision quickly and moved along the hallway toward the servants' stairs. It would be quicker to send Endicott to check on Jess and Sergeant Hobbs.

The hall that led to the kitchen was deserted as it should be to all outward appearances. Endicott was posted at the stairs, discreetly hidden away behind the closed door.

He knocked three times, the prearranged signal. There was no answer. Possibly Endicott had gone up to the exit at the second floor. He knocked once more. When there was no response he jerked the door open.

The gaslight at the wall, used to light the stairway so that servants wouldn't fall on their way up or down, had been doused. The narrow stairway was completely dark.

Burke cursed softly as he lit the mantle and turned up the flame. Where the devil was Endicott?

Light spiraled up the stairway. It was deserted. Endicott was gone. He quickly strode down the hallway to the service entry where they had come in only a short while earlier. The constable on duty turned with a jerk.

"In here, right away!" Devlin ordered.

"What is it, Inspector?"

He quickly retraced his steps to the hidden stairway. "Take up this post, and don't leave it for any reason. Is that understood?"

"Where is Constable Endicott?"

"I'd like to know that as well," Devlin muttered as he sprinted back down the hall to the opposite end of the gallery, and the wide, sweeping staircase where Hobbs had been posted. He took the stairs three at a time, an urgency spreading through him. It might be nothing at all. . . .

He found Hobbs crumbled against the wall at the landing part way up the stairs, blood staining through the front of his coat.

"Damn!" he cursed, the urgency spreading to alarm. The wounded sergeant weakly lifted his head, revealing what ap-

459

peared to be a fairly shallow wound across his throat.

"Tried to stop him, Inspector," he whispered thickly. "Came at me from behind . . . He's gone after her . . . You've got to stop him . . . !" The last sentence bubbled out in a gasp of air.

Jess tried to run from Jason.

Her thick petticoats and the heavy layers of skirt, hampered her, making her movements slow and clumsy. With a fleeting thought she realized that if she had on one of the simple woolen dresses she'd worn at Old Orchard, she might escape him.

But he knew precisely what she was trying to do, and met her at each turn, closing the distance in powerful strides.

Her gaze fastened on those hands that were capable of such horrible violence, and the knife.

She lunged away again, one of the paintings crashing to the floor. She tried to dart past the table, shoving it as hard as she could to get past. But he was much quicker, moving easily, unhindered.

A smaller table with jars of linseed oil and turpentine crashed out of the way and he swiftly moved on her.

She cried out as his gloved hand closed over the thick mass of hair at the back of her head. Her fingers flew to his hand, trying to loosen his hold as she jerked away from him. She didn't care if he tore every hair from her head.

But he held her fast, those brutal fingers twisting deeply, as he cruelly jerked her toward him and brought the blade up against her throat.

"Be still!" he hissed, so near her face, she could feel the heat of his breath against her cheek. The air shuddered out of her lungs in hard gasps. She could see the gleam of that lethal blade at the edge of her vision.

He held her rigid against him, emphasizing that it was unwise even to breathe much less struggle, as he pressed the blade deeper.

"Now, dearest Jessamyn, you will come with me," he whispered with terrifying gentleness against her cheek. "There will be no

460

exhibit today, or any other day, for I can't allow you to jeopardize my friends." His fingers loosened in her hair, then his left hand lowered, going about her waist, pinning her left arm at her side, that blade still pressed against the side of her neck.

"Come, along, my dear," he instructed. "Very slowly, and carefully. No sudden moves, or I fear I might be forced to ruin your lovely gown." He held her against him, urging her slowly toward the door in careful, controlled steps.

"Listen to me," she pleaded, tensing as she felt the blade pressed more firmly. They moved forward together, as she tried to reason with him.

"They'll stop you. Surely you must know that. They know about Devoe." She felt the slightest hesitation in his body at her back. So, he wasn't aware that they knew about Devoe's involvement.

"Everyone will know of it soon. The police will stop you." His soft laughter sent a cold chill through her blood.

"They won't stop me, my dear. Because they won't have you to tell them, and they won't have your ridiculous sketches."

She played another gamble. "I don't have the sketches. Chief Abberline kept them. You'll be exposed anyway, and all of this will be for nothing. Jason, surely you must see that!" She heard the desperation in her voice.

"They will never know, Jess. The sketches mean nothing, because they would never suspect a member of society, a peer of the realm, capable of such a crime." He leaned very close as he reached to open the door, his breath chilling against her cheek.

"I am above suspicion, dearest Jessamyn. They will never know." He opened the door and forced her out ahead of him, keeping her well in front of him.

Devlin sprinted up the last half flight of steps to the second-floor landing and moved out into the open galleria. He immediately saw them. His hand went to the revolver tucked into the belt at his waist. As they came out of the studio, he moved quickly down the carpeted galleria until he was less than twenty feet away.

"Let her go!" he ordered sharply.

461

Jason whirled around, holding Jess tightly in front of himself, a human shield, the knife pressed against her throat.

"Stand away," Jason commanded, his voice as hard and smooth as ice. "Or she will die, just like the others."

Devlin saw the blade, had expected it, yet it was all the more stunning as that lethal tip pressed into the pale softness of her throat. The man was mad. He saw it in the cold calculation of his eyes, the remote, unemotional detachment in his expression. He had killed before, without emotion, or even a shred of remorse or regret. It had been there in the chilling letters he had sent to the police and the newspaper. And he would kill again just as easily.

Devlin had cared about each of the murders. He had sworn to stop the fiend who had stalked Whitechapel with such cunning and ruthlessness, leaving no trace of his identity behind, except for occasional descriptions that led nowhere. Jess had changed that for them. And she had changed him.

It was no longer merely a professional obsession. It had now become a personal obsession.

"It ends here," Devlin warned him.

"And just who is going to stop me?" Jason asked, his voice silken.

"I'm going to stop you, and expose you for the murdering bastard that you are."

She heard the cold, brutal smile in his laughter, as Jason said, "No one will believe you. It would be your word against mine." The mocking words conveyed far more, that no one would take the word of a policeman over the word of a member of the peerage.

Devlin slowly raised the revolver and aimed it directly at him.

"A revolver? An inspector playing at a gentleman's sport?" Jason laughed cruelly. "A man should always know his limitations."

"Let her go, or you will die," Devlin assured him. His voice had gone absolutely quiet without a trace of fear.

"You're taking a very great risk, Inspector. She will be dead before you can fire that revolver." He held her directly before him.

"Aye, a risk," Devlin agreed, his blue eyes gone completely to black, his face hard, as he stared down the length of his extended arm, his hand steady.

"But you'll be dead as well. You have my word on it."

Jason laughed then. Whether it was madness or incredulity, she had no idea. Her gaze was fastened on Devlin.

There was no trace of the man she had known at Old Orchard. He was gone. In his place was the hard, tough, inspector of police who had grown up on the streets of Dublin, sold by his mother—a lady who couldn't bear the scandal of the illegitimate child she bore—into a life Jess could only imagine the horror of.

It all came to this moment, as he confronted a man who represented everything that he had hated his entire life.

He would do it, she thought with a sudden certainty, because that old hatred was the strongest emotion inside him. She squeezed her eyes tight, knowing he couldn't allow Jason to leave. She didn't want her last memory to be of the death behind his eyes.

"Jason! Don't do this!"

A beautiful woman came up the stairs behind Devlin. He immediately saw the recognition in Jess's stunned gaze as she stared past him.

"Linnie?" she whispered in disbelief, as she felt Jason react to the new, perceived threat. His body went rigid.

"Don't harm her," Lenore begged softly. "I'm the one you want. Not her. She doesn't know anything."

"If only you hadn't interfered!" his breath hissed out as his hold on Jess tightened. "No one would ever have had to know about any of it."

"No one knows anything now," Lenore Deverell's voice quavered.

"No!" Jason said, low and menacing. "It's too late. She knows too much." He jerked Jess against him, the fingers of his left hand bruising her ribs as he pressed the blade deeper.

Devlin's gaze never left Jason Deverell, even as he became aware of the woman beside him.

"Let her go!" he shouted, bringing Deverell's concentration back to him.

He watched, fear and rage burning through him, as her blood appeared at the tip of the blade, and dropped onto the collar of her gown.

"Let her go!"

Jason pulled her back hard. It would come now, she thought. They couldn't stop him, but at least Linnie was safe.

The explosion of gunfire roared through the upper galleria.

She heard her sister scream, felt the force of the blow as it shuddered through her, then the dragging weight as she fell to the floor of the galleria.

"Oh, my God!" Linnie cried out. "Jess!"

Chapter Thirty-one

Lenore Forsythe Deverell — Lady Rushmore — sat before the desk in a private office of the metropolitan police in Mayfair, not far from the Gilot Gallery. Chief Inspector Frederick Abberline sat across from her. Inspector Devlin Burke sat nearby.

Outside, the chief of the Mayfair police, representatives of the home office, C.I.D., the New Scotland Yard, and countless members of the press waited.

The young woman who sat beside her, quietly encouraged her to go on with her story, difficult as it was.

"You must tell them everything," Jess said softly.

It was finally over.

Jason Deverell — Lord Rushmore — was dead, shot and killed in a confrontation with police at the Gilot Gallery.

Jess still wore the dress she had worn to the gallery. Blood stained the collar — her blood, from the small knife wound as Jason had held her hostage. If he'd had a moment longer . . . But he had been badly shaken by Linnie's unexpected appearance at the gallery.

Her sister had risked her life to come out of hiding and warn Jess about Jason.

She looked over at Devlin. He had said little to her, except to make certain that she was unharmed after Jason was killed. The wound was small, it would heal quickly.

Sergeant Hobbs was alive. He'd been taken to Queen's Hospital so that his wounds could be cared for. He would recover. Endicott had been found in the former butler's pantry with a bad head wound, but he would recover as well.

But what of other wounds? The deeper, emotional ones that Jason's brutal actions and violent death had left behind.

Over the next hour, with Jess sitting beside her offering quiet encouragement, Lenore Deverell told them of the Hunt Club, the secret society Jason belonged to. Its secret membership included peers of the realm, distinguished members of Parliament, the titled and nobility, and the Prince of Wales.

"I was never meant to know about it. No one outside the membership is. I discovered it quite by accident," Linnie began hesitantly.

"There were rumors that the young Prince of Wales had become involved in a relationship with a young woman who was not of his class. There was even talk that the woman had a child. We all knew about it. Such things are often whispered about."

"Not the first time a member of a Royal Family has sired illegitimate children," Abberline pointed out as delicately as possible.

"The child was not the dilemma," she explained. "It seems that the Duke of Clarence had actually married the young woman, who was Roman Catholic."

Jess looked at Devlin. She saw nothing in his eyes to indicate what he must feel at the irony of the circumstances to those of his own parents.

Abberline's expression was grim. He sensed the extreme difficulty of the delicate situation. "Please go on, Lady Deverell."

"Jason . . ." she halted, and then as if she couldn't bear to even speak his name, she began again. "The members of the Hunt Club usually met at a private club here in London, but frequently they met elsewhere, often in the country, at our home.

"Late one night, my . . . husband still had not retired for the evening. I went downstairs. He and several of our guests, all gentlemen, were in the library. I overheard them speaking of a problem the Prince of Wales was having, and that they were honorbound to take care of it for him. They spoke of the young woman, Anne Crook."

She went on, knowing the horrible scandal that awaited with the truth. "I thought they perhaps meant to merely end the rela-

466

tionship. They spoke of how embarrassing it would be for the duke if anyone were to learn of it.

"Until that moment, I didn't believe the rumors. But I realized then that they must be true."

"What happened then?"

"I immediately returned to my rooms. I was determined to speak with my husband about the matter, for it seemed quite serious. But there was no opportunity as we had guests for several days. And then Anne Crook came to Deverell Hall.

"She had been warned to leave London, but she wanted desperately to contact the Duke of Clarence. She refused to believe that he would allow her to be sent away. She asked for my help. I told her I would do what I could.

"Then, after we had returned to London, Jason and his friends were out very late one evening. I was told that he was at his private club. It was well after midnight when he returned."

She stared down at her hands, clasped around Jess's.

"You must tell them everything, Linnie."

She gave Jess a tremulous smile, and then continued. "I heard his coach in the yard, and I waited for him to come up to our room. But he didn't come in the usual way. He came in through the servants' entrance instead, and remained in the kitchen for the longest time. I heard him in there, running the water at the basin, then he came upstairs.

"I startled him. He didn't expect to find me waiting for him. He had the strangest look about him — wild, frightened, in almost the same manner of a child who's very nearly been caught at some prank. I asked him what was wrong."

"What did he say?"

"He said nothing was wrong, everything was perfectly all right. Then he moved past me. I laid my hand on his arm and he turned suddenly. For a moment I thought he would strike me. That's when I saw the blood on the front of his shirt."

"Do you remember which night that was?" Abberline asked.

"Yes, it was July 18th, because I remember reading about the murder in the paper the following day."

"Anne Elizabeth Crook," Devlin recited the name of the

467

first victim, memorized from the files on the investigation.

After the terrifying encounter with Jason at the gallery, Jess thought that nothing could frighten her more. She was wrong.

For the next hour, her sister continued, telling them of her confrontation with Jason over the girl's death, discovering the horrible truth, and the fear that drove her to leave Jason without telling anyone, taking a different name, hiding from Jason and the brotherhood of friends.

"Anne Crook knew the other women," Devlin surmised. "Polly Nichols, Annie Chapman, Liz Stride, and Catherine Eddowes."

Linnie nodded. "Anne lived with Polly Nichols. Her name was mentioned in the newspaper article about Anne Crook's death."

"And you went to see her."

"I was concerned for the child. I felt responsible somehow . . ." Her voice broke. "When I returned that afternoon, my husband demanded to know where I had been. I refused to tell him, but he discovered it anyway. He frequently had me followed. He was furious." Her hands twisted in her lap.

"He said that I was to stay away from Polly Nichols. He called her dreadful names and said that she was a . . . prostitute, that she would lie about anything.

"He reminded me that I was his wife, that he would send me away forever if I persisted. Then he . . . beat me." Her voice faltered completely. Tears were streaming down Jess's cheeks as she wrapped her arms about her sister's trembling shoulders.

Devlin hated it that they had to go on, but it was necessary to know all of it.

"Polly Nichols was the second victim."

Linnie nodded as she wiped her eyes with a handkerchief. "Thank God she had sent the child away. I think at first I didn't believe that Jason could be responsible for those horrible things. But then when I read about Polly Nichols, I knew that it had to be true."

"And that's when you disappeared," Devlin concluded.

"Yes. I could tell no one for it would jeopardize them as well." She turned to Jess. "Forgive me."

"Please continue, Lady Deverell."

"I knew Jason would do everything in his power to find me, because he was afraid of what I might tell. I left without telling anyone, I took another name, and went to a place where I knew Jason would never think to look for me."

"Whitechapel. But the murders continued."

"I lived with Annie Chapman. I learned about Anne Crook's friends, who all knew of the marriage."

"Including Liz Stride and Catherine Eddowes." Devlin's voice was grim. "They died because of what they knew. What of the others who are involved?" He crossed the office and handed her the sketches Jess had made.

The first was the one she had called the Twins, because of the similarity of two descriptions. Lenore Deverell studied it.

"Adam and Charles Mainwaring."

"Good God!" Abberline muttered. She looked at the next sketch of the Watcher.

"Harry Collingwood." It was all Abberline could do to keep his silence until she was finished. She looked at the third sketch, immediately recognizing the eyes of Shadow. Emotions played across her lovely face.

Devlin saw the resemblance the moment he saw them together. There was that same wide jaw, the same shape of eyes, although different in color, the same way of holding themselves, the same modulated voice that spoke of privilege, position, and the influence of French schools. But the resemblance ended there.

Where Jess's brows and lashes were dark and her hair a rich sable color, Lenore Deverell was fair, with blond hair, gray-blue eyes, and soft golden brows. Beautiful according to the fashion of society, yet somehow a pale shadow of Jess's striking beauty.

Lady Deverell was taller than Jess, with a slenderness that hinted at fragility, carefully restrained emotions, and that innate reserve only those in society possess. Jess was like wind and smoke, all color and movement. Restraint wasn't in her nature.

"And, of course, Inspector Devoe," Abberline added to the list of those they knew to be involved. "We may never know how many others. But we have these three." He shook his head gravely.

"It will be necessary to make a statement and present our evidence to C.I.D. and Scotland Yard. We've held them back as much as possible. Lady Deverell, you are free to leave. I will have my men escort you wherever it is you wish to go so long as you remain in contact with us."

Lenore looked to Jess uncertainly. "I won't go back to Deverell Hall."

"We'll go home to Carrington Square," Jess quickly decided. She glanced at Devlin, certain that he would ask to accompany them. He did not.

He heard it in her voice—the careful distancing. She was going back to Carrington Square, back to her life as Jessamyn Forsythe, as if Jess Kelly had never existed.

"Your father is waiting," Abberline informed them. "His coach is in the alley behind the police station. He's most anxious to see both of you. I will have two of my men escort you to your residence. If you will both come this way." He rose from the desk and led them out through another door that led to the back of the police station.

The furor of dozens of conversations and shouted questions filled the station, as constables and inspectors tried to keep some order in the crowd that had quickly gathered as word spread on the street that Jack the Ripper had been killed.

Everyone wanted to know his identity, newspaper writers demanded to know which was the sketch of the murderer that had stalked Whitechapel, and several members of Scotland Yard, C.I.D., and officials of the metropolitan police waited to speak with Abberline about the case that had apparently been solved.

They were escorted outside. It was midafternoon and yet it seemed that an eternity had passed since those harrowing moments in the gallery. The coach was waiting—Vivian's coach, of which she was so proud.

Their father had obviously sent her on ahead. He stepped down from the coach and quickly assisted Lenore inside. Then he reached for Jess's hand. She hesitated, glancing back over her shoulder one last time. But no one was there.

"We must go quickly," her father urged. "It won't take them

long to discover that you've left, or that I had a coach waiting."

Her gaze came back to her father. He was changed. She saw it in his somber expression. There were no questions for now, just an urgency to leave as soon as possible. The questions would come later.

She accepted his hand and stepped inside. He took the seat opposite and the coach door was closed. But before the window shade was drawn and the signal given to the driver, Jess glanced one last time out the window. Then the shade was drawn and the coach lurched down the alley.

The questions had come. Dozens of them, over and over, for both her and Linnie.

What was Jess possibly thinking? her father had asked. How could she lie to them? In the end he had understood her motives if not her methods.

Her stepmother had been beside herself—How could she go to Whitechapel and live among those people?

Vivian had always boasted of the marvelous marriage Linnie had made—Lady Deverell, wife of a peer of the realm who was cousin to Queen Victoria.

Now Jason Deverell was dead, and the scandal surrounding his death threatened to bring Whitehall and the Royal Palace crumbling to the foundations, even though attempts had been made to conceal the names of the men involved to protect their families.

Adam and Charles Mainwaring had left London the day Jason died. It was rumored they had gone to the United States. Harry Collingwood was found at his family's country home several days later, dead of a self-inflicted gunshot wound. The Hunt Club, which had never *officially* existed, was unofficially but permanently disbanded.

Jason was buried two days earlier in a discreet ceremony. Linnie attended neither the small family memorial nor the funeral. She refused to wear black to mourn him.

She stood at the far end of the solarium, gazing out across the gardens to the front gate at Carrington Square where newspaper reporters kept up their constant vigil for some member of the family, knowing full well that Linnie was in residence.

"They're like carrion, just waiting to pick at a rotting carcass," she said with thinly disguised disgust. "Have they nothing better to write about?"

"In a few weeks, they'll all have something else to write, and distort the truth about," Jess declared across the solarium. "You will be forgotten."

"But society never forgets," Linnie murmured. "I don't believe dear Vivian shall ever recover. She's taken to her bed again."

"She may take up permanent residence," Jess responded, quite grateful for the fact that Vivian wasn't about all the time, asking questions, making deprecating remarks, passing judgment, or swooning with a new case of the vapors.

She glanced up as Linnie strode toward her. Her sister was changed. There was a poignant sadness in her exquisite features that hadn't been there before. It gave her the air of a beautiful, tragic young woman, her pale hair hanging loose about her shoulders, like molten gold against the vivid blue of her gown.

Water gurgled gently in the fountain. Mist sprayed down from thin copper pipe as it wound over the lush green plants, ferns, and palms, that defied the calendar that said it was the dead of winter in London and only four days till Christmas.

The only other sound was the gentle stroke of coarse brush against canvas as Jess tried to paint. She stopped, started again, then stopped once more, trying to get the image precisely right. Finally, she threw down her brush in complete disgust with herself.

Linnie sat in a high-back fan wicker chair that was of the Empire style. She might have been a lady of the court visiting friends in India with the lush surroundings. Her hands were folded in her lap as she contemplated her younger sister.

She frequently awoke at night with dreams from the past months. It might be several more months before she felt truly safe, not constantly watching over her shoulder. After all, her husband had tried to kill her to silence her for what she had learned about the club, Anne Crook and

472

the Prince of Wales, and the other murdered women.

She watched as Jess impatiently scrubbed at the paint on her hands. She'd never known her sister to be so obsessive about such things. Usually she painted away until her hands, apron, often her gowns, and usually her face were streaked with smudges, so intent was her concentration when she worked.

She had thanked Jess over and over. They had confided in one another, talked until the early hours of the morning, and wept in each other's arms.

There was a similarity of features between them, that when one looked at them together, it was immediately recognized, but they were very different people in many ways. Yet, she was so bonded to this person—had always been—that she couldn't imagine how she could have allowed them to be parted as they had been over the past two years.

Jason. The answer came unwilling, as it often had over the past several harrowing days. But it was done with now. She would put it behind her. But she knew there were some things that were still unresolved.

"Have you contacted your police inspector?" she asked, and watched the nervous flutter of Jess's hands—usually unnaturally steady with a brush—with a trace of bemusement.

"I . . ." there was a too-long hesitation, as if she were about to say that she didn't know what Linnie was talking about. After all, in polite society, it was perhaps less than proper for a young woman to send messages to a man. Then she threw down the cleaning cloth.

"I sent a note round to the Commercial Street station." She looked down at her hands. "He's not there. Now that the investigation is officially closed, he's taken a leave of absence. He's gone to Old Orchard."

"I see. And have you sent a wire or post there as as well?"

Jess looked up, briefly. "There didn't seem to be any reason. He could have sent a note as well." She threw down her brush.

"Another painting in the new series." Linnie observed with a small frown. "You seem to be having some difficulty with it."

473

"It's not right. The colors are all wrong, the texture doesn't work, it's stilted and artificial-looking. I've started it a half-dozen times and it still doesn't work."

Linnie nodded thoughtfully. She listened to the sounds of the fountain, the servants in the adjacent part of the house, watched Jess's maddening obsession with cleaning the brushes.

"I've decided to go away as well," she announced. Jess looked up in surprise.

"I won't remain here," Linnie explained. "It's difficult for Father . . ."

"And Vivian?" Jess suggested.

"Vivian has an unnatural preoccupation with appearances, and rumor. She liked it well enough when I was Lady Rushmore, flaunting it about all of London, using my name to influence other people. Now that I'm *that poor woman whose husband was a dreadful murderer,* she hides in her rooms, wringing her hands about what people will say. I for one, have no intention of hiding out in my rooms, here or anywhere else."

Jess smiled for the first time in days, relieved to see some of the old Linnie back, with a trace of a new, more spirited one mixed in.

"What have you decided?"

"The South of France. I leave in two days," she announced and then added excitedly, "Come with me. We shall leave all this behind for a few months, effectively tell everyone to stuff their gossip and speculation in their hat, and go on holiday." Her enthusiasm gathered momentum.

"It will be as it was when we were in school. We shall travel, stay over where we wish, go to art galleries. We can go to Provence, and be very provincial. It will be fun, Jess." Her laughter had gone to sudden sadness.

"We both deserve a little fun, don't you think? And I am a very wealthy woman. And now that the entire world knows about J.B. Dumont, you are a very respected woman. We don't need to hide from anyone any longer."

Linnie was right of course. She knew that. And there were aspects of it that seemed appealing, if only to get away from London, the scandal Jason had brought down on all of them, and her memories.

"It would be nice to get away," she admitted. "Can we be ready in such short time?"

"I've already made arrangements for my own passage. I shall simply call my solicitor and have him make the necessary changes for the two of us."

"Just the two of us? Not even Rose?" she asked, more than a little stunned that Linnie would consider going on what amounted to a grand tour without the services of a maid.

"Not even Rose. We shall muddle through ourselves, lacing our own stays, just as we did when we were girls. Oh, Jess," she said with sudden wistfulness, "I'm so very glad that you're my sister. I don't know what I would have done if you hadn't . . ."

Jess went to her then and took her hands. "I'll always be there when you need me."

The plans were made. Parker Forsythe was stunned at the thought of losing his daughters again so soon after the events of the past months. Vivian took to her bed, scandalized that they had made such a decision, to go to France, unescorted, without even a maid to see to their needs.

In the end it was all quite simply done. Jess took very little with her—a few simple gowns that could be worn in the French countryside, small personal items, brushes and canvas, and tucked inside was the sketch Mary Margaret had made of the Michaelmas tree.

The day of their departure arrived. Vivian finally roused herself enough to come downstairs to bid them farewell after Parker Forsythe declared he would have her horsewhipped if she didn't get hold of herself over the matter.

It was the first time either Jess or Linnie had heard him raise his voice to her. They had exchanged long glances across the breakfast table, along with quick smiles. That, their silent exchange declared, was more like it.

They were to travel by rail from Charing Cross to the south coast where they were to board a packet for the coast of France. Their trunks had already been sent on ahead. Vivian quietly came downstairs. Her pale, wan complexion faded the last few shades to absolute white when she saw them.

"You're not leaving dressed in that manner?" It came out in a squeak as she stared at them.

They were dressed in simple clothes, borrowed from Rose Maguire and one of the downstairs maids, a necessity of disguise given their current notoriety. Jess felt quite comfortable in the simple but serviceable wool skirt, shirtwaist, and coat, much like what she had worn when she left for Whitechapel months ago.

"I can't bear it," Vivian declared with a tremulous voice, her hand over her heart. For a acceptable young woman, she was given to more fainting spells than seemed acceptable even in fashionable circles of society.

"Good heavens!" Jess declared. "Get hold of yourself, Vivian. Or we shall march right out the front door for the whole of London to see." They had intended to leave by the servants' entrance at the back to avoid the newspaper reporters that still clustered about the front gate.

Vivian's face immediately flushed a bright color. "Well! I have never been spoken to in that manner before."

"Get used to it, Vivian," Linnie suggested with a very *Lady Rushmore* sort of smile. "Or you shall never set foot outside of this house again." It was said with all the sophistication, propriety, and delicate delivery that a lady of the court had been taught to use, and a trace of "may the devil take the consequences."

Farewells were said. Their father hugged them fondly. Vivian swooned up the stairs to her rooms.

They slipped from the house unnoticed, appearances deceiving as two *maids* with shopping baskets entered the coach at the back carriage yard.

They boarded the train at Charing Cross Station just before the last call for passengers went out, and quickly moved to their private compartment. Bags were tucked away. The train slowly pulled out of the station.

London slipped past, all the weeks and months of sadness and fear somehow disappearing along with it. They were content to let silence settle around them, the only sound the faint creaking motion of the railcar and the muted clatter of the wheels beneath them. For miles, Jess stared out the compartment window.

"Do you love him?"

Her gaze jerked to her sister at the unexpected question. Then she glanced away, trying to return to the silence.

"I married Jason for all the wrong reasons," Linnie went on, even though it was obvious Jess didn't want to discuss it. "He was the most sought-after man in London, a peer of the realm, wealthy, handsome. Every young woman wanted him, his title, and estates. But *I* married him.

"Because it was expected of me. Vivian expected it. Father expected it. From the time we wore long skirts, we were told we should marry well. That was the definition of love. We were made to believe that we would be happy if we fulfilled that expectation." She leaned across the space between the two sides of the compartment and seized Jess's hands.

"Don't you see? I believed it. I did what everyone expected of me. I thought I loved Jason." Her voice had gone to a tear-filled whisper. "I didn't know what love was. I still don't."

Vehemence flowed back into her voice. "Perhaps if I'm very lucky I may one day discover what you found with your police inspector. I pray God it will happen. Because titles and all the wealth in the world can't take the place of someone who truly loves you."

"Please stop!" Jess said, jerking her hands away. "I loved him, but he didn't love me. Don't you understand that? He didn't even write to me afterward. In the very least he could have sent a note."

"I sent you a note," Linnie reminded her. "You ignored it. Since when have you ever accepted things that simply?"

"Sometimes it is that simple," Jess informed her, recalling what Moira Callahan had once told her.

"If you believe that, then you are a fool. If you love him, go after him."

"You need me," Jess argued.

"I need for you to be happy."

At Tonbridge, the train stopped to take on passengers for the remainder of the journey to Dover.

Time condensed as miles slipped away and memories of Old Orchard returned.

Moira. Robbie. Little Jamie with his pants about his ankles. Mary Margaret with those tentative words, "Promise that you'll come back." And Devlin.

They had made love. Even now she could feel the need, sharper, more urgent than it had ever been in those few days they escaped to the cottage — the need to have him inside her, holding her, kissing her, saying to her, "Look at me, Jessie. I want to see your eyes when I'm filling you with myself."

Was it real? More real than the illusion of love her sister thought she had found?

She stared down at the painted picture Mary Margaret had pressed into her hands that last day — the picture of the Michaelmas tree, and tears filled her eyes at the sight of the tiny eggshell candle holders at the tip of each branch, holding the unlit candles.

You have to help us light the candles on Christmas night.

The train slowed. Gradually it eased to a jolting stop as it pulled into the station. The end of the line. She refolded Mary's picture and tucked it away along with the memory.

She stepped down from the train.

A sharp wind gusted about, swirling the heavy steam that plumed from beneath. She walked along the platform, her throat tight. What if she was wrong?

She looked up then, tears in her eyes. The wooden sign with the name of the destination swung back and forth, blurred so that she couldn't read it. She kept walking, hesitantly.

Then her gaze fixed on the figure of a man, wide-shouldered, slowly striding from the opposite end of the platform. She couldn't see his face. She didn't need to.

Jess picked up her skirts and ran.

Devlin caught her and pulled her into his arms. Then his hands cradled her head, pushing back the foolish-looking hat that only a London maid would wear, fingers digging into her thick hair as his mouth covered hers.

"I thought you would never come," he whispered against her lips.

"I thought you didn't want me," she gasped, laughed, then gasped again. He kissed her long and deep, his tongue sweet and restless in her mouth.

"Not want you, lass?" he asked incredulously, his eyes an intense shade of blue. "I've spent a lifetime wantin' you. I'll gladly pay another to have you. But you walked away. I couldn't bear it — the thought that everything had been nothing more than a lie. That I meant nothing to you."

She laid her fingers against his mouth, caressing the small lines etched there with his frown. "You mean everything to me. Everything." Then she took them away with her kiss.

"I can't give you a fancy home and fancy clothes, Jess."

She laughed. "I can't cook. I can't even boil water. I have the better bargain."

"Aye, but you can love, lass." His voice had gone to a harsh whisper. "For that, I can make do with burned water." Then he kissed her again, with all the promise of the love they had discovered, and love yet to be found.

"Come home, Jess. They're waiting for you." He opened his hand then as his other arm went around her. He held a small candle in the palm of his hand.

"They waited, so that you could help them light the candles on the Michaelmas tree." He folded her hand around the candle with his own.

"We'll light the candles together."